Mark Bryant, the editor of this delightful treasury of contemporary and classic country stories, was himself born in a cottage in a tiny Dorset hamlet of West Country parents. Members of his immediate family currently live in a former barn in Cumbria, a converted rural railway station in Bedfordshire, the old farm buildings of an English Heritage manor house, and between a churchyard and a medieval castle in a small Welsh border village. The author/compiler of seven books, he is also the editor of *Cat Tales for Christmas*.

Also available from Headline

Dog Tales for Christmas
Murder for Christmas
Ghosts for Christmas
Chillers for Christmas
Mystery for Christmas
Cat Tales for Christmas

Country Tales
For Christmas

edited by

Mark Bryant

HEADLINE

First published in 1994
by HEADLINE BOOK PUBLISHING

10 9 8 7 6 5 4 3 2 1

ISBN 0 7472 4709 9

Typeset by
Letterpart Limited, Reigate, Surrey

Printed and bound in Great Britain by
Cox & Wyman Ltd, Reading Berks.

HEADLINE BOOK PUBLISHING
A division of Hodder Headline PLC
338 Euston Road
London NW1 3BH

For Charlotte

Contents

Introduction

There is something deeply resonant about stories of the country-side and perhaps never more so than when told at Christmas. It is pleasant to imagine the scene. The isolated thatched farmhouse with frost-rimmed windows, a single plume of smoke from the chimney the only indication of life within. All sound deadened by a thick layer of snow as the family settle around the open hearth, snug and contented after their traditional rustic meal. And as the winter sun slowly disappears behind the treetops the youngest child carries an old leather story-book to her grand-father's side. Putting down his mulled wine, he seats her on his lap, opens the well-thumbed volume and begins to read . . .

But the countryside is, of course, more than just Christmas. There is also the springtime when brooks sparkle under hump-backed stone bridges and bluebells and daffodils sway in the breeze. When new lambs gambol and every footpath teems with rabbits, bees and butterflies. And in a few short months swallows begin to skim the air as the ripening corn turns the hillsides bronze. Then imperceptibly the cock crows ever later, the dried hay is gathered and the leaves turn yellow. The summer's heat fades, the buttercups are gone and once-green hedgerows fill with hips and haws, nuts and berries. Hunting horns echo through the woodland, a Shire horse tills stubble with its plough and fisherfolk mending their nets look up as migrating flocks head out to sea. Harvest-time is succeeded by Hallowe'en, bats flit through village churchyards, and from Penzance to John o'Groats, from Donegal to Colwyn Bay, ancient clocktowers boom out the last hours of daylight. Bolts are drawn, kettles sing on the hob and the year comes once again to its close.

This book is an anthology of some of the most evocative stories of rural life in the British Isles over the last two centuries – tales in which the landscape and its people are themselves the focus rather than being a backdrop for other events. Most areas of Britain are represented and the collection covers every aspect of the countryside, from farmyards and manor houses to poachers and parsons, and from cliffs and moors to dells and downs. All the stories are fictional and self-contained, not extracts. However, though I have tried to make the book as balanced as the limitations of length and copyright availability have allowed, for ease of reading stories written exclusively in regional dialect have generally been avoided. *Country Tales for Christmas* includes contributions by both men and women, from the nineteenth century to the present day and covers every imaginable subject, from comedy to the macabre and from romance to mystery.

So put the latch on the door, draw the curtains and settle down in a favourite chair. Then, as the last sounds fade in the world outside – in tower-block, terrace or cottage – drift away like the little girl in that old-fashioned farmhouse, listening to Grandfather telling tales of a green and pleasant land as the embers glow and the chestnuts roast . . .

Mark Bryant

The Three Strangers

THOMAS HARDY

Among the few features of agricultural England which retain an appearance but little modified by the lapse of centuries, may be reckoned the high, grassy and fuzzy downs, coombs or ewe-leases, as they are indifferently called, that fill a large area of certain countries in the south and south-west. If any mark of human occupation is met with hereon, it usually takes the form of the solitary cottage of some shepherd.

Fifty years ago such a lonely cottage stood on such a down, and may possibly be standing there now. In spite of its loneliness, however, the spot, by actual measurement, was not more than five miles from a country-town. Yet that affected it little. Five miles of irregular upland, during the long inimical seasons, with their sleets, snows, rains and mists, afford withdrawing space enough to isolate a Timon or a Nebuchadnezzar; much less, in fair weather, to please that less repellent tribe, the poets, philosophers, artists and others who 'conceive and meditate of pleasant things'.

Some old earthen camp or barrow, some clump of trees, at least some starved fragment of ancient hedge is usually taken advantage of in the erection of these forlorn dwellings. But, in the present case, such a kind of shelter had been disregarded. Higher Crowstairs, as the house was called, stood quite detached and undefended. The only reason for its precise situation seemed

1

to be the crossing of two footpaths at right angles hard by, which may have crossed there and thus for a good five hundred years. Hence the house was exposed to the elements on all sides. But, though the wind up here blew unmistakably when it did blow, and the rain hit hard whenever it fell, the various weathers of the winter season were not quite so formidable on the coomb as they were imagined to be by dwellers on low ground. The raw rimes were not so pernicious as in the hollows, and the frosts were scarcely so severe. When the shepherd and his family who tenanted the house were pitied for their sufferings from the exposure, they said that upon the whole they were less inconvenienced by 'wuzzes and flames' (hoarses and phlegms) than when they had lived by the stream of a snug neighbouring valley.

The night of 28 March 182– was precisely one of the nights that were wont to call forth these expressions of commiseration. The level rainstorm smote walls, slopes and hedges like the clothyard shafts of Senlac and Crécy. Such sheep and outdoor animals as had no shelter stood with their buttocks to the winds; while the tails of little birds trying to roost on some scraggy thorn were blown inside-out like umbrellas. The gable-end of the cottage was stained with wet, and the eavesdroppings flapped against the wall. Yet never was commiseration for the shepherd more misplaced. For that cheerful rustic was entertaining a large party in glorification of the christening of his second girl.

The guests had arrived before the rain began to fall, and they were all now assembled in the chief or living room of the dwelling. A glance into the apartment at eight o'clock on this eventful evening would have resulted in the opinion that it was as cosy and comfortable a nook as could be wished for in boisterous weather. The calling of its inhabitant was proclaimed by a number of highly polished sheep-crooks without stems that were hung ornamentally over the fireplace, the curl of each shining crook varying from the antiquated-type engraved in the patriarchal pictures of old family bibles to the most approved fashion of the last local sheep-fair. The room was lighted by half-a-dozen candles, having wicks only a trifle smaller than the grease which enveloped them, in candlesticks that were never used but at

2

high-days, holy-days, and family feasts. The lights were scattered about the room, two of them standing on the chimney-piece. This position of candles was in itself significant. Candles on the chimney-piece always meant a party.

On the hearth, in front of a back-brand to give substance, blazed a fire of thorns, that crackled 'like the laughter of the fool'.

Nineteen persons were gathered here. Of these, five women, wearing gowns of various bright hues, sat in chairs along the wall; girls shy and not shy filled the window-bench; four men, including Charley Jake the hedge-carpenter, Elijah New the parish-clerk, and John Pitcher, a neighbouring dairyman, the shepherd's father-in-law, lolled in the settle: a young man and maid, who were blushing over tentative *pourparlers* on a life-companionship, sat beneath the corner-cupboard; and an elderly engaged man of fifty or upward moved restlessly about from spots where his betrothed was not to the spot where she was. Enjoyment was pretty general, and so much the more prevailed in being unhampered by conventional restrictions. Absolute confidence in each other's good opinion begat perfect ease, while the finishing stroke of manner, amounting to a truly princely serenity, was lent to the majority by the absence of any expression or trait denoting that they wished to get on in the world, enlarge their minds, or do any eclipsing thing whatever – which nowadays so generally nips the bloom and *bonhomie* of all except the two extremes of the social scale.

Shepherd Fennel had married well, his wife being a dairyman's daughter from a vale at a distance, who brought fifty guineas in her pocket – and kept them there, till they should be required for ministering to the needs of a coming family. This frugal woman had been somewhat exercised as to the character that should be given to the gathering. A sit-still party had its advantages; but an undisturbed position of ease in chairs and settlers was apt to lead on the men to such an unconscionable deal of toping that they would sometimes fairly drink the house dry. A dancing-party was the alternative; but this, while avoiding the foregoing objection on the score of good drink, had a counterbalancing disadvantage in the matter of good victuals, the ravenous appetites engendered by the exercise causing immense havoc in the buttery. Shepherdess Fennel fell back upon the immediate plan of mingling short dances with short periods of talk and singing, so as to hinder any ungovernable rage in either. But this scheme was entirely confined to her own gentle mind: the shepherd himself was in the mood to exhibit the most reckless phases of hospitality.

The fiddler was a boy of those parts, about twelve years of age, who had a wonderful dexterity in jigs and reels, though his fingers were so small and short as to necessitate a constant shifting for the high notes, from which he scrambled back to the first position with sounds not of unmixed purity of tone. At seven the shrill tweedle-dee of this youngster had begun, accompanied by a booming ground-bass from Elijah New, the parish-clerk, who had thoughtfully brought with him his favourite musical instrument, the serpent. Dancing was instantaneous, Mrs Fennel privately enjoining the players on no account to let the dance exceed the length of a quarter of an hour.

But Elijah and the boy, in the excitement of their position, quite forgot the injunction. Moreover, Oliver Giles, a man of seventeen, one of the dancers, who was enamoured of his partner, a fair girl of thirty-three rolling years, had recklessly handed a new crown-piece to the musicians, as a bribe to keep going as long as they had muscle and wind. Mrs Fennel, seeing the steam begin to generate on the countenances of her guests, crossed over and touched the fiddler's elbow and put her hand on the serpent's mouth. But they took no notice, and fearing she might lose her character of genial hostess if she were to interfere too markedly, she retired and sat down helpless. And so the dance whizzed on with cumulative fury, the performers moving in their planet-like courses, direct and retrograde, from apogee to perigee, till the hand of the well-kicked clock at the bottom of the room had travelled over the circumference of an hour.

While these cheerful events were in course of enactment within Fennel's pastoral dwelling, an incident having considerable bearing on the party had occurred in the gloomy night without. Mrs Fennel's concern about the growing fierceness of the dance corresponded in point of time with the ascent of a human figure to the solitary hill of Higher Crowstairs from the direction of the distant town. This personage strode on through the rain without a pause, following the little-worn path which, further on in its course, skirted the shepherd's cottage.

It was nearly the time of full moon, and on this account, though the sky was lined with a uniform sheet of dripping cloud, ordinary objects out of doors were readily visible. The sad wan light revealed the lonely pedestrian to be a man of supple frame; his gait suggested that he had somewhat passed the period of perfect and instinctive agility, though not so far as to be otherwise than rapid of motion when occasion required. At a rough guess, he might have been about forty years of age. He appeared tall, but a recruiting sergeant, or other person accustomed to the judging of men's heights by the eye, would have discerned that this was chiefly owing to his gauntness, and that he was not more than five-feet-eight or –nine.

Nothwithstanding the regularity of his tread, there was caution in it, as in that of one who mentally feels his way; and despite the fact that it was not a black coat nor a dark garment of any sort that he wore, there was something about him which suggested that he naturally belonged to the black-coated tribes of men. His clothes were of fustian, and his boots hobnailed, yet in his progress he showed not the mud-accustomed bearing of hobnailed and fustianed peasantry.

By the time that he had arrived abreast of the shepherd's premises the rain came down, or rather came along, with yet more determined violence. The outskirts of the little settlement partially broke the force of wind and rain, and this induced him to stand still. The most salient of the shepherd's domestic erections was an empty sty at the forward corner of his hedgeless garden, for in these latitudes the principle of masking the homelier features of your establishment by a conventional frontage was unknown. The traveller's eye was attracted to this small building by the pallid shine of the wet slates that covered it. He turned aside, and, finding it empty, stood under the pent-roof for shelter.

While he stood, the boom of the serpent within the adjacent house, and the lesser strains of the fiddler, reached the spot as an accompaniment to the surging hiss of the flying rain on the sod, its louder beating on the cabbage-leaves of the garden, on the eight or ten beehives just discernible by the path, and its dripping from the eaves into a row of buckets and pans that had been placed under the walls of the cottage. For at Higher Crowstairs, as at all such elevated domiciles, the grand difficulty of housekeeping was an insufficiency of water; and a casual rainfall was utilized by turning out, as catchers, every utensil that the house contained. Some queer stories might be told of the contrivances for economy in suds and dish-waters that are absolutely necessitated in upland habitations during the droughts of summer. But at this season there were no such exigencies: a mere acceptance of what the skies bestowed was sufficient for an abundant store.

At last the notes of the serpent ceased and the house was silent. This cessation of activity aroused the solitary pedestrian from the reverie into which he had lapsed, and, emerging from the shed, with an apparently new intention, he walked up the path to the house-door. Arrived here, his first act was to kneel down on a large stone beside the row of vessels, and to drink a copious draught from one of them. Having quenched his thirst he rose and lifted his hand to knock, but paused with his eye upon the panel. Since the dark surface of the wood revealed absolutely nothing, it was evident that he must be mentally looking through the door, as if he wished to measure thereby all the possibilities that a house of this sort might include, and how they might bear upon the question of his entry.

In his indecision he turned and surveyed the scene around. Not a soul was anywhere visible. The garden-path stretched downward from his feet, gleaming like the track of a snail; the roof of the little well (mostly dry), the well-cover, the top rail of the garden-gate, were varnished with the same dull liquid glaze; while, far away in the vale, a faint whiteness of more than usual extent showed that the rivers were high in the meads. Beyond all this winked a few bleared lamplights through the beating drops – lights that denoted the situation of the country-town from which he had appeared to come. The absence of all notes of life in that direction seemed to clinch his intentions, and he knocked at the door.

Within, a desultory chat had taken the place of movement and musical sound. The hedge-carpenter was suggesting a song to the company, which nobody just then was inclined to undertake, so that the knock afforded a not unwelcome diversion.

'Walk in!' said the shepherd promptly.

The latch clicked upward, and out of the night our pedestrian appeared upon the door-mat. The shepherd arose, snuffed two of the nearest candles, and turned to look at him.

Their light disclosed that the stranger was dark in complexion and not unprepossessing as to feature. His hat, which for a moment he did not remove, hung low over his eyes, without concealing that they were large, open and determined, moving with a flash rather than a glance round the room. He seemed pleased with his survey, and, baring his shaggy head, said, in a rich deep voice, 'The rain is so heavy, friends, that I ask leave to come in and rest awhile.'

'To be sure, stranger,' said the shepherd. 'And faith, you've been lucky in choosing your time, for we are having a bit of a fling for a glad cause – though, to be sure, a man could hardly wish that glad cause to happen more than once a year.'

'Nor less,' spoke up a woman. 'For 'tis best to get your family over and done with, as soon as you can, so as to be all the earlier out of the fat o't.'

'And what may be this glad cause?' asked the stranger.

'A birth and christening,' said the shepherd.

The stranger hoped his host might not be made unhappy either by too many or too few of such episodes, and being invited by a gesture to pull at the mug, he readily acquiesced. His manner, which, before entering, had been so dubious, was now altogether that of a careless and candid man.

'Late to be traipsing athwart this coomb – hey?' said the engaged man of fifty.

'Late it is, master, as you say. I'll take a seat in the chimney-corner, if you have nothing to urge against it, ma'am; for I am a little moist on the side that was next the rain.'

Mrs Shepherd Fennel assented, and made room for the self-invited comer, who, having got completely inside the chimney-corner, stretched out his legs and his arms with the expansiveness of a person quite at home.

'Yes, I am rather cracked in the vamp,' he said freely, seeing that the eyes of the shepherd's wife fell upon his boots, 'and I am not well fitted either. I have had some rough times lately, and have been forced to pick up what I can get in the way of wearing, but I must find a suit better fit for working-days when I reach home.'

'One of hereabouts?' she enquired.

'Not quite that – further up the country.'

'I thought so. And so be I; and by your tongue you come from my neighbourhood.'

'But you would hardly have heard of me,' he said quickly. 'My time would be long before yours, ma'am, you see.'

This testimony to the youthfulness of his hostess had the effect of stopping her cross-examination.

'There is only one thing more wanted to make me happy,' continued the newcomer. 'And that is a little baccy, which I am sorry to say I am out of.'

'I'll fill your pipe,' said the shepherd.

'I must ask you to lend me a pipe likewise.'

'A smoker, and no pipe about 'ee?'

'I have dropped it somewhere on the road.'

The shepherd filled and handed him a new clay pipe, saying, as he did so, 'Hand me your baccy-box – I'll fill that too, now I am about it.'

The man went through the movement of searching his pockets.

'Lost that too?' said his entertainer, with some surprise.

'I am afraid so,' said the man with some confusion. 'Give it to me in a screw of paper.' Lighting his pipe at the candle with a suction that drew the whole flame into the bowl, he resettled

8

himself in the corner and bent his looks upon the faint steam from his damp legs, as if he wished to say no more.

Meanwhile, the general body of guests had been taking little notice of this visitor by reason of an absorbing discussion in which they were engaged with the band about a tune for the next dance. The matter being settled, they were about to stand up when an interruption came in the shape of another knock at the door.

At the sound of the same the man in the chimney-corner took up the poker and began stirring the brands as if doing it thoroughly were the one aim of his existence; and a second time the shepherd said, 'Walk in!' In a moment another man stood upon the straw-woven door-mat. He too was a stranger.

This individual was one of a type radically different from the first. There was more of the commonplace in his manner, and a certain jovial cosmopolitanism sat upon his features. He was several years older than the first arrival, his hair being slightly frosted, his eyebrows bristly, and his whiskers cut back from his cheeks. His face was rather full and flabby, and yet it was not altogether a face without power. A few grog-blossoms marked the neighbourhood of his nose. He flung back his long drab greatcoat, revealing that beneath it he wore a suit of cinder-grey shade throughout, large heavy seals, of some metal or other that would take a polish, dangling from his fob as his only personal ornament. Shaking the water-drops from his low-crowned glazed hat, he said, 'I must ask for a few minutes' shelter, comrades, or I shall be wetted to my skin before I get to Casterbridge.'

'Make yourself at home, master,' said the shepherd, perhaps a trifle less heartily than on the first occasion. Not that Fennel had the least tinge of niggardliness in his composition; but the room was far from large, spare chairs were not numerous, and damp companions were not altogether desirable at close quarters for the women and girls in their bright-coloured gowns.

However, the second comer, after taking off his greatcoat, and hanging his hat on a nail in one of the ceiling-beams as if he had been specially invited to put it there, advanced and sat down at

9

the table. This had been pushed so closely into the chimney-corner, to give all available room to the dancers, that its inner edge grazed the elbow of the man who had ensconced himself by the fire; and thus the two strangers were brought into close companionship. They nodded to each by way of breaking the ice of unacquaintance, and the first stranger handed his neighbour the family mug – a huge vessel of brownware, having its upper edge worn away like a threshold by the rub of whole generations of thirsty lips that had gone the way of all flesh, and bearing the following inscription burnt upon its rotund side in yellow letters:

THERE IS NO FUN
UNTiLL i CUM.

The other man, nothing loth, raised the mug to his lips, and drank on, and on, and on – till a curious blueness overspread the countenance of the shepherd's wife, who had regarded with no little surprise the first stranger's free offer to the second of what did not belong to him to dispense.

'I knew it!' said the toper to the shepherd with much satisfaction. 'When I walked up your garden before coming in, and saw the hives all of a row, I said to myself, "Where there's bees there's honey, and where there's honey there's mead." But mead of such a truly comfortable sort as this I really didn't expect to meet in my older days.' He took yet another pull at the mug, till it assumed an ominous elevation.

'Glad you enjoy it!' said the shepherd warmly.

'It is goodish mead,' assented Mrs Fennel, with an absence of enthusiasm which seemed to say that it was possible to buy praise for one's cellar at too heavy a price. 'It is trouble enough to make – and really I hardly think we shall make any more. For honey sells well, and we ourselves can make shift with a drop o' small mead and metheglin for common use from the comb-washings.'

'O, but you'll never have the heart!' reproachfully cried the stranger in cinder-grey, after taking up the mug a third time and setting it down empty. 'I love mead, when 'tis old like this, as I love to go to church o' Sundays, or to relieve the needy any day of the week.'

'Ha, ha, ha!' said the man in the chimney-corner, who, in spite of the taciturnity induced by the pipe of tobacco, could not or would not refrain from this slight testimony to his comrade's humour.

Now the old mead of those days, brewed of the purest first-year or maiden honey, four pounds to the gallon – with its due complement of white of eggs, cinnamon, ginger, cloves, mace, rosemary, yeast, and processes of working, bottling and cellaring – tasted remarkably strong; but it did not taste so strong as it actually was. Hence, presently, the stranger in cinder-grey at the table, moved by its creeping influence, unbuttoned his waistcoat, threw himself back in his chair, spread his legs, and made his presence felt in various ways.

'Well, well, as I say,' he resumed, 'I am going to Casterbridge, and to Casterbridge I must go. I should have been almost there by this time; but the rain drove me into your dwelling, and I'm not sorry for it.'

'You don't live in Casterbridge?' said the shepherd.

'Not as yet; though I shortly mean to move there.'

'Going to set up in trade, perhaps?'

'No, no,' said the shepherd's wife, 'It is easy to see that the gentleman is rich, and don't want to work at anything.'

The cinder-grey stranger paused, as if to consider whether he would accept that definition of himself. He presently rejected it by answering, ' "Rich" is not quite the word for me, dame. I do work, and I must work. And even if I only get to Casterbridge by midnight I must begin work there at eight tomorrow morning. Yes, het or wet, blow or snow, famine or sword, my day's work tomorrow must be done.'

'Poor man! Then, in spite o' seeming, you be worse off than we?' replied the shepherd's wife.

''Tis the nature of my trade, men and maidens. 'Tis the nature of my trade more than my poverty . . . But really and truly I must up and off, or I shan't get a lodging in the town.' However, the speaker did not move, and directly added, 'There's time for

11

one more draught of friendship before I go; and I'd perform it at once if the mug were not dry.'

'Here's a mug o' small,' said Mrs Fennel. 'Small we call it, though to be sure 'tis only the first wash o' the combs.'

'No,' said the stranger disdainfully. 'I won't spoil your first kindness by partaking o' your second.'

'Certainly not,' broke in Fennel. 'We don't increase and multiply every day, and I'll fill the mug again.' He went away to the dark place under the stairs where the barrel stood. The shepherdess followed him.

'Why should you do this?' she said reproachfully, as soon as they were alone. 'He's emptied it once, though it held enough for ten people; and now he's not contented wi' the small, but must needs call for more o' the strong! And a stranger unbeknown to any of us. For my part, I don't like the look o' the man at all.'

'But he's in the house, my honey; and 'tis a wet night, and a christening. Daze it, what's a cup of mead more or less? There'll be plenty more next bee-burning.'

'Very well – this time, then,' she answered, looking wistfully at the barrel. 'But what is the man's calling, and where is he one of, that he should come in and join us like this?'

'I don't know. I'll ask him again.'

The catastrophe of having the mug drained dry at one pull by the stranger in cinder-grey was effectually guarded against this time by Mrs Fennel. She poured out his allowance in a small cup, keeping the large one at a discreet distance from him. When he had tossed off his portion the shepherd renewed his enquiry about the stranger's occupation.

The latter did not immediately reply, and the man in the chimney-corner, with sudden demonstrativeness, said, 'Anybody may know my trade – I'm a wheelwright.'

'A very good trade for these parts,' said the shepherd.

'And anybody may know mine – if they've the sense to find it out,' said the stranger in cinder-grey.

'You may generally tell what a man is by his claws,' observed the hedge-carpenter, looking at his own hands. 'My fingers be as full of thorns as an old pin-cushion is of pins.'

The hands of the man in the chimney-corner instinctively sought the shade, and he gazed into the fire as he resumed his pipe. The man at the table took up the hedge-carpenter's remark, and added smartly, 'True; but the oddity of my trade is that, instead of setting a mark upon me, it sets a mark upon my customers.'

No observation being offered by anybody in elucidation of this enigma, the shepherd's wife once more called for a song. The same obstacles presented themselves as at the former time – one had no voice, another had forgotten the first verse. The stranger at the table, whose soul had now risen to a good working temperature, relieved the difficulty by exclaiming that, to start the company, he would sing himself. Thrusting one thumb into the arm-hole of his waistcoat, he waved the other hand in the air, and, with an extemporizing gaze at the shining sheep-crooks above the mantelpiece, began:

'O my trade it is the rarest one,
        Simple shepherds all—
   My trade is a sight to see;
For my customers I tie, and take them up on high,
   And waft 'em to a far countree!'

The room was silent when he had finished the verse – with one exception, that of the man in the chimney-corner, who, at the singer's word, 'Chorus!', joined him in a deep bass voice of musical relish,

      'And waft 'em to a far countree!'

Oliver Giles, John Pitcher the dairyman, the parish-clerk, the engaged man of fifty, the row of young women against the wall, seemed lost in thought not of the gayest kind. The shepherd looked meditatively on the ground, the shepherdess gazed keenly at the singer, and with some suspicion; she was doubting whether this stranger were merely singing an old song from recollection, or was composing one there and then for the

13

occasion. All were as perplexed at the obscure revelation as the guests at Belshazzar's Feast, except the man in the chimney-corner, who quietly said, 'Second verse, stranger', and smoked on.

The singer thoroughly moistened himself from his lips inwards, and went on with the next stanza as requested:

> 'My tools are but common ones,
> > Simple shepherds all—
> My tools are no sight to see;
> A little hempen string, and a post whereon to swing,
> > Are implements enough for me!'

Shepherd Fennel glanced round. There was no longer any doubt that the stranger was answering his question rhythmically. The guests one and all started back with suppressed exclamations. The young woman engaged to the man of fifty fainted half-way, and would have proceeded, but finding him wanting in alacrity for catching her she sat down trembling.

'O, he's the—!' whispered the people in the background, mentioning the name of an ominous public officer. 'He's come to do it! 'Tis to be at Casterbridge jail tomorrow – the man for sheep-stealing – the poor clock-maker we heard of, who used to live away at Shottsford and had no work to do – Timothy Summers, whose family were a-starving, and so he went out of Shottsford by the high-road, and took a sheep in open daylight, defying the farmer and the farmer's wife and the farmer's lad, and every man jack among 'em. He' (and they nodded towards the stranger of the deadly trade) 'is come from up the country to do it because there's not enough to do in his own county-town, and he's got the place here now our own county man's dead; he's going to live in the same cottage under the prison wall.'

The stranger in cinder-grey took no notice of this whispered string of observations, but again wetted his lips. Seeing that his friend in the chimney-corner was the only one who reciprocated his joviality in any way, he held out his cup towards that appreciative comrade, who also held out his own. They clinked together, the eyes of the rest of the room hanging upon the singer's actions. He parted his lips for the third verse; but at that moment another knock was audible upon the door. This time the knock was faint and hesitating.

The company seemed scared; the shepherd looked with consternation towards the entrance, and it was with some effort that he resisted his alarmed wife's deprecatory glance, and uttered for the third time the welcoming words, 'Walk in!'

The door was gently opened, and another man stood upon the mat. He, like those who had preceded him, was a stranger. This time it was a short, small personage, of fair complexion, and dressed in a decent suit of dark clothes.

'Can you tell me the way to—?' he began: then, gazing round the room to observe the nature of the company amongst whom he had fallen, his eyes lighted on the stranger in cinder-grey. It was just at the instant when the latter, who had thrown his mind into his song with such a will that he scarcely heeded the interruption, silenced all whispers and inquiries by bursting into his third verse:

> 'Tomorrow is my working day,
>   Simple shepherds all—
> Tomorrow is a working day for me;
> For the farmer's sheep is slain, and the lad who did it ta'en,
>   And on his soul may God ha' merc-y!'

The stranger in the chimney-corner, waving cups with the singer so heartily that his mead splashed over on the hearth, repeated in his bass voice as before:

> 'And on his soul may God ha' merc-y!'

All this time the third stranger had been standing in the doorway. Finding now that he did not come forward or go on speaking, the guests particularly regarded him. They noticed to their surprise that he stood before them the picture of abject terror – his knees trembling, his hand shaking so violently that the door-latch by which he supported himself rattled audibly: his white lips were parted, and his eye fixed on the merry officer of justice in the middle of the room. A moment more and he had turned, closed the door, and fled.

'What a man can it be?' said the shepherd.

The rest, between the awfulness of their late discovery and the odd conduct of this third visitor, looked as if they knew not what to think, and said nothing. Instinctively they withdrew further and further from the grim gentleman in their midst, whom some of them seemed to take for the Prince of Darkness himself, till they formed a remote circle, an empty space of floor being left between them and him—

'. . . circulus, cuius centrum diabolus.'

The room was so silent – though there were more than twenty people in it – that nothing could be heard but the patter of the rain against the window-shutters, accompanied by the occasional hiss of a stray drop that fell down the chimney into the fire, and the steady puffing of the man in the corner, who had now resumed his pipe of long clay.

The stillness was unexpectedly broken. The distant sound of a gun reverberated through the air – apparently from the direction of the county-town.

'Be jiggered!' cried the stranger who had sung the song, jumping up.

'What does that mean?' asked several.

'A prisoner escaped from the jail – that's what it means.'

All listened: the sound was repeated, and none of them spoke but the man in the chimney-corner, who said quietly, 'I've often been told that in this county they fire a gun at such times; but I never heard it till now.'

'I wonder if it is *my* man?' murmured the personage in the cinder-grey.

'Surely it is!' said the shepherd involuntarily. 'And surely we've zeed him! That little man who looked in at the door by now, and quivered like a leaf when he zeed ye and heard your song!'

. 'His teeth chattered, and the breath went out of his body,' said the dairyman.

'And his heart seemed to sink within him like a stone,' said Oliver Giles.

'And he bolted as if he'd been shot at,' said the hedge-carpenter.

'True – his teeth chattered, and his heart seemed to sink; and he bolted as if he'd been shot at,' slowly summed up the man in the chimney-corner.

'I didn't notice it,' remarked the hangman.

'We were all a-wondering what made him run off in such a fright,' faltered one of the women against the wall, 'and now 'tis explained!'

The firing of the alarm-gun went on at intervals, low and sullenly, and their suspicions became a certainty. The sinister gentleman in cinder-grey roused himself. 'Is there a constable here?' he asked, in thick tones. 'If so, let him step forward.'

The engaged man of fifty stepped quavering out from the wall, his betrothed beginning to sob on the back of the chair.

'You are a sworn constable?'

'I be, sir.'

'Then pursue the criminal at once, with assistance, and bring him back here. He can't have gone far.'

'I will, sir, I will – when I've got my staff. I'll go home and get it, and come sharp here, and start in a body.'

'Staff! – never mind your staff; the man'll be gone!'

'But I can't do nothing without my staff – can I, William, and John, and Charles Jake? No; for there's the king's royal crown a-painted on en in yaller and gold, and the lion and the unicorn, so as when I raise en up and hit my prisoner, 'tis made a lawful blow thereby. I wouldn't 'tempt to take up a man without my staff – no, not I. If I hadn't the law to gie me courage, why, instead o' my taking up him he might take up me!'

'Now, I'm a king's man myself, and can give you authority enough for this,' said the formidable officer in grey. 'Now then, all of ye, be ready. Have ye any lanterns?'

'Yes – have ye any lanterns? – I demand it!' said the constable.

'And the rest of you able-bodied—'

'Able-bodied men – yes – the rest of ye!' said the constable.

'Have you some stout staves and pitch-forks—'

'Staves and pitchforks – in the name o' the law! And take 'em in yer hands and go in quest, and do as we in authority tell ye!'

Thus aroused, the men prepared to give chase. The evidence was, indeed, though circumstantial, so convincing, that but little argument was needed to show the shepherd's guests that after what they had seen it would look very much like connivance if they did not instantly pursue the unhappy third stranger, who could not as yet have gone more than a few hundred yards over such an uneven country.

A shepherd is always well provided with lanterns; and, lighting these hastily, and with hurdle-staves in their hands, they poured out of the door, taking a direction along the crest of the hill, away from the town, the rain having fortunately a little abated.

Disturbed by the noise, or possibly by unpleasant dreams of her baptism, the child who had been christened began to cry heart-brokenly in the room overhead. These notes of grief came down through the chinks of the floor to the ears of the women below, who jumped up one by one, and seemed glad of the excuse to ascend and comfort the baby, for the incidents of the last half-hour greatly oppressed them. Thus in the space of two or three minutes the room on the ground-floor was deserted quite.

But it was not for long. Hardly had the sound of footsteps died away when a man returned round the corner of the house from the direction the pursuers had taken. Peeping in at the door, and seeing nobody there, he entered leisurely. It was the stranger of the chimney-corner, who had gone out with the rest. The motive of his return was shown by his helping himself to a cut piece of skimmer-cake that lay on a ledge beside where he had sat, and which he had apparently forgotten to take with him. He also poured out half a cup more mead from the quantity that remained, ravenously eating and drinking these as he stood. He had not finished when another figure came in just as quietly – his friend in cinder-grey.

'O – you here?' said the latter, smiling. 'I thought you had gone to help in the capture.' And this speaker also revealed the object of his return by looking solicitously round for the fascinating mug of old mead.

'And I thought you had gone,' said the other, continuing his skimmer-cake with some effort.

'Well, on second thoughts, I felt there were enough without me,' said the first confidentially, 'and such a night as it is, too. Besides, 'tis the business o' the Government to take care of its criminals – not mine.'

'True; so it is. And I felt as you did, that there were enough without me.'

'I don't want to break my limbs running over the humps and hollows of this wild country.'

'Nor I neither, between you and me.'

'These shepherd-people are used to it – simple-minded souls, you know, stirred up to anything in a moment. They'll have him ready for me before the morning, and no trouble to me at all.'

'They'll have him, and we shall have saved ourselves all labour in the matter.'

'True, true. Well, my way is to Casterbridge; and 'tis as much as my legs will do to take me that far. Going the same way?'

'No, I am sorry to say! I have to get home over there' (he nodded indefinitely to the right), 'and I feel as you do, that it is quite enough for my legs to do before bedtime.'

The other had by this time finished the mead in the mug, after which, shaking hands heartily at the door, and wishing each other well, they went their several ways.

In the meantime the company of pursuers had reached the end of the hog's-back elevation which dominated this part of the down. They had decided on no particular plan of action; and finding that the man of the baleful trade was no longer in their company, they seemed quite unable to form any such plan now. They descended in all directions down the hill, and straightway several of the party fell into the snare set by Nature for all misguided midnight ramblers over this part of the cretaceous formation. The 'lanchets', or flint slopes, which belted the escarpment at intervals of a dozen yards, took the less cautious ones unawares, and losing their footing on the rubbly steep they slid sharply downwards, the lanterns rolling from their hands to the bottom, and there lying on their sides till the horn was scorched through.

When they had again gathered themselves together, the shepherd, as the man who knew the country best, took the lead, and guided then round these treacherous inclines. The lanterns, which seemed rather to dazzle their eyes and warn the fugitive than to assist them in the exploration, were extinguished, due silence was observed; and in this more rational order they plunged into the vale. It was a grassy, briery, moist defile, affording some shelter to any person who had sought it; but the party perambulated it in vain, and ascended on the other side. Here they wandered apart, and after an interval closed together again to report progress. At the second time of closing in they found themselves near a lonely ash, the single tree on this part of the coomb, probably sown there by a passing bird some fifty years before. And here, standing a little to one side of the trunk, as motionless as the trunk itself, appeared the man they were in quest of, his outline being well defined against the sky beyond. The band noiselessly drew up and faced him.

'Your money or your life!' said the constable sternly to the still figure.

'No, no,' whispered John Pitcher. ''Tisn't our side ought to say that. That's the doctrine of vagabonds like him, and we be on the side of the law.'

'Well, well,' replied the constable impatiently; 'I must say something, mustn't I? and if you had all the weight o' this undertaking upon your mind, perhaps you'd say the wrong thing too! – Prisoner at the bar, surrender, in the name of the Father – the Crown, I mane!'

The man under the tree seemed now to notice them for the first time, and, giving them no opportunity whatever for exhibiting their courage, he strolled slowly towards them. He was, indeed, the little man, the third stranger; but his trepidation had in a great measure gone.

'Well, travellers,' he said, 'did I hear ye speak to me?'

'You did: you've got to come and be our prisoner at once!' said the constable. 'We arrest 'ee on the charge of not biding in Casterbridge jail in a decent proper manner to be hung tomorrow morning. Neighbours, do your duty, and seize the culpet!'

On hearing the charge, the man seemed enlightened, and, saying not another word, resigned himself with preternatural civility to the search-party, who, with their staves in their hands, surrounded him on all sides, and marched him back towards the shepherd's cottage.

It was eleven o'clock by the time they arrived. The light shining from the open door, a sound of men's voices within, proclaimed to them as they approached the house that some new events had arisen in their absence. On entering they discovered the shepherd's living-room to be invaded by two officers from Casterbridge jail, and a well-known magistrate who lived at the nearest country-seat, intelligence of the escape having become generally circulated.

'Gentlemen,' said the constable, 'I have brought back your man – not without risk and danger; but everyone must do his duty! He is inside this circle of able-bodied persons, who have lent me useful aid, considering their ignorance of Crown work. Men, bring forward your prisoner!' And the third stranger was led to the light.

'Who is this?' said one of the officials.

'The man,' said the constable.

'Certainly not,' said the turnkey; and the first corroborated his statement.

'But how can it be otherwise?' asked the constable. 'Or why was he so terrified at sight o' the singing instrument of the law who sat there?' Here he related the strange behaviour of the third stranger on entering the house during the hangman's song.

'Can't understand it,' said the officer coolly. 'All I know is that it is not the condemned man. He's quite a different character from this one; a gauntish fellow, with dark hair and eyes, rather good-looking, and with a musical bass voice that if you heard it once you'd never mistake as long as you lived.'

'Why, souls – 'twas the man in the chimney-corner!'

'Hey – what?' said the magistrate, coming forward after enquiring particulars from the shepherd in the background. 'Haven't you got the man after all?'

'Well, sir,' said the constable, 'he's the man we were in search of, that's true; and yet he's not the man we were in search of. For the man we were in search of was not the man we wanted, sir, if you understand my everyday way; for 'twas the man in the chimney-corner!'

'A pretty kettle of fish altogether!' said the magistrate. 'You had better start for the other man at once.'

The prisoner now spoke for the first time. The mention of the man in the chimney-corner seemed to have moved him as nothing else could so. 'Sir,' he said, stepping forward to the magistrate, 'take no more trouble about me. The time is come when I may as well speak. I have done nothing; my crime is that the condemned man is my brother. Early this afternoon I left home at Shottford to tramp it all the way to Casterbridge jail to bid him farewell. I was benighted, and called here to rest and ask the way. When I opened the door I saw before me the very man, my brother, that I thought to see in the condemned cell at Casterbridge. He was in this chimney-corner; and jammed close to him, so that he could not have got out if he had tried, was the executioner who'd come to take his life, singing a song about it and not knowing that it was his victim who was close by, joining in to save appearances. My brother looked a glance of agony at me, and I knew he meant, "Don't reveal what you see; my life depends on it." I was so terror-struck that I could hardly stand, and, not knowing what I did, I turned and hurried away.'

The narrator's manner and tone had the stamp of truth, and his story made a great impression on all around. 'And do you know where your brother is at the present time?' asked the magistrate.

'I do not. I have never seen him since I closed this door.'

'I can testify to that, for we've been between ye ever since,' said the constable.

'Where does he think to fly to? – what is his occupation?'

'He's a watch-and-clock-maker, sir.'

''A said 'a was a wheelwright – a wicked rogue,' said the constable.

'The wheels of clocks and watches he meant, no doubt,' said Shepherd Fennel. 'I thought his hands were palish for's trade.'

'Well, it appears to me that nothing can be gained by retaining this poor man in custody,' said the magistrate; 'your business lies with the other, unquestionably.'

And so the little man was released off-hand; but he looked nothing the less sad on that account, it being beyond the power of magistrate or constable to raze out the written troubles in his brain, for they concerned another whom he regarded with more solicitude than himself. When this was done, and the man had gone his way, the night was found to be so far advanced that it was deemed useless to renew the search before the next morning.

Next day, accordingly, the quest for the clever sheep-stealer became general and keen, to all appearance at least. But the intended punishment was cruelly disproportioned to the transgression, and the sympathy of a great many country-folk in that district was strongly on the side of the fugitive. Moreover, his marvellous coolness and daring in hob-and-nobbing with the hangman, under the unprecedented circumstances of the shepherd's party, won their admiration. So that it may be questioned if all those who ostensibly made themselves so busy in exploring woods and fields and lanes were quite so thorough when it came to the private examination of their own lofts and outhouses. Stories were afloat of a mysterious figure being occasionally seen in some old overgrown trackway or other, remote from turnpike roads; but when a search was instituted in any of these suspected quarters nobody was found. Thus the days and weeks passed without tidings.

In brief, the bass-voiced man of the chimney-corner was never recaptured. Some said that he went across the sea, others that he did not, but buried himself in the depths of a populous city. At any rate, the gentleman in cinder-grey never did his morning's work at Casterbridge, nor met anywhere at all, for business purposes, the genial comrade with whom he had passed an hour of relaxation in the lonely house on the coomb.

The grass has long been green on the graves of Shepherd Fennel and his frugal wife; the guests who made up the christening party have mainly followed their entertainers to the tomb; the baby in whose honour they all had met is a matron in the sere and yellow leaf. But the arrival of the three strangers at the shepherd's that night, and the details connected therewith, is a story as well known as ever in the country about Higher Crowstairs.

The Mower

H.E. BATES

In the midday heat of a June day a farm-boy was riding down a deserted meadow-lane, straddling a fat white pony. The blossoms of hawthorn had shrivelled to brown on the tall hedges flanking the lane and wild pink and white roses were beginning to open like stars among the thick green leaves. The air was heavy with the scent of early summer, the odour of the dying hawthorn bloom, the perfume of the dog-roses, the breath of ripening grass.

The boy had taken off his jacket and had hooked it over the straw victual-bag hanging from the saddle. There were bottles of beer in the bag and the jacket shaded them from the heat of the sun. The pony moved at walking-pace and the boy rode cautiously, never letting it break into a trot. As though it was necessary to be careful with the beer, he sometimes halted the pony and touched the necks of the bottles with his fingers. The bottlenecks were cool, but the cloth of his jacket was burning against his hand.

He presently steered the pony through a white gate leading from the lane to a meadow beyond. The gate was standing open and he rode the pony straight across the curving swathes of hay which lay drying in the sun. It was a field of seven or eight acres and a third of the grass had already been mown. The hay was crisp and dry under the pony's feet and the flowers that had been growing in the grass lay white and shrivelled in the sunshine.

Over on the far side of the field a man was mowing and a woman was turning the rows of grass with a hay rake. The figure of the man was nondescript and dark, and the woman was dressed in a white blouse and an old green skirt that had faded to the yellowish colour of the grass the man was mowing. The boy rode the pony towards them. The sunshine blazed down fierce and perpendicular, and there was no shade in the field except for the shadow of an ash-tree in one corner and a group of willows by a cattle-pond in another.

Everywhere was silence and the soft sound of the pony's feet in the hay and the droning of bees in the flowers among the uncut grass seemed to deepen the silence.

The woman straightened her back and, leaning on her rake, shaded her face with her hand and looked across at the boy as she heard him coming. The man went on mowing, swinging the scythe slowly and methodically, his back towards her.

The woman was dark and good-looking, with a sleek swarthy face and very high, soft red cheek-bones, like a gipsy, and a long pigtail of thick black hair which she wore twisted over her head like a snake coiled up asleep. She herself was rather like a snake also, her long body slim and supple, her black eyes liquid and bright. The boy rode up to her and dismounted. She dropped her rake and held the pony's head and ran her finger up and down its nose while he slipped from the saddle.

'Can he come?' she said.

The boy had not time to answer before the man approached, wiping the sweat from his face and neck with a dirty red handkerchief. His face was broad and thick-lipped and ponderous, his eyes were grey and simple, and the skin of his face and neck and hands was dry and tawny as an Indian's with sun and weather. He was about forty, and he walked with a slight stoop of his shoulders and a limp of his left leg, very slowly and deliberately.

'See him?' he said to the boy.

'He was up there when I got the beer,' the boy said.

26

'In the Dragon? What did he say?'

'He said he'd come.'

The woman ceased stroking the pony's nose and looked up.

'He said that yesterday,' she said.

'Ah! but you can't talk to him. He's got to have his own way,' said the man. 'Was he drunk?' he asked.

'I don't think so,' said the boy. 'He was drunk yesterday.'

The man wiped his neck impatiently and made a sound of disgust and then took out his watch. 'Half the day gone – and a damn wonder if he comes,' he muttered.

'Oh! if Ponto says he'll come,' said the woman slowly, 'he'll come. He'll come all right.'

'How do you know? He does things just when he thinks he will – and not until.'

'Oh! He'll come if he says he'll come,' she said.

The boy began to lead the pony across the field towards the ash-tree. The woman stood aside for him and then kicked her rake on a heap of hay and followed him.

The sun had crossed the zenith. The man went back to his scythe and slipped his whetstone from his pocket and laid it carefully on the mown grass. As he put on his jacket he turned and gazed at the white gate of the field. He could see no one there, and he followed the woman and the boy across the field to the ash-tree.

Under the ash tree the boy was tethering the horse in the shade and the woman was unpacking bread and cold potatoes and a meat pie. The boy had finished tethering the horse as the man came up and he was covering over the bottles of beer with a heap of hay. The sight of the beer reminded the man of something.

'You told him the beer was for him?' he asked.

'He asked me whose it was and I told him what you said,' the boy replied.

'That's all right.'

He began to unfold the sack in which the blade of his scythe had been wrapped. He spread out the sack slowly and carefully on the grass at the foot of the ash trunk and let his squat body sink down upon it heavily. The boy and the woman seated themselves on the grass at his side. He unhooked the heavy soldier's knife hanging from his belt, and unclasped it and wiped it on his trousers' knee. The woman sliced the pie. The man took his plateful of pie and bread and potatoes on his knee, and spitting his sucking-pebble from his mouth began spearing the food with the point of his knife, eating ravenously. When he did not eat with his knife he ate with his fingers, grunting and belching happily. The woman finished serving the pie, and sucking a smear of gravy from her long fingers, began to eat too.

During the eating no one spoke. The three people stared at the half-mown field. The curves of the scythed grass were beginning to whiten in the blazing sunshine. The heat shimmered and danced above the earth in the distance in little waves.

Before long the man wiped his plate with a piece of bread and swilled down his food with long drinks of cold tea from a blue can. When he had finished drinking, his head lolled back against the ash-tree and he closed his eyes. The boy lay flat on his belly, reading a sporting paper while he ate. The air was stifling and warm even under the ash-tree, and there was no sound in the noon stillness except the clink of the horse's bit as it pulled off the young green leaves of the hawthorn hedge.

But suddenly the woman sat up a little and the drowsy look on her face began to clear away. A figure of a man had appeared at the white gate and was walking across the field. He walked with a kind of swaggering uncertainty and now and then he stopped and took up a handful of mown grass and dropped it again. He was carrying a scythe on his shoulder.

She watched him intently as he skirted the standing grass and came towards the ash-tree. He halted at last within the shade of the tree and took a long look at the expanse of grass, thick with buttercups and tall bull-daisies, scattered everywhere like a white and yellow mass of stars.

'By Christ,' he muttered softly.

His voice was jocular and tipsy. The woman stood up.

'What's the matter, Ponto?' she said.

'This all he's cut?'

'That's all.'

'By Christ.'

He laid his scythe on the grass in disgust. He was a tall, thin, black-haired fellow, about thirty, lean and supple as a stoat; his sharp dark-brown eyes were filled with a roving expression, half dissolute and half cunning; the light in them was sombre with drinking. His soft red lips were full and pouting, and there was something about his face altogether conceited, easy-going and devilish. He had a curious habit of looking at things with one eye half closed in a kind of sleepy wink that was marvellously knowing and attractive. He was wearing a dark slouch hat which he had tilted back from his forehead and which gave him an air of being a little wild but sublimely happy.

Suddenly he grinned at the woman and walked over to where the man lay sleeping. He bent down and put his mouth close to his face.

'Hey, your old hoss's bolted!' he shouted.

The man woke with a start.

'Your old hoss's bolted!'

'What's that? Where did you spring from?'

'Get up, y'old sleepy guts. I wanna get this grass knocked down afore dark.'

The man got to his feet.

'Knock this lot down afore dark?'

'Yes, my old beauty. When I mow I do mow, I do.' He smiled and wagged his head. 'Me and my old dad used to mow twenty-acre fields afore dark – and start with the dew on. Twenty-acre fields. You don't know what mowin' is.'

He began to take off his jacket. He was slightly unsteady on his feet and the jacket bothered him as he pulled it off and he swore softly. He was wearing a blue-and-white shirt and a pair of dark moleskin trousers held up by a wide belt of plaited leather thongs. His whetstone rested in a leather socket hanging from the belt. He spat on his hands and slipped the whetstone from the socket and picked up his scythe and with easy, careless rhythmical swings began to whet the long blade. The woman gazed at the stroke of his arm and listened to the sharp ring of the stone against the blade with a look of unconscious admiration and pleasure on her face. The blade of the scythe was very long, tapering and slender, and it shone like silver in the freckles of sunlight coming through the ash leaves. He ceased sharpening the blade and took a swing at a tuft of bull-daisies. The blade cut the stalks crisply and the white flowers fell evenly together, like a fallen nosegay. His swing was beautiful and with the scythe in his hand the balance of his body seemed to become perfect and he himself suddenly sober, dignified and composed.

'Know what my old dad used to say?' he said.

'No.'

'Drink afore you start.'

'Fetch a bottle of beer for Ponto,' said the man to the boy at once. 'I got plenty of beer. The boy went up on the nag and fetched it.'

'That's a good job. You can't mow without beer.'

'That's right.'

'My old man used to drink twenty pints a day. God's truth. Twenty pints a day. He was a bloody champion. You can't mow without beer.'

The boy came up with a bottle of beer in his hand. Ponto took it from him mechanically, hardly looking at him. He uncorked the bottle, covered the white froth with his mouth and drank eagerly, the muscles of his neck rippling like those of a horse. He drank all the beer at one draught and threw the empty bottle into the hedge, scaring the pony.

'Whoa! damn you!' he shouted.

The pony tossed his head and quietened again. Ponto wiped his lips, and taking a step or two towards the boy, aimed the point of the scythe jocularly at his backside. The boy ran off and Ponto grinned tipsily at the woman.

'You goin' to turn the rows?' he said.

'Yes,' she said.

He looked her up and down, from the arch of her hips to the clear shape of her breasts in her blouse and the coil of her black pigtail. Her husband was walking across the field to fetch his scythe. She smiled drowsily at Ponto and he smiled in return.

'I thought you'd come,' she said softly.

His smile broadened and he stretched out his hand and let his fingers run down her bare brown throat. She quivered and breathed quickly and laughed softly in return. His eyes rested on her face with mysterious admiration and delight and he seemed suddenly very pleased about something.

'Good old Anna,' he said softly.

He walked past her and crossed the field to the expanse of unmown grass. He winked solemnly and his fingers ran lightly against her thigh as he passed her.

The woman followed him out into the sunshine and took up her rake and began to turn the rows that had been cut since early morning. When she glanced up again the men were mowing. They seemed to be mowing at the same even, methodical pace, but Ponto was already ahead. He swung his scythe with a long, light caressing sweep, smoothly and masterfully, as though his limbs had been born to mow. The grass was shaved off very close to the earth and was laid in a tidy swathe that curved gently behind him like a thick rope. On the backward stroke the grass and the buttercups and the bull-daisies were pressed gently backwards, bent in readiness to meet the forward swing that came through the grass with a soft swishing sound like the sound of indrawn breath.

The boy came and raked in the row next to the woman. Together they turned the rows and the men mowed in silence for a long time. Every time the woman looked up she looked at Ponto. He was always ahead of her husband and he moved with a kind of lusty insistence, as though he were intent on mowing the whole field before darkness fell. Her husband mowed in a stiff, awkward fashion, always limping and often whetting his scythe. The boy had taken some beer to Ponto, who often stopped to drink. She would catch the flash of the bottle tilted up in the brilliant sunshine and she would look at him meditatively as though remembering something.

As the afternoon went on, Ponto mowed far ahead of her husband, working across the field towards the pond and the willows. He began at last to mow a narrow space of grass behind the pond. She saw the swing of his bare arms through the

31

branches and then lost them again.

Suddenly he appeared and waved a bottle and shouted something.

'I'll go,' she said to the boy.

She dropped her rake and walked over to the ash-tree and found a bottle of beer. The flies were tormenting the horse and she broke off an ash bough and slipped it in the bridle. The sun seemed hotter than ever as she crossed the field with the beer, and the earth was cracked and dry under her feet. She picked up a stalk of buttercups and swung it against her skirt. The scent of the freshly mown grass was strong and sweet in the sunshine. She carried the beer close by her side, in the shadow.

Ponto was mowing a stretch of grass thirty or forty yards wide behind the pond. The grass was richer and taller than in the rest of the field and the single swathes he had cut lay as thick as corn.

She sat down on the bank of the pond under a willow until he had finished his bout of mowing. She had come up silently, and he was mowing with his back towards her, and it was not until he turned that he knew she was there.

He laid his scythe in the grass and came sidling up to her. His face was drenched in sweat and in his mouth was a stalk of totter-grass and the dark red seeds trembled as he walked. He looked at Anna with a kind of sleepy surprise.

'Good old Anna,' he said.

'You did want beer?' she said.

He smiled and sat down at her side.

She too smiled with a flash of her black eyes. He took the bottle from her hand and put one hand on her knee and caressed it gently. She watched the hand with a smile of strange, wicked, ironical amusement. He put the bottle between his knees and unscrewed the stopper.

'Drink,' he said softly.

She drank and gave him the bottle.

'Haven't seen you for ages,' she murmured.

He shrugged his shoulders and took a long drink. His hand was still on her knee and, as she played idly with the stalk of buttercups, her dark face concealed its rising passion in a look of wonderful preoccupation, as though she had forgotten him completely. He wetted his lips with his tongue and ran his hand swiftly and caressingly from her knee to her waist. Her body was stiff for one moment and then it relaxed and sank backwards into the long grass. She shut her eyes and slipped into his embrace like a snake, her face blissfully happy, her hand still clasping the stalk of buttercups, her whole body trembling.

Presently across the field came the sound of a scythe being sharpened. She whispered something quickly and struggled and Ponto got to his feet. She sat up and buttoned the neck of her blouse. She was flushed and panting, and her eyes rested on Ponto with a soft, almost beseeching look of adoration.

Ponto walked away to his scythe and picked it up and began mowing again. He mowed smoothly and with a sort of aloof indifference as though nothing had happened, and she let him mow for five or six paces before she too stood up.

'Ponto,' she whispered.

'Eh?'

'I'll come back,' she said.

She remained for a moment in an attitude of expectancy, but he did not speak or cease the swing of his arms, and very slowly she turned away and went back across the field.

She walked back to where she had left her rake. She picked up the rake and began to turn the swathes of hay again, following the boy. She worked for a long time without looking up. When at last she lifted her head and looked over towards the pond, she saw that Ponto had ceased mowing behind the pond and was cutting the grass in the open field again. He was mowing with the same easy, powerful insistence and with the same beautiful swaggering rhythm of his body, as though he could never grow tired.

They worked steadily on and the sun began to swing round behind the ash-tree and the heat began to lessen and twilight began to fall. While the two men were mowing side by side on the last strip of grass, the woman began to pack the victual-bags and put the saddle on the pony under the ash-tree.

She was strapping the girth of the saddle when she heard feet in the grass and a voice said softly:

'Any more beer?'

She turned and saw Ponto. A bottle of beer was left in the bag and she brought it out for him. He began drinking, and while he was drinking she gazed at him with rapt admiration, as though she had been mysteriously attracted out of herself by the sight of his subtle, conceited, devilish face, the memory of his embrace by the pond and the beautiful untiring motion of his arms swinging the scythe throughout the afternoon. There was something altogether trustful, foolish and abandoned about her, as though she was sublimely eager to do whatever he asked.

'Think you'll finish?' she said in a whisper.

'Easy.'

He corked the beer and they stood looking at each other. He looked at her with a kind of careless, condescending stare, half smiling. She stood perfectly still, her eyes filled with half-happy, half-frightened submissiveness.

He suddenly wiped the beer from his lips with the back of his hand and put out his arm and caught her waist and tried to kiss her.

'Not now,' she said desperately. 'Not now. He'll see. Afterwards. He'll see.'

He gave her a sort of half-pitying smile and shrugged his shoulders and walked away across the field without a word.

'Afterwards,' she called in a whisper.

She went on packing the victual-bags, the expression on her face lost and expectant. The outlines of the field and the figures of the mowers became softer and darker in the twilight. The evening air was warm and heavy with the scent of the hay.

The men ceased mowing at last. The boy had gone home and the woman led the pony across the field to where the men were waiting. Her husband was tying the sack about the blade of his scythe. She looked at Ponto with a dark, significant flash of her eyes, but he took no notice.

'You'd better finish the beer,' she said.

He took the bottle and drank it to the dregs and then hurled the bottle across the field. She tried to catch his eye, but he was already walking away over the field, as though he had never seen her.

She followed him with her husband and the pony. They came to the gate of the field and Ponto was waiting. A look of anticipation and joy shot up in her eyes.

'Why should I damn well walk?' said Ponto. 'Eh? Why should I damn well walk up this lane when I can sit on your old hoss? Lemme get up.'

He laid his scythe in the grass and while the woman held the pony he climbed into the saddle.

'Give us me scythe,' he asked. 'I can carry that. Whoa! mare, damn you!'

She picked up the scythe and gave it to him and he put it over his shoulder. She let her hand touch his knee and fixed her eyes on him with a look of enquiring eagerness, but he suddenly urged the horse forward and began to ride away up the lane.

She followed her husband out of the field. He shut the gate and looked back over the darkening field at the long black swathes of hay lying pale yellow in the dusk. He seemed pleased and he called to Ponto:

'I don't know what the Hanover we should ha' done without you, Ponto.'

Ponto waved his rein-hand with sublime conceit.

'That's nothing,' he called back. 'Me and my old dad used to mow forty-acre fields afore dark. God damn it, that's nothing. All in the day's work.'

He seized the rein again and tugged it and the horse broke into a trot, Ponto bumping the saddle and swearing and shouting as he went up the lane.

The woman followed him with her husband. He walked slowly, limping, and now and then she walked on a few paces ahead, as though trying to catch up with the retreating horse. Sometimes the horse would slow down into a walk and she would come almost to within speaking distance of Ponto, but each time the horse would break into a fresh trot and leave her as far behind again. The lane was dusky with twilight and Ponto burst into a song about a girl and a sailor.

'Hark at him,' said the husband. 'He's a Tartar. He's a Tartar.'

The rollicking voice seemed to echo over the fields with soft, deliberate mocking. The woman did not speak: but as she listened her dark face was filled with the conflicting expression of many emotions: exasperation, perplexity, jealousy, longing, hope, anger.

Love Among the Haystacks

D.H. LAWRENCE

I

The two large fields lay on a hillside facing south. Being newly cleared of hay, they were golden green, and they shone almost blindingly in the sunlight. Across the hill, half-way up, ran a high hedge, that flung its black shadow finely across the molten glow of the sward. The stack was being built just above the hedge. It was of great size, massive, but so silvery and delicately bright in tone that it seemed not to have weight. It rose dishevelled and radiant among the steady, golden-green glare of the field. A little farther back was another, finished stack.

The empty wagon was just passing through the gap in the hedge. From the far-off corner of the bottom field, where the sward was still striped grey with winrows, the loaded wagon launched forward, to climb the hill to the stack. The white dots of the hay-makers showed distinctly among the hay.

The two brothers were having a moment's rest, waiting for the load to come up. They stood wiping their brows with their arms, sighing from the heat and the labour of placing the last load. The stack they rode was high, lifting them up above the hedge-tops, and very broad, a great slightly hollowed vessel into which the sunlight poured, in which the hot, sweet scent of hay was suffocating. Small and inefficacious the brothers looked, half-submerged in the loose, great trough, lifted high up as if on an altar reared to the sun.

Maurice, the younger brother, was a handsome young fellow of twenty-one, careless and debonair, and full of vigour. His grey eyes, as he taunted his brother, were bright and baffled with a strong emotion. His swarthy face had the same peculiar smile, expectant and glad and nervous, of a young man roused for the first time in passion.

'Tha sees,' he said, as he leaned on the pommel of his fork, 'tha thowt as tha'd done me one, didna ter?' He smiled as he spoke, then fell again into his pleasant torment of musing.

'I thought nowt – tha knows so much,' retorted Geoffrey, with the touch of a sneer. His brother had the better of him. Geoffrey was a very heavy, hulking fellow, a year older than Maurice. His blue eyes were unsteady, they glanced away quickly; his mouth was morbidly sensitive. One felt him wince away, through the whole of his great body. His inflamed self-consciousness was a disease in him.

'Ah, but though, I know tha did,' mocked Maurice. 'Tha went slinkin' off' – Geoffrey winced convulsively – 'thinking as that wor the last night as any of us 'ud ha' ter stop here, an' so tha'd leave me to sleep out, though it wor thy turn—'

He smiled to himself, thinking of the result of Geoffrey's ruse.

'I didna go slinkin' off neither,' retorted Geoffrey, in his heavy, chumsy manner, wincing at the phrase. 'Didna my feyther send me to fetch some coal—'

'Oh yes, oh yes – we know all about it. But tha sees what tha missed, my lad.'

Maurice, chuckling, threw himself on his back in the bed of hay. There was absolutely nothing in his world, then, except the shallow ramparts of the stack, and the blazing sky. He clenched his fists tight, threw his arms across his face, and braced his muscles again. He was evidently very much moved, so acutely that it was hardly pleasant, though he still smiled. Geoffrey, standing behind him, could just see his red mouth, with the young moustache like black fur, curling back and showing the teeth in a smile. The elder brother leaned his chin on the pommel of his fork, looking out across the country.

Far away was the faint blue heap of Nottingham. Between, the country lay under a haze of heat, with here and there a flag of colliery smoke waving. But near at hand, at the foot of the hill, across the deep-hedged high road, was only the silence of the old church and the castle farm, among their trees. The large view only made Geoffrey more sick. He looked away, to the wagons crossing the field below him, the empty cart like a big insect moving down hill, the load coming up, rocking like a ship, the brown head of the horse ducking, the brown knees lifted and planted strenuously. Geoffrey wished it would be quick.

'Tha didna think—'

Geoffrey started, coiled within himself, and looked down at the handsome lips moving in speech below the brown arms of his brother.

'Tha didna think 'er'd be thur wi' me – or tha wouldna ha' left me to it,' Maurice said, ending with a little laugh of excited memory. Geoffrey flushed with hate, and had an impulse to set his foot on that moving, taunting mouth, which was there below him. There was silence for a time, then, in a peculiar tone of delight, Maurice's voice came again, spelling out the words, as it were:

> '*Ich bin klein, mein Herz ist rein.*
> *Ist niemand d'rin als Christ allein.*'

Maurice chuckled, then, convulsed at a twinge of recollection, keen as pain, he twisted over, pressed himself into the hay.

'Can thee say thy prayers in German?' came his muffled voice.

'I non want,' growled Geoffrey.

Maurice chuckled. His face was quite hidden, and in the dark he was going over again his last night's experiences.

'What about kissin' 'er under th'ear, Sonny,' he said, in a curious, uneasy tone. He writhed, still startled and inflamed by his first contact with love.

Geoffrey's heart swelled within him, and things went dark. He could not see the landscape.

'An' there's just a nice two-handful of her bosom,' came the low, provocative tones of Maurice, who seemed to be talking to himself.

The two brothers were both fiercely shy of women and, until this hay harvest, the whole feminine sex had been represented by their mother and in presence of any other women they were dumb louts. Moreover, brought up by a proud mother, a stranger in the country, they held the common girls as beneath them, because beneath their mother, who spoke pure English, and was very quiet. Loud-mouthed and broad-tongued the common girls were. So these two young men had grown up virgin but tormented.

Now again Maurice had the start of Geoffrey, and the elder brother was deeply mortified. There was a danger of his sinking into a morbid state, from sheer lack of living, lack of interest. The foreign governess at the Vicarage, whose garden lay beside the top field, had talked to the lads through the hedge, and had fascinated them. There was a great elder bush, with its broad creamy flowers crumbling on to the garden path, and into the field. Geoffrey never smelled elder-flower without starting and wincing, thinking of the strange foreign voice that had startled him as he mowed out with the scythe in the hedge bottom. A baby had run through the gap, and the Fräulein, calling in German, had come brushing down the flowers in pursuit. She had started so, on seeing a man standing there in the shade, that for a moment she could not move, and then she had blundered into the rake which was lying by his side. Geoffrey, forgetting she was a woman when he saw her pitch forward, had picked her up carefully, asking: 'Have you hurt you?'

Then she had broken into a laugh, and answered in German, showing him her arms, and knitting her brows. She was nettled rather badly.

'You want a dock leaf,' he said. She frowned in a puzzled fashion.

'A dock leaf?' she repeated. He had rubbed her arms with the green leaf.

And now, she had taken to Maurice. She had seemed to prefer himself at first. Now she had sat with Maurice in the moonlight, and had let him kiss her. Geoffrey sullenly suffered, making no fight.

Unconsciously, he was looking at the Vicarage garden. There she was, in a golden-brown dress. He took off his hat, and held up his right hand in greeting to her. She, a small, golden figure, waved her hand negligently from among the potato rows. He remained, arrested, in the same posture, his hat in his left hand, his right arm upraised, thinking. He could tell by the negligence of her greeting that she was waiting for Maurice. What did she think of himself? Why wouldn't she have him?

Hearing the voice of the wagoner leading the load, Maurice rose. Geoffrey still stood in the same way, but his face was sullen, and his upraised hand was slack with brooding. Maurice faced uphill. His eyes lit up and he laughed. Geoffrey dropped his own arm, watching.

'Lad?' chuckled Maurice. 'I non knowed 'er wor there.' He waved his hand clumsily. In these matters Geoffrey did better. The elder brother watched the girl. She ran to the end of the path, behind the bushes, so that she was screened from the house. Then she waved her handkerchief wildly. Maurice did not notice the manoeuvre. There was the cry of a child. The girl's figure vanished, reappeared holding up a white childish bundle, and came down the path. There she put down her charge, sped uphill to a great ash-tree, climbed quickly to a large horizontal bar that formed the fence there, and, standing poised, blew kisses with both her hands, in a foreign fashion that excited the brothers. Maurice laughed aloud, as he waved his red handkerchief.

'Well, what's the danger?' shouted a mocking voice from below. Maurice collapsed, blushing furiously.

'Now!' he called.

There was a hearty laugh from below.

The load rode up, sheered with a hiss against the stack, then

41

sank back again upon the scotches. The brothers ploughed across the mass of hay, taking the forks. Presently a big, burly man, red and glistening, climbed to the top of the load. Then he turned round, scrutinized the hillside from under his shaggy brows. He caught sight of the girl under the ash-tree.

'Oh, that's who it is,' he laughed. 'I thought it was some such bird, but I couldn't see her.'

The father laughed in a hearty, chaffing way, then began to teem the load. Geoffrey, on the stack above, received his great forkfuls, and swung them over to Maurice, who took them, placed them, building the stack. In the intense sunlight, the three worked in silence, knit together in a brief passion of work. The father stirred slowly for a moment, getting the hay from under his feet. Geoffrey waited, the blue tines of his fork glittering in expectation: the mass rose, his fork swung beneath it, there was a light clash of blades, then the hay was swept on to the stack, caught by Maurice, who placed it judiciously. One after another, the shoulders of the three men bowed and braced themselves. All wore light blue, bleached shirts, that stuck close to their backs. The father moved mechanically, his thick, rounded shoulders bending and lifting dully: he worked monotonously. Geoffrey flung away his strength. His massive shoulders swept and flung the hay extravagantly.

'Dost want to knock me ower?' asked Maurice angrily. He had to brace himself against the impact. The three men worked intensely, as if some will urged them. Maurice was light and swift at the work, but he had to use his judgement. Also, when he had to place the hay along the far ends, he had some distance to carry it. So he was too slow for Geoffrey. Ordinarily, the elder would have placed the hay as far as possible where his brother wanted it. Now, however, he pitched his forkfuls into the middle of the stack. Maurice strode swiftly and handsomely across the bed, but the work was too much for him. The other two men, clenched in their receive-and-deliver, kept up a high pitch of labour. Geoffrey still flung the hay at random. Maurice was perspiring heavily with heat and exertion, and was getting worried. Now and again, Geoffrey wiped his arm across his brow, mechanically, like an animal. Then he glanced with satisfaction at Maurice's moiled condition, and caught the next forkful.

'Wheer dost think thou'rt hollin' it, fool!' panted Maurice, as his brother flung a forkful out of reach.

'Wheer I've a mind,' answered Geoffrey.

Maurice toiled on, now very angry. He felt the sweat trickling down his body: drops fell into his long black lashes, blinding him, so that he had to stop and angrily dash his eyes clear. The veins stood out in his swarthy neck. He felt he would burst, or drop, if the work did not soon slacken off. He heard his father's fork dully scrape the cart bottom.

'There, the last,' the father panted. Geoffrey tossed the last light lot at random, took off his hat, and, steaming in the sunshine as he wiped himself, stood complacently watching Maurice struggle with clearing the bed.

'Don't you think you've got your bottom corner a bit far out?' came the father's voice from below. 'You'd better be drawing in now, hadn't you?'

'I thought you said next load,' Maurice called sulkily.

'Aye! All right. But isn't this bottom corner—?'

Maurice, impatient, took no notice.

Geoffrey strode over the stack, and struck his fork in the offending corner. 'What – here?' he bawled in his great voice.

'Aye – isn't it a bit loose?' came the irritating voice.

Geoffrey pushed his fork in the jutting corner, and, leaning his weight on the handle, shoved. He thought it shook. He thrust again with all his power. The mass swayed.

'What art up to, tha fool!' cried Maurice, in a high voice.

'Mind who tha'rt callin' a fool,' said Geoffrey, and he prepared to push again. Maurice sprang across, and elbowed his brother aside. On the yielding, swaying bed of hay, Geoffrey lost his foothold, and fell grovelling. Maurice tried the corner.

'It's solid enough,' he shouted angrily.

'Aye – all right,' came the conciliatory voice of the father, 'you do get a bit of a rest now there's such a long way to cart it,' he added reflectively.

Geoffrey had got to his feet.

'Tha'll mind who tha'rt nudging, I can tell thee,' he threatened heavily; adding, as Maurice continued to work, 'an' tha non ca's him a fool again, dost hear?'

'Not till next time,' sneered Maurice.

As he worked silently round the stack, he neared where his brother stood like a sullen statue, leaning on his fork-handle, looking out over the countryside. Maurice's heart quickened at its beat. He worked forward, until a point of his fork caught in the leather of Geoffrey's boot, and the metal rang sharply.

'Are ter going ta shift thysen?' asked Maurice threateningly. There was no reply from the great block. Maurice lifted his upper lip like a dog. Then he put out his elbow, and tried to push his brother into the stack, clear of his way.

'Who are ter shovin'?' came the deep, dangerous voice.

'Thagh,' replied Maurice, with a sneer, and straightway the two brothers set themselves against each other, like opposing bulls, Maurice trying his hardest to shift Geoffrey from his footing, Geoffrey leaning all his weight in resistance. Maurice, insecure in his footing, staggered a little, and Geoffrey's weight followed him. He went slithering over the edge of the stack.

Geoffrey turned white to the lips, and remained standing, listening. He heard the fall. Then a flush of darkness came over him, and he remained standing only because he was planted. He had not strength to move. He could hear no sound from below, was only faintly aware of a sharp shriek from a long way off. He listened again. Then he filled with sudden panic.

'Feyther!' he roared, in his tremendous voice: 'Feyther! Feyther!'

The valley re-echoed with the sound. Small cattle on the hillside looked up. Men's figures came running from the bottom field, and much nearer a woman's figure was racing across the upper field. Geoffrey waited in terrible suspense.

'Ah-h!' he heard the strange, wild voice of the girl cry out. 'Ah-h!' – and then some foreign wailing speech. Then: 'Ah-h! Are you dea-ed!'

He stood sullenly erect on the stack, not daring to go down, longing to hide in the hay, but too sullen to stoop out of sight. He heard his eldest brother come up, panting.

'Whatever's amiss!' and then the labourer, and then his father.

'Whatever have you been doing?' he heard his father ask, while yet he had not come round the corner of the stack. And then, in a low, bitter tone:

'Eh, he's done for! I'd no business to ha' put it all on the stack.'

There was a moment or two of silence, then the voice of Henry, the eldest brother, said crisply:

'He's not dead – he's coming round.'

Geoffrey heard, but was not glad. He had as lief Maurice were dead. At least that would be final: better than meeting his brother's charges, and of seeing his mother pass to the sickroom. If Maurice were killed, he himself would not explain, no, not a word, and they could hang him if they liked. If Maurice were only hurt, then everybody would know, and Geoffrey could never lift his face again. What added torture, to pass along, everybody knowing. He wanted something that he could stand back to, something definite, if it were only the knowledge that he had killed his brother. He *must* have something firm to back up to, or he would go mad. He was so lonely, he who above all needed the support of sympathy.

'No, he's comin' to, I tell you he is,' said the labourer.

'He's not dea-ed, he's not dea-ed,' came the passionate, strange sing-song of the foreign girl. 'He's not dead – no-o.'

'He wants some brandy – look at the colour of his lips,' said the crisp, cold voice of Henry. 'Can you fetch some?'

'Wha-at? Fetch?' Fräulein did not understand.

'Brandy,' said Henry, very distinct.

'Brrandy!' she re-echoed.

'You go, Bill,' groaned the father.

'Aye, I'll go,' replied Bill, and he ran across the field.

Maurice was not dead, not going to die. This Geoffrey now realised. He was glad after all that the extreme penalty was revoked. But he hated to think of himself going on. He would always shrink now. He had hoped and hoped for the time when

45

he would be careless, bold as Maurice, when he would not wince and shrink. Now he would always be the same, coiling up in himself like a tortoise with no shell.

'Ah-h! He's getting better!' came the wild voice of the Fräulein, and she began to cry, a strange sound, that startled the men, made the animal bristle within them. Geoffrey shuddered as he heard, between her sobbing, the impatient moaning of his brother as the breath came back.

The labourer returned at a run, followed by the Vicar. After the brandy, Maurice made more moaning, hiccuping noises. Geoffrey listened in torture. He heard the Vicar asking for explanations. All the united, anxious voices replied in brief phrases.

'It was that other,' cried the Fräulein. 'He knocked him over – ha!'

She was shrill and vindictive.

'I don't think so,' said the father to the Vicar, in a quite audible but private tone, speaking as if the Fräulein did not understand his English.

The Vicar addressed his children's governess in bad German. She replied in a torrent which he would not confess was too much for him. Maurice was making little moaning, sighing noises.

'Where's your pain, boy, eh?' the father asked, pathetically.

'Leave him alone a bit,' came the cool voice of Henry. 'He's winded, if no more.'

'You'd better see that no bones are broken,' said the anxious Vicar.

'It wor a blessing as he should a dropped on that heap of hay just there,' said the labourer. 'If he'd happened to ha' catched hisself on this nog o' wood 'e wouldna ha' stood much chance.'

Geoffrey wondered when he would have courage to venture down. He had wild notions of pitching himself head foremost from the stack: if he could only extinguish himself, he would be safe. Quite frantically, he longed not to be. The idea of going through life thus coiled up within himself in morbid self-consciousness, always lonely, surly, and a misery, was enough to make him cry out. What would they all think when they knew he had knocked Maurice off that high stack?

They were talking to Maurice down below. The lad had recovered in great measure, and was able to answer faintly.

'Whatever was you doin'?' the father asked gently. 'Was you playing about with our Geoffrey? – Aye, and where is he?'

Geoffrey's heart stood still.

'I dunno,' said Henry, in a curious, ironic tone.

'Go an' have a look,' pleaded the father, infinitely relieved over one son, anxious now concerning the other. Geoffrey could not bear that his eldest brother should climb up and question him in his high-pitched drawl of curiosity. The culprit doggedly set his feet on the ladder. His nailed boots slipped a rung.

'Mind yourself,' shouted the overwrought father.

Geoffrey stood like a criminal at the foot of the ladder, glancing furtively at the group. Maurice was lying, pale and slightly convulsed, upon a heap of hay. The Fräulein was kneeling beside his head. The Vicar had the lad's shirt full open down the breast, and was feeling for broken ribs. The father knelt on the other side, the labourer and Henry stood aside.

'I can't find anything broken,' said the Vicar, and he sounded slightly disappointed.

'There's nowt broken to find,' murmured Maurice, smiling.

The father started. 'Eh?' he said. 'Eh?' and he bent over the invalid.

'I say it's not hurt me,' repeated Maurice.

'What were you doing?' asked the cold, ironic voice of Henry. Geoffrey turned his head away: he had not yet raised his face.

'Nowt as I know on,' he muttered in a surly tone.

'Why!' cried Fräulein in a reproachful tone. 'I see him – knock him over!' She made a fierce gesture with her elbow. Henry curled his long moustache sardonically.

'Nay lass, niver,' smiled the wan Maurice. 'He was fur enough away from me when I slipped.'

'Oh, ah!' cried the Fräulein, not understanding.

'Yi,' smiled Maurice indulgently.

'I think you're mistaken,' said the father, rather pathetically, smiling at the girl as if she were 'wanting'.

'Oh no,' she cried. 'I *see* him.'

'Nay, lass,' smiled Maurice quietly.

She was a Pole, named Paula Jablonowsky: young, only twenty years old, swift and light as a wild cat, with a strange, wild-cat way of grinning. Her hair was blonde and full of life, all crisped into many tendrils with vitality, shaking round her face. Her fine blue eyes were peculiarly lidded, and she seemed to look piercingly, then languorously, like a wild cat. She had somewhat Slavonic cheekbones, and was very much freckled. It was evident that the Vicar, a pale, rather cold man, hated her.

Maurice lay pale and smiling in her lap, whilst she cleaved to him like a mate. One felt instinctively that they were mated. She was ready at any minute to fight with ferocity in his defence, now he was hurt. Her looks at Geoffrey were full of fierceness. She bowed over Maurice and caressed him with her foreign-sounding English.

'You say what you lai-ike,' she laughed, giving him lordship over her.

'Hadn't you better be going and looking what has become of Margery?' asked the Vicar in tones of reprimand.

'She is with her mother – I heared her. I will go in a whai-ile,' smiled the girl, coolly.

'Do you feel as if you could stand?' asked the father, still anxiously.

'Aye, in a bit,' smiled Maurice.

'You want to get up?' caressed the girl, bowing over him, till her face was not far from his.

'I'm in no hurry,' he replied, smiling brilliantly.

This accident had given him quite a strange new ease, an authority. He felt extraordinarily glad. New power had come to him all at once.

'You in no hurry,' she repeated, gathering his meaning. She smiled tenderly; she was in his service.

'She leaves us in another month – Mrs Inwood could stand no more of her,' apologized the Vicar quietly to the father.

'Why, is she—?'

'Like a wild thing – disobedient, and insolent.'

'Ha!'

The father sounded abstract.

'No more foreign governesses for me.'

Maurice stirred, and looked up at the girl.

'You stand up?' she asked brightly. 'You well?'

He laughed again, showing his teeth winsomely. She lifted his head, sprung to her feet, her hands still holding his head, then she took him under the armpits and had him on his feet before anyone could help. He was much taller than she: he grasped her strong shoulders heavily, leaned against her, and, feeling her round, firm breast doubled up against his side, he smiled, catching his breath.

'You see I'm all right,' he gasped. 'I was only winded.'

'You all right?' she cried, in great glee.

'Yes, I am.'

He walked a few steps after a moment.

'There's nowt ails me, Father,' he laughed.

'Quite well, you?' she cried in a pleading tone. He laughed outright, looked down at her, touching her cheek with his fingers.

'That's it – if tha likes.'

'If I lai-ike!' she repeated, radiant.

'She's going at the end of three weeks,' said the Vicar consolingly to the farmer.

II

While they were talking, they heard the far-off hooting of a pit.

'There goes th' loose 'a,' said Henry, coldly. 'We're *not* going to get that corner up today.'

The father looked round anxiously.

'Now, Maurice, are you sure you're all right?' he asked.

'Yes, I'm all right. Haven't I told you?'

'Then you sit down there, and in a bit you can be getting dinner out. Henry, you go on the stack. Wheer's Jim? Oh, he's minding the hosses. Bill, and you, Geoffrey, you can pick while Jim loads.'

49

Maurice sat down under the wych-elm to recover. The Fräulein had fled back. He made up his mind to ask her to marry him. He had got fifty pounds of his own, and his mother would help him. For a long time he sat musing, thinking what he would do. Then, from the float he fetched a big basket covered with a cloth, and spread the dinner. There was an immense rabbit pie, a dish of cold potatoes, much bread, a great piece of cheese, and a solid rice pudding.

These two fields were four miles from the home farm. But they had been in the hands of the Wookeys for several generations, therefore the father kept them on, and everyone looked forward to the hay harvest at Greasley: it was a kind of picnic. They brought dinner and tea in the milk-float, which the father drove over in the morning. The lads and the labourers cycled. Off and on, the harvest lasted a fortnight. As the high road from Alfreton to Nottingham ran at the foot of the fields, someone usually slept in the hay under the shed to guard the tools. The sons took it in turns. They did not care for it much, and were for that reason anxious to finish the harvest on this day. But work went slack and disjointed after Maurice's accident.

When the load was teemed, they gathered round the white cloth, which was spread under a tree between the hedge and the stack, and, sitting on the ground, ate their meal. Mrs Wookey always sent a clean cloth, and knives and forks and plates for everybody. Mr Wookey was always rather proud of this spread: everything was so proper.

'There now,' he said, sitting down jovially. 'Doesn't this look nice now – eh?'

They all sat round the white spread, in the shadow of the tree and the stack, and looked out up the fields as they ate. From their shady coolness, the gold sward seemed liquid, molten with heat. The horse with the empty wagon wandered a few yards, then stood feeding. Everything was as still as a trance. Now and again, the horse between the shafts of the load that stood propped beside the stack, jingled his loose bit as he ate. The men ate and drank in silence, the father reading the newspaper,

Maurice leaning back on a saddle, Henry reading the *Nation*, the others eating busily.

Presently 'Helloa! 'Er's 'ere again!', exclaimed Bill. All looked up. Paula was coming across the field carrying a plate.

'She's bringing something to tempt your appetite, Maurice,' said the eldest brother ironically. Maurice was midway through a large wedge of rabbit pie, and some cold potatoes.

'Aye, bless me if she's not,' laughed the father. 'Put that away, Maurice, it's a shame to disappoint her.'

Maurice looked round very shamefaced, not knowing what to do with his plate.

'Give it over here,' said Bill. 'I'll polish him off.'

'Bringing something for the invalid?' laughed the father to the Fräulein. 'He's looking up nicely.'

'I bring him some chicken, him!' She nodded her head at Maurice childishly. He flushed and smiled.

'Tha doesna mean ter bust 'im,' said Bill.

Everybody laughed aloud. The girl did not understand, so she laughed also. Maurice ate his portion very sheepishly.

The father pitied his son's shyness.

'Come here and sit by me,' he said. 'Eh, Fräulein! Is that what they call you?'

'I sit by you, Father,' she said innocently.

Henry threw his head back and laughed long and noiselessly. She settled near to the big, handsome man.

'My name,' she said, 'is Paula Jablonowsky.'

'Is what?' said the father, and the other men went into roars of laughter.

'Tell me again,' said the father. 'Your name—?'

'Paula.'

'Paula? Oh – well, it's a rum sort of name, eh? His name—' he nodded at his son.

'Maurice – I know.' She pronounced it sweetly, then laughed into the father's eyes. Maurice blushed to the roots of his hair.

They questioned her concerning her history, and made out that she came from Hanover, that her father was a shop-keeper, and that she had run away from home because she did not like

51

her father. She had gone to Paris.

'Oh,' said the father, now dubious. 'And what did you do there?'

'In school – in a young ladies' school.'

'Did you like it?'

'Oh no – no laïfe – no life!'

'What?'

'When we go out – two and two – all together – no more. Ah, no life, no life.'

'Well, that's a winder!' exclaimed the father. 'No life in Paris! And have you found much life in England?'

'No – ah no. I don't like it.' She made a grimace at the Vicarage.

'How long have you been in England?'

'Chreestmas – so.'

'And what will you do?'

'I will go to London, or to Paris. Ah, Paris! – Or get married!' She laughed into the father's eyes.

The father laughed heartily.

'Get married, eh? And who to?'

'I don't know. I am going away.'

'The country's too quiet for you?' asked the father.

'Too quiet – hm!' she nodded in assent.

'You wouldn't care for making butter and cheese?'

'Making butter – hm!' She turned to him with a glad, bright gesture. 'I like it.'

'Oh,' laughed the father. 'You would, would you?'

She nodded vehemently, with glowing eyes.

'She'd like anything in the shape of a change,' said Henry judicially.

'I think she would,' agreed the father. It did not occur to them that she fully understood what they said. She looked at them closely, then thought with bowed head.

'Hullo!' exclaimed Henry, ever the alert. A tramp was slouching towards them through the gap. He was a very seedy, slinking fellow, with a tang of horsey braggadocio about him. Small, thin and ferrety, with a week's red beard bristling on his pointed chin, he came slouching forward.

'Have yer got a bit of a job goin'?' he asked.

'A bit of a job,' repeated the father. 'Why, can't you see as we've a'most done?'

'Aye – but I noticed you was a hand short, an' I thowt as 'appen you'd gie me half a day.'

'What, are *you* any good in a hay close?' asked Henry, with a sneer.

The man stood slouching against the haystack. All the others were seated on the floor. He had an advantage.

'I could work aside any on yer,' he bragged.

'Tha looks it,' laughed Bill.

'And what's your regular trade?' asked the father.

'I'm a jockey by rights. But I did a bit o' dirty work for a boss o' mine, an' I was landed. '*E* got the benefit, *I* got kicked out. '*E* axed me – an' then 'e looked as if 'e'd never seed me.'

'Did he, though!' exclaimed the father sympathetically.

''E did that!' asserted the man.

'But we've got nothing for you,' said Henry coldly.

'What does the boss say?' asked the man, impudent.

'No, we've no work you can do,' said the father. 'You can have a bit o' something to eat, if you like.'

'I should be glad of it,' said the man.

He was given the chunk of rabbit pie that remained. This he ate greedily. There was something debased, parasitic, about him, which disgusted Henry. The others regarded him as a curiosity.

'That was nice and tasty,' said the tramp, with gusto.

'Do you want a piece of bread 'n' cheese?' asked the father.

'It'll help to fill up,' was the reply.

The man ate this more slowly. The company was embarrassed by his presence, and could not talk. All the men lit their pipes, the meal over.

'So you dunna want any help?' said the tramp at last.

'No – we can manage what bit there is to do.'

'You don't happen to have a fill of bacca to spare, do you?'

The father gave him a good pinch.

'You're all right here,' he said, looking round. They resented this familiarity. However, he filled his clay pipe and smoked with the rest.

As they were sitting silent, another figure came through the gap in the hedge, and noiselessly approached. It was a woman. She was rather small and finely made. Her face was small, very ruddy, and comely, save for the look of bitterness and aloofness that it wore. Her hair was drawn tightly back under a sailor hat. She gave an impression of cleanness, of precision and directness.

'Have you got some work?' she asked of her man. She ignored the rest. He tucked his tail between his legs.

'No, they haven't got no work for me. They've just gave me a draw of bacca.'

He was a mean crawl of a man.

'An' am I goin' to wait for you out there in the lane all day?'

'You needn't if you don't like. You could go on.'

'Well, are you coming?' she asked contemptuously. He rose to his feet in a rickety fashion.

'You needn't be in such a mighty hurry,' he said. 'If you'd wait a bit you might get summat.'

She glanced for the first time over the men. She was quite young, and would have been pretty, were she not so hard and callous-looking.

'Have you had your dinner?' asked the father.

She looked at him with a kind of anger, and turned away. Her face was so childish in its contours, contrasting strangely with her expression.

'Are you coming?' she said to the man.

'He's had his tuck-in. Have a bit, if you want it,' coaxed the father.

'What have you had?' she flashed to the man.

'He's had all what was left o' th' rabbit pie,' said Geoffrey, in an indignant, mocking tone, 'and a great hunk o' bread an' cheese.'

The young woman looked at Geoffrey, and he at her. There was a sort of kinship between them. Both were at odds with the world. Geoffrey smiled satirically. She was too grave, too deeply incensed even to smile.

'There's a cake here, though – you can have a bit o' that, said Maurice blithely.

She eyed him with scorn.

Again she looked at Geoffrey. He seemed to understand her. She turned, and in silence departed. The man remained obstinately sucking at his pipe. Everybody looked at him with hostility.

'We'll be getting to work,' said Henry, rising, pulling off his coat. Paula got to her feet. She was a little bit confused by the presence of the tramp.

'I go,' she said, smiling brilliantly. Maurice rose and followed her sheepishly.

'A good grind, eh?' said the tramp, nodding after the Fräulein. The men only half-understood him, but they hated him.

'Hadn't you better be getting off?' said Henry.

The man rose obediently. He was all slouching, parasitic insolence. Geoffrey loathed him, longed to exterminate him. He was exactly the worst foe of the hyper-sensitive: insolence without sensibility, preying on sensibility. 'Aren't you goin' to give me summat for her? It's nowt she's had all day, to my knowin'. She'll 'appen eat if I take it 'er – though she gets more than I've any knowledge of' – this with a lewd wink of jealous spite. 'And then tries to keep a tight hand on me,' he sneered, taking the bread and cheese, and stuffing it in his pocket.

III

Geoffrey worked sullenly all the afternoon, and Maurice did the horse-raking. It was exceedingly hot. So the day wore on, the atmosphere thickened, and the sunlight grew blurred. Geoffrey was picking with Bill – helping to load the wagons from the winrows. He was sulky, though extraordinarily relieved: Maurice would not tell. Since the quarrel neither brother had spoken to the other. But their silence was entirely amicable, almost affectionate. They had both been deeply moved, so much so that their ordinary intercourse was interrupted; but underneath, each felt a strong regard for the other. Maurice was peculiarly happy, his feeling of affection swimming over everything. But Geoffrey was still sullenly hostile to the most part of the world. He felt isolated. The free and easy intercommunication between the other workers left him distinctly alone. And he was a man who could not bear to stand alone, he was too much afraid of the vast confusion of life surrounding him, in which he was helpless. Geoffrey mistrusted himself with everybody.

The work went on slowly. It was unbearably hot, and everyone was disheartened.

'We s'll have getting-on-for another day of it,' said the father at tea-time, as they sat under the tree.

'Quite a day,' said Henry.

'Somebody'll have to stop, then,' said Geoffrey. 'It 'ud better be me.'

'Nay, lad, I'll stop,' said Maurice, and he hid his head in confusion.

'Stop again tonight!' exclaimed the father. 'I'd rather you went home.'

'Nay, I'm stoppin',' protested Maurice.

'He wants to do his courting,' Henry enlightened them.

The father thought seriously about it.

'I don't know . . .' he mused, rather perturbed.

But Maurice stayed. Towards eight o'clock, after sundown, the men mounted their bicycles, the father put the horse in the float, and all departed. Maurice stood in the gap of the hedge and watched them go, the cart rolling and swinging downhill, over the grass stubble, the cyclists dipping swiftly like shadows in front. All passed through the gate, there was a quick clatter of hoofs on the roadway under the lime-trees, and they were gone. The young man was very much excited, almost afraid, at finding himself alone.

Darkness was rising from the valley. Already, up the steep hill the cart-lamps crept indecisively, and the cottage windows were lit. Everything looked strange to Maurice, as if he had not seen it before. Down the hedge a large lime-tree teemed with scent that seemed almost like a voice speaking. It startled him. He caught a breath of the over-sweet fragrance, then stood still, listening expectantly.

Uphill, a horse whinnied. It was the young mare. The heavy horses went thundering across to the far hedge.

Maurice wondered what to do. He wandered round the deserted stacks restlessly. Heat came in wafts, in thick strands. The evening was a long time cooling. He thought he would go and wash himself. There was a trough of pure water in the hedge bottom. It was filled by a tiny spring that filtered over the brim of the trough down the lush hedge bottom of the lower field. All round the trough, in the upper field, the land was marshy, and there the meadowsweet stood like clots of mist, very sickly smelling in the twilight. The night did not darken, for the moon was in the sky, so that as the tawny colour drew off the heavens they remained pallid with a dimmed moon. The purple bell-flowers in the hedge went black, the ragged robin turned its pink to a faded white, the meadowsweet gathered light as if it were phosphorescent, and it made the air ache with scent.

Maurice kneeled on the slab of stone bathing his hands and arms, then his face. The water was deliciously cool. He had still an hour before Paula would come: she was not due till nine. So he decided to take his bath at night instead of waiting till morning. Was he not sticky, and was not Paula coming to talk to him? He was delighted the thought had occurred to him. As he soused his head in the trough, he wondered what the little creatures that lived in the velvety silt at the bottom would think of the taste of soap. Laughing to himself, he squeezed his cloth into the water. He washed himself from head to foot, standing in the fresh, forsaken corner of the field, where no one could see him by daylight, so that now, in the veiled grey tinge of moonlight, he was no more noticeable than the crowded flowers. The night had on a new look: he never remembered to have seen the lustrous grey sheen of it before, nor to have noticed how vital the lights looked, like live folk inhabiting the silvery spaces. And the tall trees, wrapped obscurely in their mantles, would not have surprised him had they begun to move in converse. As he dried himself, he discovered little wanderings in the air, felt on his sides soft touches and caresses that were peculiarly delicious: sometimes they startled him, and he laughed as if he were not alone. The flowers, the meadowsweet particularly, haunted him. He reached to put his hand over their fleeciness. They touched his thighs. Laughing, he gathered them and dusted himself all over with their cream dust and fragrance. For a moment he hesitated in wonder at himself: but the subtle glow in the hoary and black night reassured him. Things never had looked so personal and full of beauty, he had never known the wonder in himself before.

At nine o'clock he was waiting under the elder-bush, in a state of high trepidation, but feeling that he was worthy, having a sense of his own wonder. She was late. At a quarter-past nine she came, flitting swiftly, in her own eager way.

'No, she would *not* go to sleep,' said Paula, with a world of wrath in her tone. He laughed bashfully. They wandered out into the dim hillside field.

'I have sat – in that bedroom – for an hour, for hours,' she cried indignantly. She took a deep breath: 'Ah, breathe!' she smiled.

She was very intense, and full of energy.

'I want' – she was clumsy with the language – 'I want – I should laike – to run – there!' She pointed across the field.

'Let's run, then,' he said curiously.

'Yes!'

And in an instant she was gone. He raced after her. For all he was so young and limber, he had difficulty in catching her. At first he could scarcely see her, though he could hear the rustle of her dress. She sped with astonishing fleetness. He overtook her, caught her by the arm, and they stood panting, facing one another with laughter.

'I could win,' she asserted blithely.

'Tha couldna,' he replied, with a peculiar, excited laugh. They walked on, rather breathless. In front of them suddenly appeared the dark shapes of the three feeding horses.

'We ride a horse?' she said.

'What, bareback?' he asked.

'You say?' She did not understand.

'With no saddle?'

'No saddle – yes – no saddle.'

'Coop, lass!' he said to the mare, and in a minute he had her by the forelock, and was leading her down to the stacks, where he put a halter on her. She was a big, strong mare. Maurice seated the Fräulein, clambered himself in front of the girl, using the wheel of the wagon as a mount, and together they trotted uphill, she holding lightly round his waist. From the crest of the hill they looked round.

The sky was darkening with an awning of clouds. On the left the hill rose black and wooded, made cosy by a few lights from cottages along the highway. The hill spread to the right, and tufts of trees shut round. But in front was a great vista of night: a sprinkle of cottage candles; a twinkling cluster of lights, like an elfish fair in full swing, at the colliery, an encampment of light at a village; a red flare on the sky far off, above an iron-foundry; and in the farthest distance the dim breathing of town lights. As they watched the night stretch far out, her arms tightened round his waist, and he pressed his elbows to his side, pressing her arms closer still. The horse moved restlessly. They clung to each other.

'Tha doesna want to go right away?' he asked the girl behind him.

'I stay with you,' she answered softly, and he felt her crouching close against him. He laughed curiously. He was afraid to kiss her, though he was urged to do so. They remained still, on the restless horse, watching the small lights lead deep into the night, an infinite distance.

'I don't want to go,' he said, in a tone half pleading.

She did not answer. The horse stirred restlessly.

'Let him run,' cried Paula, 'fast!'

She broke the spell, startled him into a little fury. He kicked the mare, hit her, and away she plunged downhill. The girl clung tightly to the young man. They were riding bareback down a rough, steep hill. Maurice clung hard with hands and knees. Paula held him fast round the waist, leaning her head on his shoulders, and thrilling with excitement.

'We shall be off, we shall be off,' he cried, laughing with excitement; but she only crouched behind and pressed tight to him. The mare tore across the field. Maurice expected every moment to be flung on to the grass. He gripped with all the strength of his knees. Paula tucked herself behind him, and often wrenched him almost from his hold. Man and girl were taut with effort.

At last the mare came to a standstill, blowing. Paula slid off, and in an instant Maurice was beside her. They were both highly excited. Before he knew what he was doing, he had her in his arms, fast, and was kissing her, and laughing. They did not move for some time. Then, in silence, they walked towards the stacks.

It had grown quite dark, the night was thick with cloud. He walked with his arm round Paula's waist, she with her arm round him. They were near the stacks when Maurice felt a spot of rain.

'It's going to rain,' he said.

'Rain!' she echoed, as if it were trivial.

'I'll have to put the stack-cloth on,' he said gravely. She did not understand.

When they got to the stacks, he went round to the shed, to return staggering in the darkness under the burden of the immense and heavy cloth. It had not been used once during the hay harvest.

'What are you going to do?' asked Paula, coming close to him in the darkness.

'Cover the top of the stack with it,' he replied. 'Put it over the stack to keep the rain out.'

'Ah!' she cried, 'up there!' He dropped his burden. 'Yes,' he answered.

Fumblingly he reared the long ladder up the side of the stack. He could not see the top.

'I hope it's solid,' he said softly.

A few smart drops of rain sounded drumming on the cloth. They seemed like another presence. It was very dark indeed between the great buildings of hay. She looked up the black wall, and shrank to him.

'You carry it up there?' she asked.

'Yes,' he answered.

'I help you?' she said.

And she did. They opened the cloth. He clambered first up the steep ladder, bearing the upper part, she followed closely, carrying her full share. They mounted the shaky ladder in silence, stealthily.

IV

As they climbed the stacks a light stopped at the gate on the high road. It was Geoffrey, come to help his brother with the cloth. Afraid of his own intrusion, he wheeled his bicycle silently towards the shed. This was a corrugated-iron erection, on the opposite side of the hedge from the stacks. Geoffrey let his light go in front of him, but there was no sign from the lovers. He thought he saw a shadow slinking away. The light of the bicycle lamp sheered yellowly across the dar, catching a glint of raindrops, a mist of darkness, shadow of leaves and strokes of long grass. Geoffrey entered the shed – no one was there. He walked slowly and doggedly round to the stacks. He had passed the wagon, when he heard something sheering down upon him. Starting back under the wall of hay, he saw the long ladder slither across the side of the stack, and fall with a bruising ring.

'What wor that?' he heard Maurice, aloft, ask cautiously.

'Something fall,' came the curious, almost pleased voice of the Fräulein.

'It wor niver th' ladder,' said Maurice. He peered over the side of the stack. He lay down, looking.

'It is an' a'!' he exclaimed. 'We knocked it down with the cloth, dragging it over.'

'We fast up here?' she exclaimed with a thrill.

'We are that – without I shout and make 'em hear at the Vicarage.'

'Oh no,' she said quickly.

'I don't want to,' he replied, with a short laugh. There came a

61

swift clatter of raindrops on the cloth. Geoffrey crouched under the wall of the other stack.

'Mind where you tread – here, let me straighten this end,' said Maurice, with a peculiar intimate tone – a command and an embrace. 'We'll have to sit under it. At any rate, we shan't get wet.'

'Not get wet!' echoed the girl, pleased, but agitated.

Geoffrey heard the slide and rustle of the cloth over the top of the stack, heard Maurice telling her to 'Mind!'

'Mind!' she repeated. 'Mind! you say "Mind!" '

'Well, what if I do?' he laughed. 'I don't want you to fall over th' side, do I?' His tone was masterful, but he was not quite sure of himself.

There was silence for a moment or two.

'Maurice!' she said, plaintively.

'I'm here,' he answered, tenderly, his voice shaky with excitement that was near to distress. 'There, I've done. Now should we – we'll sit under this corner.'

'Maurice!' she was rather pitiful.

'What? You'll be all right,' he remonstrated, tenderly indignant.

'I be all raïght,' she repeated, 'I be all raïght, Maurice?'

'Tha knows tha will – I canna ca' thee Powla. Should I ca' thee Minnie?'

It was the name of a dead sister.

'Minnie?' she exclaimed in surprise.

'Aye, should I?'

She answered in full-throated German. He laughed shakily.

'Come on – come on under. But do yer wish you was safe in th' Vicarage? Should I shout for somebody?' he asked.

'I don't wish, no!' She was vehement.

'Art sure?' he insisted, almost indignantly.

'Sure – I quite sure.' She laughed.

Geoffrey turned away at the last words. Then the rain beat heavily. The lonely brother slouched miserably to the hut, where the rain played a mad tattoo. He felt very miserable, and jealous of Maurice.

His bicycle lamp, downcast, shone a yellow light on the stark floor of the shed or hut with one wall open. It lit up the trodden earth, the shafts of tools lying piled under the beam, beside the dreary grey metal of the building. He took off the lamp, shone it round the hut. There were piles of harness, tools, a big sugar box, a deep bed of hay – then the beams across the corrugated iron, all very dreary and stark. He shone the lamp into the night: nothing but the furtive glitter of raindrops through the mist of darkness, and black shapes hovering round.

Geoffrey blew out the light and flung himself on to the hay. He would put the ladder up for them in a while, when they would be wanting it. Meanwhile, he sat and gloated over Maurice's felicity. He was imaginative, and now he had something concrete to work upon. Nothing in the whole of life stirred him so profoundly, and so utterly, as the thought of this woman. For Paula was strange, foreign, different from the ordinary girls: the rousing, feminine quality seemed in her concentrated, brighter, more fascinating than in anyone he had known, so that he felt almost like a moth near a candle. He would have loved her wildly – but Maurice had got her. His thoughts beat the same course, round and round. What was it like when you kissed her, when she held you tight round the waist, how did he feel towards Maurice, did she love to touch him, was he kind and attractive to her, what did she think of himself – she merely disregarded him, as she would disregard a horse in a field; why should she do so, why couldn't he make her regard himself, instead of Maurice: he would never command a woman's regard like that, he always gave in to her too soon; if only some woman would come and take him for what he was worth, though he was such a stumbler and showed to such disadvantage, ah, what a grand thing it would be; how he would kiss her. Then round he went again in the same course, brooding almost like a madman. Meanwhile the rain drummed deep on the shed, then grew lighter and softer. There came the drip, drip of the drops falling outside.

Geoffrey's heart leaped up his chest, and he clenched himself, as a black shape crept round the post of the shed and, bowing, entered silently. The young man's heart beat so heavily, in plunges, he could not get his breath to speak. It was shock, rather than fear. The form felt towards him. He sprang up, gripped it with his great hands, panting 'Now, then!'

There was no resistance, only a little whimper of despair.

'Let me go,' said a woman's voice.

'What are you after?' he asked, in deep, gruff tones.

'I thought 'e was 'ere,' she wept despairingly, with little, stubborn sobs.

'An' you've found what you didn't expect, have you?'

At the sound of his bullying she tried to get away from him.

'Let me go,' she said.

'Who did you expect to find here?' he asked, but more his natural self.

'I expected my husband – him as you saw at dinner. Let me go.'

'Why, is it you?' exclaimed Geoffrey. 'Has he left you?'

'Let me go,' said the woman sullenly, trying to draw away. He realised that her sleeve was very wet, her arm slender under his grasp. Suddenly he grew ashamed of himself: he had no doubt hurt her, gripping her so hard. He relaxed, but did not let her go.

'An' are you searching round after that snipe as was here at dinner?' he asked. She did not answer.

'Where did he leave you?'

'I left him – 'ere. I've seen nothing of him since.'

'I s'd think it's good riddance,' he said. She did not answer. He gave a short laugh, saying.

'I should ha' thought you wouldn't ha' wanted to clap eyes on him again.'

'He's my husband – an' he's not goin' to run off if I can stop him.'

Geoffrey was silent, not knowing what to say.

'Have you got a jacket on?' he asked at last.

'What do you think? You've got hold of it.'

'You're wet through, aren't you?'

'I shouldn't be dry, comin' through the teemin' rain. But 'e's not here, so I'll go.'

'I mean,' he said humbly, 'are you wet through?'

She did not answer. He did not know what to say.

'Stop a minute,' he said, and he fumbled in his pocket for his matches. He struck a light, holding it in the hollow of his large, hard palm. He was a big man, and he looked anxious. Shedding the light on her, he saw she was rather pale, and very weary-looking. Her old sailor hat was sodden and drooping with rain. She wore a fawn-coloured jacket of smooth cloth. This jacket was black-wet where the rain had beaten, her skirt hung sodden, and dripped on to her boot. The match went out.

'Why, you're wet through!' he said.

She did not answer.

'Shall you stop in here until it gives over?' he asked. She did not answer.

''Cause if you will, you'd better take your things off, an' have th' rug. There's a horse-rug in the box.'

He waited, but she would not answer. So he lit his bicycle lamp, and rummaged in the box, pulling out a large brown blanket, striped with scarlet and yellow. She stood stock still. He shone the light on her. She was very pale, and trembling fitfully.

'Are you that cold?' he asked in concern. 'Take your jacket off, and your hat, and put this right over you.'

Mechanically, she undid the enormous fawn-coloured buttons, and unpinned her hat. With her black hair drawn back from her low, honest brow, she looked little more than a girl, like a girl driven hard with womanhood by stress of life. She was small, and natty, with neat little features. But she shivered convulsively.

'Is something a-matter with you?' he asked.

'I've walked to Bulwell and back,' she quivered, 'looking for him – an' I've not touched a thing since this morning.' She did not weep – she was too dreary-hardened to cry. He looked at her in dismay, his mouth half open: 'gormin', as Maurice would have said.

''Aven't you had nothing to eat?' he said.

Then he turned aside to the box. There, the remaining bread was kept, and the great piece of cheese, and such things as sugar and salt, with all table utensils: there was some butter.

She sat down drearily on the bed of hay. He cut her a piece of bread and butter, and a piece of cheese. This she took, but ate listlessly.

'I want a drink,' she said.

'We 'aven't got no beer,' he answered. 'My father doesn't have it.'

'I want water,' she said.

He took a can and plunged through the wet darkness, under the great black hedge, down to the trough. As he came back he saw her in the half-lit little cave sitting bunched together. The soaked grass wet his feet – he thought of her. When he gave her a cup of water, her hand touched his and he felt her fingers hot and glossy. She trembled so, she spilled the water.

'Do you feel badly?' he asked.

'I can't keep myself still – but it's only with being tired and having nothing to eat.'

He scratched his head contemplatively, waited while she ate her piece of bread and butter. Then he offered her another piece.

'I don't want it just now,' she said.

'You'll have to eat summat,' he said.

'I couldn't eat any more just now.'

He put the piece down undecidedly on the box. Then there was another long pause. He stood up with bent head. The bicycle, like a restful animal, glittered behind him, turned towards the wall. The woman sat hunched on the hay, shivering.

'Can't you get warm?' he asked.

'I shall by an' by – don't you bother. I'm taking your seat – are you stopping here all night?'

'Yes.'

'I'll be goin' in a bit,' she said.

'Nay, I non want you to go. I'm thinkin' how you could get warm.'

'Don't you bother about me,' she remonstrated, almost irritably.

'I just want to see as the stacks is all right. You take your shoes an' stockin's an' all your wet things off: you can easy wrap yourself all over in that rug, there's not so much of you.'

'It's raining – I s'll be all right – I s'll be going in a minute.'

'I've got to see as the stacks is safe. Take your wet things off.'

'Are you coming back?' she asked.

'I mightn't, not till morning.'

'Well, I s'll be gone in ten minutes, then. I've no rights to be here, an' I s'll not let anybody be turned out for me.'

'You won't be turning me out.'

'Whether or no, I shan't stop.'

'Well, shall you if I come back?' he asked. She did not answer.

He went. In a few moments, she blew the light out. The rain was falling steadily, and the night was a black gulf. All was intensely still. Geoffrey listened everywhere: no sound: save the rain. He stood between the stacks, but only heard the trickle of water, and the light swish of rain. Everything was lost in blackness. He imagined death was like that, many things dissolved in silence and darkness, blotted out, but existing. In the dense blackness he felt himself almost extinguished. He was afraid he might not find things the same. Almost frantically, he stumbled, feeling his way, till his hand touched the wet metal. He had been looking for a gleam of light.

'Did you blow the lamp out?' he asked, fearful lest the silence should answer him.

'Yes,' she answered humbly. He was glad to hear her voice. Groping into the pitch-dark shed, he knocked against the box, part of whose cover served as table. There was a clatter and a fall.

'That's the lamp, an' the knife, an' the cup,' he said. He struck a match.

'Th' cup's not broke.' He put it into the box.

'But th' oil's spilled out o' th' lamp. It always was a rotten old thing.' He hastily blew out his match, which was burning his fingers. Then he struck another light.

'You don't want a lamp, you know you don't, and I s'll be going directly, so you come an' lie down an' get your night's rest. I'm not taking any of your place.'

He looked at her by the light of another match. She was a queer little bundle, all brown, with a gaudy border folding in and

67

out, and her little face peering at him. As the match went out she saw him beginning to smile.

'I can sit right at this end,' she said. 'You lie down.'

He came and sat on the hay, at some distance from her. After a spell of silence:

'Is he really your husband?' he asked.

'He is!' she answered grimly.

'Hm!' Then there was silence again.

After a while, 'Are you warm now?'

'Why do you bother yourself?'

'I don't bother myself – do you follow him because you like him?' He put it very timidly. He wanted to know.

'I don't – I wish he was dead,' this was bitter contempt. Then doggedly: 'But he's my husband.'

He gave a short laugh.

'By God!' he said.

Again, after a while: 'Have you been married long?'

'Four years.'

'Four years – why, how old are you?'

'Twenty-three.'

'Are you turned twenty-three?'

'Last May.'

'Then you're four month older than me.' He mused over it. They were the only two voices in the pitch-black night. It was eerie silence again.

'And do you just tramp about?' he asked.

'He reckons he's looking for a job. But he doesn't like work in any shape or form. He was a stableman when I married him, at Greenhalgh's, the horse-dealers, at Chesterfield, where I was housemaid. He left that job when the baby was only two months, and I've been badgered about from pillar to post ever sin'. They say a rolling stone gathers no moss . . .'

'An' where's the baby?'

'It died when it was ten months old.'

Now the silence was clinched between them. It was quite a long time before Geoffrey ventured to say sympathetically: 'You haven't much to look forward to.'

68

'I've wished many a score time when I've started shiverin' an' shakin' at nights, as I was taken bad for death. But we're not that handy at dying.'

He was silent. 'But what ever shall you do?' he faltered.

'I s'll find him, if I drop by th' road.'

'Why?' he asked, wondering, looking her way, though he saw nothing but solid darkness.

'Because I shall. He's not going to have it all his own road.'

'But why don't you leave him?'

'Because he's *not goin' to have it all his own road*.'

She sounded very determined, even vindictive. He sat in wonder, feeling uneasy, and vaguely miserable on her behalf. She sat extraordinarily still. She seemed like a voice only, a presence.

'Are you warm now?' he asked, half afraid.

'A bit warmer – but my feet!' She sounded pitiful.

'Let me warm them with my hands,' he asked her. 'I'm hot enough.'

'No, thank you,' she said, coldly.

Then, in the darkness, she felt she had wounded him. He was writhing under her rebuff, for his offer had been pure kindness.

'They're 'appen dirty,' she said, half mocking.

'Well – mine is – an' I have a bath a'most every day,' he answered.

'I don't know when they'll get warm,' she moaned to herself.

'Well, then, put them in my hands.'

She heard him faintly rattling the match-box, and then a phosphorescent glare began to fume in his direction. Presently he was holding two smoking, blue-green blotches of light towards her feet. She was afraid. But her feet ached so, and the impulse drove her on, so she placed her soles lightly on the two blotches of smoke. His large hands clasped over her insteps, warm and hard.

'They're like ice!' he said, in deep concern.

He warmed her feet as best he could, putting them close against him. Now and again convulsive tremors ran over her. She felt his warm breath on the balls of her toes, that were bunched up in his hands. Leaning forward, she touched his hair delicately with her fingers. He thrilled. She fell to gently stroking his hair, with timid, pleasing fingertips.

'Do they feel any better?' he asked, in a low voice, suddenly lifting his face to her. This sent her hand sliding softly over his face, and her fingertips caught on his mouth. She drew quickly away. He put his hand out to find hers, in his other palm holding both her feet. His wandering hand met her face. He touched it curiously. It was wet. He put his big fingers cautiously on her eyes, into two little pools of tears.

'What's a-matter?' he asked, in a low, choked voice.

She leaned down to him, and gripped him tightly round the neck, pressing him to her bosom in a little frenzy of pain. Her bitter disillusionment with life, her unalleviated shame and degradation during the last four years, had driven her into loneliness, and hardened her till a large part of her nature was caked and sterile. Now she softened again, and her spring might be beautiful. She had been in a fair way to make an ugly old woman.

She clasped the head of Geoffrey to her breast, which heaved and fell, and heaved again. He was bewildered, full of wonder. He allowed the woman to do as she would with him. Her tears fell on his hair, as she wept noiselessly; and he breathed deep as she did. At last she let go her clasp. He put his arms round her.

'Come and let me warm you,' he said, folding her up on his knee, and lapping her with his heavy arms against himself. She was small and *câline*. He held her very warm and close. Presently she stole her arms round him.

'You *are* big,' she whispered.

He gripped her hard, started, put his mouth down wanderingly, seeking her out. His lips met her temple. She slowly, deliberately, turned her mouth to his and, with opened lips, met him in a kiss, his first love kiss.

V

It was breaking cold dawn when Geoffrey woke. The woman was still sleeping in his arms. Her face in sleep moved all his tenderness: the tight shutting of her mouth, as if in resolution to bear what was very hard to bear, contrasted so pitifully with the small mould of her features. Geoffrey pressed her to his bosom: having her, he felt he could bruise the lips of the scornful, and pass on erect, unabatable. With her to complete him, to form the core of him, he was firm and whole. Needing her so much, he loved her fervently.

Meanwhile the dawn came like death, one of those slow, livid mornings that seem to come in a cold sweat. Slowly, and painfully, the air began to whiten. Geoffrey saw it was not raining. As he was watching the ghastly transformation outside, he felt aware of something. He glanced down: she was open-eyed, watching him; she had golden brown, calm eyes, that immediately smiled into his. He also smiled, bowed softly down and kissed her. They did not speak for some time. Then:

'What's thy name?' he asked curiously.

'Lydia,' she said.

'Lydia!' he repeated, wonderingly. He felt rather shy.

'Mine's Geoffrey Wookey,' he said.

She merely smiled at him.

They were silent for a considerable time. By morning light, things look small. The huge trees of the evening were dwindling to hoary, small, uncertain things, trespassing in the sick pallor of the atmosphere. There was a dense mist, so that the light could scarcely breathe. Everything seemed to quiver with cold and sickliness.

'Have you often slept out?' he asked her.

'Not so very,' she answered.

'You won't go after *him*?' he asked.

'I s'll have to,' she replied, but she nestled in to Geoffrey. He felt a sudden panic.

'You mustn't,' he exclaimed, and she saw he was afraid for himself. She let it be, was silent.

'We couldn't get married?' he asked, thoughtfully.

'No.'

He brooded deeply over this. At length:

'Would you go to Canada with me?'

71

'We'll see what you think in two months' time,' she replied quietly, without bitterness.

'I s'll think the same,' he protested, hurt.

She did not answer, only watched him steadily. She was there for him to do as he liked with, but she would not injure his fortunes; no, not to save his soul.

'Haven't you got no relations?' he asked.

'A married sister at Crick.'

'On a farm?'

'No – married a farm labourer – but she's very comfortable. I'll go there, if you want me to, just till I can get another place in service.'

He considered this.

'Could you get on a farm?' he asked wistfully.

'Greenhalgh's was a farm.'

He saw the future brighten: she would be a help to him. She agreed to go to her sister, and to get a place of service – until spring, he said, when they would sail for Canada. He waited for her assent.

'You will come with me, then?' he asked.

'When the time comes,' she said.

Her want of faith made him bow his head: she had reason for it.

'Shall you walk to Crick, or go from Langley Mill to Ambergate? But it's only ten mile to walk. So we can go together up Hunt's Hill – you'd have to put past our lane-end, then I could easy nip down an' fetch you some money,' he said, humbly.

'I've got a half sovereign by me – it's more than I s'll want.'

'Let's see it,' he said.

After a while, fumbling under the blanket, she brought out the piece of money. He felt she was independent of him. Brooding rather bitterly, he told himself she'd forsake him. His anger gave him courage to ask:

'Shall you go in service in your maiden name?'

'No.'

He was bitterly wrathful with her – full of resentment.

'I bet I s'll niver see you again,' he said, with a short, hard laugh. She put her arms round him, pressed him to her bosom, while the tears rose to her eyes. He was reassured, but not satisfied.

'Shall you write to me tonight?'

'Yes, I will.'

'And can I write to you – who shall I write to?'

'Mrs Bredon.'

' "Bredon"!' he repeated bitterly.

He was exceedingly uneasy.

The dawn had grown quite wan. He saw the hedges drooping wet down the grey mist. Then he told her about Maurice.

'Oh, you *shouldn't*!' she said. 'You should ha' put the ladder up for them, you *should*.'

'Well – I don't care.'

'Go and do it now – and I'll go.'

'No, don't you. Stop an' see our Maurice, go on, stop an' see him – then I s'll be able to tell him.'

She consented in silence. He had her promise she would not go before he returned. She adjusted her dress, found her way to the trough, where she performed her toilet.

Geoffrey wandered round to the upper field. The stacks looked wet in the mist, the hedge was drenched. Mist rose like steam from the grass, and the near hills were veiled almost to a shadow. In the valley, some peaks of black poplar showed fairly definite, jutting up. He shivered with chill.

There was no sound from the stacks, and he could see nothing. After all, he wondered, were they up there. But he reared the ladder to the place whence it had been swept, then went down the hedge to gather dry sticks. He was breaking off thin dead twigs under a holly-tree when he heard, on the perfectly still air. 'Well I'm dashed!'

He listened intently. Maurice was awake.

'Sithee here!' the lad's voice exclaimed. Then, after a while, the foreign sound of the girl:

'What – oh, thair!'

'Aye, th' ladder's there, right enough.'

'You said it had fall down.'

'Well, I heard it drop – an' I couldna feel it nor see it.'

'You said it had fall down – you lie, you liar.'

'Nay, as true as I'm here—'

'You tell me lies – make me stay here – you tell me lies—' She was passionately indignant.

'As true as I'm standing here—' he began.

'Lies! – lies! – lies!' she cried. 'I don't believe you, never. You *mean*, you *mean, mean, mean*!'

'A' raïght, then!' he was now incensed, in his turn.

'You are bad, mean, mean, mean.'

'Are yer comin' down?' asked Maurice, coldly.

'No – I will not come with you – mean, to tell me lies.'

'Are ter comin' down?'

'No, I don't want you.'

'A' raïght, then!'

Geoffrey, peering through the holly-tree, saw Maurice negotiating the ladder. The top rung was below the brim of the stack, and rested on the cloth, so it was dangerous to approach. The Fräulein watched him from the end of the stack, where the cloth thrown back showed the light, dry hay. He slipped slightly, she screamed. When he had got on to the ladder, he pulled the cloth away, throwing it back, making it easy for her to descend.

'Now are ter comin'?' he asked.

'No!' she shook her head violently, in a pet.

Geoffrey felt slightly contemptuous of her. But Maurice waited.

'Are ter comin'?' he called.

'No,' she flashed, like a wild cat.

'All right, then I'm going.'

He descended. At the bottom, he stood holding the ladder.

'Come on, while I hold it steady,' he said.

There was no reply. For some minutes he stood patiently with his foot on the bottom rung of the ladder. He was pale, rather washed-out in his appearance, and he drew himself together with cold.

'Are ter comin', or aren't ter?' he asked at length. Still there was no reply.

'Then stop up till tha'rt ready,' he muttered, and he went away. Round the other side of the stacks he met Geoffrey.

'What, are thaïgh here?' he exclaimed.

'Bin heer a' night,' replied Geoffrey. 'I come to help thee wi' th' cloth, but I found it on, an' th' ladder down, so I thowt tha'd gone.'

'Did ter put th' ladder up?'

'I did a bit sin'.'

Maurice brooded over this. Geoffrey struggled with himself to get out his own news. At last he blurted:

'Tha knows that woman as wor here yis'day dinner – 'er come back, an' stopped i' th' shed a' night, out o' th' rain.'

'Oh – ah!' said Maurice, his eyes kindling, and a smile crossing his pallor.

'Ah' I s'll gi'e her some breakfast.'

'Oh – ah!' repeated Maurice.

'It's th' man as is good-for-nowt, not her,' protested Geoffrey. Maurice did not feel in a position to cast stones.

'Tha pleases thysen,' he said, 'what ter does.' He was very quiet, unlike himself. He seemed bothered and anxious, as Geoffrey had not seen him before.

'What's up wi' thee?' asked the elder brother, who in his own heart was glad, and relieved.

'Nowt,' was the reply.

They went together to the hut. The woman was folding the blanket. She was fresh from washing, and looked very pretty. Her hair, instead of being screwed tightly back, was coiled in a knot low down, partly covering her ears. Before, she had deliberately made herself plain-looking: now she was neat and pretty, with a sweet, womanly gravity.

'Hello. I didn't think to find you here,' said Maurice, very awkwardly, smiling. She watched him gravely without reply. 'But it was better in shelter than outside, last night,' he added.

'Yes,' she replied.

'Shall you get a few more sticks?' Geoffrey asked him. It was a new thing for Geoffrey to be leader. Maurice obeyed. He wandered forth into the damp, raw morning. He did not go to the stack, as he shrank from meeting Paula.

At the mouth of the hut, Geoffrey was making the fire. The woman got out coffee from the box: Geoffrey set the tin to boil. They were arranging breakfast when Paula appeared. She was hatless. Bits of hay stuck in her hair, and she was white-faced – altogether, she did not show to advantage.

'Ah – you!' she exclaimed, seeing Geoffrey.

'Hello!' he answered. 'You're out early.'

'Where's Maurice?'

'I dunno, he should be back directly.'

Paula was silent.

'When have you come?' she asked.

'I come last night, but I could see nobody about. I got up half an hour sin', an' put th' ladder up ready to take the stack-cloth up.'

Paula understood, and was silent. When Maurice returned with the faggots, she was crouched warming her hands. She looked up at him, but he kept his eyes averted from her. Geoffrey met the eyes of Lydia, and smiled. Maurice put his hands to the fire.

'You cold?' asked Paula tenderly.

'A bit,' he answered, quite friendly, but reserved. And all the while the four sat round the fire, drinking their smoked coffee, eating each a small piece of toasted bacon, Paula watched eagerly for the eyes of Maurice, and he avoided her. He was gentle, but would not give his eyes to her looks. And Geoffrey smiled constantly to Lydia, who watched gravely.

The German girl succeeded in getting safely into the Vicarage, her escapade unknown to anyone save the housemaid. Before a week was out, she was openly engaged to Maurice, and when her month's notice expired, she went to live at the farm.

Geoffrey and Lydia kept faith one with the other.

Malachi's Cove

ANTHONY TROLLOPE

On the northern coast of Cornwall, between Tintagel and Bossiney, down on the very margin of the sea, there lived not long since an old man who got his living by saving seaweed from the waves, and selling it for manure. The cliffs there are bold and fine, and the sea beats in upon them from the north with a grand violence. I doubt whether it be not the finest morsel of cliff scenery in England, though it is beaten by many portions of the west coast of Ireland, and perhaps also by spots in Wales and Scotland. Cliffs should be nearly precipitous, they should be broken in their outlines, and should barely admit here and there of an insecure passage from their summit to the sand at their feet. The sea should come, if not up to them, at least very near to them, and then, above all things, the water below them should be blue, and not of that dead leaden colour which is so familiar to us in England. At Tintagel all these requisites are there, except that bright blue colour which is so lovely. The cliffs themselves are bold and well broken, and the margin of sand at high water is very narrow – so narrow that at spring-tides there is barely a footing there.

Close upon this margin was the cottage or hovel of Malachi Trenglos, the old man of whom I have spoken. But Malachi, or old Glos, as he was commonly called by the people around him, had not built his house absolutely upon the sand. There was a fissure in the rock so great that at the top it formed a narrow ravine, and so complete from the summit to the base that it afforded an opening for a steep and rugged track from the top of the rock to the bottom. This fissure was so wide at the bottom that it had afforded space for Trenglos to fix his habitation on a foundation of rock, and here he had lived for many years. It was told of him that in the early days of his trade he had always carried the weed in a basket on his back to the top, but latterly he had been possessed of a donkey, which had been trained to go up and down the steep track with a single pannier over his loins, for the rocks would not permit of panniers hanging by his side; and for this assistant he had built a shed adjoining his own, and almost as large as that in which he himself resided.

But, as years went on, old Glos procured other assistance than that of the donkey, or, as I should rather say, Providence supplied him with other help; and, indeed, had it not been so, the old man must have given up his cabin and his independence and gone into the workhouse at Camelford. For rheumatism had afflicted him, old age had bowed him till he was nearly double, and by degrees he became unable to attend the donkey on its upward passage to the world above, or even to assist in rescuing the coveted weed from the waves.

At the time to which our story refers Trenglos had not been up the cliff for twelve months, and for the last six months he had done nothing towards the furtherance of his trade, except to take the money and keep it, if any of it was kept, and occasionally to shake down a bundle of fodder for the donkey. The real work of the business was done altogether by Mahala Trenglos, his granddaughter.

Mally Trenglos was known to all the farmers round the coast, and to all the small tradespeople in Camelford. She was a wild-looking, almost unearthly creature, with wild-flowing, black, uncombed hair, small in stature, with small hands and bright black eyes; but people said that she was very strong, and the children around declared that she worked day and night and knew nothing of fatigue. As to her age there were many doubts. Some said she was ten, and others five-and-twenty, but the reader may be allowed to know that at this time she had in truth passed her twentieth birthday. The old people spoke well of Mally, because she was so good to her grandfather; and it was said of her that though she carried to him a little gin and tobacco almost daily, she bought nothing for herself – and as to the gin, no one who looked at her would accuse her of meddling with that. But she had no friends and but few acquaintances among people of her own age. They said that she was fierce and ill-natured, that she had not a good word for anyone, and that she was, complete at all points, a thorough little vixen. The young men did not care for her; for, as regarded dress, all days were alike with her. She never made herself smart on Sundays. She was generally without stockings and seemed to care not at all to exercise any of those feminine attractions which might have been hers had she studied to attain them. All days were the same to her in regard to dress; and, indeed, till lately, all days had, I fear, been the same to her in other respects. Old Malachi had never been seen inside a place of worship since he had taken to live under the cliff.

But within the last two years Mally had submitted herself to the teaching of the clergyman at Tintagel, and had appeared at church on Sundays, if not absolutely with punctuality, at any rate so often that no one who knew the peculiarity of her residence was disposed to quarrel with her on that subject. But she made no difference in her dress on these occasions. She took her place on a low stone seat just inside the church door, clothed as usual in her thick red serge petticoat and loose brown serge jacket, such being the apparel which she had found to be best adapted for her hard and perilous work among the waters. She had pleaded to the clergyman, when he attacked her on the subject of church attendance with vigour, that she had got no church-going clothes. He had explained to her that she would be received there without distinction to her clothing. Mally had taken him at his word, and had gone, with a courage which certainly deserved admiration, though I doubt whether there was not mingled with it an obstinacy which was less admirable.

For people said that old Glos was rich, and that Mally might have proper clothes if she chose to buy them. Mr Polwarth, the clergyman, who, as the old man could not come to him, went down the rocks to the old man, did make some hint on the matter in Mally's absence. But old Glos, who had been patient with him on other matters, turned upon him so angrily when he made an allusion to money, that Mr Polwarth found himself obliged to give that matter up, and Mally continued to sit upon the stone bench in her short serge petticoat, with her long hair streaming down her face. She did so far sacrifice to decency on such occasions to tie up her back hair with an old shoestring. So tied it would remain through the Monday and Tuesday, but by Wednesday afternoon Mally's hair had generally managed to escape.

As to Mally's indefatigable industry there could be no manner of doubt, for the quantity of seaweed which she and the donkey amassed between them was very surprising. Old Glos, it was declared, had never collected half what Mally gathered together; but then the article was becoming cheaper, and it was necessary that the exertion should be greater. So Mally and the donkey toiled and toiled, and the seaweed came up in heaps which surprised those who looked at her little hands and light form. Was there not someone who helped her at nights, some fairy, or demon, or the like? Mally was so snappish in her answers to people that she had no right to be surprised if ill-natured things were said of her.

No one ever heard Mally Trenglos complain of her work, but about this time she was heard to make great and loud complaints of the treatment she received from some of her neighbours. It was known that she went with her plaints to Mr Polwarth; and when he could not help her, or did not give her such instant help as she needed, she went – ah, so foolishly! – to the office of a certain attorney at Camelford, who was not likely to prove himself a better friend than Mr Polwarth.

Now the nature of her injury was as follows. The place in which she collected her seaweed was a little cove – the people had come to call it Malachi's Cove from the name of the old man who lived there – which was so formed, that the margin of the sea therein could only be reached by the passage from the top down to Trenglos's hut. The breadth of the cove when the sea was out might perhaps be two hundred yards, and on each side the rocks ran out in such a way that both from north and south the domain of Trenglos was guarded from intruders. And this locality had been well chosen for its intended purpose.

There was a rush of the sea into the cove, which carried there large, drifting masses of seaweed, leaving them among the rocks when the tide was out. During the equinoctial winds of the spring and autumn the supply would never fail; and even when the sea was calm, the long, soft, salt-bedewed trailing masses of the weed, could be gathered there when they could not be found elsewhere for miles along the coast. The task of getting the weed from the breakers was often difficult and dangerous – so difficult that much of it was left to be carried away by the next incoming tide.

Mally doubtless did not gather half the crop that was there at her feet. What was taken by the returning waves she did not regret: but when interlopers came upon her cove, and gathered her wealth – her grandfather's wealth – beneath her eyes, then her heart was broken. It was this interloping, this intrusion, that drove poor Mally to the Camelford attorney. But, alas, though the Camelford attorney took Mally's money, he could do nothing for her, and her heart was broken!

She had an idea, in which no doubt her grandfather shared, that the path to the cove was, at any rate, their property. When she was told that the cove, and the sea running into the cove, were not the freeholds of her grandfather, she understood that the statement might be true. But what then as to the use of the path? Who had made the path what it was? Had she not painfully, wearily, with exceeding toil, carried up bits of rock with her own little hands, that her grandfather's donkey might have footing for his feet? Had she not scraped together crumbs of earth along the face of the cliff that she might make easier to the animal the track of that rugged way? And now, when she saw big farmers' lads coming down with other donkeys – and, indeed, there was one who came with a pony; no boy, but a young man, old enough to know better than rob a poor old man and a young girl – she reviled the whole human race, and swore that the Camelford attorney was a fool.

Any attempt to explain to her that there was still weed enough for her was worse than useless. Was it not all hers and his, or, at any rate, was not the sole way to it his and hers? And was not her trade stopped and impeded? Had she not been forced to back her laden donkey down, twenty yards she said, but it had, in truth, been five, because Farmer Gunliffe's son had been in the way with his thieving pony? Farmer Gunliffe had wanted to buy her weed at his own price, and because she had refused he had set on his thieving son to destroy her in this wicked way.

'I'll hamstring the beast the next time as he's down here!' said Mally to old Glos, while the angry fire literally streamed from her eyes.

Farmer Gunliffe's small homestead – he held about fifty acres of land, was close by the village of Tintagel, and not a mile from the cliff. The seawrack, as they call it, was pretty well the only manure within his reach, and no doubt he thought it hard that he should be kept from using it by Mally Trenglos and her obstinacy.

'There's heaps of other coves, Barty,' said Mally to Barty Gunliffe, the farmer's son.

'But none so nigh, Mally, nor yet none that fills 'emselves as this place.'

Then he explained to her that he would not take the weed that came up close to hand. He was bigger than she was, and stronger, and would get it from the outer rocks, with which she never meddled. Then, with scorn in her eye, she swore that she could get it where he durst not venture, and repeated her threat of hamstringing the pony. Barty laughed at her wrath, jeered at her because of her wild hair, and called her a mermaid.

'I'll mermaid you!' she cried. 'Mermaid, indeed! I wouldn't be a man to come and rob a poor girl and an old cripple. But you're no man, Barty Gunliffe! You're not half a man.'

Nevertheless, Bartholomew Gunliffe was a very fine young fellow as far as the eye went. He was about five feet eight inches high, with strong arms and legs, with light curly brown hair and blue eyes. His father was but in a small way as a farmer, but, nevertheless, Barty Gunliffe was well thought of among the girls around. Everybody liked Barty – excepting only Mally Trenglos and she hated him like poison.

Barty, when he was asked why so good-natured a lad as he persecuted a poor girl and an old man, threw himself upon the justice of the thing. It wouldn't do at all, according to his view, that any single person should take upon himself to own that which God Almighty sent as the common property of all. He would do Mally no harm, and so he had told her. But Mally was a vixen – a wicked little vixen; and she must be taught to have a civil tongue in her head. When once Mally would speak him civil as he went for weed, he would get his father to pay the old man some sort of toll for the use of the path.

'Speak him civil?' said Mally. 'Never; not while I have a tongue in my mouth!' and I fear old Glos encouraged her rather than otherwise in her view of the matter.

But her grandfather did not encourage her to hamstring the pony. Hamstringing a pony would be a serious thing, and old Glos thought it might be very awkward for both of them if Mally were put into prison. He suggested, therefore, that all manner of impediments should be put in the way of the pony's feet, surmising that the well-trained donkey might be able to work in spite of them. And Barty Gunliffe, on his next descent, did find the passage very awkward when he came near to Malachi's hut, but he made his way down, and poor Mally saw the lumps of rock at which she had laboured so hard pushed on one side or rolled out of the way with a steady persistency of injury towards herself that almost drove her frantic.

'Well, Barty, you're a nice boy,' said old Glos, sitting in the doorway of the hut, as he watched the intruder.

'I ain't a-doing no harm to none as doesn't harm me,' said Barty. 'The sea's free to all, Malachi.'

'And the sky's free to all, but I mustn't get up on the top of your big barn to look at it,' said Mally, who was standing among the rocks with a long hook in her hand. The long hook was the tool with which she worked in dragging the weed from the waves. 'But you ain't got no justice, nor yet no sperrit, or you wouldn't come here to vex an old man like he.'

'I didn't want to vex him, nor yet to vex you, Mally. You let me be for a while, and we'll be friends yet.'

'Friends!' exclaimed Mally. 'Who'd have the likes of you for a friend? What are you moving them stones for? Them stones belongs to grandfather.' And in her wrath she made a movement as though she were going to fly at him.

'Let him be, Mally,' said the old man; 'let him be. He'll get his punishment. He'll come to be drowned some day if he comes down here when the wind is in-shore.'

'That he may be drowned then!' said Mally, in her anger. 'If he was in the big hole there among the rocks, and the sea running in at half-tide, I wouldn't lift a hand to help him out.'

'Yes, you would, Mally; you'd fish me up with your hook like a big stick of seaweed.'

She turned from him with scorn as he said this, and went into the hut. It was time for her to get ready for her work, and one of the great injuries done her lay in this – that such a one as Barty Gunliffe should come and look at her during her toil among the breakers.

It was an afternoon in April, and the hour was something after four o'clock. There had been a heavy wind from the north-west all the morning, with gusts of rain, and the sea-gulls had been in and out of the cove all the day, which was a sure sign to Mally that the incoming tide would cover the rocks with weed.

The quick waves were now returning with wonderful celerity over the low reefs, and the time had come at which the treasure must be seized, if it was to be garnered on that day. By seven o'clock it would be growing dark, at nine it would be high water, and before daylight the crop would be carried out again if not collected. All this Mally understood very well, and some of this Barty was beginning to understand also.

As Mally came down with her bare feet, bearing her long hook in her hand, she saw Barty's pony standing patiently on the sand, and in her heart she longed to attack the brute. Barty at this moment, with a common three-pronged fork in his hand, was standing down on a large rock, gazing forth towards the waters. He had declared that he would gather the weed only at places which were inaccessible to Mally, and he was looking out that he might settle where he would begin.

'Let 'un be, let 'un be,' shouted the old man to Mally, as he saw her take a step towards the beast, which she hated almost as much as she hated the man.

Hearing her grandfather's voice through the wind, she desisted from her purpose, if any purpose she had had, and went forth to her work. As she passed down the cove, and scrambled in among the rocks, she saw Barty still standing on his perch; out beyond, the white-curling waves were cresting and breaking themselves with violence, and the wind was howling among the caverns and abutments of the cliff.

Every now and then there came a squall of rain, and though there was sufficient light, the heavens were black with clouds. A scene more beautiful might hardly be found by those who love the glories of the coast. The light for such objects was perfect. Nothing could exceed the grandeur of the colours – the blue of the open sea, the white of the breaking waves, the yellow sands, or the streaks of red and brown which gave such richness to the cliff.

But neither Mally nor Barty were thinking of such things as these. Indeed they were hardly thinking of their trade after its ordinary forms. Barty was meditating how he might best accomplish his purpose of working beyond the reach of Mally's feminine powers, and Mally was resolving that wherever Barty went she would go farther.

And, in many respects, Mally had the advantage. She knew every rock in the spot, and was sure of those which gave a good foothold, and sure also of those which did not. And then her activity had been made perfect by practice for the purpose to which it was to be devoted. Barty, no doubt, was stronger than she, and quite as active. But Barty could not jump among the waves from one stone to another as she could do, nor was he as yet able to get aid in his work from the very force of the water as she could get it. She had been hunting seaweed in that cove since she had been an urchin of six years old, and she knew every hole and corner and every spot of vantage. The waves were her friends, and she could use them. She could measure their strength, and knew when and where it would cease.

Mally was great down in the salt pools of her own cove – great, and very fearless. As she watched Barty make his way forward from rock to rock, she told herself, gleefully, that he was going astray. The curl of the wind as it blew into the cove would not carry the weed up to the northern buttresses of the cove; and then there was the great hole just there – the great hole of which she had spoken when she wished him evil.

And now she went to work, hooking up the dishevelled hairs of the ocean, and landing many a cargo on the extreme margin of the sand, from whence she would be able in the evening to drag it back before the invading waters would return to reclaim the spoil.

And on his side also Barty made his heap up against the northern buttresses of which I have spoken. Barty's heap became big and still bigger, so that he knew, let the pony work as he might, he could not take it all up that evening. But still it was not as large as Mally's heap. Mally's hook was better than his fork, and Mally's skill was better than his strength. And when he failed in some haul Mally would jeer at him with a wild, weird laughter, and shriek to him through the wind that he was not half a man. At first he answered her with laughing words, but before long, as she boasted of her success and pointed to his failure, he became angry, and then he answered her no more. He became angry with himself, in that he missed so much of the plunder before him.

The broken sea was full of the long straggling growth which the waves had torn up from the bottom of the ocean, but the masses were carried past him, away from him – nay, once or twice over him; and then Mally's weird voice would sound in his ear, jeering him. The gloom among the rocks was now becoming thicker and thicker, the tide was beating in with increased strength, and the gusts of wind came with quicker and greater violence. But still he worked on. While Mally worked he would work, and he would work for some time after she was driven in. He would not be beaten by a girl.

The great hole was now full of water, but of water which seemed to be boiling as though in a pot. And the pot was full of floating masses – large treasures of seaweed which were thrown to and fro upon its surface, but lying there so thick that one would seem almost able to rest upon it without sinking.

Mally knew well how useless it was to attempt to rescue aught from the fury of that boiling cauldron. The hole went in under the rocks, and the side of it towards the shore lay high, slippery and steep. The hole, even at low water, was never empty; and Mally believed that there was no bottom to it. Fish thrown in there could escape out to the ocean, miles away – so Mally in her softer moods would tell the visitors to the cove. She knew the hole well. Poulnadioul she was accustomed to call it; which was supposed, when translated, to mean that this was the hole of the Evil One. Never did Mally attempt to make her own of weed which had found its way into that pot.

But Barty Gunliffe knew no better, and she watched him as he endeavoured to steady himself on the treacherously slippery edge of the pool. He fixed himself there and made a haul, with some small success. How he managed it she hardly knew, but she stood still for a while watching him anxiously, and then she saw him slip. He slipped, and recovered himself – slipped again, and again recovered himself.

'Barty, you fool!' she screamed, 'if you get yourself pitched in there, you'll never come out no more.'

Whether she simply wished to frighten him, or whether her heart relented and she had thought of his danger with dismay, who shall say? She could not have told herself. She hated him as much as ever – but she could hardly have wished to see him drowned before her eyes.

'You go on, and don't mind me,' said he, speaking in a hoarse angry tone.

'Mind you! – who minds you?' retorted the girl. And then she again prepared herself for work.

But as she went down over the rocks with her long hook balanced in her hands, she suddenly heard a splash, and, turning quickly round saw the body of her enemy tumbling amidst the eddying waves in the pool. The tide had now come up so far that every succeeding wave washed into it and over it from the side nearest to the sea, and then ran down again back from the rocks, as the rolling wave receded, with a noise like the fall of a cataract. And then, when the surplus water had retreated for a moment, the surface of the pool would be partly calm, though the fretting bubbles would still boil up and down, and there was ever a simmer on the surface, as though, in truth, the cauldron were heated. But this time of comparative rest was but a moment, for the succeeding breaker would come up almost as soon as the foam of the preceding one had gone, and then again the waters would be dashed upon the rocks, and the sides would echo with the roar of the angry wave.

Instantly Mally hurried across to the edge of the pool, crouching down upon her hands and knees for security as she did so. As a wave receded, Barty's head and face were carried round near to her, and she could see that his forehead was covered with blood. Whether he were alive or dead she did not know. She had seen nothing but his blood, and the light-coloured hair of his head lying amidst the foam. Then his body was drawn along by the suction of the retreating wave; but the mass of water that escaped was not on this occasion large enough to carry the man out with it.

Instantly Mally was at work with her hook, and getting it fixed into his coat, dragged him towards the spot on which she was kneeling. During the half minute of repose she got him so close that she could touch his shoulder. Straining herself down, laying herself over the long bending handle of the hook, she strove to grasp him with her right hand. But she could not do it; she could only touch him.

Then came the next breaker, forcing itself on with a roar, looking to Mally as though it must certainly knock her from her resting-place, and destroy them both. But she had nothing for it but to kneel, and hold by her hook.

What prayer passed through her mind at that moment for herself or for him, or for that old man who was sitting unconsciously up at the cabin, who can say? The great wave came and rushed over her as she lay almost prostrate, and when the water was gone from her eyes, and the tumult of the foam, and the violence of the roaring breaker had passed by her, she found herself at her length upon the rock, while his body had been lifted up, free from her hook, and was lying upon the slippery ledge, half in the water and half out of it. As she looked at him, in that instant, she could see that his eyes were open and that he was struggling with his hands.

'Hold by the hook, Barty,' she cried, pushing the stick of it before him, while she seized the collar of his coat in her hands.

Had he been her brother, her lover, her father she could not have clung to him with more of the energy of despair. He did contrive to hold by the stick which she had given him, and when the succeeding wave had passed by, he was still on the ledge. In the next moment she was seated a yard or two above the hole, in comparative safety, while Barty lay upon the rocks with his still bleeding head resting upon her lap.

What could she do now? She could not carry him; and in fifteen minutes the sea would be up where she was sitting. He was quite insensible, and very pale, and the blood was coming slowly – very slowly – from the wound on his forehead. Ever so gently she put her hand upon his hair to move it back from his face; and then she bent over his mouth to see if he breathed, and as she looked at him she knew that he was beautiful.

What would she not give that he might live? Nothing now was so precious to her as his life – as this life which she had so far rescued from the waters. But what could she do? Her grandfather could scarcely get himself down over the rocks, if indeed he could succeed in doing so much as that. Could she drag the wounded man backwards, if it were only a few feet, so that he might lie above the reach of the waves till further assistance could be procured?

She set herself to work and she moved him, almost lifting him. As she did so she wondered at her own strength, but she was very strong at that moment. Slowly, tenderly, falling on the rocks herself so that he might fall on her, she got him back to the margin of the sand, to a spot which the waters would not reach for the next two hours.

Here her grandfather met them, having seen at last what had happened from the door.

'Dada,' she said, 'he fell into the pool yonder, and was battered against the rocks. See there at his forehead.'

'Mally, I'm thinking that he's dead already,' said old Glos, peering down over the body.

'No, Dada; he is not dead; but mayhap he's dying. But I'll go at once up to the farm.'

'Mally,' said the old man, 'look at his head. They'll say we murdered him.'

'Who'll say so? Who'll lie like that? Didn't I pull him out of the hole?'

'What matters that? His father'll say we killed him.'

It was manifest to Mally that whatever anyone might say hereafter, her present course was plain before her. She must run up the path to Gunliffe's farm and get the necessary assistance. If the world were as bad as her grandfather said, it would be so bad that she would not care to live longer in it. But be that as it might, there was no doubt as to what she must do now.

So away she went as fast as her naked feet could carry her up the cliff. When at the top she looked round to see if any person might be within ken, but she saw no one. So she ran with all her speed along the headland of the cornfield which led in the direction of old Gunliffe's house, and as she drew near to the homestead she saw that Barty's mother was leaning on the gate. As she approached she attempted to call, but her breath failed her for any purpose of loud speech, so she ran on till she was able to grasp Mrs Gunliffe by the arm.

'Where's himself?' she said, holding her hand upon her beating heart that she might husband her breath.

'Who is it you mean?' said Mrs Gunliffe, who participated in the family feud against Trenglos and his granddaughter. 'What does the girl clutch me for in that way?'

'He's dying then, that's all.'

'Who is dying? Is it old Malachi? If the old man's bad, we'll send someone down.'

'It ain't Dada; it's Barty! Where's himself? where's the master?' But by this time Mrs Gunliffe was in an agony of despair, and was calling out for assistance lustily. Happily Gunliffe, the father, was at hand, and with him a man from the neighbouring village.

'Will you not send for the doctor?' said Mally. 'Oh, man, you should send for the doctor!'

Whether any orders were given for the doctor she did not know, but in a very few minutes she was hurrying across the field again towards the path to the cove, and Gunliffe with the other man and his wife were following her.

As Mally went along she recovered her voice, for their step was not so quick as hers, and that which to them was a hurried movement, allowed her to get her breath again. And as she went she tried to explain to the father what had happened, saying but little, however, of her own doings in the matter. The wife hung behind listening, exclaiming every now and again that her boy was killed, and then asking wild questions as to his being yet alive. The father, as he went, said little. He was known as a silent, sober man, well spoken of for diligence and general conduct, but supposed to be stern and very hard when angered.

As they drew near to the top of the path the other man whispered something to him, and then he turned round upon Mally and stopped her.

'If he has come by his death between you, your blood shall be taken for his,' said he.

Then the wife shrieked out that her child had been murdered, and Mally, looking round into the faces of the three, saw that her grandfather's words had come true. They suspected her of having taken the life, in saving which she had nearly lost her own.

She looked round at them with awe in her face, and then, without saying a word, preceded them down the path. What had she to answer when such a charge as that was made against her? If they chose to say that she pushed him into the pool and hit him with her hook as he lay amidst the waters, how could she show that it was not so?

Poor Mally knew little of the law of evidence, and it seemed to her that she was in their hands. But as she went down the steep track with a hurried step – a step so quick that they could not keep up with her – her heart was very full – very full and very high. She had striven for the man's life as though he had been her brother. The blood was yet not dry on her own legs and arms, where she had torn them in his service. At one moment she had felt sure that she would die with him in that pool. And now they said that she had murdered him! It may be that he was not dead and what would he say if ever he should speak again? Then she thought of that moment when his eyes had opened, and he had seemed to see her. She had no fear for herself, for her heart was very high. But it was full also – full of scorn, disdain and wrath.

When she had reached the bottom, she stood close to the door of the hut waiting for them, so that they might precede her to the other group, which was there in front of them, at a little distance on the sand.

'He is there, and Dada is with him. Go and look at him,' said Mally.

The father and mother ran on stumbling over the stones, but Mally remained behind by the door of the hut.

Barty Gunliffe was lying on the sand where Mally had left him, and old Malachi Trenglos was standing over him, resting himself with difficulty upon a stick.

'Not a move he's made since she left him,' said he; 'not a move. I put his head on the old rug as you see, and I tried 'un with a drop of gin, but he wouldn't take it – he wouldn't take it.'

'Oh, my boy! my boy!' said the mother, throwing herself beside her son upon the sand.

'Haud your tongue, woman,' said the father, kneeling down slowly by the lad's head, 'whimpering that way will do 'un no good.'

Then, having gazed for a minute or two upon the pale face beneath him, he looked up sternly into that of Malachi Trenglos.

The old man hardly knew how to bear this terrible inquisition.

'He would come,' said Malachi; 'he brought it all upon hisself.'

'Who was it struck him?' said the father.

'Sure he struck hisself, as he fell among the breakers.'

'Liar!' said the father, looking up at the old man.

'They have murdered him! – they have murdered him!' shrieked the mother.

'Haud your peace, woman!' said the husband again. 'They shall give us blood for blood.'

Mally, leaning against the corner of the hovel, heard it all, but did not stir. They might say what they liked. They might make it out to be murder. They might drag her and her grandfather to Camelford gaol, and then to Bodmin, and the gallows; but they could not take from her the conscious feeling that was her own. She had done her best to save him – her very best. And she had saved him!

She remembered her threat to him before they had gone down on the rocks together, and her evil wish. Those words had been very wicked; but since that she had risked her life to save his. They might say what they pleased of her, and do what they pleased. She knew what she knew.

Then the father raised his son's head and shoulders in his arms, and called on the others to assist him in carrying Barty towards the path. They raised him between them carefully and tenderly, and lifted their burden on towards the spot at which Mally was standing. She never moved, but watched them at their work; and the old man followed them, hobbling after them with his crutch.

When they had reached the end of the hut she looked upon Barty's face, and saw that it was very pale. There was no longer blood upon the forehead, but the great gash was to be seen there plainly, with its jagged cut, and the skin livid and blue round the orifice. His light brown hair was hanging back, as she had made it to hang when she had gathered it with her hand after the big wave had passed over them. Ah, how beautiful he was in Mally's eyes with that pale face, and the sad scar upon his brow! She turned her face away, that they might not see her tears; but she did not move, nor did she speak.

But now, when they had passed the end of the hut, shuffling along with their burden, she heard a sound which stirred her. She roused herself quickly from her leaning posture, and stretched forth her head as though to listen; then she moved to follow them. Yes, they had stopped at the bottom of the path, and had again laid the body on the rocks. She heard that sound again, as of a long, long sigh, and then, regardless of any of them, she ran to the wounded man's head.

'He is not dead,' she said. 'There; he is not dead.'

As she spoke Barty's eyes opened, and he looked about him.

'Barty, my boy, speak to me,' said the mother.

Barty turned his face upon his mother, smiled, and then stared about him wildly.

'How is it with thee, lad?' said his father. Then Barty turned his face again to the latter voice, and as he did so his eyes fell upon Mally.

'Mally!' he said, 'Mally!'

It could have wanted nothing further to any of those present to teach them that, according to Barty's own view of the case, Mally had not been his enemy; and, in truth, Mally herself wanted no further triumph. That word had vindicated her, and she withdrew back to the hut.

'Dada,' she said. 'Barty is not dead, and I'm thinking they won't say anything more about our hurting him.'

Old Glos shook his head. He was glad the lad hadn't met his death there; he didn't want the young man's blood, but he knew what folk would say. The poorer he was the more sure the world would be to trample on him. Mally said what she could to comfort him, being full of comfort herself.

She would have crept up to the farm if she dared, to ask how Barty was. But her courage failed her when she thought of that, so she went to work again, dragging back the weed she had saved to the spot at which on the morrow she would load the donkey. As she did this she saw Barty's pony still standing patiently under the rock; so she got a lock of fodder and threw it down before the beast.

It had become dark down in the cove, but she was still dragging back the seaweed when she saw the glimmer of a lantern coming down the pathway. It was a most unusual sight, for lanterns were not common down in Malachi's Cove. Down came the lantern rather slowly – much more slowly than she was in the habit of descending, and then through the gloom she saw the figure of a man standing at the bottom of the path. She went up to him, and saw that it was Mr Gunliffe, the father.

'Is that Mally?' said Gunliffe.

'Yes, it is Mally; and how is Barty, Mr Gunliffe?'

'You must come to 'un yourself, now at once,' said the farmer. 'He won't sleep a wink till he's seed you. You must not say but you'll come.'

'Sure I'll come if I'm wanted,' said Mally.

Gunliffe waited a moment, thinking that Mally might have to prepare herself, but Mally needed no preparation. She was dripping with salt water from the weed which she had been dragging, and her elfin locks were streaming wildly from her head; but, such as she was, she was ready.

'Dada's in bed,' she said, 'and I can go now if you please.'

Then Gunliffe turned round and followed her up the path, wondering at the life which this girl led so far away from all her sex. It was now dark night, and he had found her working at the very edge of the rolling waves by herself, in the darkness, while the only human being who might seem to be her protector had already gone to his bed.

When they were at the top of the cliff Gunliffe took her by her hand, and led her along. She did not comprehend this, but she made no attempt to take her hand from his. Something he said about falling on the cliffs, but it was muttered so lowly that Mally hardly understood him. But in truth the man knew that she had saved his boy's life, and that he had injured her instead of thanking her. He was now taking her to his heart, and as words were wanting to him, he was showing his love after this silent fashion. He held her by the hand as though she were a child, and Mally tripped along at his side asking him no questions.

When they were at the farmyard gate he stopped there for a moment.

'Mally, my girl,' he said, 'he'll not be content till he sees thee, but thou must not stay long wi' him, lass. Doctor says he's weak like, and wants sleep badly.'

Mally merely nodded her head, and then they entered the house. Mally had never been within it before, and looked about with wondering eyes at the furniture of the big kitchen. Did any idea of her future destiny flash upon her then, I wonder? But she did not pause here a moment, but was led up to the bedroom above stairs, where Barty was lying on his mother's bed.

'Is it Mally herself?' said the voice of the weak youth.

'It's Mally herself,' said the mother, 'so now you can say what you please.'

'Mally,' said he, 'Mally, it's along of you that I'm alive this moment.'

'I'll not forget it on her,' said the father, with his eyes turned away from her. 'I'll never forget it on her.'

'We hadn't a one but only him,' said the mother, with her apron up to her face.

'Mally, you'll be friends with me now?' said Barty.

To have been made lady of the manor of the cove for ever, Mally couldn't have spoken a word now. It was not only that the words and presence of the people there cowed her and made her speechless, but the big bed, and the looking-glass, and the unheard-of wonders of the chamber, made her feel her own insignificance. But she crept up to Barty's side, and put her hand upon his.

'I'll come and get the weed, Mally; but it shall be all for you,' said Barty.

'Indeed, you won't then, Barty dear,' said the mother; 'you'll never go near the awesome place again. What would we do if you were took from us?'

'He mustn't go near the hole if he does,' said Mally, speaking at last in a solemn voice, and imparting the knowledge which she had kept to herself while Barty was her enemy; ''specially not if the wind's any way from the nor'ard.'

'She'd better go down now,' said the father.

Barty kissed the hand which he held, and Mally, looking at him as he did so, thought that he was like an angel.

'You'll come and see us tomorrow, Mally?' said he.

To this she made no answer, but followed Mrs Gunliffe out of the room. When they were down in the kitchen the mother had tea for her, and thick milk, and a hot cake – all the delicacies which the farm could afford. I don't know that Mally cared much for the eating and drinking that night, but she began to think that the Gunliffes were good people – very good people. It was better thus, at any rate, than being accused of murder and carried off to Camelford prison.

'I'll never forget it on her – never,' the father had said.

Those words stuck to her from that moment, and seemed to sound in her ears all the night. How glad she was that Barty had come down to the cove – oh, yes, how glad! There was no question of his dying now, and as for the blow on his forehead, what harm was that to a lad like him?

'But father shall go with you,' said Mrs Gunliffe, when Mally prepared to start for the cove by herself. Mally, however, would not hear of this. She could find her way to the cove whether it was light or dark.

'Mally, thou art my child now, and I shall think of thee so,' said the mother, as the girl went off by herself.

Mally thought of this too, as she walked home. How could she become Mrs Gunliffe's child; ah, how?

I need not, I think, tell the tale any further. That Mally did become Mrs Gunliffe's child, and how she became so the reader will understand; and in process of time the big kitchen and all the wonders of the farmhouse were her own. The people said that Bart Gunliffe had married a mermaid out of the sea; but when it was said in Mally's hearing I doubt whether she liked it; and when Barty himself would call her a mermaid she would frown at him, and throw about her black hair, and pretend to cuff him with her little hand.

Old Glos was brought up to the top of the cliff, and lived his few remaining days under the roof of Mr Gunliffe's house; and as for the cove and the right of seaweed, from that time forth all that has been supposed to attach itself to Gunliffe's farm, and I do not know that any of the neighbours are prepared to dispute the right.

Christmas at Cold Comfort Farm

STELLA GIBBONS

It was Christmas Eve. Dusk, a filthy mantle, lay over Sussex when the Reverend Silas Hearsay, Vicar of Howling, set out to pay his yearly visit to Cold Comfort Farm. Earlier in the afternoon he had feared he would not be Guided to go there, but then he had seen a crate of British port-type wine go past the Vicarage on the grocer's boy's bicycle, and it could only be going, by that road, to the farmhouse. Shortly afterwards he was Guided to go, and set out upon his bicycle.

The Starkadders, of Cold Comfort Farm, had never got the hang of Christmas, somehow, and on Boxing Day there was always a run on the Howling Pharmacy for lint, bandages and boracic powder. So the Vicar was going up there, as he did every year, to show them the ropes a bit. (It must be explained that these events took place some years before the civilizing hand of Flora Poste had softened and reformed the Farm and its rude inhabitants.)

After removing two large heaps of tussocks which blocked the lane leading to the Farm and thereby releasing a flood of muddy, icy water over his ankles, the Vicar wheeled his machine on towards the farmhouse, reflecting that those tussocks had never fallen there from the dung-cart of Nature. It was clear that someone did not want him to come to the place. He pushed his bicycle savagely up the hill, muttering.

The farmhouse was in silence and darkness. He pulled the ancient hell-bell (once used to warn excommunicated persons to stay away from Divine Service) hanging outside the front door, and waited.

For a goodish bit nothing happened. Suddenly a window far above his head was flung open and a voice wailed into the twilight—

'No! No! No!'

And the window slammed shut again.

'You're making a mistake, I'm sure,' shouted the Vicar, peering up into the webby thongs of the darkness. 'It's me. The Rev. Silas Hearsay.'

There was a pause. Then—

'Beant you postman?' asked the voice, rather embarrassed.

'No, no, of course not; come, come!' laughed the Vicar, grinding his teeth.

'I be comin',' retorted the voice. 'Thought it were postman after his Christmas Box.' The window slammed again. After a very long time indeed the door suddenly opened and there stood Adam Lambsbreath, oldest of the farm servants, peering up at the Reverend Hearsay by the light of a lonely rushdip (so called because you dipped it in grease and rushed to wherever you were going before it went out).

'Is anyone at home? May I enter?' enquired the Vicar, entering, and staring scornfully round the desolate kitchen, at the dead blue ashes in the grate, the thick dust on hanch and beam, the feathers blowing about like fun everywhere. Yet even here there were signs of Christmas, for a withered branch of holly stood in a shapeless vessel on the table. And Adam himself . . . there was something even more peculiar than usual about him.

'Are you ailing, man?' asked the Vicar irritably, kicking a chair out of the way and perching himself on the edge of the table.

'Nay, Rev., I be niver better,' piped the old man. '*The older the berry, The more it makes merry.*'

'Then why,' thundered the Vicar, sliding off the table and walking on tiptoe towards Adam with his arms held at full length above his head, 'are you wearing three of Mrs Starkadder's red shawls?'

Adam stood his ground.

'I mun have a red courtepy, master. Can't be Santa Claus wi'out a red courtepy,' he said. 'Iverybody knows that. Ay, the hand o' Fate lies heavy on us all, Christmas and all the year round alike, but I thought I'd bedight meself as Santa Claus, so I did, just to please me little Elfine. And this night at midnight I be goin' around fillin' the stockin's, if I'm spared.'

The Vicar laughed contemptuously.

'So that were why I took three o' Mrs Starkadder's red shawls,' concluded Adam.

'I suppose you have never thought of God in terms of Energy? No, it is too much to expect.' The Reverend Hearsay re-seated himself on the table and glanced at his watch. 'Where in Energy's name *is* everybody? I have to be at the Assembly Rooms to read a paper on "The Future of the Father Fixation" at eight, and I've got to feed first. If nobody's coming, I'd rather go.'

'Won't ee have a dram o' swede wine first?' a deep voice asked, and a tall woman stepped over the threshold, followed by a little girl of twelve or so with yellow hair and clear, beautiful features. Judith Starkadder dropped her hat on the floor and leant against the table, staring listlessly at the Vicar.

'No swede wine, I thank you,' snapped the Reverend Hearsay. He glanced keenly round the kitchen in search of the British port-type, but there was no sign of it. 'I came up to discuss an article with you and yours. An article in *Home Anthropology*.'

''Twere good of ee, Reverend,' she said tiredly.

'It is called *Christmas: From Religious Festival to Shopping Orgy*. Puts the case for Peace and Good Will very sensibly. Both good for trade. What more can you want?'

'Nothing,' she said, leaning her head on her hand.

'But I see,' the Vicar went on furiously, in a low tone and glaring at Adam, 'that here, as everywhere else, the usual childish wish-fantasies are in possession. Stars, shepherds, manger, stockings, fir-trees, puddings . . . Energy help you all! I wish you good night, and a prosperous Christmas.'

He stamped out of the kitchen, and slammed the door after him with such violence that he brought a slate down on his back tyre and cut it open, and he had to walk home, arriving there too late for supper before setting out for Godmere.

After he had gone, Judith stared into the fire without speaking, and Adam busied himself with scraping the mould from a jar of mincemeat and picking some things which had fallen into it out of a large crock of pudding which he had made yesterday.

Elfine, meanwhile, was slowly opening a small brown paper parcel which she had been nursing, and at last revealed a small and mean-looking doll dressed in a sleazy silk dress and one under-garment that did not take off. This she gently nursed, talking to it in a low, sweet voice.

'Who gave you that, child?' asked her mother idly.

'I told you, Mother. Uncle Micah and Aunt Rennett and Aunt Prue and Uncle Harkaway and Uncle Ezra.'

'Treasure it. You will not get many such.'

'I know, Mother; I do. I love her very much, dear, dear Caroline,' and Elfine gently put a kiss on the doll's face.

'Now, missus, have ee got the Year's Luck? Can't make puddens wi'out the Year's Luck,' said Adam, shuffling forward.

'It's somewhere here. I forget—'

She turned her shabby handbag upside down, and there fell out on the table the following objects:

A small coffin-nail.
A menthol cone.
Three bad sixpences.
A doll's cracked looking-glass.
A small roll of sticking-plaster.

Adam collected these objects and ranged them by the pudding-basin.

'Ay, them's all there,' he muttered. 'Him as gets the sticking-plaster'll break a limb; the menthol cone means as you'll be blind wi' headache, the bad coins means as you'll lose all yer money, and him as gets the coffin-nail will die afore the New Year. The mirror's seven years' bad luck for someone. Aie! In ye go, curse ye!' and he tossed the objects into the pudding, where they were not easily nor long distinguishable from the main mass.

'Want a stir, missus? Come, Elfine, my popelot, stir long, stir firm, your meat to earn,' and he handed her the butt of an old rifle, once used by Fig Starkadder in the Gordon Riots.

Judith turned from the pudding with what is commonly described as a gesture of loathing, but Elfine took the rifle butt and stirred the mixture once or twice.

'Ay, now tes all mixed,' said the old man, nodding with satisfaction. 'Tomorrer we'll boil un fer a good hour, and un'll be done.'

'Will an hour be enough?' said Elfine. 'Mrs Hawk-Monitor up at Hautcouture Hall boils hers for eight hours, and another four on Christmas Day.'

'How do ee know?' demanded Adam. 'Have ee been runnin' wi' that young goosepick Mus' Richard again?'

'You shut up. He's awfully decent.'

'Tisn't decent to run wi' a young popelot all over the Downs in all weathers.'

'Well, it isn't any of your business, so shut up.'

After an offended pause, Adam said:

'Well, niver fret about puddens. None of 'em here has iver tasted any puddens but mine, and they won't know no different.'

At midnight, when the farmhouse was in darkness save for the faint flame of a nightlight burning steadily beside the bed of Harkaway, who was afraid of bears, a dim shape might have been seen moving stealthily along the corridor from bedroom to bedroom. It wore three red shawls pinned over its torn nightshirt and carried over its shoulder a nosebag (the property of Viper the gelding), distended with parcels. It was Adam, bent on putting into the stockings of the Starkadders the presents which he had made or bought with his savings. The presents were chiefly swedes, beetroots, mangel-wurzels and turnips, decorated with coloured ribbons and strips of silver paper from tea packets.

'Ay,' muttered the old man, as he opened the door of the room where Meriam, the hired girl, was sleeping over the Christmas week. 'An apple for each will make 'em retch, a couple o' nuts will warm their wits.'

The next instant he stepped back in astonishment. There was a light in the room and there, sitting bolt upright in bed beside her slumbering daughter, was Mrs Beetle.

Mrs Beetle looked steadily at Adam, for a minute or two. Then she observed:

'Some 'opes.'

'Nay, niver say that, soul,' protested Adam, moving to the bedrail where hung a very fully fashioned salmon-pink silk stocking with ladders all down it. ''Tisn't so. Ee do know well that I looks on the maidy as me own child.'

Mrs Beetle gave a short laugh and adjusted a curler. 'You better not let Agony 'ear you, 'intin' I dunno wot,' said Mrs Beetle. ''Urry up and put yer rubbish in there, I want me sleep out; I got to be up at cock-wake ter-morrer.'

Adam put a swede, an apple and a small pot in the stocking and was tip-toeing away when Mrs Beetle, raising her head from the pillow, enquired:

'Wot's that you've give 'er?'

'Eye-shadow,' whispered Adam hoarsely, turning at the door.

'*Wot?*' hissed Mrs Beetle, inclining her head in an effort to hear. ''Ave you gorn crackers?'

'Eye-shadow. To put on the maidy's eyes. 'Twill give that touch o' glamour as be irresistible; it do say so on pot.'

'Get out of 'ere, you old trouble-maker! Don't she 'ave enough bother resistin' as it is, and then you go and give 'er . . . 'ere, wait till I—' and Mrs Beetle was looking around for something to throw as Adam hastily retreated.

'And I'll lay you ain't got no present fer me, ter make matters worse,' she called after him.

Silently he placed a bright new tin of beetle-killer on the washstand and shuffled away.

His experiences in the apartments of the other Starkadders were no more fortunate, for Seth was busy with a friend and was so furious at being interrupted that he threw his riding-boots at the old man, Luke and Mark had locked their door and could be heard inside roaring with laughter at Adam's discomfiture, and Amos was praying, and did not even get up off his knees or open his eyes as he discharged at Adam the goat-pistol which he kept over by his bed. And everybody else had such enormous holes in their stockings that the small presents Adam put in them fell through on to the floor along with the big ones, and when the Starkadders got up in the morning and rushed round to the foot of the bed to see what Santa had brought, they stubbed their toes on the turnips and swedes and walked on the smaller presents and smashed them to smithereens.

So what with one thing and another everybody was in an even worse temper than usual when the family assembled round the long table in the kitchen for the Christmas dinner about half-past two the next afternoon. They would all have sooner been in some place else, but Mrs Ada Doom (Grandmother Doom, known as Grummer) insisted on them all being there, and as they did not want her to go mad and bring disgrace on the House of Starkadder, there they had to be.

One by one they came in, the men from the fields with soil on their boots, the women fresh from hennery and duck filch with eggs in their bosoms that they gave to Mrs Beetle who was just making the custard. Everybody had to work as usual on Christmas Day, and no one had troubled to put on anything handsomer than their usual workaday clouts stained with mud and plough-oil. Only Elfine wore a cherry-red jersey over her dark skirt and had pinned a spray of holly on herself. An aunt, a distant aunt named Mrs Poste, who lived in London, had unexpectedly sent her the pretty jersey. Prue and Letty had stuck sixpenny artificial posies in their hair, but they only looked wild and queer.

At last all were seated and waiting for Ada Doom.

'Come, come, mun we stick here like jennets i' the trave?' demanded Micah at last. 'Amos, Reuben, do ee carve the turkey. If so be as we wait much longer, 'twill be shent, and the sausages, too.'

Even as he spoke, heavy footsteps were heard approaching the head of the stairs, and everybody at once rose to their feet and looked towards the door.

The low-ceilinged room was already half in dusk, for it was a cold, still Christmas Day, without much light in the grey sky, and the only other illumination came from the dull fire, half-buried under a tass of damp kindling.

Adam gave a last touch to the pile of presents, wrapped in hay and tied with bast, which he had put round the foot of the withered thorn-branch that was the traditional Starkadder Christmas-tree, hastily rearranged one of the tufts of sheep's-wool that decorated its branches, straightened the raven's skeleton that adorned its highest branch in place of a fairy-doll or star, and shuffled into his place just as Mrs Doom reached the foot of the stairs, leaning on her daughter Judith's arm. Mrs Doom struck at him with her stick in passing as she went slowly to the head of the table.

'Well, well. What are we waiting for? Are you all mishooden?' she demanded impatiently as she seated herself. 'Are you all here? All? Answer me!' banging her stick.

'Ay, Grummer,' rose the low, dreary drone from all sides of the table. 'We be all here.'

'Where's Seth?' demanded the old woman, peering sharply on either side of the long row.

'Gone out,' said Harkaway briefly, shifting a straw in his mouth.

'What for?' demanded Mrs Doom.

There was an ominous silence.

'He said he was going to fetch something, Grandmother,' at last said Elfine.

'Ay. Well, well, no matter, so long as he comes soon. Amos, carve the bird. Ay, would it were a vulture, 'twere more fitting! Reuben, fling these dogs the fare my bounty provides. Sausages . . . pah! Mince-pies . . . what a black-bitter mockery it all is! Every almond, every raisin, is wrung from the dry, dying soil and paid for with sparse greasy notes grudged alike by bank and buyer. Come, Ezra, pass the ginger wine! Be gay, spawn! Laugh, stuff yourselves, gorge and forget, you rat-heaps! Rot you all!' and she fell back in her chair, gasping and keeping one eye on the British port-type that was now coming up the table.

'Tes one of her bad days,' said Judith tonelessly. 'Amos, will you pull a cracker wi' me? We were lovers . . . once.'

'Hush, woman.' He shrank back from the proffered treat. 'Tempt me not wi' motters and paper caps. Hell is paved wi' such.' Judith smiled bitterly and fell silent.

Reuben, meanwhile, had seen to it that Elfine got the best bit of the turkey (which is not saying much) and had filled her glass with port-type wine and well-water.

The turkey gave out before it got to Letty, Prue, Susan, Phoebe, Jane and Rennett, who were huddled together at the foot of the table, and they were making do with Brussels sprouts as hard as bullets drenched with weak gravy, and home-brewed braket. There was silence in the kitchen except for the sough of swallowing, the sudden suck of drinking.

'WHERE IS SETH?' suddenly screamed Mrs Doom, flinging down her turkey-leg and glaring round.

Silence fell; everyone moved uneasily, not daring to speak in case they provoked an outburst. But at that moment the cheerful, if unpleasant, noise of a motor-cycle was heard outside, and in another moment it stopped at the kitchen door. All eyes were turned in that direction, and in another moment in came Seth.

'Well, Grummer! Happen you thought I was lost!' he cried impudently, peeling off his boots and flinging them at Meriam, the hired girl, who cowered by the fire gnawing a sausage skin.

Mrs Doom silently pointed to his empty seat with the turkey-leg, and he sat down.

'She hev had an outhees. Ay, 'twas terrible,' reproved Judith in a low tone as Seth seated himself beside her.

'Niver mind, I ha' something here as will make her chirk like a mellet,' he retorted, and held up a large brown-paper parcel. 'I ha' been to the Post Office to get it.'

'Ah, gie it me! Aie, my lost pleasurings! Tes none I get, nowadays; gie it me now!' cried the old woman eagerly.

'Nay, Grummer. Ee must wait till pudden time,' and the young man fell on his turkey ravenously.

When everyone had finished, the women cleared away and

poured the pudding into a large dusty dish, which they bore to the table and set before Judith.

'Amos? Pudding?' she asked listlessly. 'In a glass or on a plate?'

'On plate, on plate, woman,' he said feverishly, bending forward with a fierce glitter in his eye. ''Tes easier to see the Year's Luck so.'

A stir of excitement now went through the company, for everybody looked forward to seeing everybody else drawing ill-luck from the symbols concealed in the pudding. A fierce, attentive silence fell. It was broken by a wail from Reuben—

'The coin – the coin! Wala wa!' and he broke into deep, heavy sobs. He was saving up to buy a tractor, and the coin meant, of course, that he would lose all his money during the year.

'Never mind, Reuben, dear,' whispered Elfine, slipping an arm round his neck. 'You can have the penny Father gave me.'

Shrieks from Letty and Prue now announced that they had received the menthol cone and the sticking-plaster, and a low mutter of approval greeted the discovery by Amos of the broken mirror.

Now there was only the coffin-nail, and a ghoulish silence fell on everybody as they dripped pudding from their spoons in a feverish hunt for it; Ezra was running his through a tea-strainer.

But no one seemed to have got it.

'Who has the coffin-nail? Speak, you draf-saks!' at last demanded Mrs Doom.

'Not I.' 'Nay.' 'Niver sight nor snitch of it,' chorused everybody.

'Adam!' Mrs Doom turned to the old man. 'Did you put the coffin-nail into the pudding?'

'Ay, mistress, that I did – didn't I, Miss Judith, didn't I, Elfine, my liddle lovesight?'

'He speaks truth for once, Mother.'

'Yes, he did, Grandmother. I saw him.'

'*Then where is it?*' Mrs Doom's voice was low and terrible and her gaze moved slowly down the table, first on one side and then the other, in search of signs of guilt, while everyone cowered over their plates.

Everyone, that is, except Mrs Beetle, who continued to eat a sandwich that she had taken out of a cellophane wrapper, with every appearance of enjoyment.

'Carrie Beetle!' shouted Mrs Doom.

'I'm 'ere,' said Mrs Beetle.

'Did you take the coffin-nail out of the pudding?'

'Yes, I did.' Mrs Beetle leisurely finished the last crumb of sandwich and wiped her mouth with a clean handkerchief. 'And will again, if I'm spared till next year.'

'You . . . you . . . you . . .' choked Mrs Doom, rising in her chair and beating the air with her clenched fists. 'For two hundred years . . . Starkadders . . . coffin-nails in puddings . . . and now . . . you . . . dare . . .'

'Well, I 'ad enough of it las' year,' retorted Mrs Beetle. 'That pore old soul Ernest Dolour got it, as well you may remember—'

'That's right. Cousin Ernest,' nodded Mark Dolour. 'Got a job workin' on the oil-field down Henfield way. Good money, too.'

'Thanks to me, if he 'as,' retorted Mrs Beetle. 'If I 'adn't put it up to you, Mark Dolour, you'd 'ave let 'im die. All of you was 'angin' over the pore old soul waitin' for 'im to 'and in 'is dinner pail, and Micah (wot's old enough to know better, 'eaven only knows) askin' 'im could 'e 'ave 'is wrist-watch if anything was to 'appen to 'im . . . it fair got me down. So I says to Mark, why don't yer go down and 'ave a word with Mr Earthdribble the undertaker in Howling and get 'im to tell Ernest it weren't a proper coffin-nail at all, it were a throw-out, so it didn't count. The bother we 'ad! Shall I ever ferget it! Never again, I says to meself. So this year there ain't no coffin-nail. I fished it out o' the pudden meself. Parss the water, please.'

'Where is it?' whispered Mrs Doom, terribly. 'Where is this year's nail, woman?'

'Down the—' Mrs Beetle checked herself, and coughed, 'down the well,' concluded Mrs Beetle firmly.

'Niver fret, Grummer, I'll get it up fer ee! Me and the water voles, we can dive far and deep!' and Urk rushed from the room, laughing wildly.

'There ain't no need,' called Mrs Bettle after him. 'But anything to keep you an' yer rubbishy water voles out of mischief!' And Mrs Bettle went into a cackle of laughter, alternately slapping her knee and Caraway's arm, and muttering, 'Oh, cor, wait till I tell Agony! "Dive far and deep." Oh, cor!' After a minute's uneasy silence—

'Grummer.' Seth bent winningly towards the old woman, the large brown-paper parcel in his hand. 'Will you see your present now?'

'Aye, boy, aye. Let me see it. You're the only one that has thought of me, the only one.'

Seth was undoing the parcel, and now revealed a large book, handsomely bound in red leather with gilt lettering.

'There, Grummer. 'Tis the year's numbers o' *The Milk Producers' Weekly Bulletin and Cowkeepers' Guide*. I collected un for ee, and had un bound. Art pleased?'

'Ay. 'Tis handsome enough. A graceful thought,' muttered the old lady, turning the pages. Most of them were pretty battered, owing to her habit of rolling up the paper and hitting anyone with it who happened to be within reach.

''Tis better so. 'Tis heavier. Now I can *throw* it.'

The Starkadders so seldom saw a clean and handsome object at the farmhouse (for Seth was only handsome) that they now crept round, fascinated, to examine the book with murmurs of awe. Among them came Adam, but no sooner had he bent over the book than he recoiled from it with a piercing scream.

'Aie! . . . aie! aie!'

'What's the matter, dotard?' screamed Mrs Doom, jabbing at him with the volume. 'Speak, you kaynard!'

'Tes calf! Tes bound in calf! And tes our Pointless's calf, as she had last Lammastide, as was sold at Godmere to Farmer Lust!' cried Adam, falling to the floor. At the same instant, Luke hit Micah in the stomach, Harkaway pushed Ezra into the fire, Mrs Doom flung the bound volume of *The Milk Producers' Weekly*

Bulletin and Cowkeepers' Guide at the struggling mass, and the Christmas dinner collapsed into indescribable confusion.

In the midst of the uproar, Elfine, who had climbed on to the table, glanced up at the window as though seeking help, and saw a laughing face looking at her, and a hand in a yellow string glove beckoning with a riding-crop. Swiftly she darted down from the table and across the room, and out through the half-open door, slamming it after her.

Dick Hawk-Monitor, a sturdy boy astride a handsome pony, was out in the yard.

'Hallo!' she gasped. 'Oh, Dick, I am glad to see you!'

'I thought you never would see me – what on earth's the matter in there?' he asked curiously.

'Oh, never mind them, they're always like that. Dick, do tell me, what presents did you have?'

'Oh, a rifle, and a new saddle, and a fiver – lots of things. Look here, Elfine, you mustn't mind, but I brought you—'

He bent over the pony's neck and held out a sandwich box, daintily filled with slices of turkey, a piece of pudding, a tiny mince-pie and a crystallized apricot.

'Thought your dinner mightn't be very—' he ended gruffly.

'Oh, Dick, it's lovely! Darling little . . . what is it?'

'Apricot. Crystallized fruit. Look here, let's go up to the usual place, shall we? – and I'll watch you eat it.'

'But you must have some, too.'

'Man! I'm stoked up to the brim now! But I dare say I could manage a bit more. Here, you catch hold of Rob Roy, and he'll help you up the hill.'

He touched the pony with his heels and it trotted on towards the snow-streaked Downs, Elfine's yellow hair flying out like a shower of primroses under the grey sky of winter.

The Man Who Went Too Far

E.F. BENSON

The little village of St Faith's nestles in a hollow of wooded hill up on the north bank of the River Fawn in the county of Hampshire, huddling close round its grey Norman church as if for spiritual protection against the fays and fairies, the trolls and 'little people', who might be supposed still to linger in the vast empty spaces of the New Forest, and to come after dusk and do their doubtful businesses. Once outside the hamlet you may walk in any direction (so long as you avoid the high road which leads to Brockenhurst) for the length of a summer afternoon without seeing sign of human habitation, or possibly even catching sight of another human being. Shaggy wild ponies may stop their feeding for a moment as you pass, the white scuts of rabbits will vanish into their burrows, a brown viper perhaps will glide from your path into a clump of heather, and unseen birds will chuckle in the bushes, but it may easily happen that for a long day you will see nothing human. But you will not feel in the least lonely; in summer, at any rate, the sunlight will be gay with butterflies, and the air thick with all those woodland sounds which like instruments in an orchestra combine to play the great symphony of the yearly festival of June. Winds whisper in the birches, and sigh among the firs; bees are busy with their redolent labour among the heather, a myriad birds chirp in the green temples of the forest trees, and the voice of the river prattling over stony places, bubbling into pools, chuckling and gulping round corners, gives you the sense that many presences and companions are near at hand.

Yet, oddly enough, though one would have thought that these benign and cheerful influences of wholesome air and spaciousness of forest were very healthful comrades for a man, in so far as Nature can really influence this wonderful human genus which has in these centuries learned to defy her most violent storms in its well-established houses, to bridle her torrents and make them light its streets, to tunnel her mountains and plough her seas, the inhabitants of St Faith's will not willingly venture into the forest after dark. For in spite of the silence and loneliness of the hooded night it seems that a man is not sure in what company he may suddenly find himself, and though it is difficult to get from these villagers any very clear story of occult appearances, the feeling is widespread. One story indeed I have heard with some definiteness, the tale of a monstrous goat that has been seen to skip with hellish glee about the woods and shady places, and this perhaps is connected with the story which I have here attempted to piece together. It too is well known to them; for all remember the young artist who died here not long ago, a young man, or so he struck the beholder, of great personal beauty, with something about him that made men's faces to smile and brighten when they looked on him. His ghost they will tell you 'walks' constantly by the stream and through the woods which he loved so, and in especial it haunts a certain house, the last of the village, where he lived, and its garden in which he was done to death. For my part I am inclined to think that the terror of the Forest dates chiefly from that day. So, such as the story is, I have set it forth in connected form. It is based partly on the accounts of the villagers, but mainly on that of Darcy, a friend of mine and a friend of the man with whom these events were chiefly concerned.

The day had been one of untarnished midsummer splendour, and as the sun drew near to its setting, the glory of the evening grew every moment more crystalline, more miraculous. West-ward from St Faith's the beechwood which stretched for some miles towards the heathery upland beyond already cast its veil of clear shadow over the red roofs of the village, but the spire of the grey church, over-topping all, still pointed a flaming orange finger into the sky. The River Fawn, which runs below, lay in sheets of sky-reflected blue, and wound its dreamy devious course round the edge of this wood, where a rough two-planked bridge crossed from the bottom of the garden of the last house in the village, and communicated by means of a little wicker gate with the wood itself. Then once out of the shadow of the wood the stream lay in flaming pools of the molten crimson of the sunset, and lost itself in the haze of woodland distances.

This house at the end of the village stood outside the shadow, and the lawn which sloped down to the river was still flecked with sunlight. Garden-beds of dazzling colour lined its gravel walks, and down the middle of it ran a brick pergola, half-hidden in clusters of rambler-rose and purple with starry clematis. At the bottom end of it, between two of its pillars, was slung a hammock containing a shirt-sleeved figure.

The house itself lay somewhat remote from the rest of the village, and a footpath leading across two fields, now tall and fragrant with hay, was its only communication with the high road. It was low-built, only two storeys in height and, like the garden, its walls were a mass of flowering roses. A narrow stone terrace ran along the garden front, over which was stretched an awning, and on the terrace a young silent-footed manservant was busy with the laying of the table for dinner. He was neat-handed and quick with his job, and having finished it he went back into the house, and reappeared again with a large rough bath-towel on his arm. With this he went to the hammock in the pergola.

'Nearly eight, sir,' he said.

'Has Mr Darcy come yet?' asked a voice from the hammock.

'No, sir.'

'If I'm not back when he comes, tell him that I'm just having a bathe before dinner.'

The servant went back to the house, and after a moment or two Frank Halton struggled to a sitting posture, and slipped out on to the grass. He was of medium height and rather slender in build, but the supple ease and grace of his movements gave the impression of great physical strength: even his descent from the hammock was not an awkward performance. His face and hands were of very dark complexion, either from constant exposure to wind and sun, or, as his black hair and dark eyes tended to show, from some strain of southern blood. His head was small, his face of an exquisite beauty of modelling, while the smoothness of its contour would have led you to believe that he was a beardless lad still in his teens. But something, some look which living and experience alone can give, seemed to contradict that, and finding yourself completely puzzled as to his age, you would next moment probably cease to think about that, and only look at this glorious specimen of young manhood with wondering satisfaction.

He was dressed as became the season and the heat, and wore only a shirt open at the neck, and a pair of flannel trousers. His head, covered very thickly with a somewhat rebellious crop of short curly hair, was bare as he strolled across the lawn to the bathing-place that lay below. Then for a moment there was silence, then the sound of splashed and divided waters, and presently after, a great shout of ecstatic joy, as he swam upstream with the foamed water standing in a frill round his neck. Then after some five minutes of limb-stretching struggle with the flood, he turned over on his back, and with arms thrown wide, floated downstream, ripple-cradled and inert. His eyes were shut, and between half-parted lips he talked gently to himself.

'I am one with it,' he said to himself, 'the river and I, I and the river. The coolness and splash of it is I, and the water-herbs that wave in it are I also. And my strength and my limbs are not mine but the river's. It is all one, all one, dear Fawn.'

A quarter of an hour later he appeared again at the bottom of the lawn, dressed as before, his wet hair already drying into its crisp short curls again. There he paused a moment, looking back at the stream with the smile with which men look on the face of a friend, then turned towards the house. Simultaneously his servant came to the door leading on to the terrace, followed by a man who appeared to be some half-way through the fourth decade of his years. Frank and he saw each other across the bushes and garden-beds and, each quickening his step, they met suddenly face to face round an angle of the garden walk, in the fragrance of syringa.

'My dear Darcy,' cried Frank, 'I am charmed to see you.'

But the other stared at him in amazement.

'Frank!' he exclaimed.

'Yes, that is my name,' he said, laughing: 'what is the matter?'

Darcy took his hand.

'What have you done to yourself?' he asked. 'You are a boy again.'

'Ah, I have a lot to tell you,' said Frank. 'Lots that you will hardly believe, but I shall convince you—'

He broke off suddenly, and held up his hand.

'Hush, there is my nightingale,' he said.

The smile of recognition and welcome with which he had greeted his friend faded from his face, and a look of rapt wonder took its place, as of a lover listening to the voice of his beloved. His mouth parted slightly, showing the white line of teeth, and his eyes looked out and out till they seemed to Darcy to be focused on things beyond the vision of man. Then something perhaps startled the bird, for the song ceased.

'Yes, lots to tell you,' he said. 'Really I am delighted to see you. But you look rather white and pulled down; no wonder after that fever. And there is to be no nonsense about this visit. It is June now, you stop here till you are fit to begin work again. Two months at least.'

'Ah, I can't trespass quite to that extent.'

Frank took his arm and walked him down the grass.

'Trespass? Who talks of trespass? I shall tell you quite openly when I am tired of you, but you know when we had the studio together, we used not to bore each other. However, it is ill talking of going away on the moment of your arrival. Just a stroll to the river, and then it will be dinner-time.'

Darcy took out his cigarette case, and offered it to the other.

Frank laughed.

'No, not for me. Dear me, I suppose I used to smoke once. How very odd!'

'Given it up?'

'I don't know. I suppose I must have. Anyhow I don't do it now. I would as soon think of eating meat.'

'Another victim on the smoking altar of vegetarianism?'

'Victim?' asked Frank. 'Do I strike you as such?'

He paused on the margin of the stream and whistled softly. Next moment a moorhen made its splashing flight across the river, and ran up the bank. Frank took it very gently in his hands and stroked its head, as the creature lay against his shirt.

'And is the house among the reeds still secure?' he half-crooned to it. 'And is the missus quite well, and are the neighbours flourishing? There, dear, home with you,' and he flung it into the air.

'That bird's very tame,' said Darcy, slightly bewildered.

'It is rather,' said Frank, following its flight.

During dinner Frank chiefly occupied himself in bringing himself up-to-date in the movements and achievements of this old friend whom he had not seen for six years. Those six years, it now appeared, had been full of incident and success for Darcy; he had made a name for himself as a portrait painter which bade fair to outlast the vogue of a couple of seasons, and his leisure time had been brief. Then some four months previously he had been through a severe attack of typhoid, the result of which as concerns this story was that he had come down to this seques-tered place to recruit.

'Yes, you've got on,' said Frank at the end. 'I always knew you would. ARA with more in prospect. Money? You roll in it, I suppose, and, oh Darcy, how much happiness have you had all these years? That is the only imperishable possession. And how much have you learned? Oh, I don't mean in Art. Even I could have done well in that.'

Darcy laughed.

'Done well? My dear fellow, all I have learned in these six years you knew, so to speak, in your cradle. Your old pictures fetch huge prices. Do you never paint now?'

Frank shook his head.

'No, I'm too busy,' he said.

'Doing what? Please tell me. That is what everyone is forever asking me.'

'Doing? I suppose you would say I do nothing.'

Darcy glanced up at the brilliant young face opposite him.

'It seems to suit you, that way of being busy,' he said. 'Now, it's your turn. Do you read? Do you study? I remember you saying that it would do us all – all us artists, I mean – a great deal of good if we would study any one human face carefully for a year, without recording a line. Have you been doing that?'

Frank shook his head again.

'I mean exactly what I say,' he said. 'I have been *doing* nothing. And I have never been so occupied. Look at me; have I not done something to myself to begin with?'

'You are two years younger than I,' said Darcy, 'at least you used to be. You therefore are thirty-nine. But had I never seen you before I should say you were just twenty. But was it worth while to spend six years of greatly occupied life in order to look twenty? Seems rather like a woman of fashion.'

Frank laughed boisterously.

'First time I've ever been compared to that particular bird of prey,' he said. 'No, that has not been my occupation – in fact I am only very rarely conscious that one effect of my occupation has been that. Of course, it must have been if one comes to think of it. It is not very important. Quite true my body has become young. But that is very little; I have become young.'

Darcy pushed back his chair and sat sideways to the table looking at the other.

'Has that been your occupation then?' he asked.

'Yes, that anyhow is one aspect of it. Think what youth means! It is the capacity for growth: mind, body, spirit, all grow, all get stronger, all have a fuller, firmer life every day. That is something, considering that every day that passes after the ordinary man reaches the full-blown flower of his strength, weakens his hold on life. A man reaches his prime, and remains, we say, in his prime for ten years, or perhaps twenty. But after his primest prime is reached, he slowly, insensibly weakens. These are the signs of age in you, in your body, in your art probably, in your mind. You are less electric than you were. But I, when I reach my prime – I am nearing it – ah, you shall see.'

The stars had begun to appear in the blue velvet of the sky, and to the east the horizon seen above the black silhouette of the village was growing dove-coloured with the approach of moonrise. White moths hovered dimly over the garden-beds, and the footsteps of night tip-toed through the bushes. Suddenly Frank rose.

'Ah, it is the supreme moment,' he said softly. 'Now more than at any other time the current of life, the eternal imperishable current runs so close to me that I am almost enveloped in it. Be silent a minute.'

He advanced to the edge of the terrace and looked out, standing stretched with arms outspread. Darcy heard him draw a long breath into his lungs, and after many seconds expel it again. Six or eight times he did this, then turned back into the lamplight.

'It will sound to you quite mad, I expect,' he said, 'but if you want to hear the soberest truth I have ever spoken and shall ever speak, I will tell you about myself. But come into the garden if it is not too damp for you. I have never told anyone yet, but I shall like to tell you. It is long, in fact, since I have even tried to classify what I have learned.'

They wandered into the fragrant dimness of the pergola, and sat down. Then Frank began:

'Years ago, do you remember,' he said, 'we used often to talk about the decay of joy in the world. Many impulses, we settled, had contributed to this decay, some of which were good in themselves, others that were quite completely bad. Among the good things, I put what we may call certain Christian virtues: renunciation, resignation, sympathy with suffering, and the desire to relieve sufferers. But out of those things spring very bad ones, useless renunciations, asceticism for its own sake, mortification of the flesh with nothing to follow, no corresponding gain that is, and that awful and terrible disease which devastated England some centuries ago, and from which by heredity of spirit we suffer now, Puritanism. That was a dreadful plague, the brutes held and taught that joy and laughter and merriment were evil: it was the most profane and wicked doctrine. Why, what is the commonest crime one sees? A sullen face. That is the truth of the matter.

'Now all my life I have believed that we are intended to be happy, that joy is of all gifts the most divine. And when I left London, abandoned my career, such as it was, I did so because I intended to devote my life to the cultivation of joy, and, by continuous and unsparing effort, to be happy. Among people, and in constant intercourse with others, I did not find it possible; there were too many distractions in towns and work-rooms, and also too much suffering. So I took one step backwards or forwards, as you may choose to put it, and went straight to Nature, to trees, birds, animals, to all those things which quite clearly pursue one aim only, which blindly follow the great Nature instinct to be happy without any care at all for morality, or human law or divine law. I wanted, you understand, to get all joy first-hand and unadulterated, and I think it scarcely exists among men; it is obsolete.'

Darcy turned in his chair.

'Ah, but what makes birds and animals happy?' he asked. 'Food, food and mating.'

Frank laughed gently in the stillness.

'Do not think I became a sensualist,' he said. 'I did not make that mistake. For the sensualist carries his miseries pick-a-back, and round his feet is wound the shroud that shall soon enwrap him. I may be mad, it is true, but I am not so stupid anyhow as to have tried that. No, what is it that makes puppies play with their own tails, that sends cats on their prowling ecstatic errands at night?'

He paused a moment.

121

'So I went to Nature,' he said. 'I sat down here in this New Forest, sat down fair and square, and looked. That was my first difficulty, to sit here quiet without being bored, to wait without being impatient, to be receptive and very alert, though for a long time nothing particular happened. The change, in fact, was slow in those early stages.'

'Nothing happened?' asked Darcy, rather impatiently, with the sturdy revolt against any new idea which to the English mind is synonymous with nonsense. 'Why, what in the world *should* happen?'

Now Frank as he had known him was the most generous but most quick-tempered of mortal men; in other words his anger would flare to a prodigious beacon, under almost no provocation, only to be quenched again under a gust of no less impulsive kindliness. Thus the moment Darcy had spoken, an apology for his hasty question was half-way up his tongue. But there was no need for it to have travelled even so far, for Frank laughed again with kindly, genuine mirth.

'Oh, how I should have resented that a few years ago,' he said. 'Thank goodness that resentment is one of the things I have got rid of. I certainly wish that you should believe my story – in fact, you are going to – but that you at this moment should imply that you do not does not concern me.'

'Ah, your solitary sojournings have made you inhuman,' said Darcy, still very English.

'No, human,' said Frank. 'Rather more human, at least rather less of an ape.'

'Well, that was my first quest,' he continued, after a moment, 'the deliberate and unswerving pursuit of joy, and my method: the eager contemplation of Nature. As far as motive went, I daresay it was purely selfish, but as far as effect goes, it seems to me about the best thing one can do for one's fellow-creatures, for happiness is more infectious than smallpox. So, as I said, I sat down and waited; I looked at happy things, zealously avoided the sight of anything unhappy, and by degrees a little trickle of the happiness of this blissful world began to filter into me. The trickle grew more abundant, and now, my dear fellow, if I could for a moment divert from me into you one half of the torrent of joy that pours through me day and night, you would throw the world, art, everything aside, and just live, exist. When a man's body dies, it passes into trees and flowers. Well, that is what I have been trying to do with my soul before death.'

The servant had brought into the pergola a table with syphons and spirits, and had set a lamp upon it. As Frank spoke he leaned forward towards the other, and Darcy for all his matter-of-fact common sense could have sworn that his companion's face shone, was luminous in itself. His dark brown eyes glowed from within, the unconscious smile of a child irradiated and transformed his face. Darcy felt suddenly excited, exhilarated.

'Go on,' he said. 'Go on. I can feel you are somehow telling me sober truth. I daresay you are mad; but I don't see that that matters.'

Frank laughed again.

'Mad?' he said. 'Yes, certainly, if you wish. But I prefer to call it sane. However, nothing matters less than what anybody chooses to call things. God never labels his gifts; He just puts them into our hands; just as He put animals in the Garden of Eden, for Adam to name if he felt disposed.

'So by the continual observance and study of things that were happy,' continued he, 'I got happiness, I got joy. But seeking it, as I did, from Nature, I got much more which I did not seek, but stumbled upon originally by accident. It is difficult to explain, but I will try.

'About three years ago I was sitting one morning in a place I will show you tomorrow. It is down by the river brink, very green, dappled with shade and sun, and the river passes there through some little clumps of reeds. Well, as I sat there, doing nothing, but just looking and listening, I heard the sound quite distinctly of some flute-like instrument playing a strange unending melody. I thought at first it was some musical yokel on the highway and did not pay much attention. But before long the strangeness and indescribable beauty of the tune struck me. It never repeated itself, but it never came to an end, phrase after phrase ran its sweet course, it worked gradually and inevitably up to a climax, and having attained it, it went on; another climax was reached and another and another. Then with a sudden gasp of wonder I localized where it came from. It came from the reeds and from the sky and from the trees. It was everywhere, it was the sound of life. It was, my dear Darcy, as the Greeks would have said, it was Pan playing on his pipes, the voice of Nature. It was the life-melody, the world-melody.'

Darcy was far too interested to interrupt, though there was a question he would have liked to ask, and Frank went on:

'Well, for the moment I was terrified, terrified with the impotent horror of nightmare, and I stopped my ears and just ran from the place and got back to the house panting, trembling, literally in a panic. Unknowingly, for at that time I only pursued joy, I had begun, since I drew my joy from Nature, to get in touch with Nature. Nature, Force, God, call it what you will, had drawn across my face a little gossamer web of essential life. I saw that when I emerged from my terror, and I went very humbly back to where I had heard the Pan-pipes. But it was nearly six months before I heard them again.'

'Why was that?' asked Darcy.

'Surely because I had revolted, rebelled, and worst of all been frightened. For I believe that just as there is nothing in the world which so injures one's body as fear, so there is nothing that so much shuts up the soul. I was afraid, you see, of the one thing in the world which has real existence. No wonder its manifestation was withdrawn.'

'And after six months?'

'After six months one blessed morning I heard the piping again. I wasn't afraid that time. And since then it has grown louder, it has become more constant. I now hear it often, and I can put myself into such an attitude towards Nature that the pipes will almost certainly sound. And never yet have they played the same tune, it is always something new, something fuller, richer, more complete than before.'

'What do you mean by "such an attitude towards Nature"?' asked Darcy.

'I can't explain that; but by translating it into a bodily attitude it is this.'

Frank sat up for a moment quite straight in his chair, then slowly sunk back with arms outspread and head drooped.

'That,' he said, 'an effortless attitude, but open, resting, receptive. It is just that which you must do with your soul.'

Then he sat up again.

'One word more,' he said, 'and I will bore you no further . . . Nor unless you ask me questions shall I talk about it again. You will find me, in fact, quite sane in my mode of life. Birds and beasts you will see behaving somewhat intimately with me, like that moorhen, but that is all. I will walk with you, ride with you, play golf with you, and talk with you on any subject you like. But I wanted you on the threshold to know what has happened to me. And one thing more will happen.'

He paused again, and a slight look of fear crossed his eyes.

'There will be a final revelation,' he said, 'a complete and blinding stroke which will throw open to me, once and for all, the full knowledge, the full realisation and comprehension that I am one, just as you are, with life. In reality there is no "me", no "you", no "it". Everything is part of the one and only thing which is life. I know that that is so, but the realisation of it is not yet mine. But it will be, and on that day, so I take it, I shall see Pan. It may mean death, the death of my body, that is, but I don't care. It may mean immortal, eternal life lived here and now and for ever. Then having gained that, ah, my dear Darcy, I shall preach such a gospel of joy, showing myself as the living proof of the truth, that Puritanism, the dismal religion of sour races, shall vanish like a breath of smoke, and be dispersed and disappear in the sunlit air. But first the full knowledge must be mine.'

Darcy watched his face narrowly.

'You are afraid of that moment,' he said.

Frank smiled at him.

'Quite true; you are quick to have seen that. But when it comes I hope I shall not be afraid.'

For some little time there was silence; then Darcy rose.

'You have bewitched me, you extraordinary boy,' he said. 'You have been telling me a fairy-story, and I find myself saying, "Promise me it is true".'

'I promise you that,' said the other.

'And I know I shan't sleep,' added Darcy.

Frank looked at him with a sort of mild wonder as if he scarcely understood.

'Well, what does that matter?' he said.

'I assure you it does. I am wretched unless I sleep.'

'Of course I can make you sleep if I want,' said Frank in a rather bored voice.

'Well, do.'

'Very good: go to bed. I'll come upstairs in ten minutes.'

Frank busied himself for a little after the other had gone, moving the table back under the awning of the verandah and quenching the lamp. Then he went with his quick silent tread upstairs and into Darcy's room. The latter was already in bed, but very wide-eyed and wakeful, and Frank with an amused smile of indulgence, as for a fretful child, sat down on the edge of the bed.

'Look at me,' he said, and Darcy looked.

'The birds are sleeping in the brake,' said Frank softly, 'and the winds are asleep. The sea sleeps, and the tides are but the heaving of its breast. The stars swing slow, rocked in the great cradle of the Heavens, and—'

He stopped suddenly, gently blew out Darcy's candle, and left him sleeping.

Morning brought to Darcy a flood of hard common sense, as clear and crisp as the sunshine that filled his room. Slowly as he woke he gathered together the broken threads of the memories of the evening which had ended, so he told himself, in a trick of common hypnotism. That accounted for it all; the whole strange talk he had had was under a spell of suggestion from the extraordinary vivid boy who had once been a man; all his own excitement, his acceptance of the incredible had been merely the effect of a stronger, more potent will imposed on his own. How strong that will was, he guessed from his own instantaneous obedience to Frank's suggestion of sleep. And armed with impenetrable common sense he came down to breakfast. Frank had already begun, and was consuming a large plateful of porridge and milk with the most prosaic and healthy appetite.

'Slept well?' he asked.

'Yes, of course. Where did you learn hypnotism?'

'By the side of the river.'

'You talked an amazing quantity of nonsense last night,' remarked Darcy, in a voice prickly with reason.

'Rather. I felt quite giddy. Look, I remembered to order a dreadful daily paper for you. You can read about money markets or politics or cricket matches.'

Darcy looked at him closely. In the morning light Frank looked even fresher, younger, more vital than he had done the night before, and the sight of him somehow dented Darcy's armour of common sense.

'You are the most extraordinary fellow I ever saw,' he said. 'I want to ask you some more questions.'

'Ask away,' said Frank.

For the next day or two Darcy plied his friend with many questions, objections and criticisms on the theory of life, and gradually got out of him a coherent and complete account of his experience. In brief, then, Frank believed that 'by lying naked', as he put it, to the force which controls the passage of the stars, the breaking of a wave, the budding of a tree, the love of a youth and maiden, he had succeeded in a way hitherto undreamed of in possessing himself of the essential principle of life. Day by day, so he thought, he was getting nearer to, and in closer union with, the great power itself which caused all life to be, the spirit of nature, of Force, or the spirit of God. For himself, he confessed to what others would call paganism; it was sufficient for him that there existed a principle of life. He did not worship it, he did not pray to it, he did not praise it. Some of it existed in all human beings, just as it existed in trees and animals; to realise and make living to himself the fact that it was all one, was his sole aim and object.

Here perhaps Darcy would put in a word of warning.

'Take care,' he said. 'To see Pan meant death, did it not?'

Frank's eyebrows would rise at this.

'What does that matter?' he said. 'True, the Greeks were always right, and they said so, but there is another possibility. For the nearer I get to it, the more living, the more vital and young I become.'

'What then do you expect the final revelation will do for you?'

'I have told you,' said he. 'It will make me immortal.'

But it was not so much from speech and argument that Darcy grew to grasp his friend's conception, as from the ordinary conduct of his life. They were passing, for instance, one morning down the village street, when an old woman, very bent and decrepit, but with an extraordinary cheerfulness of face, hobbled out from her cottage. Frank instantly stopped when he saw her.

'You old darling! How goes it all?' he said.

But she did not answer, her dim old eyes were riveted on his face; she seemed to drink in like a thirsty creature the beautiful radiance which shone there. Suddenly she put her two withered old hands on his shoulders.

'You're just the sunshine itself,' she said, and he kissed her and passed on.

But scarcely a hundred yards further a strange contradiction of such tenderness occurred. A child running along the path towards them fell on its face and set up a dismal cry of fright and pain. A look of horror came into Frank's eyes, and, putting his fingers in his ears, he fled at full speed down the street, and did not pause till he was out of hearing. Darcy, having ascertained that the child was not really hurt, followed him in bewilderment.

'Are you without pity then?' he asked.

Frank shook his head impatiently.

'Can't you see?' he asked. 'Can't you understand that that sort of thing – pain, anger, anything unlovely – throws me back, retards the coming of the great hour! Perhaps when it comes I shall be able to piece that side of life on to the other, on to the true religion of joy. At present I can't.'

'But the old woman. Was she not ugly?'

Frank's radiance gradually returned.

'Ah, no. She was like me. She longed for joy, and knew it when she saw it, the old darling.'

Another question suggested itself.

'Then what about Christianity?' asked Darcy.

'I can't accept it. I can't believe in any creed of which the central doctrine is that God who is joy should have had to suffer. Perhaps it was so; in some inscrutable way I believe it may have been so, but I don't understand how it was possible. So I leave it alone; my affair is joy.'

They had come to the weir above the village, and the thunder of riotous cool water was heavy in the air. Trees dipped into the translucent stream with slender trailing branches, and the meadow where they stood was starred with midsummer blossomings. Larks shot up carolling into the crystal dome of blue, and a thousand voices of June sang round them. Frank, bare-headed as was his wont, with his coat slung over his arm and his shirt-sleeves rolled up above the elbow, stood there like some beautiful wild animal with eyes half-shut and mouth half-open, drinking in the scented warmth of the air. Then suddenly he flung himself face downwards on the grass at the edge of the stream, burying his face in the daisies and cowslips, and lay stretched there in wide-armed ecstasy, with his long fingers pressing and stroking the dewy herbs of the field. Never before had Darcy seen him thus fully possessed by his idea; his caressing fingers, his half-buried face pressed close to the grass, even the clothed lines of his figure were instinct with a vitality that somehow was different from that of other men. And some faint glow from it reached Darcy, some thrill, some vibration from that charged recumbent body passed to him, and for a moment he understood as he had not understood before, despite his persistent questions and the candid answers they received, how real, and how realised by Frank, his idea was.

Then suddenly the muscles in Frank's neck became stiff and alert, and he half-raised his head.

'The Pan-pipes, the Pan-pipes,' he whispered. 'Close, oh, so close.'

Very slowly, as if a sudden movement might interrupt the melody, he raised himself and leaned on the elbow of his bent arm. His eyes opened wider, the lower lids drooped as if he focused his eyes on something very far away, and the smile on his face broadened and quivered like sunlight on still water, till the exultance of its happiness was scarcely human. So he remained motionless and rapt for some minutes, then the look of listening died from his face, and he bowed his head, satisfied.

'Ah, that was good,' he said. 'How is it possible you did not hear? Oh, you poor fellow! Did you really hear nothing?'

A week of this outdoor and stimulating life did wonders in restoring to Darcy the vigour and health which his weeks of fever had filched from him, and as his normal activity and higher pressure of vitality returned, he seemed to himself to fall even more under the spell which the miracle of Frank's youth cast over him. Twenty times a day he found himself saying to himself suddenly at the end of some ten minutes' silent resistance to the absurdity of Frank's idea: 'But it isn't possible; it can't be possible,' and from the fact of his having to assure himself so frequently of this, he knew that he was struggling and arguing with a conclusion which already had taken root in his mind. For in any case a visible living miracle confronted him, since it was equally impossible that this youth, this boy, trembling on the verge of manhood, was thirty-five. Yet such was the fact.

July was ushered in by a couple of days of blustering and fretful rain, and Darcy, unwilling to risk a chill, kept to the house. But to Frank this weeping change of weather seemed to have no bearing on the behaviour of man, and he spent his days exactly as he did under the suns of June, lying in his hammock, stretched on the dripping grass, or making huge rambling excursions into the forest, the birds hopping from tree to tree after him, to return in the evening, drenched and soaked, but with the same unquenchable flame of joy burning within him. 'Catch cold?' he would ask; 'I've forgotten how to do it, I think. I suppose it makes one's body more sensitive always to sleep out-of-doors. People who live indoors always remind me of something peeled and skinless.'

'Do you mean to say you slept out-of-doors last night in that deluge?' asked Darcy. 'And where, may I ask?'

Frank thought a moment.

'I slept in the hammock till nearly dawn,' he said. 'For I remember the light blinked in the east when I awoke. Then I went – where did I go – oh, yes, to the meadow where the Pan-pipes sounded so close a week ago. You were with me, do you remember? But I always have a rug if it is wet.'

And he went whistling upstairs.

Somehow that little touch, his obvious effort to recall where he had slept, brought strangely home to Darcy the wonderful romance of which he was the still half-incredulous beholder. Sleep till close on dawn in a hammock, then the tramp – or probably scamper – underneath the windy and weeping heavens to the remote and lonely meadow by the weir! The picture of other such nights rose before him; Frank sleeping perhaps by the bathing-place under the filtered twilight of the stars, or the white blaze of moonshine, a stir and awakening at some dead hour, perhaps a space of silent wide-eyed thought, and then a wandering through the hushed wood to some other dormitory, alone with his happiness, alone with the joy and the life that suffused and enveloped him, without other thought or desire or aim except the hourly and never-ceasing communion with the joy of Nature.

They were in the middle of dinner that night, talking on indifferent subjects, when Darcy suddenly broke off in the middle of a sentence.

'I've got it,' he said. 'At last I've got it.'

'I congratulate you,' said Frank. 'But what?'

'The radical unsoundness of your idea. It is this: "All Nature from highest to lowest is full, crammed full of suffering; every living organism in Nature preys on another, yet in your aim to get close to, to be one with Nature, you leave suffering altogether out; you run away from it, you refuse to recognize it." And you are waiting, you say, for the final revelation.'

Frank's brow clouded slightly.

'Well,' he asked, rather wearily.

'Cannot you guess then when the final revelation will be? In joy you are supreme. I grant you that; I did not know a man

131

could be so master of it. You have learned perhaps practically all that Nature can teach. And if, as you think, the final revelation is coming to you, it will be the revelation of horror, suffering, death, pain in all its hideous forms. Suffering does exist: you hate it and fear it.'

Frank held up his hand.

'Stop; let me think,' he said.

There was silence for a long minute.

'That never struck me,' he said at length. 'It is possible that what you suggest is true. Does the sight of Pan mean that, do you think? Is it that Nature, take it altogether, suffers horribly, suffers to a hideous inconceivable extent? Shall I be shown all the suffering?'

He got up and came round to where Darcy sat.

'If it is so, so be it,' he said. 'Because, my dear fellow, I am near, so splendidly near to the final revelation. Today the pipes have sounded almost without pause. I have even heard the rustle in the bushes, I believe, of Pan's coming. I have seen, yes, I saw today, the bushes pushed aside as if by a hand, and a piece of a face, not human, peered through. But I was not frightened, at least I did not run away this time.'

He took a turn up to the window and back again.

'Yes, there is suffering all through,' he said, 'and I have left it all out of my search. Perhaps, as you say, the revelation will be that. And in that case, it will be good-bye. I have gone on one line. I shall have gone too far along one road, without having explored the other. But I can't go back now. I wouldn't if I could; not a step would I retrace! In any case, whatever the revelation is, it will be God. I'm sure of that.'

The rainy weather soon passed, and with the return of the sun Darcy again joined Frank in long rambling days. It grew extraordinarily hotter, and with the fresh bursting of life, after the rain, Frank's vitality seemed to blaze higher and higher. Then, as is the habit of the English weather, once evening clouds began to bank themselves up in the west, the sun went down in a glare of coppery thunder-rack, and the whole earth broiling

132

under an unspeakable oppression and sultriness paused and panted for the storm. After sunset the remote fires of lightning began to wink and flicker on the horizon, but when bed-time came the storm seemed to have moved no nearer, though a very low unceasing noise of thunder was audible. Weary and oppressed by the stress of the day, Darcy fell at once into a heavy uncomforting sleep.

He woke suddenly into full consciousness, with the din of some appalling explosion of thunder in his ears, and sat up in bed with racing heart. Then for a moment, as he recovered himself from the panic-land which lies between sleeping and waking, there was silence, except for the steady hissing of rain on the shrubs outside his window. But suddenly that silence was shattered and shredded into fragments by a scream from somewhere close at hand outside in the black garden, a scream of supreme and despairing terror. Again and once again it shrilled up, and then a babble of awful words was interjected. A quivering sobbing voice that he knew said:

'My God, oh, my God; oh, Christ!'

And then followed a little mocking, bleating laugh. Then was silence again; only the rain hissed on the shrubs.

All this was but the affair of a moment, and without pause either to put on clothes or light a candle, Darcy was already fumbling at his door-handle. Even as he opened it he met a terror-stricken face outside, that of the manservant who carried a light.

'Did you hear?' he asked.

The man's face was bleached to a dull shining whiteness.

'Yes, sir,' he said. 'It was the master's voice.'

Together they hurried down the stairs and through the dining room where an orderly table for breakfast had already been laid, and out on to the terrace. The rain for the moment had been utterly stayed, as if the tap of the heavens had been turned off, and under the lowering black sky, not quite dark, since the moon rode somewhere serene behind the conglomerated thunder-clouds, Darcy stumbled into the garden, followed by the servant with the candle. The monstrous leaping shadow of himself was cast before him on the lawn; lost and wandering odours of rose and lily and damp earth were thick about him, but more pungent was some sharp and acrid smell that suddenly reminded him of a certain châlet in which he had once taken refuge in the Alps. In the blackness of the hazy light from the sky, and the vague tossing of the candle behind him, he saw that the hammock in which Frank so often lay was tenanted. A gleam of white shirt was there, as if a man were sitting up in it, but across that there was an obscure dark shadow, and as he approached the acrid odour grew more intense.

He was now only some few yards away, when suddenly the black shadow seemed to jump into the air, then came down with tappings of hard hoofs on the brick path that ran down to the pergola, and with frolicsome skippings galloped off into the bushes. When that was gone Darcy could see quite clearly that a shirted figure sat up in the hammock. For one moment, from sheer terror of the unseen, he hung on his step, and the servant joining him they walked together to the hammock.

It was Frank. He was in shirt and trousers only, and he sat up with braced arms. For one half-second he stared at them, his face a mask of horrible contorted terror. His upper lip was drawn back so that the gums of the teeth appeared, and his eyes were focused not on the two who approached him, but on something quite close to him. His nostrils were widely expanded, as if he panted for breath, and terror incarnate and repulsion and deathly anguish ruled dreadful lines on his smooth cheeks and forehead. Then even as they looked the body sank backwards, and the ropes of the hammock wheezed and strained.

Darcy lifted him out and carried him indoors. Once he thought there was a faint convulsive stir of the limbs that lay with so dead a weight in his arms, but when they got inside, there was no trace of life. But the look of supreme terror and agony of fear had gone from his face, a boy tired with play but still smiling in his sleep was the burden he laid on the floor. His eyes had closed, and the beautiful mouth lay in smiling curves, even as when a few mornings ago, in the meadow by the weir, it had quivered to the music of the unheard melody of Pan's pipes. Then they looked further.

Frank had come back from his bathe before dinner that night in his usual costume of shirt and trousers only. He had not dressed, and during dinner, so Darcy remembered, he had rolled up the sleeves of his shirt to above the elbow. Later, as they sat and talked after dinner on the close sultriness of the evening, he had unbuttoned the front of his shirt to let what little breath of wind there was play on his skin. The sleeves were rolled up now, the front of the shirt was unbuttoned, and on his arms and on the brown skin of his chest were strange discolorations which grew momently more clear and defined, till they saw that the marks were pointed prints, as if caused by the hoofs of some monstrous goat that had leaped and stamped upon him.

The Shooting Party

VIRGINIA WOOLF

She got in and put her suitcase in the rack, and the brace of
pheasants on top of it. Then she sat down in the corner. The
train was rattling through the Midlands, and the fog, which came
in when she opened the door, seemed to enlarge the carriage and
set the four travellers apart. Obviously M.M. – those were the
initials on the suitcase – had been staying the weekend with a
shooting party, obviously, for she was telling over the story now,
lying back in her corner. She did not shut her eyes. But clearly
she did not see the man opposite, nor the coloured photograph of
York Minster. She must have heard, too, what they had been
saying. For as she gazed, her lips moved; now and then she
smiled. And she was handsome; a cabbage rose; a russet apple;
tawny; but scarred on the jaw – the scar lengthened when she
smiled. Since she was telling over the story she must have been a
guest there, and yet, dressed as she was, out of fashion as women
dressed, years ago, in pictures in fashion plates of sporting
newspapers, she did not seem exactly a guest, nor yet a maid.
Had she had a basket with her she would have been the woman
who breeds fox-terriers; the owner of the Siamese cat; someone
connected with hounds and horses. But she had only a suitcase
and pheasants. Somehow therefore she must have wormed her
way into the room that she was seeing through the stuffing of the
carriage, and the man's bald head, and the picture of York

Minster. And she must have listened to what they were saying, for now, like somebody imitating the noise that someone else makes, she made a little click at the back of her throat: 'Chk. Chk.' Then she smiled.

'Chk,' said Miss Antonia, pinching her glasses on her nose. The damp leaves fell across the long windows of the gallery; one or two stuck, fish-shaped, and lay like inlaid brown wood upon the window-panes. Then the trees in the Park shivered, and the leaves, flaunting down, seemed to make the shiver visible – the damp brown shiver.

'Chk,' Miss Antonia sniffed again, and pecked at the flimsy white stuff that she held in her hands, as a hen pecks nervously, rapidly, at a piece of white bread.

The wind sighed. The room was draughty. The doors did not fit, nor the windows. Now and then a ripple, like a reptile, ran under the carpet. On the carpet lay panels of green and yellow, where the sun rested, and then the sun moved and pointed a finger as if in mockery at a hole in the carpet and stopped. And then on it went, the sun's feeble but impartial finger, and lay upon the coat of arms over the fireplace – gently illumined the shield; the pendant grape; the mermaid; and the spears. Miss Antonia looked up as the light strengthened. Vast lands, so they said, the old people had owned – her forefathers – the Rashleighs. Over there. Up the Amazons. Freebooter. Voyagers. Sacks of emeralds. Nosing round the islands. Taking captives. Maidens. There she was, all scales from the tail to the waist. Miss Antonia grinned. Down struck the finger of the sun and her eye went with it. Now it rested on a silver frame; on a photograph; on an egg-shaped baldish head; on a lip that stuck out under the moustache; and the name 'Edward' written with a flourish beneath.

'The King . . .' Miss Antonia muttered, turning the film of white upon her knee, 'had the Blue Room,' she added with a toss of her head. The light faded.

Out in the King's Ride the pheasants were being driven across the noses of the guns. Up they spurted from the underwood like heavy rockets, reddish purple rockets, and as they rose the guns cracked in order, eagerly, sharply, as if a line of dogs had suddenly barked. Tufts of white smoke held together for a moment; then gently dissolved themselves, faded and dispersed.

In the deep-cut road beneath the hanger a cart stood, laid already with soft warm bodies, with limp claws, and still lustrous eyes. The birds seemed alive still, but swooning under their rich damp feathers. They looked relaxed and comfortable, stirring slightly, as if they slept upon a warm bank of soft feathers on the floor of the cart.

Then the Squire, with the hang-dog, purple-stained face, in the shabby gaiters, cursed and raised his gun.

Miss Antonia stitched on. Now and then a tongue of flame reached round the grey log that stretched from one bar to another across the grate; ate it greedily, then died out, leaving a white bracelet where the bark had been eaten off. Miss Antonia looked up for a moment, stared wide-eyed, instinctively, as a dog stares at a flame. Then the flame sank and she stitched again.

Then, silently, the enormously high door opened. Two lean men came in, and drew a table over the hole in the carpet. They went out; they came in. They laid a cloth upon the table. They went out; they came in. They brought a green baize basket of knives and forks; and glasses; and sugar casters; and salt-cellars; and bread; and a silver vase with three chrysanthemums in it. And the table was laid. Miss Antonia stitched on.

Again the door opened, pushed feebly this time. A little dog trotted in, a spaniel, nosing nimbly; it paused. The door stood open. And then, leaning on her stick, heavily, old Miss Rashleigh entered. A white shawl, diamond-fastened, clouded her baldness. She hobbled; crossed the room; hunched herself in the high-backed chair by the fireside. Miss Antonia went on stitching.

'Shooting,' she said at last.

Old Miss Rashleigh nodded. 'In the King's Ride,' she said. She gripped her stick. They sat waiting.

The shooters had moved now from the King's Ride to the Home

Woods. They stood in the purple ploughed field outside. Now and then a twig snapped; leaves came whirling. But above the mist and the smoke was an island of blue – faint blue, pure blue – alone in the sky. And in the innocent air, as if straying alone like a cherub, a bell from a far hidden steeple frolicked, gambolled, then faded. Then again up shot the rockets, the reddish purple pheasants. Up and up they went. Again the guns barked; the smoke balls formed; loosened, dispersed. And the busy little dogs ran nosing nimbly over the fields; and the warm damp bodies, still languid and soft, as if in a swoon, were bunched together by the men in gaiters and flung into the cart.

'There!' grunted Milly Masters, the housekeeper, throwing down her glasses. She was stitching too in the small dark room that overlooked the stable-yard. The jersey, the rough woollen jersey for her son, the boy who cleaned the church, was finished. 'The end o' that!' she muttered. Then she heard the cart. Wheels ground on the cobbles. Up she got. With her hands to her hair, her chestnut-coloured hair, she stood in the yard, in the wind.

'Coming!' she laughed, and the scar on her cheek lengthened. She unbolted the door of the game room as Wing, the keeper, drove the cart over the cobbles. The birds were dead now, their claws gripped tight, though they gripped nothing. The leathery eyelids were creased greyly over their eyes. Mrs Masters the housekeeper, Wing the gamekeeper, took bunches of dead birds by the neck and flung them down on the slate floor of the game larder. The slate floor became smeared and spotted with blood. The pheasants looked smaller now, as if their bodies had shrunk together. Then Wing lifted the tail of the cart and drove in the pins which secured it. The sides of the cart were stuck about with little grey-blue feathers, and the floor was smeared and stained with blood. But it was empty.

'The last of the lot!' Milly Masters grinned as the cart drove off.

'Luncheon is served, ma'am,' said the butler. He pointed at the table; he directed the footman. The dish with the silver cover was placed precisely there where he pointed. They waited, the butler and the footman.

Miss Antonia laid her white film upon the basket; put away her silk; her thimble; stuck her needle through a piece of flannel; and hung her glasses on a hook upon her breast. Then she rose.

'Luncheon!' she barked in old Miss Rashleigh's ear. One second later old Miss Rashleigh stretched her leg out; gripped her stick; and rose too. Both old women advanced slowly to the table; and were tucked in by the butler and the footman, one at this end, one at that. Off came the silver cover. And there was the pheasant, featherless, gleaming; the thighs tightly pressed to its side; and little mounds of breadcrumbs were heaped at either end.

Miss Antonia drew the carving-knife across the pheasant's breast firmly. She cut two slices and laid them on a plate. Deftly the footman whipped it from her, and old Miss Rashleigh raised her knife. Shots rang out in the wood under the window.

'Coming?' said old Miss Rashleigh, suspending her fork.

The branches flung and flaunted on the trees in the Park.

She took a mouthful of pheasant. Falling leaves flicked the windowpane; one or two stuck to the glass.

'In the Home Woods, now,' said Miss Antonia. 'Hugh's last shoot.' She drew her knife down the other side of the breast. She added potatoes and gravy, Brussels sprouts and bread sauce methodically in a circle round the slices on her plate. The butler and the footman stood watching, like servants at a feast. The old ladies ate quietly; silently; nor did they hurry themselves; methodically they cleaned the bird. Bones only were left on their plates. Then the butler drew the decanter towards Miss Antonia, and paused for a moment with his head bent.

'Give it here, Griffiths,' said Miss Antonia, and took the carcass in her fingers and tossed it to the spaniel beneath the table. The butler and the footman bowed and went out.

'Coming closer,' said Miss Rashleigh, listening. The wind was rising. A brown shudder shook the air; leaves flew too fast to stick. The glass rattled in the windows.

'Birds wild,' Miss Antonia nodded, watching the helter-skelter.

Old Miss Rashleigh filled her glass. As they sipped their eyes became lustrous like half-precious stones held to the light. Slate-blue were Miss Rashleigh's; Miss Antonia's red, like port. And their laces and their flounces seemed to quiver, as if their bodies were warm and languid underneath their feathers as they drank.

'It was a day like this, d'you remember?' said old Miss Rashleigh, fingering her glass. 'They brought him home . . . a bullet through his heart. A bramble, so they said. Tripped. Caught his foot . . .' She chuckled as she sipped her wine.

'And John . . .' said Miss Antonia. 'The mare, they said, put her foot in a hole. Died in the field. The hunt rode over him. He came home, too, on a shutter . . .' They sipped again.

'Remember Lily?' said old Miss Rashleigh. 'A bad 'un.' She shook her head. 'Riding with a scarlet tassel on her cane . . .'

'Rotten at the heart!' cried Miss Antonia. 'Remember the Colonel's letter? "Your son rode as if he had twenty devils in him – charged at the head of his men." . . . Then one white devil – ah hah!' She sipped again.

'The men of our house . . .' began Miss Rashleigh. She raised her glass. She held it high, as if she toasted the mermaid carved in plaster on the fireplace. She paused. The guns were barking. Something cracked in the woodwork. Or was it a rat running behind the plaster?

'Always women . . .' Miss Antonia nodded. 'The men of our house. Pink and white Lucy at the Mill – d'you remember?'

'Ellen's daughter at the Goat and Sickle,' Miss Rashleigh added.

'And the girl at the tailor's,' Miss Antonia murmured, 'where Hugh bought his riding-breeches, the little dark shop on the right . . .'

' . . . that used to be flooded every winter. It's *his* boy,' Miss Antonia chuckled, leaning towards her sister, 'that cleans the church.'

There was a crash. A slate had fallen down the chimney. The great log had snapped in two. Flakes of plaster fell from the shield above the fireplace.

'Falling,' old Miss Rashleigh chuckled, 'falling.'

'And who,' said Miss Antonia, looking at the flakes on the carpet, 'who's to pay?'

Crowing like old babies, indifferent, reckless, they laughed; crossed to the fireplace, and sipped their sherry by the wood ashes and the plaster until each glass held only one drop of wine, reddish purple, at the bottom. And this the old women did not wish to part with so it seemed; for they fingered their glasses, as they sat side by side by the ashes; but they never raised them to their lips.

'Milly Masters in the still room,' began old Miss Rashleigh. 'She's our brother's . . .'

A shot barked beneath the window. It cut the string that held the rain. Down it poured, down, down, down, in straight rods whipping the windows. Light faded from the carpet. Light faded in their eyes too, as they sat by the white ashes listening. Their eyes became like pebbles, taken from water; grey stones dulled and dried. And their hands gripped their hands like the claws of dead birds gripping nothing. And they shrivelled as if the bodies inside the clothes had shrunk. Then Miss Antonia raised her glass to the mermaid. It was the last toast, the last drop; she drank it off. 'Coming!' she croaked, and slapped the glass down. A door banged below. Then another. Then another. Feet could be heard trampling, yet shuffling, along the corridor towards the gallery.

'Closer! Closer!' grinned Miss Rashleigh, baring her three yellow teeth.

The immensely high door burst open. In rushed three great hounds and stood panting. Then there entered, slouching, the Squire himself in shabby gaiters. The dogs pressed round him, tossing their heads, snuffling at his pockets. Then they bounded forward. They smelt the meat. The floor of the gallery waved like a wind-lashed forest with the tails and backs of the great questing hounds. They snuffed the table. They pawed the cloth. Then with a wild neighing whimper they flung themselves upon the little yellow spaniel who was gnawing the carcass under the table.

'Curse you, curse you!' howled the Squire. But his voice was weak, as if he shouted against a wind. 'Curse you, curse you!' he shouted, now cursing his sisters.

Miss Antonia and Miss Rashleigh rose to their feet. The great dogs had seized the spaniel. They worried him, they mauled him with their great yellow teeth. The Squire swung a leather knotted tawse this way, that way, cursing the dogs, cursing his sisters, in the voice that sounded so loud yet so weak. With one lash he curled to the ground the vase of chrysanthemums. Another caught old Miss Rashleigh on the cheek. The old woman staggered backwards. She fell against the mantelpiece. Her stick, striking wildly, struck the shield above the fireplace. She fell with a thud upon the ashes. The shield of the Rashleighs crashed from the wall. Under the mermaid, under the spears, she lay buried.

The wind lashed the panes of glass; shots volleyed in the Park and a tree fell. And then King Edward in the silver frame slid, toppled and fell too.

The grey mist had thickened in the carriage. It hung down like a veil; it seemed to put the four travellers in the corners at a great distance from each other, though in fact they were as close as a third-class railway carriage could bring them. The effect was strange. The handsome, if elderly, the well-dressed, if rather shabby woman who had got into the train at some station in the Midlands seemed to have lost her shape. Her body had become all mist. Only her eyes gleamed, changed, lived all by themselves it seemed; eyes without a body; blue-grey eyes seeing something invisible. In the misty air they shone out, they moved, so that in the sepulchral atmosphere – the windows were blurred, the lamps haloed with fog – they were like lights dancing, will-o'-the-wisps that move, people say, over the graves of unquiet sleepers in churchyards. An absurd idea? Mere fancy! Yet after all since there is nothing that does not leave some residue, and memory is a light that dances in the mind when the reality is buried, why should not the eyes there, gleaming, moving, be the ghost of a family, of an age, of a civilisation dancing over the grave?

The train slowed down. One after another lamps stood up; held their yellow heads erect for a second; then were felled. Up they stood again as the train slid into the station. The lights massed and blazed. And the eyes in the corner? They were shut; the lids were closed. They saw nothing. Perhaps the light was too strong. And of course in the full blaze of the station lamps it was plain – she was quite an ordinary piece of business – something connected with a cat or a horse or a dog. She reached for her suitcase, rose, and took the pheasants from the rack. But did she, all the same, as she opened the carriage door and stepped out, murmur, 'Chk. Chk.' as she passed?

Half a Life-time Ago

ELIZABETH GASKELL

I

Half a life-time ago, there lived in one of the Westmorland dales a single woman, of the name of Susan Dixon. She was the owner of the small farmhouse where she resided, and of some thirty or forty acres of land by which it was surrounded. She had also an hereditary right to a sheep-walk, extending to the wild fells that overhang Blea Tarn. In the language of the country, she was a Stateswoman. Her house is yet to be seen on the Oxenfell road, between Skelwith and Coniston. You go along a moorland track, made by the carts that occasionally came for turf from the Oxenfell. A brook babbles and prattles by the wayside, giving you a sense of companionship, which relieves the deep solitude in which this way is usually traversed. Some miles on this side of Coniston there is a farmstead – a grey stone house, and a square of farm-buildings surrounding a green space of rough turf, in the midst of which stands a mighty, funereal umbrageous yew, making a solemn shadow, as of death, in the very heart and centre of the light and heat of the brightest summer day. On the side away from the house, this yard slopes down to a dark-brown pool, which is supplied with fresh water from the overflowings of a stone cistern, into which some rivulet of the brook before mentioned continually and melodiously falls bubbling. The cattle drink out of this cistern. The household bring their pitchers and fill them with drinking-water by a dilatory, yet pretty, process. The water-carrier brings with her a leaf of the hound's-tongue fern, and, inserting it in the crevice of the grey rock, makes a cool, green spout for the sparkling stream.

The house is no specimen, at the present day, of what it was in the life-time of Susan Dixon. Then, every small diamond-pane in the windows glittered with cleanliness. You might have eaten off the floor; you could see yourself in the pewter plates and the polished oaken awmry, or dresser, of the state kitchen into which you entered. Few strangers penetrated further than this room. Once or twice, wandering tourists, attracted by the lonely picturesqueness of the situation, and the exquisite cleanliness of the house itself, made their way into this house-place, and offered money enough (as they thought) to tempt the hostess to receive them as lodgers. They would give no trouble, they said; they would be out rambling or sketching all day long; would be perfectly content with a share of the food which she provided for herself; or would procure what they required from the Water-head Inn at Coniston. But no liberal sum – no fair words – moved her from her stony manner, or her monotonous tone of indifferent refusal. No persuasion could induce her to show any more of the house than that first room; no appearance of fatigue procured for the weary an invitation to sit down and rest; and if one more bold and less delicate did so without being asked, Susan stood by, cold and apparently deaf, or only replying by the briefest monosyllables, till the unwelcome visitor had departed. Yet those with whom she had dealings, in the way of selling her cattle or her farm produce, spoke of her as keen after a bargain – a hard one to have to do with; and she never spared herself exertion or fatigue, at market or in the field, to make the most of her produce. She led the haymakers with her swift, steady rake, and her noiseless evenness of motion. She was about among the earliest in the market, examining samples of oats, pricing them, and then turning with grim satisfaction to her own cleaner corn.

She was served faithfully and long by those who were rather her fellow-labourers than her servants. She was even and just in her dealings with them. If she was peculiar and silent, they knew her, and knew that she might be relied on. Some of them had known her from her childhood; and deep in their hearts was an unspoken – almost unconscious – pity for her; for they knew her story, though they never spoke of it.

Yes, the time had been when that tall, gaunt, hard-featured, angular woman – who never smiled, and hardly ever spoke an unnecessary word – had been a fine-looking girl, bright-spirited and rosy; and when the hearth at the Yew Nook had been as bright as she, with family love and youthful hope and mirth. Fifty or fifty-one years ago, William Dixon and his wife Margaret were alive; and Susan, their daughter, was about eighteen years old – ten years older than the only other child, a boy named after his father. William and Margaret Dixon were rather superior people, of a character belonging – as far as I have seen – exclusively to the class of Westmorland and Cumberland states-men – just, independent, upright; not given to much speaking; kind-hearted, but not demonstrative; disliking change, and new ways, and new people; sensible and shrewd; each household self-contained, and its members having little curiosity as to their neighbours, with whom they rarely met for any social inter-course, save at the stated times of sheep-shearing and Christmas; having a certain kind of sober pleasure in amassing money, which occasionally made them miserable (as they call miserly people up in the north) in their old age; reading no light or ephemeral literature, but the grave, solid books brought round by the pedlars (such as the *Paradise Lost* and *Regained*, *The Death of Abel*, *The Spiritual Quixote*, and *The Pilgrim's Progress*, were to be found in nearly every house; the men occasionally going off laking, i.e. playing, i.e. drinking for days together, and having to be hunted up by anxious wives, who dared not leave their husbands to the chances of the wild precipitous roads, but walked miles and miles, lantern in hand, in the dead of night, to discover and guide the solemnly drunken husband home; who had a dreadful headache the next day, and the day after that came forth as grave, and sober, and virtuous-looking as if there were no such things as malt and spirituous liquors in the world; and

149

who were seldom reminded of their misdoings by their wives, to whom such occasional outbreaks were as things of course, when once the immediate anxiety produced by them was over. Such were – such are – the characteristics of a class now passing away from the face of the land, as their compeers, the yeomen, have done before them. Of such was William Dixon. He was a shrewd, clever farmer, in his day and generation, when shrewdness was rather shown in the breeding and rearing of sheep and cattle than in the cultivation of land. Owing to this character of his, statesmen from a distance, from beyond Kendal, or from Borrowdale, of greater wealth than he, would send their sons to be farm-servants for a year or two with him, in order to learn some of his methods before setting up on land of their own. When Susan, his daughter, was about seventeen, one Michael Hurst was farm-servant at Yew Nook. He worked with the master, and lived with the family, and was in all respects treated as an equal, except in the field. His father was a wealthy statesman at Wythburne, up beyond Grasmere; and through Michael's servitude the families had become acquainted, and the Dixons went over to the High Beck sheep-shearing, and the Hursts came down by Red Bank and Loughrig Tarn and across the Oxenfell when there was the Christmas-tide feasting at Yew Nook. The fathers strolled round the fields together, examined cattle and sheep, and looked knowingly over each other's horses. The mothers inspected the dairies and household arrangements, each openly admiring the plans of the other, but secretly preferring their own. Both fathers and mothers cast a glance from time to time at Michael and Susan, who were thinking of nothing less than farm or dairy, but whose unspoken attachment was, in all ways, so suitable and natural a thing that each parent rejoiced over it, although with characteristic reserve it was never spoken about – not even between husband and wife.

Susan had been a strong, independent, healthy girl; a clever help to her mother, and a spirited companion to her father; more of a man in her (as he often said) than her delicate little brother ever would have. He was his mother's darling, although she loved Susan well. There was no positive engagement between

Michael and Susan – I doubt whether even plain words of love had been spoken; when one winter-time Margaret Dixon was seized with inflammation consequent upon a neglected cold. She had always been strong and notable, and had been too busy to attend to the earliest symptoms of illness. It would go off, she said to the woman who helped in the kitchen; or if she did not feel better when they had got the hams and bacon out of hand, she would take some herb-tea and nurse up a bit. But Death could not wait till the hams and bacon were cured: he came on with rapid strides, and shooting arrows of portentous agony. Susan had never seen illness – never knew how much she loved her mother till now, when she felt a dreadful, instinctive certainty that she was losing her. Her mind was thronged with recollecions of the many times she had slighted her mother's wishes; her heart was full of the echoes of careless and angry replies that she had spoken. What would she not now give to have opportunities of service and obedience, and trials of her patience and love, for that dear mother who lay gasping in torture! And yet Susan had been a good girl and an affectionate daughter.

The sharp pain went off, and delicious ease came on; yet still her mother sunk. In the midst of this languid peace she was dying. She motioned Susan to her bedside, for she could only whisper; and then; while the father was out of the room, she spoke as much to the eager, hungering eyes of her daughter by the motion of her lips, as by the slow, feeble sounds of her voice.

'Susan, lass, thou must not fret. It is God's will, and thou wilt have a deal to do. Keep Father straight if thou canst; and if he goes out Ulverstone ways, see that thou meet him before he gets to the Old Quarry. It's a dree bit for a man who has had a drop. As for lile Will' – here the poor woman's face began to work and her fingers to move nervously as they lay on the bed-quilt – 'lile Will will miss me most of all. Father's often vexed with him because he's not a quick, strong lad; he is not, my poor lile chap. And Father thinks he's saucy, because he cannot always stomach oat-cake and porridge. There's better than three pounds in th' old black teapot on the top shelf of the cupboard. Just keep a piece of loaf-bread by you, Susan dear, for Will to come to when he's not taken his breakfast. I have, may be, spoilt him; but there'll be no one to spoil him now.'

She began to cry a low, feeble cry, and covered up her face that Susan might not see her. That dear face! those precious moments while yet the eyes could look out with love and intelligence. Susan laid her head down close by her mother's ear.

'Mother, I'll take tent of Will. Mother, do you hear? He shall not want ought I can give or get for him, least of all the kind words which you had ever ready for us both. Bless you! bless you! my own mother.'

'Thou'lt promise me that, Susan, wilt thou? I can die easy if thou'lt take charge of him. But he's hardly like other folk; he tries Father at times, though I think Father'll be tender of him when I'm gone, for my sake. And, Susan, there's one thing more. I never spoke of it for fear of the bairn being called a tell-tale, but I just comforted him up. He vexes Michael at times, and Michael has struck him before now. I did not want to make a stir; but he's not strong, and a word from thee, Susan, will go a long way with Michael.'

Susan was as red now as she had been pale before; it was the first time that her influence over Michael had been openly acknowledged by a third person, and a flash of joy came athwart the solemn sadness of the moment. Her mother had spoken too much, and now came on the miserable faintness. She never spoke again coherently; but when her children and her husband stood by her bedside, she took lile Will's hand and put it into Susan's, and looked at her with imploring eyes. Susan clasped her arms round Will, and leaned her head upon his curly little one, and vowed within herself to be as a mother to him.

Henceforward she was all in all to her brother. She was a more spirited and amusing companion to him than his mother had been, from her greater activity, and perhaps, also, from her originality of character, which often prompted her to perform her habitual actions in some new and racy manner. She was tender to lile Will when she was prompt and sharp with everybody else – with Michael most of all; for somehow the girl

152

felt that, unprotected by her mother, she must keep up her own dignity, and not allow her lover to see how strong a hold he had upon her heart. He called her hard and cruel, and left her so; and she smiled softly to herself, when his back was turned, to think how little he guessed how deeply he was loved. For Susan was merely comely and fine-looking; Michael was strikingly handsome, admired by all the girls for miles round, and quite enough of a country coxcomb to know it and plume himself accordingly. He was the second son of his father; the eldest would have High Beck farm, of course, but there was a good penny in the Kendal bank in store for Michael. When harvest was over, he went to Chapel Langdale to learn to dance; and at night, in his merry moods, he would do his steps on the flag-floor of the Yew Nook kitchen, to the secret admiration of Susan, who had never learned dancing, but who flouted him perpetually, even while she admired, in accordance with the rule she seemed to have made for herself about keeping him at a distance so long as he lived under the same roof with her. One evening he sulked at some saucy remark of hers; he sitting in the chimney-corner with his arms on his knees, and his head bent forwards, lazily gazing into the wood-fire on the hearth, and luxuriating in rest after a hard day's labour; she sitting among the geraniums on the long, low window-seat, trying to catch the last slanting rays of the autumnal light to enable her to finish stitching a shirt-collar for Will, who lounged full-length on the flats at the other side of the hearth to Michael, poking the burning wood from time to time with a long hazel-stick to bring out the leap of glittering sparks.

'And if you can dance a threesome reel, what good does it do ye?' asked Susan, looking askance at Michael, who had just been vaunting his proficiency. 'Does it help you plough, or reap, or even climb the rocks to take a raven's nest? If I were a man, I'd be ashamed to give in to such softness.'

'If you were a man, you'd be glad to do anything which made the pretty girls stand round and admire.'

'As they do to you, eh! Ho, Michael, that would not be my way o' being a man!'

'What would then?' asked he, after a pause, during which he

had expected in vain that she would go on with her sentence. No answer.

'I should not like you as a man, Susy; you'd be too hard and headstrong.'

'Am I hard and headstrong?' asked she, with as indifferent a tone as she could assume, but which yet had a touch of pique in it. His quick ear detected the inflexion.

'No, Susy! You're wilful at times, and that's right enough. I don't like a girl without spirit. There's a mighty pretty girl come to the dancing-class; but she is all milk-and-water. Her eyes never flash like yours when you're put out; why, I can see them flame across the kitchen like a cat's in the dark. Now, if you were a man, I should feel queer before those looks of yours; as it is, I rather like them, because—'

'Because what?' asked she, looking up and perceiving that he had stolen close up to her.

'Because I can make all right in this way,' said he, kissing her suddenly.

'Can you?' said she, wrenching herself out of his grasp and panting, half with rage. 'Take that, by way of proof that making right is none so easy.' And she boxed his ears pretty sharply. He went back to his seat discomfited and out of temper. She could no longer see to look, even if her face had not burnt and her eyes dazzled, but she did not choose to move her seat, so she still preserved her stooping attitude and pretended to go on sewing.

'Eleanor Hebthwaite may be milk-and-water,' muttered he, 'but— Confound thee, lad! what art doing?' exclaimed Michael, as a great piece of burning wood was cast into his face by an unlucky poke of Will's. 'Thou great lounging, clumsy chap, I'll teach thee better!' and with one or two good, round kicks he sent the lad whimpering away into the back-kitchen. When he had a little recovered himself from his passion, he saw Susan standing before him, her face looking strange and almost ghastly by the reversed position of the shadows, arising from the fire-light shining upwards right under it.

'I tell thee what, Michael,' said she, 'that lad's motherless, but not friendless.'

'His own father leathers him, and why should not I, when he's given me such a burn on my face?' said Michael, putting up his hand to his cheek as if in pain.

'His father's his father, and there is nought more to be said. But if he did burn thee, it was by accident, and not o' purpose, as thou kicked him; it's a mercy if his ribs are not broken.'

'He howls loud enough, I'm sure. I might ha' kicked many a lad twice as hard and they'd ne'er ha' said ought but "damn ye", but yon lad must needs cry out like a stuck pig if one touches him,' replied Michael, sullenly.

Susan went back to the window-seat, and looked absently out of the window at the drifting clouds for a minute or two, while her eyes filled with tears. Then she got up and made for the outer door which led into the back-kitchen. Before she reached it, however, she heard a low voice, whose music made her thrill, say—

'Susan, Susan!'

Her heart melted within her, but it seemed like treachery to her poor boy, like faithlessness to her dead mother, to turn to her lover while the tears which he had caused to flow were yet unwiped on Will's cheeks. So she seemed to take no heed, but passed into the darkness and, guided by the sobs, she found her way to where Willie sat crouched among disused tubs and churns.

'Come out wi' me, lad,' and they went into the orchard, where the fruit-trees were bare of leaves, but ghastly in their tattered covering of grey moss: and the soughing November wind came with long sweeps over the fells till it rattled among the crackling boughs, underneath which the brother and sister sat in the dark; he in her lap, and she hushing his head against her shoulder.

'Thou should'st na' play wi' fire. It's a naughty trick. Thou'lt suffer for it in worse ways nor this before thou'st done, I'm afeared. I should ha' hit thee twice as lungeous kicks as Mike, if I'd been in his place. He did na' hurt thee, I am sure,' she assumed, half as a question.

'Yes! but he did. He turned me quite sick.' And he let his head fall languidly down on his sister's breast.

'Come lad! come lad!' said she, anxiously. 'Be a man. It was not much that I saw. Why, when first the red cow came, she kicked me far harder for offering to milk her before her legs were tied. See thee! here's a peppermint-drop, and I'll make thee a pasty tonight; and don't give way so, for it hurts me sore to think that Michael has done thee any harm, my pretty.'

Willie roused himself up, and put back the wet and ruffled hair from his heated face; and he and Susan rose up, and hand-in-hand went towards the house, walking slowly and quietly except for a kind of sob which Willie could not repress. Susan took him to the pump and washed his tear-stained face, till she thought she had obliterated all traces of the recent disturbance, arranging his curls for him, and then she kissed him tenderly, and led him in, hoping to find Michael in the kitchen, and make all straight between them. But the blaze had dropped down into darkness; the wood was a heap of grey ashes in which the sparks ran hither and thither; but, even in the groping darkness, Susan knew by the sinking at her heart that Michael was not there. She threw another brand on the hearth and lighted the candle, and sat down to her work in silence. Willie cowered on his stool by the side of the fire, eyeing his sister from time to time, and sorry and oppressed, he knew not why, by the sight of her grave, almost stern face. No one came. They two were in the house alone. The old woman who helped Susan with the household work had gone out for the night to some friend's dwelling. William Dixon, the father, was up on the fells seeing after his sheep. Susan had no heart to prepare the evening meal.

'Susy, darling, are you angry with me?' said Willie, in his little piping, gentle voice. He had stolen up to his sister's side. 'I won't never play with fire again; and I'll not cry if Michael does kick me. Only don't look so like dead mother – don't – don't – please don't!' he exclaimed, hiding his face on her shoulder.

'I'm not angry, Willie,' said she. 'Don't be feared on me. You want your supper, and you shall have it; and don't you be feared on Michael. He shall give reason for every hair of your head that he touches – he shall.'

When William Dixon came home, he found Susan and Willie

sitting together, hand-in-hand, and apparently pretty cheerful. he bade them go to bed, for that he would sit up for Michael; and the next morning, when Susan came down, she found that Michael had started an hour before with the cart for lime. It was a long day's work; Susan knew it would be late, perhaps later than on the preceding night, before he returned – at any rate, past her usual bed-time; and on no account would she stop up a minute beyond that hour in the kitchen, whatever she might do in her bedroom. Here she sat and watched till past midnight; and when she saw him coming up the brow with the carts, she knew full well, even in that faint moonlight, that his gait was the gait of a man in liquor. But though she was annoyed and mortified to find in what way he had chosen to forget her, the fact did not disgust or shock her as it would have done many a girl, even at that day, who had not been brought up as Susan had, among a class who considered it no crime, but rather a mark of spirit, in a man to get drunk occasionally. Nevertheless, she chose to hold herself very high all the next day when Michael was, perforce, obliged to give up any attempt to do heavy work, and hung about the out-buildings and farm in a very disconsolate and sickly state. Willie had far more pity on him than Susan. Before evening, Willie and he were fast, and on his side, ostentatious friends. Willie rode the horses down to water; Willie helped him to chop wood. Susan sat gloomily at her work, hearing an indistinct but cheerful conversation going on in the shippon, while the cows were being milked. She almost felt irritated with her little brother, as if he were a traitor, and had gone over to the enemy in the very battle that she was fighting in his cause. She was alone with no one to speak to, while they prattled on, regardless if she were glad or sorry.

Soon Willie burst in. 'Susan! Susan! come with me; I've something so pretty to show you. Round the corner of the barn – run! run!' (He was dragging her along, half reluctant, half desirous of some change in that weary day.) Round the corner of the barn; and there caught hold of by Michael, who stood there awaiting her.

'O Willie!' cried she, 'you naughty boy. There is nothing

pretty – what have you brought me here for? Let me go; I won't be held.'

'Only one word. Nay, if you wish it so much, you may go,' said Michael, suddenly loosing his hold as she struggled. But, now she was free, she only drew off a step or two, murmuring something about Willie.

'You are going, then?' said Michael, with seeming sadness. 'You won't hear me say a word of what is in my heart.'

'How can I tell whether it is what I should like to hear?' replied she, still drawing back.

'That is just what I want you to tell me; I want you to hear it, and then to tell me whether you like it or not.'

'Well, you may speak,' replied she, turning her back, and beginning to plait the hem of her apron.

He came close to her.

'I'm sorry I hurt Willie the other night. He has forgiven me. Can you?'

'You hurt him very badly,' she replied. 'But you are right to be sorry. I forgive you.'

'Stop, stop!' said he, laying his hand upon her arm. 'There is something more I've got to say. I want you to be my – what is it they call it, Susan?'

'I don't know,' said she, half-laughing, but trying to get away with all her might now; and she was a strong girl, but she could not manage it.

'You do. My – what is it I want you to be?'

'I tell you I don't know, and you had best be quiet, and just let me go in, or I shall think you're as bad now as you were last night.'

'And how did you know what I was last night? It was past twelve when I came home. Were you watching? Ah, Susan! be my wife, and you shall never have to watch for a drunken husband. If I were your husband, I would come straight home, and count every minute an hour till I saw your bonny face. Now you know what I want you to be. I ask you to be my wife. Will you, my own dear Susan?'

She did not speak for some time. Then she only said, 'Ask

Father.' And now she was really off like a lapwing round the corner of the barn, and up in her own little room, crying with all her might, before the triumphant smile had left Michael's face where he stood.

The 'Ask Father' was a mere form to be gone through. Old Daniel Hurst and William Dixon had talked over what they could respectively give their children long before this; and that was the parental way of arranging such matters. When the probable amount of worldly gear that he could give his child had been named by each father, the young folk, as they said, might take their own time in coming to the point which the old men, with the prescience of experience, saw that they were drifting to; no need to hurry them, for they were both young, and Michael, though active enough, was too thoughtless, old Daniel said, to be trusted with the entire management of a farm. Meanwhile, his father would look about him, and see after all the farms that were to be let.

Michael had a shrewd notion of this preliminary understanding between the fathers, and so felt less daunted than he might otherwise have done at making the application for Susan's hand. It was all right, there was not an obstacle; only a deal of good advice, which the lover thought might have as well been spared, and which it must be confessed he did not much attend to, although he assented to every part of it. Later that day Susan was called downstairs, and slowly came dropping into view down the steps which led from the two family apartments into the house-place. She tried to look composed and quiet, but it could not be done. She stood side by side with her lover, with her head drooping, her cheeks burning, not daring to look up or move, while her father made the newly bethrothed a somewhat formal address in which he gave his consent, and many a piece of worldly wisdom beside. Susan listened as well as she could for the beating of her heart; but when her father solemnly and sadly referred to his own lost wife, she could keep from sobbing no longer; but, throwing her apron over her face, she sat down on the bench by the dresser, and fairly gave way to pent-up tears. Oh, how strangely sweet to be comforted as she was comforted,

159

by tender caress, and many a low-whispered promise of love! Her father sat by the fire, thinking of the days that were gone; Willie was still out of doors; but Susan and Michael felt no one's presence or absence – they only knew they were together as bethrothed husband and wife.

In a week, or two, they were formally told of the arrangements to be made in their favour. A small farm in the neighbourhood happened to fall vacant; and Michael's father offered to take it for him, and be responsible for the rent for the first year, while William Dixon was to contribute a certain amount of stock, and both fathers were to help towards the furnishing of the house. Susan received all this information in a quiet, indifferent way; she did not care much for any of these preparations, which were to hurry her through the happy hours; she cared least of all for the money amount of dowry and of substance. It jarred on her to be made the confidante of occasional slight repinings of Michael's, as one by one his future father-in-law set aside a beast or a pig for Susan's portion, which were not always the best animals of their kind upon the farm. But he also complained of his own father's stinginess, which somewhat, though not much, alleviated Susan's dislike to being awakened out of her pure dream of love to the consideration of worldly wealth.

But in the midst of all this bustle, Willie moped and pined. He had the same chord of delicacy running through his mind that made his body feeble and weak. He kept out of the way, and was apparently occupied in whittling and carving uncouth heads on hazel-sticks in an outhouse. But he positively avoided Michael, and shrunk away even from Susan. She was too much occupied to notice this at first. Michael pointed it out to her, saying with a laugh—

'Look at Willie! he might be a cast-off lover and jealous of me, he looks so dark and downcast at me.' Michael spoke this jest out loud, and Willie burst into tears, and ran out of the house.

'Let me go, let me go!' said Susan (for her lover's arm was round her waist). 'I must go to him if he's fretting. I promised mother I would.' She pulled herself away, and went in search of the boy. She sought in byre and barn, through the orchard, where indeed in this leafless winter-time there was no great concealment, up into the room where the wool was usually stored in the later summer, and at last she found him, sitting at bay, like some hunted creature, up behind the wood-stack.

'What are ye gone for, lad, and me seeking you everywhere?' asked she, breathless.

'I did not know you would seek me. I've been away many a time, and no one has cared to seek me,' said he, crying afresh.

'Nonsense,' replied Susan, 'don't be so foolish, ye little good-for-nought.' But she crept up to him in the hole he had made underneath the great brown sheafs of wood, and squeezed herself down by him. 'What for should folk seek after you, when you get away from them whenever you can?' asked she.

'They don't want me to stay. Nobody wants me. If I go with father, he says I hinder more than I help. You used to like to have me with you. But now, you've taken up with Michael, and you'd rather I was away; and I can just hide away; but I cannot stand Michael jeering at me. He's got you to love him and that might serve him.'

'But I love you, too, dearly, lad!' said she, putting her arm round his neck.

'Which on us do you like best?' said he, wistfully, after a little pause, putting her arm away, so that he might look in her face, and see if she spoke truth.

She went very red.

'You should not ask such questions. They are not fit for you to ask, nor for me to answer.'

'But mother bade you love me!' said he, plaintively.

'And so I do. And so I ever will do. Lover nor husband shall come betwixt thee and me, lad – ne'er a one of them. That I promise thee (as I promised mother before), in the sight of God and with her hearkening now, if ever she can hearken to earthly word again. Only I cannot abide to have thee fretting, just because my heart is large enough for two.'

'And thou'lt love me always?'

'Always, and ever. And the more – the more thou'lt love Michael,' said she, dropping her voice.

'I'll try,' said the boy, sighing, for he remembered many a harsh word and blow of which his sister knew nothing. She would have risen up to go away, but he held her tight, for here and now she was all his own, and he did not know when such a time might come again. So the two sat crouched-up and silent, till they heard the horn blowing at the field-gate, which was the summons home to any wanderers belonging to the farm, and at this hour of the evening signified that supper was ready. Then the two went in.

II

Susan and Michael were to be married in April. He had already gone to take possession of his new farm, three or four miles away from Yew Nook – but that is neighbouring, according to the acceptation of the word in that thinly populated district – when William Dixon fell ill. He came home one evening, complaining of headache and pains in his limbs, but seemed to loathe the posset which Susan prepared for him; the treacle-posset which was the homely country remedy against an incipient cold. He took to his bed with a sensation of exceeding weariness, and an odd, unusual looking-back to the days of his youth, when he was a lad living with his parents, in this very house.

The next morning he had forgotten all his life since then, and did not know his own children; crying, like a newly-weaned baby, for his mother to come and soothe away his terrible pain. The doctor from Coniston said it was the typhus-fever, and warned Susan of its infectious character, and shook his head over his patient. There were no friends near to come and share her anxiety; only good, kind old Peggy, who was faithfulness itself, and one or two labourers' wives, who would fain have helped her, had not their hands been tied by their responsibility to their own families. But, somehow, Susan neither feared nor flagged. As for fear, indeed, she had no time to give way to it, for every energy of both body and mind was required. Besides, the young have had too little experience of the danger of infection to dread it much. She did indeed wish, from time to time, that Michael

162

had been at home to have taken Willie over to his father's at High Beck; but then, again, the lad was docile and useful to her, and his fecklessness in many things might make him be harshly treated by strangers; so, perhaps, it was as well that Michael was away at Appleby fair, or even beyond that – gone into Yorkshire after horses.

Her father grew worse; and the doctor insisted on sending over a nurse from Coniston. Not a professional nurse – Coniston could not have supported such a one; but a widow who was ready to go where the doctor sent her for the sake of the payment. When she came, Susan suddenly gave way; she was felled by the fever herself, and lay unconscious for long weeks. Her consciousness returned to her one spring afternoon; early spring; April – her wedding-month. There was a little fire burning in the small corner-grate, and the flickering of the blaze was enough for her to notice in her weak state. She felt that there was someone sitting on the window-side of her bed, behind the curtain, but she did not care to know who it was; it was even too great a trouble for her languid mind to consider who it was likely to be. She would rather shut her eyes, and melt off again into the gentle luxury of sleep. The next time she wakened, the Coniston nurse perceived her movement, and made her a cup of tea, which she drank with eager relish; but still they did not speak, and once more Susan lay motionless – not asleep, but strangely, pleasantly conscious of all the small chamber and household sounds; the fall of a cinder on the hearth, the fitful singing of the half-empty kettle, the cattle tramping out to the field again after they had been milked, the aged step on the creaking stair – old Peggy's, as she knew. It came to her door; it stopped; the person outside listened for a moment, and then lifted the wooden latch, and looked in. The watcher by the bedside arose, and went to her. Susan would have been glad to see Peggy's face once more, but was far too weak to turn, so she lay and listened.

'How is she?' whispered one trembling, aged voice.

'Better,' replied the other. 'She's been awake, and had a cup of tea. She'll do now.'

'Has she asked after him?'

'Hush! No; she has not spoken a word.'

'Poor lass! poor lass!'

The door was shut. A weak feeling of sorrow and self-pity came over Susan. What was wrong? Whom had she loved? And dawning, dawning, slowly rose the sun of her former life, and all particulars were made distinct to her. She felt that some sorrow was coming to her, and cried over it before she knew what it was, or had strength enough to ask. In the dead of night – and she had never slept again – she softly called to the watcher, and asked—

'Who?'

'Who what?' replied the woman, with a conscious affright, ill-veiled by a poor assumption of ease. 'Lie still, there's a darling, and go to sleep. Sleep's better for you than all the doctor's stuff.'

'Who?' repeated Susan. 'Something is wrong. Who?'

'Oh, dear!' said the woman. 'There's nothing wrong. Willie has taken the turn, and is doing nicely.'

'Father?'

'Well, he's all right now,' she answered, looking another way, as if seeking for something.

'Then it's Michael! Oh, me! oh, me!' She set up a succession of weak, plaintive, hysterical cries before the nurse could pacify her, by declaring that Michael had been at the house not three hours before to ask after her, and looked as well and as hearty as ever man did.

'And you heard of no harm to him since?' enquired Susan.

'Bless the lass, no, for sure! I've ne'er heard his name named since I saw him go out of the yard as stout a man as ever trod shoe-leather.'

It was well, as the nurse said afterwards to Peggy, that Susan had been so easily pacified by the equivocating answer in respect to her father. If she had pressed the questions home in his case as she did in Michael's, she would have learnt that he was dead and buried more than a month before. It was well, too, that in her weak state of convalescence (which lasted long after this first day of consciousness) her perceptions were not sharp enough to observe the sad change that had taken place in Willie. His bodily strength returned, his appetite was something enormous, but his eyes wandered continually; his regard could not be arrested; his speech became slow, impeded and incoherent. People began to say that the fever had taken away the little wit Willie Dixon had ever possessed, and that they feared that he would end in being a 'natural', as they call an idiot in the Dales.

The habitual affection and obedience to Susan lasted longer than any other feeling that the boy had had previous to his illness; and, perhaps, this made her be the last to perceive what everyone else had long anticipated. She felt the awakening rude when it did come. It was in this wise:

One June evening, she sat out of doors under the yew-tree, knitting. She was pale still from her recent illness; and her languor, joined to the fact of her black dress, made her look more than usually interesting. She was no longer the buoyant self-sufficient Susan, equal to every occasion. The men were bringing in the cows to be milked, and Michael was about in the yard giving orders and directions with somewhat the air of a master, for the farm belonged of right to Willie, and Susan had succeeded to the guardianship of her brother. Michael and she were to be married as soon as she was strong enough – so, perhaps, his authoritative manner was justified; but the labourers did not like it, although they said little. They remembered him a stripling on the farm, knowing far less than they did, and often glad to shelter his ignorance of all agricultural matters behind their superior knowledge. They would have taken orders from Susan with far more willingness; nay! Willie himself might have commanded them; and from the old hereditary feeling towards the owners of land, they would have obeyed him with far greater cordiality than they now showed to Michael. But Susan was tired with even three rounds of knitting, and seemed not to notice, or to care, how things went on around her; and Willie – poor Willie! – there he stood lounging against the door-sill, enormously grown and developed, to be sure, but with restless eyes and ever-open mouth, and every now and then setting up a strange kind of howling cry, and then smiling vacantly to himself at the sound he had made. As the two old labourers passed him, they looked at each other ominously, and shook their heads.

'Willie, darling,' said Susan, 'don't make that noise – it makes my head ache.'

She spoke feebly, and Willie did not seem to hear; at any rate, he continued his howl from time to time.

'Hold thy noise, wilt 'a?' said Michael, roughly, as he passed near him, and threatening him with his fist. Susan's back was turned to the pair. The expression on Willie's face changed from vacancy to fear, and he came shambling up to Susan, and put her arm round him, and, as if protected by that shelter, he began making faces at Michael. Susan saw what was going on, and, as if now first struck by the strangeness of her brother's manner, she looked anxiously at Michael for an explanation. Michael was irritated at Willie's defiance of him, and did not mince the matter.

'It's just that the fever has left him silly – he never was as wise as other folk, and now I doubt if he will ever get right.'

Susan did not speak, but she went very pale, and her lip quivered. She looked long and wistfully at Willie's face, as he watched the motion of the ducks in the great stable-pool. He laughed softly to himself every now and then.

'Willie likes to see the ducks go overhead,' said Susan, instinctively adopting the form of speech she would have used to a young child.

'Willie, boo! Willie, boo!' he replied, clapping his hands, and avoiding her eye.

'Speak properly, Willie,' said Susan, making a strong effort at self-control, and trying to arrest his attention.

'You know who I am – tell me my name!' She grasped his arm almost painfully tight to make him attend. Now he looked at her, and, for an instant, a gleam of recognition quivered over his face; but the exertion was evidently painful, and he began to cry at the vainness of the effort to recall her name. He hid his face upon her shoulder with the old affectionate trick of manner. She put him gently away, and went into the house into her own little bedroom. She locked the door, and did not reply at all to Michael's calls for her, hardly spoke to old Peggy, who tried to tempt her out to receive some homely sympathy, and through the open casement there still came the idiotic sound of 'Willie, boo! Willie, boo!'

III

After the stun of the blow came the realization of the consequences. Susan would sit for hours trying patiently to recall and piece together fragments of recollection and consciousness in her brother's mind. She would let him go and pursue some senseless bit of play, and wait until she could catch his eye or his attention again; when she would resume her self-imposed task. Michael complained that she never had a word for him, or a minute of time to spend with him now; but she only said she must try, while there was yet a chance, to bring back her brother's lost wits. As for marriage in this state of uncertainty, she had no heart to think of it. Then Michael stormed, and absented himself for two or three days; but it was of no use. When he came back, he saw that she had been crying till her eyes were all swollen up, and he gathered from Peggy's scoldings (which she did not spare him) that Susan had eaten nothing since he went away. But she was as inflexible as ever.

'Not just yet. Only not just yet. And don't say again that I do not love you,' said she, suddenly hiding herself in his arms.

And so matters went on through August. The crop of oats was gathered in; the wheat-field was not ready as yet, when one fine day Michael drove up in a borrowed shandry, and offered to take Willie for a ride. His manner, when Susan asked him where he was going to, was rather confused; but the answer was straight and clear enough.

He had business in Ambleside. He would never lose sight of the lad, and have him back safe and sound before dark. So Susan let him go.

Before night they were at home again: Willie in high delight at a little rattling, paper windmill that Michael had bought for him in the street, and striving to imitate this new sound with perpetual buzzings. Michael, too, looked pleased. Susan knew

167

the look, although afterwards she remembered that he had tried to veil it from her, and had assumed a grave appearance of sorrow whenever he caught her eye. He put up his horse; for, although he had three miles further to go, the moon was up – the bonny harvest-moon – and he did not care how late he had to drive on such a road by such a light. After the supper which Susan had prepared for the travellers was over, Peggy went upstairs to see Willie safe in bed; for he had to have the same care taken of him that a little child of four years old requires.

Michael drew near to Susan.

'Susan,' he said, 'I took Will to see Dr Preston, at Kendal. He's the first doctor in the county. I thought it were better for us – for you – to know at once what chance there were for him.'

'Well!' said Susan, looking eagerly up. She saw the same strange glance of satisfaction, the same instant change to apparent regret and pain. 'What did he say?' said she. 'Speak! can't you?'

'He said he would never get better of his weakness.'

'Never!'

'No; never. It's a long word, and hard to bear. And there's worse to come, dearest. The doctor thinks he will get badder from year to year. And he said, if he was us – you – he would send him off in time to Lancaster Asylum. They've ways there both of keeping such people in order and making them happy. I only tell you what he said,' continued he, seeing the gathering storm in her face.

'There was no harm in his saying it,' she replied, with great self-constraint, forcing herself to speak coldly instead of angrily. 'Folk is welcome to their opinions.'

They sat silent for a minute or two, her breast heaving with suppressed feeling.

'He's counted a very clever man,' said Michael, at length.

'He may be. He's none of my clever men, nor am I going to be guided by him, whatever he may think. And I don't thank them that went and took my poor lad to have such harsh notions formed about him. If I'd been there, I could have called out the sense that is in him.'

'Well! I'll not say more tonight, Susan. You're not taking it rightly, and I'd best be gone, and leave you to think it over. I'll not deny they are hard words to hear, but there's sense in them, as I take it; and I reckon you'll have to come to 'em. Anyhow, it's a bad way of thanking me for my pains, and I don't take it well in you, Susan,' said he, getting up, as if offended.

'Michael, I'm beside myself with sorrow. Don't blame me, if I speak sharp. He and me is the only ones, you see. And mother did so charge me to have a care of him! And this is what he's come to, poor lile chap!' She began to cry, and Michael to comfort her with caresses.

'Don't,' said she. 'It's no use trying to make me forget poor Willie is a natural. I could hate myself for being happy with you, even for just a little minute. Go away, and leave me to face it out.'

'And you'll think it over, Susan, and remember what the doctor says?'

'I can't forget it,' said she. She meant she could not forget what the doctor had said about the hopelessness of her brother's case; Michael had referred to the plan of sending Willie away to an asylum, or madhouse, as they were called in that day and place. The idea had been gathering force in Michael's mind for some time; he had talked it over with his father, and secretly rejoiced over the possession of the farm and land which would then be his in fact, if not in law, by right of his wife. He had always considered the good penny her father could give her in his catalogue of Susan's charms and attractions. But of late he had grown to esteem her as the heiress of Yew Nook. He, too, should have land like his brother – land to possess, to cultivate, to make profit from, to bequeath. For some time he had wondered that Susan had been so much absorbed in Willie's present, that she had never seemed to look forward to his future, state. Michael had long felt the boy to be a trouble; but of late he had absolutely loathed him. His gibbering, his uncouth gestures, his loose, shambling gait, all irritated Michael inexpressibly. He did not come near the Yew Nook for a couple of days. He thought that he would leave her time to become anxious to see him and reconciled to his plan. They were strange, lonely days to Susan.

They were the first she had spent face to face with the sorrows that had turned her from a girl into a woman; for hitherto Michael had never let twenty-four hours pass by without coming to see her since she had had the fever. Now that he was absent, it seemed as though some cause of irritation was removed from Will, who was much more gentle and tractable than he had been for many weeks. Susan thought that she observed him making efforts at her bidding, and there was something piteous in the way in which he crept up to her, and looked wistfully in her face, as if asking her to restore him the faculties that he felt to be wanting.

'I never will let thee go, lad. Never! There's no knowing where they would take thee to, or what they could do with thee. As it says in the Bible, "Nought but death shall part thee and me".'

The countryside was full, in those days, of stories of the brutal treatment offered to the insane; stories that were, in fact, but too well founded, and the truth of one of which only would have been a sufficient reason for the strong prejudice existing against all such places. Each succeeding hour that Susan passed, alone, or with the poor affectionate lad for her sole companion, served to deepen her solemn resolution never to part with him. So, when Michael came, he was annoyed and surprised by the calm way in which she spoke, as if following Dr Preston's advice was utterly and entirely out of the question. He had expected nothing less than a consent, reluctant it might be, but still a consent; and he was extremely irritated. He could have repressed his anger, but he chose rather to give way to it; thinking that he could thus best work upon Susan's affection, so as to gain his point. But, somehow, he over-reached himself; and now he was astonished in his turn at the passion of indignation that she burst into.

'Thou wilt not bide in the same house with him, say'st thou? There's no need for thy biding, as far as I can tell. There's solemn reason why I should bide with my own flesh and blood, and keep to the word I pledged my mother on her death-bed; but, as for thee, there's no tie that I know on to keep thee fro' going to America or Botany Bay this very night, if that were thy inclination. I will have no more of your threats to make me send my bairn away. If thou marry me, thou'lt help me to take charge of Willie. If thou doesn't choose to marry me on those terms – why! I can snap my fingers at thee, never fear. I'm not so far gone in love as that. But I will not have thee, if thou say'st in such a hectoring way that Willie must go out of the house – and the house his own too – before thou'lt set foot in it. Willie bides here, and I bide with him.'

'Thou hast maybe spoken a word too much,' said Michael, pale with rage. 'If I am free, as thou say'st, to go to Canada or Botany Bay, I reckon I'm free to live where I like, and that will not be with a natural who may turn into a madman some day, for aught I know. Choose between him and me, Susy, for I swear to thee, thou shan't have both.'

'I have chosen,' said Susan, now perfectly composed and still. 'Whatever comes of it, I bide with Willie.'

'Very well,' replied Michael, trying to assume an equal composure of manner. 'Then I'll wish you a very good night.' He went out of the house-door, half-expecting to be called back again; but, instead, he heard a hasty step inside, and a bolt drawn.

'Whew!' said he to himself, 'I think I must leave my lady alone for a week or two, and give her time to come to her senses. She'll not find it so easy as she thinks to let me go.'

So he went past the kitchen-window in nonchalant style, and was not seen again at Yew Nook for some weeks. How did he pass the time? For the first day or two, he was unusually cross with all things and people that came athwart him. Then wheat-harvest began, and he was busy, and exultant about his heavy crop. Then a man came from a distance to bid for the lease of his farm, which, by his father's advice, had been offered for sale, as he himself was so soon likely to remove to the Yew Nook. He had so little idea that Susan really would remain firm to her determination, that he at once began to haggle with the man who came after his farm, showed him the crop just got in, and managed skilfully enough to make a good bargain for himself. Of course, the bargain had to be sealed at the public-house; and the companions he met with there soon became friends enough to tempt him into Langdale, where again he met with Eleanor Hebthwaite.

How did Susan pass the time? For the first day or so, she was too angry and offended to cry. She went about her household duties in a quick, sharp, jerking, yet absent way; shrinking one moment from Will, overwhelming him with remorseful caresses the next. The third day of Michael's absence, she had the relief of a good fit of crying; and after that, she grew softer and more tender; she felt how harshly she had spoken to him, and remembered how angry she had been. She made excuses for him. It was no wonder, she said to herself, that he had been vexed with her; and no wonder he would not give in, when she had never tried to speak gently or to reason with him. She was to blame, and she would tell him so, and tell him once again all that her mother had bade her to be to Willie, and all the horrible stories she had heard about madhouses, and he would be on her side at once.

And so she watched for his coming, intending to apologize as soon as ever she saw him. She hurried over her household work, in order to sit quietly at her sewing, and hear the first distant sound of his well-known step or whistle. But even the sound of her flying needle seemed too loud – perhaps she was losing an exquisite instant of anticipation; so she stopped sewing, and looked longingly out through the geranium leaves, in order that her eye might catch the first stir of the branches in the wood-path by which he generally came. Now and then a bird might spring out of the covert; otherwise the leaves were heavily still in the sultry weather of early autumn. Then she would take up her sewing, and, with a spasm of resolution, she would determine that a certain task should be fulfilled before she would again allow herself the poignant luxury of expectation. Sick at heart was she when the evening closed in, and the chances of that day diminished. Yet she stayed up longer than usual, thinking that if he were coming – if he were only passing along the distant road – the sight of a light in the window might encourage him to make his appearance even at that late hour, while seeing the house all darkened and shut up might quench any such intention.

Very sick and weary at heart, she went to bed; too desolate and despairing to cry, or make any moan. But in the morning hope came afresh. Another day – another chance! And so it went on for weeks. Peggy understood her young mistress's sorrow full well, and respected it by her silence on the subject. Willie seemed happier now that the irritation of Michael's presence was removed; for the poor idiot had a sort of antipathy to Michael, which was a kind of heart's echo to the repugnance in which the latter held him. Altogether, just at this time, Willie was the happiest of the three.

As Susan went into Coniston, to sell her butter, one Saturday, some inconsiderate person told her that she had seen Michael Hurst the night before. I said inconsiderate, but I might rather have said unobservant; for anyone who had spent half-an-hour in Susan Dixon's company might have seen that she disliked having any reference made to the subjects nearest her heart, were they joyous or grievous. Now she went a little paler than usual (and she had never recovered her colour since she had had the fever), and tried to keep silence. But an irrepressible pang forced out the question—

'Where?'

'At Thomas Applethwaite's, in Langdale. They had a kind of harvest-home, and he were there among the young folk, very thick wi' Nelly Hebthwaite, old Thomas's niece. Thou'lt have to look after him a bit, Susan!'

She neither smiled nor sighed. The neighbour who had been speaking to her was struck with the grey stillness of her face. Susan herself felt how well her self-command was obeyed by every little muscle, and said to herself in her Spartan manner, 'I can bear it without either wincing or blenching.' She went home early, at a tearing, passionate pace, trampling and breaking through all obstacles of briar or bush. Willie was moping in her absence – hanging listlessly on the farmyard gate to watch for her. When he saw her, he set up one of his strange, inarticulate cries, of which she was now learning the meaning, and came towards her with his loose, galloping run, head and limbs all shaking and wagging with pleasant excitement. Suddenly she turned from him, and burst into tears. She sat down on a stone by the wayside, not a hundred yards from home, and buried her face in her hands, and gave way to a passion of pent-up sorrow; so terrible and full of agony were her low cries, that the idiot stood by her, aghast and silent. All his joy gone for the time, but not, like her joy, turned into ashes. Some thought struck him. Yes! the sight of her woe made him think, great as the exertion was. He ran, and stumbled, and shambled home, buzzing with his lips all the time. She never missed him. He came back in a trice, bringing with him his cherished paper windmill, bought on that fatal day when Michael had taken him into Kendal to have his doom of perpetual idiocy pronounced. He thrust it into Susan's face, her hands, her lap, regardless of the injury his frail plaything thereby received. He leapt before her to think how he had cured all heart-sorrow, buzzing louder than ever. Susan looked up at him, and that glance of her sad eyes sobered him. He began to whimper, he knew not why: and she now, comforter in her turn, tried to soothe him by twirling his windmill. But it was broken; it made no noise; it would not go round. This seemed to afflict Susan more than him. She tried to make it right, although she saw the task was hopeless; and while she did so, the tears rained down unheeded from her bent head on the paper toy.

'It won't do,' said she, at last. 'It will never do again.' And somehow, she took the accident and her words as omens of the love that was broken, and that she feared could never be pieced together more. She rose up and took Willie's hand, and the two went slowly in to the house.

To her surprise, Michael Hurst sat in the house-place. The house-place is a sort of better kitchen, where no cookery is done, but which is reserved for state occasions. Michael had gone in there because he was accompanied by his only sister, a woman older than himself, who was well married beyond Keswick, and who now came for the first time to make acquaintance with Susan. Michael had primed his sister with his wishes regarding Will, and the position in which he stood with Susan; and arriving at Yew Nook in the absence of the latter, he had not scrupled to conduct his sister into the guest-room, as he held Mrs Gale's worldly position in respect and admiration, and therefore wished her to be favourably impressed with all the signs of property which he was beginning to consider as Susan's greatest charms. He had secretly said to himself, that if Eleanor Hebthwaite and Susan Dixon were equal in point of riches, he would sooner have Eleanor by far. He had begun to consider Susan as a termagant; and when he thought of his intercourse with her, recollections of her somewhat warm and hasty temper came far more readily to his mind than any remembrance of her generous, loving nature.

And now she stood face to face with him; her eyes tear-swollen, her garments dusty, and here and there torn in consequence of her rapid progress through the bushy by-paths. She did not make a favourable impression on the well-clad Mrs Gale, dressed in her best silk gown, and therefore unusually susceptible to the appearance of another. Nor were Susan's manners gracious or cordial. How could they be, when she remembered what had passed between Michael and herself the last time they met? For her penitence had faded away under the daily disappointment of these last weary weeks.

But she was hospitable in substance. She bade Peggy hurry on the kettle, and busied herself among the tea-cups, thankful that the presence of Mrs Gale, as a stranger, would prevent the immediate recurrence to the one subject which she felt must be present in Michael's mind as well as in her own. But Mrs Gale was withheld by no such feelings of delicacy. She had come ready-primed with the case, and had undertaken to bring the girl to reason. There was no time to be lost. It had been prearranged between the brother and sister that he was to stroll out into the farmyard before his sister introduced the subject; but she was so confident in the success of her arguments, that she must needs have the triumph of a victory as soon as possible; and, accordingly, she brought a hail-storm of good reasons to bear upon Susan. Susan did not reply for a long time; she was so indignant at this intermeddling of a stranger in the deep family sorrow and shame. Mrs Gale thought she was gaining the day, and urged her arguments more pitilessly. Even Michael winced for Susan, and wondered at her silence. He shrunk out of sight, and into the shadow, hoping that his sister might prevail, but annoyed at the hard way in which she kept putting the case.

Suddenly Susan turned round from the occupation she had pretended to be engaged in, and said to him in a low voice, which yet not only vibrated itself, but made its hearers thrill through all their obtuseness—

'Michael Hurst! does your sister speak truth, think you?'

Both women looked at him for his answer; Mrs Gale without anxiety, for had she not said the very words they had spoken together before; had she not used the very arguments that he himself had suggested? Susan, on the contrary, looked to his answer as settling her doom for life; and in the gloom of her eyes you might have read more despair than hope.

He shuffled his position. He shuffled in his words.

'What is it you ask? My sister has said many things.'

'I ask you,' said Susan, trying to give a crystal clearness both to her expressions and her pronunciation, 'if, knowing as you do how Will is afflicted, you will help me to take that charge of him which I promised my mother on her death-bed that I would do; and which means, that I shall keep him always with me, and do all in my power to make his life happy. If you will do this, I will be your wife; if not, I remain unwed.'

'But he may get dangerous; he can be but a trouble; his being here is a pain to you, Susan, not a pleasure.'

'I ask you for either yes or no,' said she, a little contempt at his evading her question mingling with her tone. He perceived it, and it nettled him.

'And I have told you. I answered your question the last time I was here. I said I would ne'er keep house with an idiot; no more I will. So now you've gotten your answer.'

'I have,' said Susan. And she sighed deeply.

'Come, now,' said Mrs Gale, encouraged by the sigh; 'one would think you don't love Michael, Susan, to be so stubborn in yielding to what I'm sure would be best for the lad.'

'Oh! she does not care for me,' said Michael. 'I don't believe she ever did.'

'Don't I? Haven't I?' asked Susan, her eyes blazing out fire. She left the room directly, and sent Peggy in to make the tea; and catching at Will, who was lounging about in the kitchen, she went upstairs with him and bolted herself in, straining the boy to her heart, and keeping him almost breathless, lest any noise she made might cause him to break out into the howls and sounds which she could not bear that those below should hear.

A knock at the door. It was Peggy.

'He wants for to see you, to wish you good-bye.'

'I cannot come. Oh, Peggy, send them away.'

It was her only cry for sympathy; and the old servant understood it. She sent them away, somehow; not politely, as I have been given to understand.

'Good go with them,' said Peggy, as she grimly watched their retreating figures. 'We're rid of bad rubbish, anyhow.' And she turned into the house, with the intention of making ready some refreshment for Susan, after her hard day at the market, and her harder evening. But in the kitchen, to which she passed through the empty house-place, making a face of contemptuous dislike at the used tea-cups and fragments of a meal yet standing there, she found Susan, with her sleeves tucked up and her working apron on, busied in preparing to make clap-bread, one of the hardest and hottest domestic tasks of a Daleswoman. She looked up, and first met and then avoided Peggy's eye; it was too full of sympathy. Her own cheeks were flushed, and her own eyes were dry and burning.

'Where's the board, Peggy? We need clap-bread; and, I reckon, I've time to get through with it tonight.' Her voice had a sharp, dry tone in it, and her motions a jerking angularity about them.

Peggy said nothing, but fetched her all that she needed. Susan beat her cakes thin with vehement force. As she stooped over them, regardless even of the task in which she seemed so much occupied, she was surprised by a touch on her mouth of something – what she did not see at first. It was a cup of tea, delicately sweetened and cooled, and held to her lips, when exactly ready, by the faithful old woman. Susan held it off a hand's breadth, and looked into Peggy's eyes, while her own filled with the strange relief of tears.

'Lass!' said Peggy, solemnly, 'thou hast done well. It is not long to bide, and then the end will come.'

'But you are very old, Peggy,' said Susan, quivering.

'It is but a day sin' I were young,' replied Peggy; she stopped the conversation by again pushing the cup with gentle force to Susan's dry and thirsty lips. When she had drunken she fell again to her labour, Peggy heating the hearth, and doing all that she knew would be required, but never speaking another word. Willie basked close to the fire, enjoying the animal luxury of warmth, for the autumn evenings were beginning to be chilly. It was one o'clock before they thought of going to bed on that memorable night.

IV

The vehemence with which Susan Dixon threw herself into occupation could not last for ever. Times of languor and remembrance would come – times when she recurred with a passionate yearning to bygone days, the recollection of which was so vivid and delicious, that it seemed as though it were the reality, and the present bleak bareness the dream. She smiled anew at the magical sweetness of some touch or tone which in memory she felt and heard, and drank the delicious cup of poison, although at the very time she knew what the consequences of racking pain would be.

'This time, last year,' thought she, 'we went nutting together – this very day last year; just such a day as today. Purple and gold were the lights on the hills; the leaves were just turning brown; here and there on the sunny slopes the stubble-fields looked tawny; down in a cleft of yon purple slate-rock the beck fell like a silver glancing thread; all just as it is today. And he climbed the slender, swaying nut-trees, and bent the branches for me to gather; or made a passage through the hazel copses, from time to time claiming a toll. Who could have thought he loved me so little? – who? – who?'

Or, as the evening closed in, she would allow herself to imagine that she heard his coming step, just so that she might recall the feeling of exquisite delight which had passed by without the due and passionate relish at the time. Then she would wonder how she could have had the strength, the cruel, self-piercing strength, to say what she had done; to stab herself with that stern resolution, of which the scar would remain till her dying day. It might have been right; but, as she sickened, she wished she had not instinctively chosen the right. How luxurious a life haunted by no stern sense of duty must be! And many led this kind of life; why could not she? Oh, for one hour again of his sweet company! If he came now, she would agree to whatever he proposed.

It was a fever of the mind. She passed through it, and came out healthy, if weak. She was capable once more of taking pleasure in following an unseen guide through briar and brake. She returned with tenfold affection to her protecting care of Willie. She acknowledged to herself that he was to be her all-in-all in life. She made him her constant companion. For his sake, as the real owner of Yew Nook, and she as his steward and guardian, she began that course of careful saving, and that love of acquisition, which afterwards gained for her the reputation of being miserly. She still thought that he might regain a scanty portion of sense – enough to require some simple pleasures and excitement, which would cost money. And money should not be wanting. Peggy rather assisted her in the formation of her parsimonious habits than otherwise; economy was the order of the district, and a certain degree of respectable avarice the characteristic of her age. Only Willie was never stinted nor hindered of anything that the two women thought could give him pleasure, for want of money.

There was one gratification which Susan felt was needed for the restoration of her mind to its more healthy state, after she had passed through the whirling fever, when duty was as nothing, and anarchy reigned: a gratification – that, somehow, was to be her last burst of unreasonableness; of which he knew and recognized pain as the sure consequence. She must see him once more – herself unseen.

The week before the Christmas of this memorable year, she

went out in the dusk of the early winter evening, wrapped close in shawl and cloak. She wore her dark shawl under her cloak, putting it over her head in lieu of a bonnet; for she knew that she might have to wait long in concealment. Then she tramped over the wet fell-path, shut in by misty rain for miles and miles, till she came to the place where he was lodging; a farmhouse in Langdale, with a steep, stony lane leading up to it: this lane was entered by a gate out of the main road, and by the gate were a few bushes – thorns; but from them the leaves had fallen, and they offered no concealment: an old wreck of a yew-tree grew among them, however, and underneath that Susan cowered down, shrouding her face, of which the colour might betray her, with a corner of her shawl. Long did she wait; cold and cramped she became, too damp and stiff to change her posture readily. And after all, he might never come! But, she would wait till daylight, if need were; and she pulled out a crust, with which she had providently supplied herself. The rain had ceased – a dull, still, brooding weather had succeeded; it was a night to hear distant sounds. She heard horses' hooves striking and splashing on the stones, and in the pools of the road at her back. Two horses; not well-ridden, or evenly guided, as she could tell.

Michael Hurst and a companion drew near; not tipsy, but not sober. They stopped at the gate to bid each other a maudlin farewell. Michael stooped forward to catch the latch with the hook of the stick which he carried; he dropped the stick, and it fell with one end close to Susan – indeed, with the slightest change of posture she could have opened the gate for him. He swore a great oath, and struck his horse with his closed fist, as if that animal had been to blame; then he dismounted, opened the gate, and fumbled about for his stick. When he had found it (Susan had touched the other end) his first use of it was to flog his horse well, and she had much ado to avoid its kicks and plunges. Then, still swearing, he staggered up the lane, for it was evident he was not sober enough to remount.

By daylight Susan was back and at her daily labours at Yew Nook. When the spring came, Michael Hurst was married to

Eleanor Hebthwaite. Others, too, were married, and christenings made their firesides merry and glad; or they travelled, and came back after long years with many wondrous tales. More rarely, perhaps, a Dalesman changed his dwelling. But to all households more change came than to Yew Nook. There the seasons came round with monotonous sameness; or, if they brought mutation, it was of a slow, and decaying, and depressing kind. Old Peggy died. Her silent sympathy, concealed under much roughness, was a loss to Susan Dixon. Susan was not yet thirty when this happened, but she looked a middle-aged, not to say an elderly woman. People affirmed that she had never recovered her complexion since that fever, a dozen years ago, which killed her father, and left Will Dixon an idiot. But besides her grey sallowness, the lines in her face were strong, and deep, and hard. The movements of her eyeballs were slow and heavy; the wrinkles at the corners of her mouth and eyes were planted firm and sure; not an ounce of unnecessary flesh was there on her bones – every muscle started strong and ready for use. She needed all this bodily strength, to a degree that no human creature, now Peggy was dead, knew of: for Willie had grown up large and strong in body, and, in general, docile enough in mind; but, every now and then, he became first moody, and then violent. These paroxysms lasted but a day or two; and it was Susan's anxious care to keep their very existence hidden and unknown. It is true, that occasional passers-by on that lonely road heard sounds at night of knocking about of furniture, blows, and cries, as of some tearing demon within the solitary farmhouse; but these fits of violence usually occurred in the night: and whatever had been their consequence, Susan had tidied and redded up all signs of aught unusual before the morning. For, above all, she dreaded lest someone might find out in what danger and peril she occasionally was, and might assume a right to take away her brother from her care. The one idea of taking charge of him had deepened and deepened with the years. It was graven into her mind as the object for which she lived. The sacrifice she had made for this object only made it more precious to her. Besides, she separated the idea of the docile, affectionate, loutish, indolent Will, and kept it distinct from the terror which the demon that occasionally possessed him inspired her with. The one was her flesh and her blood – the child of her dead mother; the other was some fiend who came to torture and convulse the creature she so loved. She believed that she fought her brother's battle in holding those tearing hands, in binding whenever she could those uplifted restless arms prompt and prone to do mischief. All the time she subdued him with her cunning or her strength, she spoke to him in pitying murmurs, or abused the third person, the fiendish enemy, in no unmeasured tones. Towards morning the paroxysm was exhausted, and he would fall asleep, perhaps only to waken with evil and renewed vigour. But when he was laid down, she would sally out to taste the fresh air, and to work off her wild sorrow in cries and mutterings to herself. The early labourers saw her gestures at a distance, and thought her as crazed as the idiot-brother who made the neighbourhood a haunted place. But did any chance person call at Yew Nook later on in the day, he would find Susan Dixon cold, calm, collected; her manner curt, her wits keen.

Once this fit of violence lasted longer than usual. Susan's strength both of mind and body was nearly worn out; she wrestled in prayer that somehow it might end before she, too, was driven mad; or, worse, might be obliged to give up her life's aim, and consign Willie to a madhouse. From that moment of prayer (as she afterwards superstitiously thought) Willie calmed – and then he drooped – and then he sank – and, last of all, he died in reality from physical exhaustion.

But he was so gentle and tender as he lay on his dying bed; such strange, child-like gleams of returning intelligence came over his face, long after the power to make his dull, inarticulate sounds had departed, that Susan was attracted to him by a stronger tie than she had ever felt before. It was something to have even an idiot loving her with dumb, wistful, animal affection; something to have any creature looking at her with such beseeching eyes, imploring protection from the insidious enemy stealing on. And yet she knew that to him death was no enemy, but a true friend, restoring light and health to his poor clouded mind. It was to her that death was an enemy; to her, the survivor, when Willie died; there was no one to love her. Worse doom still, there was no one left on earth for her to love.

You now know why no wandering tourist could persuade her to receive him as a lodger; why no tired traveller could melt her heart to afford him rest and refreshment; why long habits of seclusion had given her a moroseness of manner, and how care for the interests of another had rendered her keen and miserly.

But there was a third act in the drama of her life.

V

In spite of Peggy's prophecy that Susan's life should not seem long, it did seem wearisome and endless, as the years slowly uncoiled their monotonous circles. To be sure, she might have made a change for herself, but she did not care to do it. It was, indeed, more than 'not caring', which merely implies a certain degree of *vis inertiae* to be subdued before an object can be attained, and that the object itself does not seem to be of sufficient importance to call out the requisite energy. On the contrary, Susan exerted herself to avoid change and variety. She had a morbid dread of new faces, which originated in her desire to keep poor dead Willie's state a profound secret. She had a contempt for new customs; and, indeed, her old ways prospered so well under her active hand and vigilant eye, that it was difficult to know how they could be improved upon. She was regularly present in Coniston market with the best butter and the earliest chickens of the season. Those were the common farm produce that every farmer's wife about had to sell; but Susan, after she had disposed of the more feminine articles, turned to on the man's side. A better judge of a horse or cow there was not in all the country round. Yorkshire itself might have attempted to jockey her, and would have failed. Her corn was sound and clean; her potatoes well preserved to the latest spring. People began to talk of the hoards of money Susan Dixon must have laid up somewhere; and one young ne'er-do-weel of a farmer's son undertook to make love to the woman of forty, who looked fifty-five, if a day. He made up to her by opening a gate on the road-path home, as she was riding on a bare-backed horse, her purchase not an hour ago. She was off before him, refusing his civility; but the remounting was not so easy, and rather than fail she did not choose to attempt it. She walked, and he walked alongside, improving his opportunity, which, as he vainly thought, had been consciously granted to him. As they drew near Yew Nook, he ventured on some expression of wish to keep company with her. His words were vague and clumsily arranged. Susan turned round and coolly asked him to explain himself. He took courage, as he thought of her reputed wealth, and expressed his wishes this second time pretty plainly. To his surprise, the reply she made was in a series of smart strokes across his shoulders, administered through the medium of a supple hazel-switch.

'Take that!' said she, almost breathless, 'to teach thee how thou darest make a fool of an honest woman old enough to be thy mother. If thou com'st a step nearer the house, there's a good horse-pool, and there's two stout fellows who'll like no better fun than ducking thee. Be off wi' thee.'

And she strode into her own premises, never looking round to see whether he obeyed her injunction or not.

Sometimes three or four years would pass over without her hearing Michael Hurst's name mentioned. She used to wonder at such times whether he were dead or alive. She would sit for hours by the dying embers of her fire on a winter's evening, trying to recall the scenes of her youth; trying to bring up living pictures of the faces she had then known – Michael's most especially. She thought it was possible, so long had been the lapse of years, that she might now pass by him in the street unknowing and unknown. His outward form she might not recognize, but himself she should feel in the thrill of her whole being. He could not pass her unawares.

What little she did hear about him, all testified a downward tendency. He drank – not at stated times when there was no other work to be done, but continually, whether it was seed-time or harvest. His children were all ill at the same time; then one died, while the others recovered, but were poor sickly things. No one dared to give Susan any direct intelligence of her former lover; many avoided all mention of his name in her presence; but a few spoke out either in indifference to, or ignorance of, those bygone days. Susan heard every word, every whisper, every sound that related to him. But her eye never changed, nor did a muscle of her face move.

Late one November night she sat over her fire; not a human being besides herself in the house; none but she had ever slept there since Willie's death. The farm-labourers had foddered the cattle and gone home hours before. There were crickets chirping all round the warm hearth-stones; there was the clock ticking with the peculiar beat Susan had known from her childhood, and which then and ever since she had oddly associated with the idea of a mother and child talking together, one loud tick, and quick – a feeble, sharp one following.

The day had been keen, and piercingly cold. The whole lift of heaven seemed a dome of iron. Black and frost-bound was the earth under the cruel east wind. Now the wind had dropped, and as the darkness had gathered in, the weather-wise old labourers prophesied snow. The sounds in the air arose again, as Susan sat still and silent. They were of a different character to what they had been during the prevalence of the east wind. Then they had been shrill and piping; now they were like low distant growling; not unmusical, but strangely threatening. Susan went to the window, and drew aside the little curtain. The whole world was white – the air was blinded with the swift and heavy fall of snow. At present it came down straight, but Susan knew those distant sounds in the hollows and gulleys of the hills portended a driving wind and a more cruel storm. She thought of her sheep; were they all folded? the new-born calf, was it bedded well? Before the drifts were formed too deep for her to pass in and out – and by the morning she judged that they would be six or seven feet deep – she would go out and see after the comfort of her beasts. She took a lantern, and tied a shawl over her head, and went out into the open air. She had tenderly provided for all her animals, and was returning, when, borne on the blast as if some spirit-cry – for it seemed to come rather down from the skies than from any creature standing on earth's level – she heard a voice of agony; she could not distinguish words; it seemed rather as if some bird of prey was being caught in the whirl of the icy wind, and torn and tortured by its violence. Again! up high above! Susan put down her lantern, and shouted loud in return; it was an instinct, for if the creature were not human, which she had doubted but a moment before, what good could her responding cry do? And her cry was seized on by the tyrannous wind, and borne farther away in the opposite direction to that from which the call of agony had proceeded. Again she listened; no sound: then again it rang through space; and this time she was sure it was human. She turned into the house, and heaped turf and wood on the fire, which, careless of her own sensations, she had allowed to fade and almost die out. She put a new candle in her lantern; she changed her shawl for a maud, and leaving the door on the latch, she sallied out. Just at the moment when her ear first encountered the weird noises of the storm, on issuing forth into the open air, she thought she heard the words, 'Oh God! Oh help!' They were a guide to her, if words they were, for they came straight from a rock not a quarter of a mile from Yew Nook, but only to be reached, on account of its precipitous character, by a roundabout path. Thither she steered, defying wind and snow; guided by here a thorn-tree, there an old, doddered oak, which had not quite lost their identity under the whelming mask of snow. Now and then she stopped to listen; but never a word or sound heard she, till right from where the copse-wood grew thick and tangled at the base of the rock, round which she was winding, she heard a moan. Into the brake – all snow in appearance – almost a plain of snow looked on from the little eminence where she stood – she plunged, breaking down the bush, stumbling, bruising herself, fighting her way; her lantern held between her teeth, and she herself using head as well as hands to butt away a passage, at whatever cost of bodily injury. As she climbed or staggered, owing to the unevenness of the snow-covered ground, where the briars and weeds of years were tangled and matted together, her foot felt something strangely soft and yielding. She lowered her lantern; there lay a man, prone on his face, nearly covered by the fast-falling flakes; he must have fallen from the rock above, as, not knowing of the circuitous path, he had tried to descend its steep, slippery face. Who could tell? it was no time for thinking. Susan lifted him up with her wiry strength; he gave no help – no sign of life; but for all that he might be alive: he was still warm; she tied her maud round him; she fastened the lantern to her apron-string; she held him tight: half-carrying, half-dragging – what did a few bruises signify to him, compared to dear life, to precious life! She got him through the brake, and down the path. There, for an instant, she stopped to take breath; but, as if stung by the Furies, she pushed on again with almost superhuman strength. Clasping him round the waist, and leaning his dead weight against the lintel of the door, she tried to undo the latch; but now, just at this moment, a trembling faintness came over her, and a fearful dread took possession of her – that here, on the very threshold of her home, she might be found dead, and buried under the snow, when the farm-servants came in the morning. This terror stirred her up to one more effort. Then she and her companion were in the warmth of the quiet haven of that kitchen; she laid him on the settle, and sank on the floor by his side. How long she remained in this swoon she could not tell; not very long she judged by the fire, which was still red and sullenly glowing when she came to herself. She lighted the candle, and bent over her late burden to ascertain if indeed he were dead. She stood long gazing. The man lay dead. There could be no doubt about it. His filmy eyes glared at her, unshut. But Susan was not one to be affrighted by the stony aspect of death. It was not that; it was the bitter, woeful recognition of Michael Hurst!

She was convinced he was dead; but after a while she refused to believe in her conviction. She stripped off his wet outer-garments with trembling, hurried hands. She brought a blanket down from her own bed; she made up the fire. She swathed him in fresh, warm wrappings, and laid him on the flags before the fire, sitting herself at his head, and holding it in her lap, while she tenderly wiped his loose, wet hair, curly still, although its colour had changed from nut-brown to iron-grey since she had seen it last. From time to time she bent over the face afresh, sick, and fain to believe that the flicker of the fire-light was some slight convulsive motion. But the dim, staring eyes struck chill to her heart. At last she ceased her delicate, busy cares; but she still held the head softly, as if caressing it. She thought over all the possibilities and chances in the mingled yarn of their lives that might, by so slight a turn, have ended far otherwise. If her mother's cold had been early tended, so that the responsibility as to her brother's weal or woe had not fallen upon her, if the fever had not taken such rough, cruel hold on Will; nay, if Mrs Gale, that hard, worldly sister, had not accompanied him on his last visit to Yew Nook – his very last before this fatal, stormy night; if she had heard his cry – a cry uttered by those pale, dead lips with such wild, despairing agony, not yet three hours ago! – Oh! if she had but heard it sooner, he might have been saved before that blind, false step had precipitated him down the rock! In going over this weary chain of unrealized possibilities, Susan learnt the force of Peggy's words. Life was short, looking back upon it. It seemed but yesterday since all the love of her being had been poured out, and run to waste. The intervening years – the long monotonous years that had turned her into an old woman before her time – were but a dream.

The labourers coming in the dawn of the winter's day were surprised to see the fire-light through the low kitchen-window. They knocked, and hearing a moaning answer, they entered, fearing, that something had befallen their mistress. For all the explanation they got were these words—

'It is Michael Hurst. He was belated, and fell down the Raven's Crag. Where does Eleanor, his wife, live?'

How Michael Hurst got to Yew Nook no one but Susan ever knew. They thought he had dragged himself there, with some sore, internal bruise sapping away his minuted life. They could not have believed the superhuman exertion which had first sought him out, and then dragged him hither. Only Susan knew of that.

She gave him into the charge of her servants, and went out and saddled her horse. Where the wind had drifted the snow on one side, and the road was clear and bare, she rode, and rode fast; where the soft, deceitful heaps were massed up, she dismounted and led her steed, plunging in deep, with fierce energy, the pain at her heart urging her onwards with a sharp, digging spur.

The grey, solemn, winter's noon was more night-like than the depth of summer's night; dim-purple brooded the low skies over the white earth, as Susan rode up to what had been Michael Hurst's abode while living. It was a small farmhouse, carelessly kept outside, slatternly tended within. The pretty Nelly Hebthwaite was pretty still; her delicate face had never suffered from any long-enduring feeling. If anything, its expression was that of plaintive sorrow; but the soft, light hair had scarcely a tinge of grey; the wood-rose tint of complexion yet remained, if not so brilliant as in youth; the straight nose, the small mouth were untouched by time. Susan felt the contrast even at that moment. She knew that her own skin was weather-beaten, furrowed, brown – that her teeth were gone, and her hair grey and ragged. And yet she was not two years older than Nelly – she had not been plain, in youth, when she took account of these things. Nelly stood wondering at the strange-enough horse-woman, who stopped and panted at the door, holding her horse's bridle and refusing to enter.

'Where is Michael Hurst?' asked Susan, at last.

'Well, I can't rightly say. He should have been at home last night, but he was off, seeing after a public-house to be let at Ulverstone, for our farm does not answer, and we were thinking—'

'He did not come home last night?' said Susan, cutting short the story, and half-affirming, half-questioning, by way of letting in a ray of the awful light before she let it full in, in its consuming wrath.

'No! he'll be stopping somewhere out Ulverston ways. I'm sure we've need of him at home, for I've no one but lile Tommy to help me tend the beasts. Things have not gone well with us, and we don't keep a servant now. But you're trembling all over, ma'am. You'd better come in, and take something warm, while your horse rests. That's the stable-door, to your left.'

189

Susan took her horse there; loosened his girths, and rubbed him down with a wisp of straw. Then she looked about her for hay; but the place was bare of food, and smelt damp and unused. She went to the house, thankful for the respite, and got some clap-bread, which she mashed up for the horse in a pailful of luke-warm water. Every moment was a respite, and yet every moment made her dread the more the task that lay before her. It would be longer than she thought at first. She took the saddle off, and hung about her horse, which seemed, somehow, more like a friend than anything else in the world. She laid her cheek against his neck, and rested there, before returning to the house for the last time.

Eleanor had brought down one of her own gowns, which hung on a chair against the fire, and had made her unknown visitor a cup of hot tea. Susan could hardly bear all these little attentions: they choked her, and yet she was so wet, so weak with fatigue and excitement, that she could neither resist by voice nor by action. Two children stood awkwardly about, puzzled at the scene, and even Eleanor began to wish for some explanation of who her strange visitor was.

'You've, maybe, heard him speaking of me? I'm called Susan Dixon.'

Nelly coloured, and avoided meeting Susan's eye.

'I've heard other folk speak of you. He never named your name.'

This respect of silence came like balm to Susan: balm not felt or heeded at the time it was applied, but very grateful in its effect for all that.

'He is at my house,' continued Susan, determined not to stop or quaver in the operation – the pain which must be inflicted.

'At your house? Yew Nook?' questioned Eleanor, surprised. 'How came he there?' – half jealously. 'Did he take shelter from the coming storm? Tell me – there is something – tell me, woman!'

'He took no shelter. Would to God he had!'

'Oh! would to God! would to God!' shrieked out Eleanor, learning all from the woeful import of those dreary eyes. Her cries thrilled through the house; the children's piping wailings and passionate cries of 'Daddy! Daddy!' pierced into Susan's very marrow. But she remained as still and tearless as the great round face upon the clock.

At last, in a lull of crying, she said – not exactly questioning – but as if partly to herself—

'You loved him, then?'

'Loved him! he was my husband! He was the father of three bonny bairns that lie dead in Grasmere Churchyard. I wish you'd go, Susan Dixon, and let me weep without your watching me! I wish you'd never come near the place.'

'Alas! alas! it would not have brought him to life. I would have laid down my own to save his. My life has been so very sad! No one would have cared if I had died. Alas! alas!'

The tone in which she said this was so utterly mournful and despairing that it awed Nelly into quiet for a time. But by-and-by she said, 'I would not turn a dog out to do it harm; but the night is clear, and Tommy shall guide you to the Red Cow. But, Oh! I want to be alone. If you'll come back tomorrow, I'll be better, and I'll hear all, and thank you for every kindness you have shown him – and I do believe you've showed him kindness – though I don't know why.'

Susan moved heavily and strangely.

She said something – her words came thick and unintelligible. She had had a paralytic stroke since she had last spoken. She could not go, even if she would. Nor did Eleanor, when she became aware of the state of the case, wish her to leave. She had her laid on her own bed, and weeping silently all the while for her lost husband, she nursed Susan like a sister. She did not know what her guest's worldly position might be; and she might never be repaid. But she sold many a little trifle to purchase such small comforts as Susan needed. Susan, lying still and motionless, learnt much. It was not a severe stroke; it might be the forerunner of others yet to come, but at some distance of time. But for the present she recovered, and regained much of her former health. On her sick-bed she matured her plans. When she returned to Yew Nook, she took Michael Hurst's widow and children with her to live there, and fill up the haunted hearth with living forms that should banish the ghosts.

And so it fell out that the latter days of Susan Dixon's life were better than the former.

Philippa's Fox-Hunt

EDITH SOMERVILLE & MARTIN ROSS

No one can accuse Philippa and me of having married in haste. As a matter of fact, it was but little under five years from that autumn evening on the river when I had said what is called in Ireland 'the hard word', to the day in August when I was led to the altar by my best man, and was subsequently led away from it by Mrs Sinclair Yeates. About two years out of the five had been spent by me at Shreelane in ceaseless warfare with drains, eaveshoots, chimneys, pumps; all those fundamentals, in short, that the ingenuous and improving tenant expects to find established as a basis from which to rise to higher things. As far as rising to higher things went, frequent ascents to the roof to search for leaks summed up my achievements; in fact, I suffered so general a shrinkage of my ideals that the triumph of making the hall door-bell ring blinded me to the fact that the rat-holes in the hall floor were nailed up with pieces of tin biscuit boxes, and that the casual visitor could, instead of leaving a card, have easily written his name in the damp on the walls.

Philippa, however, proved adorably callous to these and similar shortcomings. She regarded Shreelane and its floundering, foundering *ménage* of incapables in the light of a gigantic picnic in a foreign land; she held long conversations daily with Mrs Cadogan, in order, as she informed me, to acquire the language; without any ulterior domestic intention she engaged kitchenmaids because of the beauty of their eyes, and house-maids because they had such delightfully picturesque old mothers, and she declined to correct the phraseology of the parlourmaid, whose painful habit it was to whisper 'Do ye choose cherry or clarry?' when proffering the wine. Fast-days, perhaps, afforded my wife her first insight into the sterner realities of Irish housekeeping. Philippa had what are known as High Church proclivities, and took the matter seriously.

'I don't know how we are to manage for the servants' dinner tomorrow, Sinclair,' she said, coming to my office one Thursday morning; 'Julia says she "promised God this long time that she wouldn't eat an egg on a fast-day", and the kitchenmaid says she won't eat herrings "without they're fried with onions", and Mrs Cadogan says she will "not go to them extremes for servants".'

'I should let Mrs Cadogan settle the menu herself,' I suggested.

'I asked her to do that,' replied Philippa, 'and she only said she "thanked God *she* had no appetite!" '

The lady of the house here fell away into unseasonable laughter.

I made the demoralizing suggestion that, as we were going away for a couple of nights, we might safely leave them to fight it out, and the problem was abandoned.

Philippa had been much called on by the neighbourhood in all its shades and grades, and daily she and her trousseau frocks presented themselves at hall doors of varying dimensions in due acknowledgement of civilities. In Ireland, it may be noted, the process known in England as 'summering and wintering' a newcomer does not obtain; sociability and curiosity alike forbid delay. The visit to which we owed our escape from the intricacies of the fast-day was to the Knoxes of Castle Knox, relations in some remote and tribal way of my landlord, Mr Flurry of that ilk. It involved a short journey by train, and my wife's longest basket-trunk; it also, which was more serious, involved my being lent a horse to go out cubbing the following morning.

At Castle Knox we sank into an almost forgotten environment of draught-proof windows and doors, of deep carpets, of silent servants instead of clattering belligerents. Philippa told me afterwards that it had only been by an effort that she had restrained herself from snatching up the train of her wedding-gown as she paced across the wide hall on little Sir Valentine's arm. After three weeks at Shreelane she found it difficult to remember that the floor was neither damp nor dusty.

I had the good fortune to be of the limited number of those who got on with Lady Knox, chiefly, I imagine, because I was as a worm before her, and thankfully permitted her to do all the talking.

'Your wife is extremely pretty,' she pronounced autocratically, surveying Philippa between the candle-shades; 'does she ride?'

Lady Knox was a short, square lady, with a weather-beaten face, and an eye decisive from long habit of taking her own line across country and elsewhere. She would have made a very imposing little coachman, and would have caused her stable helpers to rue the day they had had the presumption to be born; it struck me that Sir Valentine sometimes did so.

'I'm glad you like her looks,' I replied, 'as I fear you will find her thoroughly despicable otherwise; for one thing, she not only can't ride, but she believes that I can!'

'Oh, come, you're not as bad as all that!' my hostess was good enough to say; 'I'm going to put you up on Sorcerer tomorrow, and we'll see you at the top of the hunt – if there is one. That young Knox hasn't a notion how to draw these woods.'

'Well, the best run we had last year out of this place was with Flurry's hounds,' struck in Miss Sally, sole daughter of Sir Valentine's house and home, from her place half-way down the table. It was not difficult to see that she and her mother held different views on the subject of Mr Flurry Knox.

'I call it a criminal thing in anyone's great-great-grandfather to rear up a preposterous troop of sons and plant them all out in his own country,' Lady Knox said to me with apparent irrelevance. 'I detest collaterals. Blood may be thicker than water, but it is also a great deal nastier. In this country I find that fifteenth cousins consider themselves near relations if they live within twenty miles of one!'

Having before now taken in the position with regard to Flurry Knox, I took care to accept these remarks as generalities, and turned the conversation to other themes.

'I see Mrs Yeates is doing wonders with Mr Hamilton,' said Lady Knox presently, following the direction of my eyes, which had strayed away to where Philippa was beaming upon her left-hand neighbour, a mildewed-looking old clergyman, who was delivering a long dissertation, the purport of which we were happily unable to catch.

'She has always had a gift for the Church,' I said.

'Not curates?' said Lady Knox, in her deep voice.

I made haste to reply that it was the elders of the Church who were venerated by my wife.

'Well, she has her fancy in old Eustace Hamilton; he's elderly enough!' said Lady Knox. 'I wonder if she'd venerate him as much if she knew that he had fought with his sister-in-law, and they haven't spoken for thirty years! though for the matter of that,' she added, 'I think it shows his good sense!'

'Mrs Knox is rather a friend of mine,' I ventured.

'Is she? H'm! Well, she's not one of mine!' replied my hostess, with her usual definiteness. 'I'll say one thing for her, I believe, she's always been a sportswoman. She's very rich, you know, and they say she only married old Badger Knox to save his hounds from being sold to pay his debts, and then she took the horn from him and hunted them herself. Has she been rude to your wife yet? No? Oh, well, she will. It's a mere question of time. She hates all English people. You know the story they tell of her? She was coming from London, and when she was getting her ticket the man asked if she had said a ticket for York. "No, thank God, Cork!" says Mrs Knox.'

'Well, I rather agree with her!' said I; 'but why did she fight with Mr Hamilton?'

'Oh, nobody knows. I don't believe they know themselves! Whatever it was, the old lady drives five miles to Fortwilliam every Sunday, rather than go to his church, just outside her own back gates,' Lady Knox said with a laugh like a terrier's bark. 'I wish I'd fought with him myself,' she continued. 'He gives us forty minutes every Sunday.'

As I struggled into my boots the following morning, I felt that Sir Valentine's acid confidences on cub-hunting, bestowed on me at midnight, did credit to his judgement. 'A very moderate amusement, my dear Major,' he had said, in his dry little voice; 'you should stick to shooting. No one expects you to shoot before daybreak.'

It was six o'clock as I crept downstairs, and found Lady Knox and Miss Sally at breakfast, with two lamps on the table, and a foggy daylight oozing in from under the half-raised blinds. Philippa was already in the hall, pumping up her bicycle, in a state of excitement at the prospect of her first experience of hunting that would have been more comprehensible to me had she been going to ride a strange horse, as I was. As I bolted my food I saw the horses being led past the windows, and a faint twang of a horn told that Flurry Knox and his hounds were not far off.

Miss Sally jumped up.

'If I'm not on the Cockatoo before the hounds come up, I shall never get there!' she said, hobbling out of the room in the toils of her safety habit. Her small, alert face looked very childish under her riding-hat; the lamp-light struck sparks out of her thick coil of golden-red hair; I wondered how I had ever thought her like her prim little father.

She was already on her white cob when I got to the hall door, and Flurry Knox was riding over the glistening wet grass with his hounds, while his whip, Dr Jerome Hickey, was having a stirring time with the young entry and the rabbit-holes. They moved on without stopping, up a back avenue, under tall and dripping trees, to a thick laurel covert, at some little distance from the house. Into this the hounds were thrown, and the usual period of fidgety inaction set in for the riders, of whom all told, there were about half a dozen. Lady Knox, square and solid, on her big, confidential iron-grey, was near me, and her eyes were on me and my mount; with her rubicund face and white collar she was more than ever like a coachman.

'Sorcerer looks as if he suits you well,' she said, after a few minutes of silence, during which the hounds rustled and cracked steadily through the laurels; 'he's a little high on the leg, and so are you, you know, so you show each other off.'

Sorcerer was standing like a rock, with his good-looking head in the air and his eyes fastened on the covert. His manners, so far, had been those of a perfect gentleman, and were in marked contrast to those of Miss Sally's cob, who was sidling, hopping and snatching unappeasably at his bit. Philippa had disappeared from view down the avenue ahead. The fog was melting, and the sun threw long blades of light through the trees; everything was quiet, and in the distance the curtained windows of the house marked the warm repose of Sir Valentine, and those of the party who shared his opinion of cubbing.

'Hark! hark to cry there!'

It was Flurry's voice, away at the other side of the covert. The rustling and brushing through the laurels became more vehement, then passed out of hearing.

'He never will leave his hounds alone,' said Lady Knox disapprovingly.

Miss Sally and the Cockatoo moved away in a series of heraldic capers towards the end of the laurel plantation, and at the same moment I saw Philippa on her bicycle shoot into view on the drive ahead of us.

'I've seen a fox!' she screamed, white with what I believe to have been personal terror, though she says it was excitement; 'it passed quite close to me!'

'What way did he go?' bellowed a voice which I recognized as Dr Hickey's, somewhere in the deep of the laurels.

'Down the drive!' returned Philippa, with a pea-hen quality in her tones with which I was quite unacquainted.

An electrifying screech of 'Gone away!' was projected from the laurels by Dr Hickey.

'Gone away!' chanted Flurry's horn at the top of the covert.

'This is what he calls cubbing!' said Lady Knox, 'a mere farce!' but none the less she loosed her sedate monster into a canter.

Sorcerer got his hind legs under him, and hardened his crest against the bit, as we all hustled along the drive after the flying figure of my wife. I knew very little about horses, but I realized that even with the hounds tumbling hysterically out of the covert, Sorcerer comported himself with the manners of the best society. Up a side road I saw Flurry Knox opening half of a gate and cramming through it; in a moment we also had crammed through, and the turf of a pasture field was under our feet. Dr Hickey leaned forward and took hold of his horse; I did likewise, with the trifling difference that my horse took hold of me, and I steered for Flurry Knox with single-hearted purpose, the hounds, already a field ahead, being merely an exciting and noisy accompaniment of this endeavour. A heavy stone wall was the first occurrence of note. Flurry chose a place where the top was loose, and his clumsy-looking brown mare changed feet on the rattling stones like a fairy. Sorcerer came at it, tense and as collected as a bow at full stretch, and sailed steeply into the air; I saw the wall far beneath me, with an unsuspected ditch on the far side, and I felt my hat following me at the full stretch of its guard as we swept over it, then, with a long slant, we descended to earth some sixteen feet from where we had left it, and I was the possessor of the gratifying fact that I had achieved a good-sized 'fly', and had not perceptibly moved in my saddle. Subsequent disillusioning experience has taught me that but few horses jump like Sorcerer, so gallantly, so sympathetically, and with such supreme mastery of the subject; but none the less the enthusiasm that he imparted to me has never been extinguished, and that October morning ride revealed to me the unsuspected intoxication of fox-hunting.

Behind me I heard the scrabbling of the Cockatoo's little hooves among the loose stone, and Lady Knox, galloping on my left, jerked a maternal chin over her shoulder to mark her daughter's progress. For my part, had there been an entire circus behind me, I was far too much occupied with ramming on my hat and trying to hold Sorcerer, to have looked round, and all my spare faculties were devoted to steering for Flurry, who had taken a right-handed turn, and was at that moment surmounting a bank of uncertain and briary aspect. I surmounted it also, with the swiftness and simplicity for which the Quaker's methods of bank jumping had not prepared me, and two or three fields, traversed at the same steeplechase pace, brought us to a road and to an abrupt check. There, suddenly, were the hounds, scrambling in baffled silence down into the road from the opposite bank, to look for the line they had overrun, and there, amazingly, was Philippa, engaged in excited converse with several men with spades over their shoulders.

'Did ye see the fox, boys?' shouted Flurry, addressing the group.

'We did! we did!' cried my wife and her friends in chorus; 'he ran up the road!'

'We'd be badly off without Mrs Yeates!' said Flurry, as he whirled his mare round and clattered up the road with a hustle of hounds after him.

It occurred to me as forcibly as any mere earthly thing can occur to those who are wrapped in the sublimities of a run, that, for a young woman who had never before seen a fox out of a cage at the Zoo, Philippa was taking to hunting very kindly. Her cheeks were a most brilliant pink, her blue eyes shone.

'Oh, Sinclair!' she exclaimed, 'they say he's going for Aussolas, and there's a road I can ride all the way!'

'Ye can, miss! Sure we'll show you!' chorused her cortège.

Her foot was on the pedal ready to mount. Decidedly my wife was in no need of assistance from me.

Up the road a hound gave a yelp of discovery, and flung himself over a stile into the fields; the rest of the pack went squealing and jostling after him, and I followed Flurry over one of those infinitely varied erections, pleasantly termed 'gaps' in Ireland. On this occasion the gap was made of three razor-edged slabs of slate leaning against an iron bar, and Sorcerer conveyed to me his thorough knowledge of the matter by a lift of his hind quarters that made me feel as I were being skilfully kicked downstairs. To what extent I looked it, I cannot say, nor providentially can Philippa, as she had already started. I only know that undeserved good luck restored to me my stirrup before Sorcerer got away with me in the next field.

What followed was, I am told, a very fast fifteen minutes; for me time was not; the empty fields rushed past uncounted, fences came and went in a flash, while the wind sang in my ears, and the dazzle of the early sun was in my eyes. I saw the hounds occasionally, sometimes pouring over a green bank, as the charging breaker lifts and flings itself, sometimes driving across a field, as the white tongues of foam slide racing over the sand; and always ahead of me was Flurry Knox, going as a man goes who knows his country, who knows his horse, and whose heart is wholly and absolutely in the right place.

Do what I would, Sorcerer's implacable stride carried me closer and closer to the brown mare, till, as I thundered down the slope of a long field, I was not twenty yards behind Flurry. Sorcerer had stiffened his neck to iron, and to slow him down was beyond me; but I fought his head away to the right, and found myself coming hard and steady at a stone-faced bank with broken ground in front of it. Flurry bore away to the left, shouting something that I did not understand. That Sorcerer shortened his stride at the right moment was entirely due to his own judgement; standing well away from the jump, he rose like a stag out of the tussocky ground, and as he swung my twelve stone six into the air the obstacle revealed itself to him and me as consisting not of one bank but of two, and I have often been asked to state the width of the *bohireen*, and can only reply that in my opinion it was at least eighteen feet; Flurry Knox and Dr Hickey, who did not jump it, say that it is not more than five. What Sorcerer did with it I cannot say; the sensation was of a towering flight with a kick back in it, a biggish drop, and a landing on cee-springs, still on the downhill grade. That was how one of the best horses in Ireland took one of Ireland's most ignorant riders over a very nasty place.

A sombre line of fir-wood lay ahead, rimmed with a grey wall, and in another couple of minutes we had pulled up on the Aussolas road, and were watching the hounds struggling over the wall into Aussolas demesne.

'No hurry now,' said Flurry, turning in his saddle to watch the Cockatoo jump into the road, 'he's to ground in the big earth inside. Well, Major, it's well for you that's a big-jumped horse. I thought you were a dead man a while ago when you faced him at the *bohireen*!'

I was disclaiming intention in the matter when Lady Knox and the others joined us.

'I thought you told me your wife was no sportswoman,' she said to me, critically scanning Sorcerer's legs for cuts the while, 'but when I saw her a minute ago she had abandoned her bicycle and was running across country like—'

'Look at her now!' interrupted Miss Sally. 'Oh! – oh!' In the interval between these exclamations my incredulous eyes beheld my wife in mid air, hand in hand with a couple of stalwart country boys, with whom she was leaping in unison from the top of a bank on to the road.

Everyone, even the saturnine Dr Hickey, began to laugh; I rode back to Philippa, who was exchanging compliments and congratulations with her escort.

'Oh, Sinclair!' she cried, 'wasn't it splendid? I saw you jumping, and everything! Where are they going now?'

'My dear girl,' I said, with marital disapproval, 'you're killing yourself. Where's your bicycle?'

'Oh, it's punctured in a sort of lane, back there. It's all right; and then they' – she breathlessly waved her hand at her attendants – 'they showed me the way.'

'Begor! you proved very good, miss!' said a grinning cavalier.

'Faith she did!' said another, polishing his shining brow with his white flannel coat-sleeve, 'she lepped like a haarse!'

'And may I ask how you propose to go home?' said I.

'I don't know and I don't care! I'm not going home!' She cast an entirely disobedient eye at me. 'And your eyeglass is hanging down your back and your tie is bulging out over your waistcoat!'

The little group of riders had begun to move away.

'We're going on into Aussolas,' called out Flurry; 'come on, and make my grandmother give you some breakfast, Mrs Yeates; she always has it at eight o'clock.'

The front gates were close at hand, and we turned in under the tall beech-trees, with the unswept leaves rustling round the horses' feet, and the lovely blue of the October morning sky filling the spaces between smooth grey branches and golden leaves. The woods rang with the voices of the hounds, enjoying an untrammelled rabbit hunt, while the Master and the Whip, both on foot, strolled along unconcernedly with their bridles over their arms, making themselves agreeable to my wife, an occasional touch of Flurry's horn, or a crack of Dr Hickey's whip just indicating to the pack that the authorities still took a friendly interest in their doings.

Down a grassy glade in the wood a party of old Mrs Knox's young horses suddenly swept into view, headed by an old mare, who, with her tail over her back, stampeded ponderously past our cavalcade, shaking and swinging her handsome old head, while her youthful friends bucked and kicked and snapped at each other round her with the ferocious humour of their kind.

'Here, Jerome, take the horn,' said Flurry to Dr Hickey; 'I'm going to see Mrs Yeates up to the house, the way these tomfools won't gallop on top of her.'

From this point it seems to me that Philippa's adventures are more worthy of record than mine, and as she has favoured me with a full account of them, I venture to think my version may be relied on.

Mrs Knox was already at breakfast when Philippa was led, quaking, into her formidable presence. My wife's acquaintance with Mrs Knox was, so far, limited to a state visit on either side, and she found but little comfort in Flurry's assurances that his grandmother wouldn't mind if he brought all the hounds in to breakfast, coupled with the statement that she would put her eyes on sticks for the Major.

Whatever the truth of this may have been, Mrs Knox received her guest with an equanimity quite unshaken by the fact that her boots were in the fender instead of on her feet, and that a couple of shawls of varying dimensions and degrees of age did not conceal the inner presence of a magenta flannel dressing-jacket. She installed Philippa at the table and plied her with food, oblivious as to whether the needful implements with which to eat it were forthcoming or no. She told Flurry where a vixen had reared her family, and she watched him ride away, with some biting comment on his mare's hocks screamed after him from the window.

The dining-room at Aussolas Castle is one of the many rooms in Ireland in which Cromwell is said to have stabled his horse (and probably no one would have objected less than Mrs Knox had she been consulted in the matter). Philippa questions if the room had ever been tidied up since, and she endorses Flurry's observation that 'there wasn't a day in the year you wouldn't get feeding for a hen and chickens on the floor'. Opposite to Philippa, on a Louis Quinze chair, sat Mrs Knox's woolly dog, its suspicious little eyes peering at her out of their setting of pink lids and dirty white wool. A couple of young horses outside the windows tore at the matted creepers on the walls, or thrust faces that were half-shy, half-impudent, into the room. Portly pigeons waddled to and fro on the broad window-sill, sometimes flying in to perch on the picture-frames, while they kept up incessantly a hoarse and pompous cooing.

Animals and children are, as a rule, alike destructive to conversation; but Mrs Knox, when she chose, *bien entendu*, could have made herself agreeable in a Noah's Ark, and Philippa has a gift of sympathetic attention that personal experience has taught me to regard with distrust as well as respect, while it has often made me realize the worldly wisdom of Kingsley's injunction:

'Be good, sweet maid, and let who will be clever.'

Family prayers, declaimed by Mrs Knox with alarming austerity, followed close on breakfast, Philippa and a vinegar-faced hench-woman forming the family. The prayers were long, and through the open window as they progressed came distantly a whoop or two; the declamatory tones staggered a little, and then continued at a distinctly higher rate of speed.

'Ma'am! Ma'am!' whispered a small voice at the window.

Mrs Knox made a repressive gesture and held on her way. A

sudden outcry of hounds followed, and the owner of the whisper, a small boy with a face freckled like a turkey's egg, darted from the window and dragged a donkey and bath-chair into view. Philippa admits to having lost the thread of the discourse, but she thinks that the 'Amen' that immediately ensued can hardly have come in its usual place. Mrs Knox shut the book abruptly, scrambled up from her knees, and said, 'They've found!'

In a surprisingly short space of time she had added to her attire her boots, a fur cape and a garden hat, and was in the bath-chair, the small boy stimulating the donkey with the success peculiar to his class, while Philippa hung on behind.

The woods of Aussolas are hilly and extensive, and on that particular morning it seemed that they held as many foxes as hounds. In vain was the horn blown and the whips cracked, small rejoicing parties of hounds, each with a fox of its own, scoured to and fro: every labourer in the vicinity had left his work, and was sedulously heading every fox with yells that would have befitted a tiger hunt, and sticks and stones when occasion served.

'Will I pull out as far as the big rosydandhrum, ma'am?' enquired the small boy; 'I seen three of the dogs go in it, and they yowling.'

'You will,' said Mrs Knox, thumping the donkey on the back with her umbrella; 'here Jeremiah Regan! Come down out of that with that pitchfork! Do you want to kill the fox, you fool?'

'I do not, your honour, ma'am,' responded Jeremiah Regan, a tall young countryman, emerging from a bramble brake.

'Did you see him?' said Mrs Knox eagerly.

'I seen himself and his ten pups drinking below at the lake ere yestherday, your honour, ma'am, and he as big as a chestnut horse!' said Jeremiah.

'Faugh! Yesterday!' snorted Mrs Knox; 'go on to the rhododendrons, Johnny!'

The party, reinforced by Jeremiah and the pitchfork, progressed at a high rate of speed along the shrubbery path, encountering *en route* Lady Knox, stooping on to her horse's neck under the sweeping branches of the laurels.

205

'Your horse is too high for my coverts, Lady Knox,' said the lady of the manor, with a malicious eye at Lady Knox's flushed face and dinged hat; 'I'm afraid you will be left behind like Absalom when the hounds go away!'

'As they never do anything here but hunt rabbits,' retorted her ladyship. 'I don't think that's likely.'

Mrs Knox gave her donkey another whack, and passed on.

'Rabbits, my dear!' she said scornfully to Philippa. 'That's all she knows about it. I declare it disgusts me to see a woman of that age making such a Judy of herself! Rabbits indeed!'

Down in the thicket of rhododendron everything was very quiet for a time. Philippa strained her eyes in vain to see any of the riders; the horn-blowing and the whip-cracking passed on almost out of hearing. Once or twice a hound worked through the rhododendrons, glanced at the party, and hurried on, immersed in business. All at once, Johnny, the donkey-boy, whispered excitedly:

'Look at he! Look at he!' and pointed to a boulder of grey rock that stood out among the dark evergreens. A big yellow cub was crouching on it; he instantly slid into the shelter of the bushes, and the irrepressible Jeremiah, uttering a rending shriek, plunged into the thicket after him. Two or three hounds came rushing at the sound, and after this Philippa says she finds some difficulty in recalling the proper order of events; chiefly, she confesses, because of the wholly ridiculous tears of excitement that blurred her eyes.

'We ran,' she said, 'we simply tore, and the donkey galloped, and as for that old Mrs Knox, she was giving cracked screams to the hounds all the time, and they were screaming too; and then somehow we were all out on the road!'

What seems to have occurred was that three couple of hounds, Jeremiah Regan, and Mrs Knox's equipage, amongst them somehow hustled the cub out of Aussolas demesne and up on to a hill on the farther side of the road. Jeremiah was sent back by his mistress to fetch Flurry, and the rest of the party pursued a thrilling course along the road, parallel with that of the hounds, who were hunting slowly through the gorse on the hill-side.

'Upon my honour and word, Mrs Yeates, my dear, we have the hunt to ourselves!' said Mrs Knox to the panting Philippa, as they pounded along the road. 'Johnny, d'ye see the fox?'

'I do, ma'am!' shrieked Johnny, who possessed the usual field-glass vision bestowed upon his kind. 'Look at him over-right us on the hill above! Hi! The spotty dog have him! No, he's gone from him! *Gwan o' that!*' This to the donkey, with blows that sounded like the beating of carpets, and produced rather more dust.

They had left Aussolas some half a mile behind, when, from a strip of wood on their right, the fox suddenly slipped over the bank on to the road just ahead of them, ran up it for a few yards, and whisked in at a small entrance gate, with the three couple of hounds yelling on a red-hot scent, not thirty yards behind. The bath-chair party whirled in at their heels, Philippa and the donkey considerably blown, Johnny scarlet through his freckles, but as fresh as paint, the old lady blind and deaf to all things save the chase. The hounds went raging through the shrubs beside the drive, and away down a grassy slope towards a shallow glen, in the bottom of which ran a little stream, and after them over the grass bumped the bath-chair. At the stream they turned sharply and ran up the glen towards the avenue, which crossed it by means of a rough stone viaduct.

''Pon me conscience, he's into the old culvert!' exclaimed Mrs Knox; 'there was one of my hounds choked there once, long ago! Beat on the donkey, Johnny!'

At this juncture Philippa's narrative again becomes incoherent, not to say breathless. She is, however, positive that it was somewhere about here that the upset of the bath-chair occurred, but she cannot be clear as to whether she picked up the donkey or Mrs Knox, or whether she herself was picked up by Johnny while Mrs Knox picked up the donkey. From my knowledge of Mrs Knox I should say she picked up herself and no one else. At all events, the next salient point is the palpitating moment when Mrs Knox, Johnny and Philippa successively applying an eye to the opening of the culvert by which the stream trickled under the viaduct, while five dripping hounds bayed and leaped around them, discovered by more senses than that of sight that the fox was in it, and furthermore that one of the hounds was in it too.

'There's a strong grating before him at the far end,' said Johnny, his head in at the mouth of the hole, his voice sounding as if he were talking into a jug, 'the two of them's fighting in it; they'll be choked surely!'

'Then don't stand gabbing there, you little fool, but get in and pull the hound out!' exclaimed Mrs Knox, who was balancing herself on a stone in the stream.

'I'd be in dread, ma'am,' whined Johnny.

'Balderdash!' said the implacable Mrs Knox. 'In with you!'

I understand that Philippa assisted Johnny into the culvert, and presume that it was in so doing that she acquired the two Robinson Crusoe bare footprints which decorated her jacket when I next met her.

'Have you got hold of him yet, Johnny?' cried Mrs Knox up the culvert.

'I have, ma'am, by the tail,' responded Johnny's voice, sepulchral in the depths.

'Can you stir him, Johnny?'

'I cannot, ma'am, and the wather is rising in it.'

'Well, please God, they'll not open the mill-dam!' remarked Mrs Knox philosophically to Philippa, as she caught hold of Johnny's dirty ankles. 'Hold on to the tail, Johnny!'

She hauled, with, as might be expected, no appreciable result. 'Run, my dear, and look for somebody, and we'll have that fox yet!'

Philippa ran, whither she knew not, pursued by fearful visions of bursting mill-dams, and maddened foxes at bay. As she sped up the avenue she heard voices, robust male voices, in a shrubbery, and made for them. Advancing along an embowered walk towards her was what she took for one wild instant to be a funeral; a second glance showed her that it was a party of clergymen of all ages, walking by twos and three in the dappled shade of the over-arching trees. Obviously she had intruded her sacrilegious presence into a Clerical Meeting. She acknowledges that at this awe-inspiring spectacle she faltered, but the thought of Johnny, the hound, and the fox, suffocating, possibly drowning together in the culvert, nerved her. She does not remember what she said or how she said it, but I fancy she must have conveyed to them the impression that old Mrs Knox was being drowned, as she immediately found herself heading a charge of the Irish Church towards the scene of disaster.

Fate has not always used me well, but on this occasion it was mercifully decreed that I and the other members of the hunt should be privileged to arrive in time to see my wife and her rescue party precipitating themselves down the glen.

'Holy Biddy!' ejaculated Flurry, 'is she running a paper-chase with all the parsons? But look! For pity's sake will you look at my grandmother and my Uncle Eustace?'

Mrs Knox and her sworn enemy the old clergyman, whom I had met at dinner the night before, were standing, apparently in the stream, tugging at two bare legs that projected from a hole in the viaduct, and arguing at the top of their voices. The bath-chair lay on its side with the donkey grazing beside it, on the bank a stout archdeacon was tendering advice, and the hounds danced and howled round the entire group.

'I tell you, Eliza, you had better let the archdeacon try,' thundered Mr Hamilton.

'Then I tell you I will not!' vociferated Mrs Knox, with a tug at the end of the sentence that elicited a subterranean lament from Johnny. 'Now who was right about the second grating? I told you so twenty years ago!'

Exactly as Philippa and her rescue party arrived, the efforts of Mrs Knox and her brother-in-law triumphed. The struggling, sopping form of Johnny was slowly drawn from the hole, drenched, speechless, but clinging to the stern of a hound, who, in its turn, had its jaws fast in the hind quarters of a limp, yellow cub.

'Oh, it's dead!' wailed Philippa, 'I *did* think I should have been in time to save it!'

'Well, if that doesn't beat all!' said Dr Hickey.

The Cobweb

SAKI

The farmhouse kitchen probably stood where it did as a matter of accident or haphazard choice, yet its situation might have been planned by a master-strategist in farmhouse architecture. Dairy and poultry-yard, and herb garden, and all the busy places of the farm seemed to lead by easy access into its wide-flagged haven, where there was room for everything and where muddy boots left traces that were easily swept away. And yet, for all that it stood so well in the centre of human bustle, its long, latticed window, with the wide window seat, built into an embrasure beyond the huge fireplace, looked out on a wild spreading view of hill and heather and wooded combe. The window nook made almost a little room in itself, quite the pleasantest room in the farm as far as situation and capabilities went. Young Mrs Ladbruk, whose husband had just come into the farm by way of inheritance, cast covetous eyes on this snug corner, and her fingers itched to make it bright and cosy with chintz curtains and bowls of flowers, and a shelf or two of old china. The musty farm parlour, looking out to a prim, cheerless garden imprisoned within high, blank walls, was not a room that lent itself readily either to comfort or decoration.

'When we are more settled I shall work wonders in the way of making the kitchen habitable,' said the young woman to her occasional visitors. There was an unspoken wish in those words,

211

a wish which was unconfessed as well as unspoken. Emma Ladbruk was the mistress of the farm; jointly with her husband she might have her say, and to a certain extent her way, in ordering its affairs. But she was not mistress of the kitchen.

On one of the shelves of an old dresser, in company with chipped sauce-boats, pewter jugs, cheese-graters, and paid bills, rested a worn and ragged Bible, on whose front page was the record, in faded ink, of a baptism dated ninety-four years ago. 'Martha Crale' was the name written on that yellow page. The yellow, wrinkled old dame who hobbled and muttered about the kitchen, looking like a dead autumn leaf which the winter winds still pushed hither and thither, had once been Martha Crale; for seventy odd years she had been Martha Mountjoy. For longer than anyone could remember she had pattered to and fro between oven and wash-house and dairy, and out to chicken-run and garden, grumbling and muttering and scolding, but working unceasingly. Emma Ladbruk, of whose coming she took as little notice as she would of a bee wandering in at a window on a summer's day, used at first to watch her with a kind of frightened curiosity. She was so old and so much a part of the place, it was difficult to think of her exactly as a living thing. Old Shep, the white-nozzled, stiff-limbed collie, waiting for his time to die, seemed almost more human than he withered, dried-up old woman. He had been a riotous, roystering puppy, mad with the joy of life, when she was already a tottering, hobbling dame; now he was just a blind, breathing carcass, nothing more, and she still worked with frail energy, still swept and baked and washed, fetched and carried. If there were something in these wise old dogs that did not perish utterly with death, Emma used to think to herself, what generations of ghost-dogs there must be out on those hills, that Martha had reared and fed and tended and spoken a last good-bye word to in that old kitchen. And what memories she must have of human generations that had passed away in her time. It was difficult for anyone, let alone a stranger like Emma, to get her to talk of the days that had been; her shrill, quavering speech was of doors that had been left unfastened, pails that had got mislaid, calves whose feeding-time was overdue, and the various little faults and lapses that chequer a farmhouse routine. Now and again, when election time came round, she would unstore her recollections of the old names round which the fight had waged in the days gone by. There had been a Palmerston, that had been a name down Tiverton way; Tiverton was not a far journey as the crow flies, but to Martha it was almost a foreign country. Later there had been Northcotes and Aclands, and many other newer names that she had forgotten; the names changed, but it was always Libruls and Toories, Yellows and Blues. And they always quarrelled and shouted as to who was right and who was wrong. The one they quarrelled about most was a fine old gentleman with an angry face – she had seen his picture on the walls. She had seen it on the floor too, with a rotten apple squashed over it, for the farm had changed its politics from time to time. Martha had never been on one side or the other; none of 'they' had ever done the farm a stroke of good. Such was her sweeping verdict, given with all a peasant's distrust of the outside world.

When the half-frightened curiosity had somewhat faded away, Emma Ladbruk was uncomfortably conscious of another feeling towards the old woman. She was a quaint old tradition, lingering about the place, she was part and parcel of the farm itself, she was something at once pathetic and picturesque – but she was dreadfully in the way. Emma had come to the farm full of plans for little reforms and improvements, in part the result of training in the newest ways and methods, in part the outcome of her own ideas and fancies. Reforms in the kitchen region, if those deaf old ears could have been induced to give them even a hearing, would have met with short shrift and scornful rejection, and the kitchen region spread over the zone of dairy and market business and half the work of the household. Emma, with the latest science of dead-poultry dressing at her fingertips, sat by, an unheeded watcher, while old Martha trussed the chickens for the market-stall as she had trussed them for nearly four-score years – all leg and no breast. And the hundred hints anent effective cleaning and labour-lightening and the things that make for wholesomeness which the young woman was ready to impart or to put into action dropped away into nothingness before that wan, muttering, unheeding presence. Above all, the coveted window corner, that was to be a dainty, cheerful oasis in the gaunt old kitchen, stood now choked and lumbered with a litter of odds and ends that Emma, for all her nominal authority, would not have dared or cared to displace; over them seemed to be spun the protection of something that was like a human cobweb. Decidedly Martha was in the way. It would have been an unworthy meanness to have wished to see the span of that brave old life shortened by a few paltry months, but as the days sped by Emma was conscious that the wish was there, disowned though it might be, lurking at the back of her mind.

She felt the meanness of the wish come over her with a qualm of self-reproach one day when she came into the kitchen and found an unaccustomed state of things in that usually busy quarter. Old Martha was not working. A basket of corn was on the floor by her side, and out in the yard the poultry were beginning to clamour a protest of overdue feeding-time. But Martha sat huddled in a shrunken bunch on the window-seat, looking out with her dim old eyes as though she saw something stranger than the autumn landscape.

'Is anything the matter, Martha,' asked the young woman.

''Tis death, 'tis death-a-coming,' answered the quavering voice; 'I knew 'twere coming. I knew it. 'Tweren't for nothing that old Shep's been howling all morning. An' last night I heard the screech-owl give the death-cry, and there was something white as run across the yard yesterday; 'tweren't a cat nor a stoat, 'twere something. The fowls knew 'twere something; they all drew off to one side. Ay, there's been warnings. I knew it were a-coming.'

The young woman's eyes clouded with pity. The old thing sitting there so white and shrunken had once been a merry, noisy child, playing about in lanes and hay-lofts and farmhouse garrets; that had been eighty-odd years ago, and now she was just a frail old body cowering under the approaching chill of the death that was coming at last to take her. It was not probable that much could be done for her, but Emma hastened away to get assistance and counsel. Her husband, she knew, was down at a tree-felling some little distance off, but she might find some other intelligent soul who knew the old woman better than she did. The farm, she soon found out, had that faculty common to farmyards of swallowing up and losing its human population. The poultry followed her in interested fashion, and swine grunted interrogations at her from behind the bars of their sties, but barnyard and rickyard, orchard and stables and dairy, gave no reward to her search. Then, as she retraced her steps towards the kitchen, she came suddenly on her cousin, young Mr Jim, as everyone called him, who divided his time between amateur horse-dealing, rabbit-shooting and flirting with the farm maids.

'I'm afraid old Martha is dying,' said Emma. Jim was not the sort of person to whom one had to break news gently.

'Nonsense,' he said; 'Martha means to live to a hundred. She told me so, and she'll do it.'

'She may be actually dying at this moment, or it may just be the beginning of the break-up,' persisted Emma, with a feeling of contempt for the slowness and dullness of the young man.

A grin spread over his good-natured features.

'It don't look like it,' he said, nodding towards the yard. Emma turned to catch the meaning of his remark. Old Martha stood in the middle of a mob of poultry scattering handfuls of grain around her. The turkey-cock, with the bronzed sheen of his feathers and the purple-red of his wattles, the gamecock with the glowing metallic lustre of his Eastern plumage, the hens, with their ochres and buffs and umbers and their scarlet combs, and the drakes, with their bottle-green heads, made a medley of rich colour, in the centre of which the old woman looked like a withered stalk standing amid the riotous growth of gaily hued flowers. But she threw the grain deftly amid the wilderness of beaks, and her quavering voice carried as far as the two people who were watching her. She was still harping on the theme of death coming to the farm.

'I knew 'twere a-coming. There's been signs an' warnings.'

'Who's dead, then, old Mother?' called out the young man.

''Tis young Mister Ladruk,' she shrilled back; 'they've just a-carried his body in. Run out of the way of a tree that was coming down an' ran hisself on to an iron post. Dead when they picked un up. Ay, I knew 'twere coming.'

And she turned to fling a handful of barley at a belated group of guinea-fowl that came racing towards her.

The farm was a family property, and passed to the rabbit-shooting cousin as the next-of-kin. Emma Ladruk drifted out of its history as a bee that had wandered in at an open window might flit its way out again. On a cold grey morning she stood waiting with her boxes already stowed in the farm cart, till the last of the market produce should be ready, for the train she was to catch was of less importance than the chickens and butter and eggs that were to be offered for sale. From where she stood she could see an angle of the long latticed window that was to have been cosy with curtains and gay with bowls of flowers. Into her mind came the thought that for months, perhaps for years, long after she had been utterly forgotten, a white, unheeding face would be seen peering out through those latticed panes, and a weak muttering voice would be heard quavering up and down those flagged passages. She made her way to a narrow barred casement that opened into the farm larder, Old Martha was standing at a table trussing a pair of chickens for the market stall as she had trussed them for nearly four-score years.

A View From a Hill

M.R. JAMES

How pleasant it can be, alone in a first-class railway carriage, on the first day of a holiday that is to be fairly long, to dawdle through a bit of English country that is unfamiliar, stopping at every station. You have a map open on your knee, and you pick out the villages that lie to right and left by their church towers. You marvel at the complete stillness that attends your stoppage at the stations, broken only by a footstep crunching the gravel. Yet perhaps that is best experienced after sundown, and the traveller I have in mind was making his leisurely progress on a sunny afternoon in the latter half of June.

He was in the depths of the country. I need not particularize further than to say that if you divided the map of England into four quarters, he would have been found in the south-western of them.

He was a man of academic pursuits, and his term was just over. He was on his way to meet a new friend, older than himself. The two of them had first met on an official inquiry in town, had found that they had many tastes and habits in common, liked each other, and the result was an invitation from Squire Richards to Mr Fanshawe which was now taking effect.

The journey ended about five o'clock. Fanshawe was told by a cheerful country porter that the car from the Hall had been up to the station and left a message that something had to be fetched

217

from half a mile farther on, and would the gentleman please to wait a few minutes till it came back? 'But I see,' continued the porter, 'as you've got your bysticle, and very like you'd find it pleasanter to ride up to the 'All yourself. Straight up the road 'ere, and then first turn to the left – it ain't above two mile – and I'll see as your things is put in the car for you. You'll excuse me mentioning it, only I thought it were a nice evening for a ride. Yes, sir, very seasonable weather for the haymakers: let me see, I have your bike ticket. Thank you, sir; much obliged: you can't miss your road, etc., etc.'

The two miles to the Hall were just what was needed, after the day in the train, to dispel somnolence and impart a wish for tea. The Hall, when sighted, also promised just what was needed in the way of a quiet resting-place after days of sitting on committees and college-meetings. It was neither excitingly old nor depressingly new. Plastered walls, sash-windows, old trees, smooth lawns, were the features which Fanshawe noticed as he came up the drive. Squire Richards, a burly man of sixty-odd, was awaiting him in the porch with evident pleasure.

'Tea first,' he said, 'or would you like a longer drink? No? All right, tea's ready in the garden. Come along, they'll put your machine away. I always have tea under the lime-tree by the stream on a day like this.'

Nor could you ask for a better place. Midsummer afternoon, shade and scent of a vast lime-tree, cool, swirling water within five yards. It was long before either of them suggested a move. But about six, Mr Richards sat up, knocked out his pipe, and said: 'Look here, it's cool enough now to think of a stroll if you're inclined? All right: then what I suggest is that we walk up the park and get on to the hillside, where we can look over the country. We'll have a map, and I'll show you where things are; and you can go off on your machine, or we can take the car, according as you want exercise or not. If you're ready, we can start now and be back well before eight, taking it very easy.'

'I'm ready. I should like my stick, though, and have you got any field-glasses? I lent mine to a man a week ago, and he's gone off Lord knows where and taken them with him.'

Mr Richards pondered. 'Yes,' he said, 'I have, but they're not things I use myself, and I don't know whether the ones I have will suit you. They're old-fashioned, and about twice as heavy as they make 'em now. You're welcome to have them, but *I* won't carry them. By the way, what do you want to drink after dinner?'

Protestations that anything would do were overruled, and a satisfactory settlement was reached on the way to the front hall, where Mr Fanshawe found his stick, and Mr Richards, after thoughtful pinching of his lower lip, resorted to a drawer in the hall-table, extracted a key, crossed to a cupboard in the panelling, opened it, took a box from the shelf, and put it on the table. 'The glasses are in there,' he said, 'and there's some dodge of opening it, but I've forgotten what it is. You try.'

Mr Fanshawe accordingly tried. There was no keyhole, and the box was solid, heavy and smooth: it seemed obvious that some part of it would have to be pressed before anything could happen. 'The corners,' said he to himself, 'are the likely places; and infernally sharp corners they are too,' he added, as he put his thumb in his mouth after exerting force on a lower corner.

'What's the matter?' said the Squire.

'Why, your disgusting Borgia box has scratched me, drat it,' said Fanshawe. The Squire chuckled unfeelingly. 'Well, you've got it open, anyway,' he said.

'So I have! Well, I don't begrudge a drop of blood in a good cause, and here are the glasses. They *are* pretty heavy, as you said, but I think I'm equal to carrying them.'

'Ready?' said the Squire. 'Come on then, we go out by the garden.'

So they did, and passed out into the park, which sloped decidedly upwards to the hill which, as Fanshawe had seen from the train, dominated the country. It was a spur of a larger range that lay behind. On the way, the Squire, who was great on earthworks, pointed out various spots where he detected or imagined traces of war-ditches and the like. 'And here,' he said, stopping on a more or less level plot with a ring of large trees, 'is Baxter's Roman villa.'

'Baxter?' said Mr Fanshawe.

'I forgot; you don't know about him. He was the old chap I got those glasses from. I believe he made them. He was an old watchmaker down in the village, a great antiquary. My father gave him leave to grub about where he liked; and when he made a find he used to lend him a man or two to help him with the digging. He got a surprising lot of things together, and when he died – I dare say it's ten or fifteen years ago – I bought the whole lot and gave them to the town museum. We'll run in one of these days, and look over them. The glasses came to me with the rest, but of course I kept them. If you look at them, you'll see they're more or less amateur work – the body of them; naturally the lenses weren't his making.'

'Yes, I see they are just the sort of thing that a clever workman in a different line of business might turn out. But I don't see why he made them so heavy. And did Baxter actually find a Roman villa here?'

'Yes, there's a pavement turfed over, where we're standing: it was too rough and plain to be worth taking up, but of course there are drawings of it: and the small things and pottery that turned up were quite good of their kind. An ingenious chap, old Baxter: he seemed to have a quite out-of-the-way instinct for these things. He was invaluable to our archaeologists. He used to shut up his shop for days at a time, and wander off over the district, marking down places, where he scented anything, on the Ordnance map; and he kept a book with fuller notes of the places. Since his death, a good many of them have been sampled, and there's always been something to justify him.'

'What a good man!' said Mr Fanshawe.

'Good?' said the Squire, pulling up brusquely.

'I meant useful to have about the place,' said Mr Fanshawe. 'But was he a villain?'

'I don't know about that either,' said the Squire; 'but all I can say is, if he was good, he wasn't lucky. And he wasn't liked: I didn't like him,' he added, after a moment.

'Oh?' said Fanshawe interrogatively.

'No, I didn't; but that's enough about Baxter: besides, this is the stiffest bit, and I don't want to talk and walk as well.'

Indeed it was hot, climbing a slippery grass slope that evening.

'I told you I should take you the short way,' panted the Squire, 'and I wish I hadn't. However, a bath won't do us any harm when we get back. Here we are, and there's the seat.'

A small clump of old Scots firs crowned the top of the hill; and, at the edge of it, commanding the cream of the view, was a wide and solid seat, on which the two disposed themselves, and wiped their brows, and regained breath.

'Now, then,' said the Squire, as soon as he was in a condition to talk connectedly, 'this is where your glasses come in. But you'd better take a general look round first. My word! I've never seen the view look better.'

Writing as I am now with a winter wind flapping against dark windows and a rushing, tumbling sea within a hundred yards, I find it hard to summon up the feelings and words which will put my reader in possession of the June evening and the lovely English landscape of which the Squire was speaking.

Across a broad level plain they looked upon ranges of great hills, whose uplands – some green, some furred with woods – caught the light of a sun, westering but not yet low. And all the plain was fertile, though the river which traversed it was nowhere seen. There were copses, green wheat, hedges and pasture-land: the little compact white moving cloud marked the evening train. Then the eye picked out red farms and grey houses, and nearer home scattered cottages, and then the Hall, nestled under the hill. The smoke of chimneys was very blue and straight. There was a smell of hay in the air: there were wild roses on bushes hard by. It was the acme of summer.

After some minutes of silent contemplation, the Squire began to point out the leading features, the hills and valleys, and told where the towns and villages lay. 'Now,' he said, 'with the glasses you'll be able to pick out Fulnaker Abbey. Take a line across that big green field, then over the wood beyond it, then over the farm on the knoll.'

'Yes, yes,' said Fanshawe, 'I've got it. What a fine tower!'

'You must have got the wrong direction,' said the Squire; 'there's not much of a tower about there that I remember, unless it's Oldbourne Church that you've got hold of. And if you call that a fine tower, you're easily pleased.'

'Well, I do call it a fine tower,' said Fanshawe, the glasses still at his eyes, 'whether it's Oldbourne or any other. And it must belong to a largish church; it looks to me like a central tower – four big pinnacles at the corners, and four smaller ones between. I must certainly go over there. How far is it?'

'Oldbourne's about nine miles, or less,' said the Squire. 'It's a long time since I've been there, but I don't remember thinking much of it. Now I'll show you another thing.'

Fanshawe had lowered the glasses, and was still gazing in the Oldbourne direction. 'No,' he said, 'I can't make out anything with the naked eye. What was it you were going to show me?'

'A good deal more to the left – it oughtn't to be difficult to find. Do you see a rather sudden knob of a hill with a thick wood on top of it? It's in a dead line with that single tree on the top of the big ridge.'

'I do,' said Fanshawe, 'and I believe I could tell you without much difficulty what it's called.'

'Could you now?' said the Squire. 'Say on.'

'Why, Gallows Hill,' was the answer.

'How did you guess that?'

'Well, if you don't want it guessed, you shouldn't put up a dummy gibbet and a man hanging on it.'

'What's that?' said the Squire abruptly. 'There's nothing on that hill but wood.'

'On the contrary,' said Fanshawe, 'there's a largish expanse of grass on the top and your dummy gibbet in the middle; and I thought there was something on it when I looked first. But I see there's nothing – or is there? I can't be sure.'

'Nonsense, nonsense, Fanshawe, there's no such thing as a dummy gibbet, or any other sort, on that hill. And it's thick wood – a fairly young plantation. I was in it myself not a year ago. Hand me the glasses, though I don't suppose I can see anything.' After a pause: 'No, I thought not: they won't show a thing.'

Meanwhile Fanshawe was scanning the hill – it might be only two or three miles away. 'Well, it's very odd,' he said, 'it does look exactly like a wood without the glass.' He took it again. 'That *is* one of the oddest effects. The gibbet is perfectly plain, and the grass field, and there even seem to be people on it, and carts, or *a* cart, with men in it. And yet when I take the glass away, there's nothing. It must be something in the way this afternoon light falls: I shall come up earlier in the day when the sun's full on it.'

'Did you say you saw people and a cart on that hill?' said the Squire incredulously. 'What should they be doing there at this time of day, even if the trees have been felled? Do talk sense – look again.'

'Well, I certainly thought I saw them. Yes, I should say there were a few, just clearing off. And now – by Jove, it does look like something hanging on the gibbet. But these glasses are so beastly heavy I can't hold them steady for long. Anyhow, you can take it from me there's no wood. And if you'll show me the road on the map, I'll go there tomorrow.'

The Squire remained brooding for some little time. At last he rose and said, 'Well, I suppose that will be the best way to settle it. And now we'd better be getting back. Bath and dinner is my idea.' And on the way back he was not very communicative.

They returned through the garden, and went into the front hall to leave sticks, etc., in their due place. And here they found the aged butler Patten evidently in a state of some anxiety. 'Beg pardon, Master Henry,' he began at once, 'but someone's been up to mischief here, I'm much afraid.' He pointed to the open box which had contained the glasses.

'Nothing worse than that, Patten?' said the Squire. 'Mayn't I take out my own glasses and lend them to a friend? Bought with my own money, you recollect? At old Baxter's sale, eh?'

Patten bowed, unconvinced. 'Oh, very well, Master Henry, as long as you know who it was. Only I thought proper to name it, for I didn't think that box'd been off its shelf since you first put it there; and, if you'll excuse me, after what happened . . .' The voice was lowered, and the rest was not audible to Fanshawe. The Squire replied with a few words and a gruff laugh, and called on Fanshawe to come and be shown his room. And I do not think that anything else happened that night which bears on my story.

Except, perhaps, the sensation which invaded Fanshawe in the small hours that something had been let out which ought not to have been let out. It came into his dreams. He was walking in a garden which he seemed half to know, and stopped in front of a rockery made of old wrought stones, pieces of window tracery from a church, and even bits of figures. One of these moved his curiosity: it seemed to be a sculptured capital with scenes carved on it. He felt he must pull it out, and worked away, and, with an ease that surprised him, moved the stones that obscured it aside, and pulled out the block. As he did so, a tin label fell down by his feet with a little clatter. He picked it up and read on it: 'On no account move this stone. Yours sincerely, J. Patten.' As often happens in dreams, he felt that this injunction was of extreme importance; and with an anxiety that amounted to anguish he looked to see if the stone had really been shifted. Indeed it had; in fact, he could not see it anywhere. The removal had disclosed the mouth of a burrow, and he bent down to look into it. Something stirred in the blackness, and then, to his intense horror, a hand emerged – a clean right hand in a neat cuff and coat-sleeve, just in the attitude of a hand that means to shake yours. He wondered whether it would not be rude to let it alone. But, as he looked at it, it began to grow hairy and dirty and thin, and also to change its pose and stretch out as if to take hold of his leg. At that he dropped all thought of politeness, decided to run, screamed and woke himself up.

This was the dream he remembered; but it seemed to him (as, again, it often does) that there had been others of the same import before, but not so insistent. He lay awake for some little time, fixing the details of the last dream in his mind, and wondering in particular what the figures had been which he had seen or half seen on the carved capital. Something quite incongruous, he felt sure; but that was the most he could recall.

Whether because of the dream, or because it was the first day of his holiday, he did not get up very early; nor did he at once plunge into the exploration of the country. He spent a morning, half lazy, half instructive, in looking over the volumes of the

County Archaeological Society's transactions, in which were many contributions from Mr Baxter on finds of flint implements, Roman sites, ruins of monastic establishments – in fact, most departments of archaeology. They were written in an odd, pompous, only half-educated style. If the man had had more early schooling, thought Fanshawe, he would have been a very distinguished antiquary; or he might have been (he thus qualified his opinion a little later), but for a certain love of opposition and controversy, and, yes, a patronizing tone as of one possessing superior knowledge, which left an unpleasant taste. He might have been a very respectable artist. There was an imaginary restoration and elevation of a priory church which was very well conceived. A fine pinnacled central tower was a conspicuous feature of this; it reminded Fanshawe of that which he had seen from the hill, and which the Squire had told him must be Oldbourne. But it was not Oldbourne; it was Fulnaker Priory. 'Oh, well,' he said to himself, 'I suppose Oldbourne Church may have been built by Fulnaker monks, and Baxter had copied Oldbourne tower. Anything about it in the letterpress? Ah, I see it was published after his death – found among his papers.'

After lunch the Squire asked Fanshawe what he meant to do.

'Well,' said Fanshawe, 'I think I shall go out on my bike about four as far as Oldbourne and back by Gallows Hill. That ought to be a round trip of about fifteen miles, oughtn't it?'

'About that,' said the Squire, 'and you'll pass Lambsfield and Wanstone, both of which are worth looking at. There's a little stained glass at Lambsfield and the stone at Wanstone.'

'Good,' said Fanshawe, 'I'll get tea somewhere, and may I take the glasses? I'll strap them on my bike, on the carrier.'

'Of course, if you like,' said the Squire. 'I really ought to have some better ones. If I go into the town today, I'll see if I can pick up some.'

'Why should you trouble to do that if you can't use them yourself?' said Fanshawe.

'Oh, I don't know; one ought to have a decent pair; and – well, old Patten doesn't think those are fit to use.'

'Is he a judge?'

'He's got some tale: I don't know: something about old Baxter. I've promised to let him tell me about it. It seems very much on his mind since last night.'

'Why? Did he have a nightmare like me?'

'He had something: he was looking like an old man this morning, and he said he hadn't closed an eye.'

'Well, let him save up his tale till I come back.'

'Very well, I will if I can. Look here, are you going to be late? If you get a puncture eight miles off and have to walk home, what then? I don't trust these bicycles: I shall tell them to give us cold things to eat.'

'I shan't mind that, whether I'm late or early. But I've got things to mend punctures with. And now I'm off.'

It was just as well that the Squire had made that arrangement about a cold supper, Fanshawe thought, and not for the first time, as he wheeled his bicycle up the drive at about nine o'clock. So also the Squire thought and said, several times, as he met him in the hall, rather pleased at the confirmation of his want of faith in bicycles than sympathetic with his hot, weary, thirsty, and indeed haggard, friend. In fact, the kindest thing he found to say was: 'You'll want a long drink tonight? Cider-cup do? All right. Hear that, Patten? Cider-cup, iced, lots of it.' Then to Fanshawe, 'Don't be all night over your bath.'

By half-past nine they were at dinner, and Fanshawe was reporting progress, if progress it might be called.

'I got to Lambsfield very smoothly, and saw the glass. It is very interesting stuff, but there's a lot of lettering I couldn't read.'

'Not with glasses?' said the Squire.

'Those glasses of yours are no manner of use inside a church – or inside anywhere, I suppose, for that matter. But the only places I took 'em into were churches.'

'H'm! Well, go on,' said the Squire.

'However, I took some sort of a photograph of the window, and I dare say an enlargement would show what I want. Then Wanstone; I should think that stone was a very out-of-the-way thing, only I don't know about that class of antiquities. Has

226

anybody opened the mound it stands on?'

'Baxter wanted to, but the farmer wouldn't let him.'

'Oh, well, I should think it would be worth doing. Anyhow, the next thing was Fulnaker and Oldbourne. You know, it's very odd about that tower I saw from the hill. Oldbourne Church is nothing like it, and of course there's nothing over thirty feet high at Fulnaker, though you can see it had a central tower. I didn't tell you, did I? that Baxter's fancy drawing of Fulnaker shows a tower exactly like the one I saw.'

'So you thought, I dare say,' put in the Squire.

'No, it wasn't a case of thinking. The picture actually *reminded* me of what I'd seen, and I made sure it was Oldbourne, well before I looked at the title.'

'Well, Baxter had a very fair idea of architecture. I dare say what's left made it easy for him to draw the right sort of tower.'

'That may be it, of course, but I'm doubtful if even a professional could have got it so exactly right. There's absolutely nothing left at Fulnaker but the bases of the piers which supported it. However, that isn't the oddest thing.'

'What about Gallows Hill?' said the Squire. 'Here, Patten, listen to this. I told you what Mr Fanshawe said he saw from the hill.'

'Yes, Master Henry, you did; and I can't say I was so much surprised, considering.'

'All right, all right. You keep that till afterwards. We want to hear what Mr Fanshawe saw today. Go on, Fanshawe. You turned to come back by Ackford and Thorfield, I suppose?'

'Yes, and I looked into both the churches. Then I got to the turning which goes to the top of Gallows Hill; I saw that if I wheeled my machine over the field at the top of the hill I could join the home road on this side. It was about half-past six when I got to the top of the hill, and there was a gate on my right, where it ought to be, leading into the belt of plantation.'

'You hear that, Patten? A belt, he says.'

'So I thought it was – a belt. But it wasn't. You were quite right, and I was hopelessly wrong. I *cannot* understand it. The whole top is planted quite thick. Well, I went on into this wood, wheeling and dragging my bike, expecting every minute to come to a clearing, and then my misfortunes began. Thorns, I suppose; first I realized that the front tyre was slack, then the back. I couldn't stop to do more than try to find the punctures and mark them; but even that was hopeless. So I ploughed on, and the farther I went, the less I liked the place.'

'Not much poaching in that cover, eh, Patten?' said the Squire.

'No, indeed, Master Henry: there's very few cares to go—'

'No, I know: never mind that now. Go on, Fanshawe.'

'I don't blame anybody for not caring to go there. I know I had all the fancies one least likes: steps crackling over twigs behind me, indistinct people stepping behind trees in front of me, yes, and even a hand laid on my shoulder. I pulled up very sharp at that and looked round, but there really was no branch or bush that could have done it. Then, when I was just about at the middle of the plot, I was convinced that there was someone looking down on me from above – and not with any pleasant intent. I stopped again, or at least slackened my pace, to look up. And as I did, down I came, and barked my shins abominably on, what do you think? a block of stone with a big square hole in the top of it. And within a few paces there were two others just like it. The three were set in a triangle. Now, can you make out what they were put there for?'

'I think I can,' said the Squire, who was now very grave and absorbed in the story. 'Sit down, Patten.'

It was just in time, for the old man was supporting himself by one hand, and leaning heavily on it. He dropped into a chair, and said in a very tremulous voice, 'You didn't go between them stones, did you, sir?'

'I did *not*,' said Fanshawe, emphatically. 'I dare say I was an ass, but as soon as it dawned on me where I was, I just shouldered my machine and did my best to run. It seemed to me as if I was in an unholy evil sort of graveyard, and I was most profoundly thankful that it was one of the longest days and still sunlight. Well, I had a horrid run, even if it was only a few hundred yards. Everything caught on everything: handles and spokes and carrier and pedals – caught in them viciously, or I fancied so. I fell over at least five times. At last I saw the hedge, and I couldn't trouble to hunt for the gate.'

'There *is* no gate on my side,' the Squire interpolated.

'Just as well I didn't waste time, then. I dropped the machine over somehow and went into the road pretty near head-first; some branch or something got my ankle at the last moment. Anyhow, there I was out of the wood, and seldom more thankful or more generally sore. Then came the job of mending my punctures. I had a good outfit and I'm not at all bad at the business; but this was an absolutely hopeless case. It was seven when I got out of the wood, and I spent fifty minutes over one tyre. As fast as I found a hole and put on a patch, and blew it up, it went flat again. So I made up my mind to walk. That hill isn't three miles away, is it?'

'Not more across country, but nearer six by road.'

'I thought it must be. I thought I couldn't have taken well over an hour over less than five miles, even leading a bike. Well, there's my story: where's yours and Patten's?'

'Mine? I've no story,' said the Squire. 'But you weren't very far out when you thought you were in a graveyard. There must be a good few of them up there, Patten, don't you think? They left 'em there when they fell to bits, I fancy.'

Patten nodded, too much interested to speak.

'Now then, Patten,' said the Squire, 'you've heard what sort of a time Mr Fanshawe's been having. What do you make of it? Anything to do with Mr Baxter? Fill yourself a glass of port, and tell us.'

'Ah, that done me good, Master Henry,' said Patten, after absorbing what was before him. 'If you really wish to know what were in my thoughts, my answer would be clear in the affirmative. Yes,' he went on, warming to his work, 'I should say as Mr Fanshawe's experiences of today were very largely doo to the person you named. And I think, Master Henry, as I have some title to speak, in view of me 'aving been many years on speaking terms with him, and swore in to be jury on the Coroner's inquest near this time ten years ago, you being then, if you carry your mind back, Master Henry, travelling abroad, and no one 'ere to represent the family.'

'Inquest?' said Fanshawe. 'An inquest on Mr Baxter, was there?'

'Yes, sir, on – on that very person. The facts as led up to that occurrence was these. The deceased was, as you may have gathered, a very peculiar individual in 'is 'abits – in my idear, at least, but all must speak as they find. He lived very much to himself, without neither chick nor child, as the saying is. And how he passed away his time was what very few could orfer a guess at.'

'He lived unknown, and few could know when Baxter ceased to be,' said the Squire to his pipe.

'I beg pardon, Master Henry, I was just coming to that. But when I say how he passed away his time – to be sure we know 'ow intent he was in rummaging and ransacking out all the 'istry of the neighbourhood and the number of things he'd managed to collect together – well, it was spoke of for miles round as Baxter's Museum, and many a time when he might be in the mood, and I might have an hour to spare, have he showed me his pieces of pots and what-not, going back by his account to the times of the ancient Romans. However, you know more about that than what I do, Master Henry: only what I was a-going to say was this, as know what he might and interesting as he might be in his talk, there was something about the man – well, for one thing, no one ever remember to see him in church nor yet chapel at service-time. And that made talk. Our rector he never come in the house but once. "Never ask me what the man said"; that was all anybody could ever get out of *him*. Then how did he spend his nights, particularly about this season of the year? Time and again the labouring men'd meet him coming back as they went out to their work, and he'd pass 'em by without a word, looking, they says, like someone straight out of the asylum. They'd see the whites of his eyes all round. He'd have a fish-basket with him, that they noticed, and he always come the same road. And the talk got to be that he'd made himself some business, and that not the best kind – well, not so far from where you was at seven o'clock this evening, sir.

'Well, now, after such a night as that, Mr Baxter he'd shut up the shop, and the old lady that did for him had orders not to come in; and knowing what she did about his language, she took care to obey them orders. But one day it so happened, about three o'clock in the afternoon, the house being shut up as I said, there come a most fearful to-do inside, and smoke out of the windows, and Baxter crying out seemingly in an agony. So the man as lived next door he run round to the back premises and burst the door in, and several others come too. Well, he tell me he never in all his life smelt such a fearful – well, odour, as what there was in that kitchen-place. It seem as if Baxter had been boiling something in a pot and overset it on his leg. There he laid on the floor, trying to keep back the cries, but it was more than he could manage, and when he seen the people come in – oh, he was in a nice condition: if his tongue warn't blistered worse than his leg it warn't his fault. Well, they picked him up, and got him into a chair, and run for the medical man, and one of 'em was going to pick up the pot, and Baxter, he screams out to let it alone. So he did, but he couldn't see as there was anything in the pot but a few old brown bones. Then they says 'Dr Lawrence'll be here in a minute, Mr Baxter; he'll soon put you to rights.' And then he was off again. He must be got up to his room, he couldn't have the doctor come in there and see all that mess – they must throw a cloth over it – anything – the tablecloth out of the parlour; well, so they did. But that must have been poisonous stuff in that pot, for it was pretty near on two months before Baxter were about agin. Beg pardon, Master Henry, was you going to say something?'

'Yes, I was,' said the Squire. 'I wonder you haven't told me all this before. However, I was going to say I remember old Lawrence telling me he'd attended Baxter. He was a queer card, he said. Lawrence was up in the bedroom one day, and picked up a little mask covered with black velvet, and put it on in fun and went to look at himself in the glass. He hadn't time for a proper look, for old Baxter shouted out to him from the bed: "Put it down, you fool! Do you want to look through a dead man's eyes?" and it startled him so that he did put it down, and then he asked Baxter what he meant. And Baxter insisted on him handing it over, and said the man he bought it from was dead, or some such nonsense. But Lawrence felt it as he handed it over, and he declared he was sure it was made out of the front of a skull. He bought a distilling apparatus at Baxter's sale, he told me, but he could never use it: it seemed to taint everything, however much he cleaned it. But go on, Patten.'

'Yes, Master Henry, I'm nearly done now, and about time, too, for I don't know what they'll think about me in the servants' 'all. Well, this business of the scalding was some few years before Mr Baxter was took, and he got about again, and went on just as he'd used. And one of the last jobs he done was finishing up them actual glasses what you took out last night. You see he'd made the body of them some long time, and got the pieces of glass for them, but there was somethink wanted to finish 'em, whatever it was, I don't know, but I picked up the frame one day, and I says: "Mr Baxter, why don't you make a job of this?" And he says, "Ah, when I've done that, you'll hear news, you will: there's going to be no such pair of glasses as mine when they're filled and sealed," and there he stopped, and I says: "Why, Mr Baxter, you talk as if they was wine bottles: filled and sealed – why, where's the necessity for that?" "Did I say filled and sealed?" he says. "O, well, I was suiting my conversation to my company." Well, then come round this time of year, and one fine evening, I was passing his shop on my way home, and he was standing on the step, very pleased with hisself, and he says: "All right and tight now: my best bit of work's finished, and I'll be out with 'em tomorrow." "What, finished them glasses?" I says, "might I have a look at them?" "No, no," he says, "I've put 'em to bed for tonight, and when I do show 'em you, you'll have to pay for peepin', so I tell you." And that, gentlemen, were the last words I heard that man say.

'That were the 17th of June, and just a week after, there was a funny thing happened, and it was doo to that as we brought in "unsound mind" at the inquest, for barring that, no one as knew

Baxter in business could anyways have laid that against him. But George Williams, as lived in the next house, and do now, he was woke up that same night with a stumbling and tumbling about in Mr Baxter's premises, and he got out o' bed, and went to the front window on the street to see if there was any rough customers about. And it being a very light night, he could make sure as there was not. Then he stood and listened, and he hear Mr Baxter coming down his front stair one step after another very slow, and he got the idear as it was like someone bein' pushed or pulled down and holdin' on to everythin' he could. Next thing he hear the street door come open, and out come Mr Baxter into the street in his day-clothes, 'at and all, with his arms straight down by his sides, and talking to hisself, and shakin' his head from one side to the other, and walking in a peculiar way that he appeared to be going as it were against his own will. George Williams put up the window, and hear him say: "Oh mercy, gentlemen!" and then he shut up sudden as if, he said, someone clapped his hand over his mouth, and Mr Baxter threw his head back, and his hat fell off. And Williams see his face looking something pitiful, so as he couldn't keep from calling out to him: "Why, Mr Baxter, ain't you well?" and he was goin' to offer to fetch Dr Lawrence to him, only he heard the answer: "'Tis best you mind your own business. Put in your head." But whether it were Mr Baxter said it so hoarse-like and faint, he never could be sure. Still there weren't no one but him in the street, and yet Williams was that upset by the way he spoke that he shrank back from the window and went and sat on the bed. And he heard Mr Baxter's step go on and up the road, and after a minute or more he couldn't help but look out once more and he seen him going along the same curious way as before. And one thing he recollected was that Mr Baxter never stopped to pick up his 'at when it fell off, and yet there it was on his head. Well, Master Henry, that was the last anybody see of Mr Baxter, leastways for a week or more. There was a lot of people said he was called off on business, or made off because he'd got into some scrape, but he was well known for miles round, and none of the railway-people not the public-house people hadn't seen him;

and then ponds was looked into and nothink found; and at last one evening Fakes the keeper come down from over the hill to the village, and he says he seen the Gallows Hill planting black with birds, and that were a funny thing, because he never seen no sign of a creature there in his time. So they looked at each other a bit, and first one says: "I'm game to go up," and another says: "So am I, if you are," and half a dozen of 'em set out in the evening time, and took Dr Lawrence with them, and you know, Master Henry, there he was between them three stones with his neck broke.'

Useless to imagine the talk which this story set going. It is not remembered. But before Patten left them, he said to Fanshawe: 'Excuse me, sir, but did I understand as you took out them glasses with you today? I thought you did; and might I ask, did you make use of them at all?'

'Yes. Only to look at something in a church.'

'Oh, indeed, you took 'em into the church, did you, sir?'

'Yes, I did; it was Lambsfield Church. By the way, I left them strapped on to my bicycle, I'm afraid, in the stable-yard.'

'No matter for that, sir. I can bring them in the first thing tomorrow, and perhaps you'll be so good as to look at 'em then.'

Accordingly, before breakfast, after a tranquil and well-earned sleep, Fanshawe took the glasses into the garden and directed them to a distant hill. He lowered them instantly, and looked at top and bottom, worked the screws, tried them again and yet again, shrugged his shoulders and replaced them on the hall-table.

'Patten,' he said, 'they're absolutely useless. I can't see a thing: it's as if someone had stuck a black wafer over the lens.'

'Spoilt my glasses, have you?' said the Squire. 'Thank you: the only ones I've got.'

'You try them yourself,' said Fanshawe, 'I've done nothing to them.'

So after breakfast the Squire took them out to the terrace and stood on the steps. After a few ineffectual attempts, 'Lord, how heavy they are!' he said impatiently, and in the same instant dropped them on the stones, and the lens splintered and the barrel cracked: a little pool of liquid formed on the stone slab. It was inky black, and the odour that rose from it is not to be described.

'Filled and sealed, eh?' said the Squire. 'If I could bring myself to touch it, I dare say we should find the seal. So that's what came of his boiling and distilling, is it? Old Ghoul!'

'What in the world do you mean?'

'Don't you see, my good man? Remember what he said to the doctor about looking through dead men's eyes? Well, this was another way of it. But they didn't like having their bones boiled, I take it, and the end of it was they carried him off whither he would not. Well, I'll get a spade, and we'll bury this thing decently.'

As they smoothed the turf over it, the Squire, handing the spade to Patten, who had been a reverential spectator, remarked to Fanshawe: 'It's almost a pity you took that thing into the church: you might have seen more than you did. Baxter had them for a week, I make out, but I don't see that he did much in the time.'

'I'm not sure,' said Fanshawe, 'there is that picture of Fulnaker Priory Church.'

The Enemies

DYLAN THOMAS

It was morning in the green acres of the Jarvis valley, and Mr
Owen was picking the weeds from the edges of his garden path.
A great wind pulled at his beard, the vegetable world roared
under his feet. A rook had lost itself in the sky, and was making a
noise to its mate; but the mate never came, and the rook flew into
the west with a woe in its beak. Mr Owen, who had stood up to
ease his shoulders and look at the sky, observed how dark the
wings beat against the red sun. In her draughty kitchen Mrs
Owen grieved over the soup. Once, in past days, the valley had
housed the cattle alone; the farm-boys came down from the hills
to holla at the cattle and to drive them to be milked; but no
stranger set foot in the valley. Mr Owen, walking lonely through
the country, had come upon it at the end of a late summer
evening when the cattle were lying down still, and the stream
that divided it was speaking over the pebbles. Here, thought Mr
Owen, I will build a small house with one storey, in the middle of
the valley, set around by a garden. And, remembering clearly the
way he had come along the winding hills, he returned to his
village and the questions of Mrs Owen. So it came about that a
house with one storey was built in the green fields; a garden was
dug and planted, and a low fence put up around the garden to
keep the cows from the vegetables.

That was early in the year. Now summer and autumn had gone

over; the garden had blossomed and died; there was frost at the weeds. Mr Owen bent down again, tidying the path, while the wind blew back the heads of the nearby grasses and made an oracle of each green mouth. Patiently he strangled the weeds; up came the roots, making war in the soil around them; insects were busy in the holes where the weeds had sprouted, but, dying between his fingers, they left no stain. He grew tired of their death, and tireder of the fall of the weeds. Up came the roots, down went the cheap, green heads.

Mrs Owen, peering into the depths of her crystal, had left the soup to bubble on unaided. The ball grew dark, then lightened as a rainbow moved within it. Growing hot like a sun, and cooling again like an arctic star, it shone in the folds of her dress where she held it lovingly. The tea leaves in her cup at breakfast had told of a dark stranger. What would the crystal tell her? Mrs Owen wondered.

Up came the roots, and a crooked worm, disturbed by the probing of the fingers, wriggled blind in the sun. Of a sudden the valley filled all its hollows with the wind, with the voice of the roots, with the breathing of the nether sky. Not only a mandrake screams; torn roots have their cries; each weed Mr Owen pulled out of the ground screamed like a baby. In the village behind the hill the wind would be raging, the clothes on the garden lines would be set to strange dances. And women with shapes in their wombs would feel a new knocking as they bent over the steamy tubs. Life would go on in their veins, in the bones, the binding flesh, that had their seasons and their weathers even as the valley binding the house about with the flesh of the green grass.

The ball, like an open grave, gave up its dead to Mrs Owen. She stared on the lips of women and the hairs of men that wound into a pattern on the face of the crystal world. But suddenly the patterns were swept away, and she could see nothing but the shapes of the Jarvis hills. A man with a black hat was walking down the paths into the invisible valley beneath. If he walked any nearer he would fall into her lap. 'There's a man with a black hat walking on the hills,' she called through the window. Mr Owen smiled and went on weeding.

It was at this time that the Reverend Mr Davies lost his way; he had been losing it most of the morning, but now he had lost it altogether, and stood perturbed under a tree on the rim of the Jarvis hills. A great wind blew through the branches, and a great grey-green earth moved unsteadily beneath him. Wherever he looked the hills stormed up to the sky, and wherever he sought to hide from the wind he was frightened by the darkness. The farther he walked, the stranger was the scenery around him; it rose to undreamed-of heights, and then fell down again into a valley no bigger than the palm of his hand. And the trees walked like men. By a divine coincidence he reached the rim of the hills just as the sun reached the centre of the sky. With the wide world rocking from horizon to horizon, he stood under a tree and looked down into the valley. In the fields was a little house with a garden. The valley roared around it, the wind leapt at it like a boxer, but the house stood still. To Mr Davies it seemed as though the house had been carried out of a village by a large bird and placed in the very middle of the tumultuous universe.

But as he climbed over the craggy edges and down the side of the hill, he lost his place in Mrs Owen's crystal. A cloud displaced his black hat, and under the cloud walked a very old phantom, a shape of air with stars all frozen in its beard, and a half-moon for a smile. Mr Davies knew nothing of this as the stones scratched his hands. He was old, he was drunk with the wine of the morning, but the stuff that came out of his cuts was a human blood.

Nor did Mr Owen, with his face near the soil and his hands on the necks of the screaming weeds, know of the transformation in the crystal. He had heard Mrs Owen prophesy the coming of the black hat, and had smiled as he always smiled at her faith in the powers of darkness. He had looked up when she called, and, smiling, had returned to the clearer call of the ground. 'Multiply, multiply,' he had said to the worms disturbed in their channelling, and had cut the brown worms in half so that the halves might breed and spread their life over the garden and go out, contaminating, into the fields and the bellies of the cattle.

Of this Mr Davies knew nothing. He saw a young man with a

beard bent industriously over the garden soil; he saw that the house was a pretty picture, with the face of a pale young woman pressed up against the window. And, removing his black hat, he introduced himself as the rector of a village some ten miles away.

'You are bleeding,' said Mr Owen.

Mr Davies's hands, indeed, were covered in blood.

When Mrs Owen had seen to the rector's cuts, she sat him down in the armchair near the window, and made him a strong cup of tea.

'I saw you on the hill,' she said and he asked her how she had seen him, for the hills are high and a long way off.

'I have good eyes,' she answered.

He did not doubt her. Her eyes were the strangest he had seen.

'It is quiet here,' said Mr Davies.

'We have no clock,' she said, and laid the table for three.

'You are very kind.'

'We are kind to those that come to us.'

He wondered how many came to the lonely house in the valley, but did not question her for fear of what she would reply. He guessed she was an uncanny woman loving the dark because it was dark. He was too old to question the secrets of darkness, and now, with the black suit torn and wet and his thin hands bound with the bandages of the stranger woman, he felt older than ever. The winds of the morning might blow him down, and the sudden dropping of the dark be blind in his eyes. Rain might pass through him as it passes through the body of a ghost. A tired, white-haired old man, he sat under the window, almost invisible against the panes and the white cloth of the chair.

Soon the meal was ready, and Mr Owen came in unwashed from the garden.

'Shall I say grace?' asked Mr Davies when all three were seated around the table.

Mrs Owen nodded.

'O Lord God Almighty, bless this our meal,' said Mr Davies. Looking up as he continued his prayer, he saw that Mr and Mrs Owen had closed their eyes. 'We thank Thee for the bounties that Thou hast given us.' And he saw that the lips of Mr and Mrs

Owen were moving softly. He could not hear what they said, but he knew that the prayers they spoke were not his prayers.

'Amen,' said all three together.

Mr Owen, proud in his eating, bent over the plate as he had bent over the complaining weed. Outside the window was the brown body of the earth, the green skin of the grass, and the breasts of the Jarvis hills; there was a wind that chilled the animal earth, and a sun that had drunk up the dews on the fields; there was creation sweating out of the pores of the trees; and the grains of sand on far-away seashores would be multiplying as the sea rolled over them. He felt the coarse foods on his tongue; there was a meaning in the rind of the meat, and a purpose in the lifting of food to mouth. He saw, with a sudden satisfaction, that Mrs Owen's throat was bare.

She, too, was bent over her plate, but was letting the teeth of her fork nibble at the corners of it. She did not eat, for the old powers were upon her, and she dared not lift up her head for the greenness of her eyes. She knew by the sound which way the wind blew in the valley; she knew the stage of the sun by the curve of the shadows on the cloth. Oh, that she could take her crystal, and see within it the stretches of darkness gathering in her mind, drawing in the light around her. There was a ghost on her left; with all her strength she drew in the intangible light that moved around him, and mixed it in her dark brains.

Mr Davies, like a man sucked by a bird, felt desolation in his veins, and, in a sweet delirium, told of his adventures on the hills, of how it had been cold and blowing, and how the hills went up and down. He had been lost, he said, and had found a dark retreat to shelter from the bullies in the wind; but the darkness had frightened him, and he had walked again on the hills where the morning tossed him about like a ship on the sea. Wherever he went he was blown in the open or frightened in the narrow shades. There was nowhere, he said pityingly, for an old man to go. Loving his parish, he had loved the surrounding lands, but the hills had given under his feet or plunged him into the air. And, loving his God, he had loved the darkness where men of old had worshipped the dark invisible. But now the hill caves were full of shapes and voices that mocked him because he was old.

'He is frightened of the dark,' thought Mrs Owen, 'the lovely dark.' With a smile, Mr Owen thought: 'He is frightened of the worm in the earth, of the copulation in the tree, of the living grease in the soil.' They looked at the old man, and saw that he was more ghostly than ever. The window behind him cast a ragged circle of light round his head.

Suddenly Mr Davies knelt down to pray. He did not understand the cold in his heart nor the fear that bewildered him as he knelt, but, speaking his prayers for deliverance, he stared up at the shadowed eyes of Mrs Owen and at the smiling eyes of her husband. Kneeling on the carpet at the head of the table, he stared in bewilderment at the dark mind and the gross dark body. He stared and he prayed, like an old god beset by his enemies.

Aunt Deborah

MARY RUSSELL MITFORD

A crosser old woman than Mrs Deborah Thornby was certainly not to be found in the whole village of Hilton. Worth, in country phrase, a power of money, and living (to borrow another rustic expression) upon her means, the exercise of her extraordinary faculty for grumbling and scolding seemed the sole occupation of her existence, her only pursuit, solace, and amusement; and really it would have been a great pity to have deprived the poor woman of a pastime so consolatory to herself, and which did harm to nobody: her family consisting only of an old labourer, to guard the house, take care of her horse, her cow, and her chaise and cart, and work in the garden, who was happily, for his comfort, stone deaf, and could not hear her vituperation; and of a parish girl of twelve, to do the indoor work, who had been so used to be scolded all her life, that she minded the noise no more than a miller minds the clack of his mill, or than people who live in a churchyard mind the sound of the church bells, and would probably, from long habit, have felt some miss of the sound had it ceased, of which, by the way, there was small danger, so long as Mrs Deborah continued in this life. Her crossness was so far innocent that it hurt nobody except herself. But she was also cross-grained, and that evil quality is unluckily apt to injure other people; and did so very materially in the present instance.

Mrs Deborah was the only daughter of old Simon Thornby, of

Chalcott great farm; she had had one brother, who having married the rosy-cheeked daughter of the parish clerk, a girl with no portion except her modesty, her good-nature and her prettiness, had been discarded by his father, and after trying various ways to gain a living, and failing in all, had finally died broken-hearted, leaving the unfortunate clerk's daughter, rosy-cheeked no longer, and one little boy, to the tender mercy of his family. Old Simon showed none. He drove his son's widow from the door as he had before driven off his son; and when he also died, an event which occurred within a year or two, bequeathed all his property to his daughter Deborah.

This bequest was exceedingly agreeable to Mrs Deborah (for she was already of an age to assume that title), who valued money, not certainly for the comforts and luxuries which it may be the means of procuring, nor even for its own sake, as the phrase goes, but for that which, to a woman of her temper, was perhaps the highest that she was capable of enjoying: the power which wealth confers over all who are connected with or dependent on its possessor.

The principal subjects of her despotic dominion were the young widow and her boy, whom she placed in a cottage near her own house, and with whose comfort and happiness she dallied pretty much as a cat plays with the mouse which she has got into her clutches, and lets go only to catch again, or an angler with the trout which he has fairly hooked, and merely suffers to struggle in the stream until it is sufficiently exhausted to bring to land. She did not mean to be cruel, but she could not help it; so poor mice were mocked with the semblance of liberty, although surrounded by restraint; and the awful paw seemingly sheathed in velvet, whilst they were in reality never out of reach of the horrors of the pat.

It sometimes, however, happens that the little mouse makes her escape from Madam Pussy at the very moment when she seems to have the unlucky trembler actually within her claws; and so it occurred in the present instance.

The dwelling to which Mrs Deborah retired after the death of her father, was exceedingly romantic and beautiful in point of situation. It was a small but picturesque farmhouse, on the very banks of the Loddon, a small branch of which, diverging from the parent stream, and crossed by a pretty footbridge, swept round the homestead, the orchard and garden, and went winding along the water meadows in a thousand glittering meanders, until it was lost in the rich woodlands which formed the background of the picture. In the month of May, when the orchard was full of its rosy and pearly blossoms, a forest of lovely bloom, the meadows yellow with cowslips, and the clear brimming river, bordered by the golden tufts of the water ranunculus, and garlanded by the snowy flowers of the hawthorn and the wild cherry, the thin wreath of smoke curling from the tall, old-fashioned chimneys of the pretty irregular building, with its porch and its bay-windows, and gable-ends full of light and shadow – in that month of beauty it would be difficult to imagine a more beautiful or a more English landscape.

On the other side of the narrow winding road parted from Mrs Deborah's demesne by a long, low bridge of many arches, stood a little rustic mill, and its small low-browed cottage, with its own varied background of garden and fruit trees, and thickly wooded meadows, extending in long perspective, a smiling verdant valley of many miles.

Now Chalcott mill, reckoned by everybody else the prettiest point in her prospect, was to Mrs Deborah not merely an eye-sore, but a heart-sore, not on its own account; cantankerous as she was, she had no quarrel with the innocent buildings, but for the sake of its inhabitants.

Honest John Stokes, the miller, was her cousin-german. People did say, that some forty years before there had been question of a marriage between the parties; and really they both denied the thing with so much vehemence and fury, that one should almost be tempted to believe there was some truth in the report. Certain it is, that if they had been that wretched thing a mismatched couple, and had gone on snarling together all their lives, they could not have hated each other more zealously. One shall not often meet with anything so perfect in its way as that aversion. It was none of your silent hatreds that never come to words; nor of your civil hatreds, that veil themselves under smooth phrases and smiling looks. Their ill-will was frank, open, and above-board. They could not afford to come to an absolute breach, because it would have deprived them of the pleasure of quarrelling; and in spite of the frequent complaints they were wont to make of their near neighbourhood, I am convinced that they derived no small gratification from the opportunities which it afforded them of saying disagreeable things to each other.

And yet Mr John Stokes was a well-meaning man, and Mrs Deborah Thornby was not an ill-meaning woman. But she was, as I have said before, cross in the grain; and he – why he was one of those plain-dealing personages who will speak their whole mind, and who pique themselves upon that sort of sincerity which is comprised in telling to another all the ill that they have ever heard, or thought, or imagined, concerning him; in repeating, as if it were a point of duty, all the harm that one neighbour says of another, and in denouncing, as if it were a sin, whatever the unlucky person whom they address may happen to do, or to leave undone.

'I am none of your palavering chaps, to flummer over an old vixen for the sake of her strong-box. I hate such falseness. I speak the truth and care for no man,' quoth John Stokes.

And accordingly John Stokes never saw Mrs Deborah Thornby but he saluted her, pretty much as his mastiff accosted her favourite cat: erected his bristles, looked at her with savage bloodshot eyes, showed his teeth, and vented a sound something between a snarl and a growl; whilst she (like the four-footed tabby), set up her back and spat at him in return.

They met often, as I have said, for the enjoyment of quarrelling; and as whatever he advised she was pretty sure *not* to do, it is probable that his remonstrances in favour of her friendless relations served to confirm her in the small tyranny which she exercised towards them.

Such being the state of feeling between these two jangling cousins, it may be imagined with what indignation Mrs Deborah found John Stokes, upon the death of his wife, removing her widowed sister-in-law from the cottage in which she had placed her, and bringing her home to the mill, to officiate as his housekeeper, and take charge of a lovely little girl, his only child. She vowed one of those vows of anger which I fear are oftener kept than the vows of love, to strike both mother and son out of her will (by the way, she had a superstitious horror of that disagreeable ceremony, and even the temptation of choosing new legatees whenever the old displeased her, had not been sufficient to induce her to make one – the threat did as well), and never to speak to either of them again as long as she lived.

She proclaimed this resolution at the rate of twelve times an hour (that is to say, once in five minutes), every day for a fortnight; and in spite of her well-known caprice, there seemed for once in her life reason to believe that she would keep her word.

Those prudent and sagacious persons who are so good as to take the superintendence of other people's affairs, and to tell by the look of the foot where the shoe pinches and where it does not, all united in blaming the poor widow for withdrawing herself and her son from Mrs Deborah's protection. But besides that no human being can adequately estimate the misery of leading a life of dependence upon one to whom scolding was as the air she breathed, without it she must die, a penurious dependence too, which supplied grudgingly the humblest wants, and yet would not permit the exertions by which she would joyfully have endeavoured to support herself; besides the temptation to exchange Mrs Deborah's incessant maundering for the miller's rough kindness, and her scanty fare for the coarse plenty of his board; besides these homely but natural temptations, hardly to be adequately allowed for by those who have past their lives amidst smiling kindness and luxurious abundance; besides these motives she had a stronger and dearer one in her desire to rescue her boy from the dangers of an enforced and miserable idleness, and to put him in the way of earning his bread by honest industry.

Through the interest of his grandfather, the parish-clerk, the little Edward had been early placed in the Hilton free school, where he had acquitted himself so much to the satisfaction of the master, that at twelve years old he was the head boy of the foundation, and took precedence of the other nine-and-twenty wearers of the full-skirted blue coats, leathern belts and tasselled caps, in the various arts of reading, writing, cyphering and mensuration. He could flourish a swan without ever taking his pen from the paper. Nay, there is little doubt but from long habit he could have flourished it blindfold, like the man who had so often modelled the wit of Ferney in breadcrumbs, that he could produce little busts of Voltaire with his hands under the table; he had not his equal in Practice or the Rule of Three, and his piece, when sent round at Christmas, was the admiration of the whole parish.

Unfortunately, his arrival at this pre-eminence was also the signal of his dismissal from the free school. He returned home to his mother, and as Mrs Deborah, although hourly complaining of the expense of supporting a great lubberly boy in idleness, refused to apprentice him to any trade, and even forbade his finding employment in helping her deaf man of all work to cultivate her garden, which the poor lad, naturally industrious and active, begged her permission to do, his mother, considering that no uncertain expectations of money at the death of his kinswoman could counterbalance the certain evil of dragging on his days in penury and indolence during her life, wisely determined to betake herself to the mill, and accept John Stokes's offer of sending Edward to a friend in town, for the purpose of being placed with a civil engineer; a destination with which the boy himself – a fine intelligent youth, by the way, tall and manly, with black eyes that talked and laughed, and curling dark hair – was delighted in every point of view. He longed for a profession for which he had a decided turn; he longed to see the world as personified by the city of cities, the unparagoned London; and he longed more than either to get away from Aunt Deborah, the storm of whose vituperation seemed ringing in his ears so long as he continued within the sight of her dwelling. One would think the clerk of the mill and the prattle of his pretty cousin Cicely might have drowned it, but it did not. Nothing short of leaving the spinster fifty miles behind, and setting the great city between him and her, could efface the impression.

'I hope I am not ungrateful,' thought Edward to himself, as he was trudging London-ward after taking a tender leave of all at the mill; 'I hope I am not ungrateful. I do not think I am, for I would give my right arm ay, or my life, if it would serve master John Stokes or please dear Cissy. But really I do hope never to come within hearing of Aunt Deborah again, she storms so. I wonder whether all old women are so cross, I don't think my mother will be, nor Cissy. I am sure Cissy won't. Poor Aunt Deborah! I suppose she can't help it.' And with this indulgent conclusion, Edward wended on his way.

Aunt Deborah's mood was by no means so pacific. She stayed at home fretting, fuming, and chaffing, and storming herself hoarse – which, as the people at the mill took care to keep out of earshot, was all so much good scolding thrown away. The state of things since Edward's departure had been so decisive, that even John Stokes thought it wiser to keep himself aloof for a time; and although they pretty well guessed that she would take measures to put in effect her threat of disinheritance, the first outward demonstration came in the shape of a young man (gentleman I suppose he called himself – ay, there is no doubt but he wrote himself 'Esquire') who attended her to church a few Sundays after, and was admitted to the honour of sitting in the same pew.

Nothing could be more unlike our friend Edward than the stranger. Fair, freckled, light-haired, light-eyed, with invisible eyebrows and eyelashes, insignificant in feature, pert and perking in expression, and in figure so dwarfed and stunted, that though in point of age he had evidently attained his full growth (if one may use the expression of such a he-doll), Robert at fifteen would have made two of him – such was the new favourite. So far as appearance went, for certain, Mrs Deborah had not changed for the better.

Gradually it oozed out, as, somehow or other, news like water will find a vent, however small the cranny – by slow degrees it came to be understood that Mrs Deborah's visitor was a certain Mr Adolphus Lynfield, clerk to an attorney of no great note in the good town of Belford Regis, and nearly related, as he affirmed, to the Thornby family.

Upon hearing these findings, John Stokes, the son of old Simon Thornby's sister, marched across the road, and finding the door upon the latch, entered unannounced into the presence of his enemy.

'I think it my duty to let you know, cousin Deborah, that this here chap's an impostor – a sham – and that you are a fool,' was his conciliatory opening. 'Search the register. The Thornbys have been yeomen of this parish ever since the time of Elizabeth – more shame to you for forcing the last of the race to seek his bread elsewhere; and if you can find such a name as Lynfield amongst 'em, I'll give you leave to turn me into a pettifogging lawyer – that's all. Saunderses, and Symondses, and Stokeses, and Mays, you'll find in plenty, but never a Lynfield. Lynfield, quotha! it sounds like a made-up name in a story-book! And as for 'Dolphus, why there never was anything like it in all the generation, except my good old great aunt Dolly, and that stood for Dorothy. All our names have been Christian-like and English, Toms, and Jacks, and Jems, and Bills, and Sims, and Neds – poor fellow! None of your outlandish 'Dolphuses. Dang it, I believe the foolish woman likes the chap the better for having a name she can't speak! Remember, I warn you he's a sham!' And off strode the honest miller, leaving Mrs Deborah too angry for reply, and confirmed both in her prejudice and prepossession by the natural effect of that spirit of contradiction which formed so large an ingredient in her composition, and was not wholly wanting in that of John Stokes.

Years passed away, and in spite of frequent ebbs and flows, the tide of Mrs Deborah's favour continued to set towards Mr Adolphus Lynfield. Once or twice, indeed, report had said that he was fairly discarded, but the very appearance of the good miller, anxious to improve the opportunity for his protégé, had been sufficient to determine his cousin to reinstate Mr Adolphus in her good graces. Whether she really liked him is doubtful. He entertained too good an opinion of himself to be very successful in gaining that of other people.

That the gentleman was not deficient in 'left-handed wisdom', was proved pretty clearly by most of his actions; for instance, when routed by the downright miller from the position which he had taken up of a near kinsman by the father's side, he, like an able tactician, wheeled about and called cousins with Mrs Deborah's mother; and as that good lady happened to have borne the very general, almost universal, name of Smith, which is next to anonymous, even John Stokes could not dislodge him from that entrenchment. But he was not always so dextrous. Cunning in him lacked the crowning perfection of hiding itself under the appearance of honesty. His art never looked like nature. It stared you in the face, and could not deceive the dullest observer. His very flattery had a tone of falseness that affronted the person flattered; and Mrs Deborah, in particular, who did not want for shrewdness, found it so distasteful, that she would certainly have discarded him upon that one ground of offence, had not her love of power been unconsciously propitiated by the perception of the efforts which he made, and the degradation to which he submitted, in the vain attempt to please her. She liked the homage offered to '*les beaux yeux de sa cassette*', pretty much as a young beauty likes the devotion extorted by her charms, and for the sake of the incense tolerates the worshipper.

Nevertheless there were moments when the conceit which I have mentioned as the leading characteristic of Mr Adolphus Lynfield had well nigh banished him from Chalcott. Piquing himself on the variety and extent of his knowledge, the universality of his genius, he of course paid the penalty of other universal geniuses, by being in no small degree superficial. Not content with understanding every trade better than those who had followed it all their lives, he had a most unlucky propensity to put his devices into execution, and as his information was, for the most part, picked up from the column headed 'Varieties' in the county newspaper, where of course there is some chaff mingled with the grain, and as the figments in question were generally ill understood and imperfectly recollected, it is really surprising that the young gentleman did not occasion more mischief than actually occurred by the quips and quiddities which he delighted to put in practice whenever he met with anyone simple enough to permit the exercise of his talents.

Some damage he did effect by his experiments, as Mrs Deborah found to her cost. He killed a bed of old-fashioned spice cloves, the pride of her heart, by salting the ground to get rid of the worms. Her broods of geese also, and of turkeys, fell victims to a new and infallible mode of feeding, which was to make them twice as fat in half the time. Somehow or other, they all died under the operation. So did half a score of fine apple-trees, under an improved method of grafting; whilst a magnificent brown Bury pear, that covered one end of the house, perished of the grand discovery of severing the bark to increase the crop. He lamed Mrs Deborah's old horse, by doctoring him for a prick in shoeing, and ruined her favourite cow, the best milch cow in the county, by a most needless attempt to increase her milk.

Now these mischances and misdemeanours, aye, or the half of them, would undoubtedly have occasioned Mr Adolphus's dismissal, and the recall of poor Edward, every account of whom was in the highest degree favourable, had the worthy miller been able to refrain from lecturing his cousin upon her neglect of the one, and her partiality for the other. It was really astonishing that John Stokes, a man of sagacity in all other respects, never could understand that scolding was, of all devisable processes, the least likely to succeed in carrying his point with one who was such a proficient in that accomplishment that if the old penalty for female scolds, the ducking-stool, had continued in fashion, she would have stood an excellent chance of attaining to that distinction. But so it was. The same blood coursed through their veins, and his tempestuous good-will and her fiery anger took the same form of violence and passion.

Nothing but these lectures *could* have kept Mrs Deborah constant in the train of such a trumpery, jiggetting, fidgetty little personage as Mr Adolphus – the more especially as her heart was assailed in its better and softer parts by the quiet respectfulness of Mrs Thornby's demeanour, who never forgot that she had experienced her protection in the hour of need, and by the irresistible good-nature of Cicely, a smiling, rosy, sunny-looking creature, whose only vocation in the world seemed to be the trying to make everybody as happy as herself.

Mrs Deborah (with such a humanizing taste, she could not, in spite of her cantankerous temper, be all bad) loved flowers; and Cicely, a rover of the woods and fields from early childhood, and no despicable practical gardener, took care to keep her beaupots constantly supplied, from the first snowdrop to the last China rose. Nothing was too large for Cicely's good-will, nothing too small. Huge chimney jars of lilacs, laburnums, horse-chestnuts, peonies, and the golden and gorgeous double furze, china jugs filled with magnificent double stocks and rich wallflowers, with their bitter-sweet odour, like the taste of orange marmalade, pinks, sweet-peas, and mignonette, from her own little garden; or woodland posies, that might beseem the hand of the Faerie Queen, composed of those gems of flowers, the scarlet pimpernel, and the blue anagallis, the rosy star of the wild geranium, with its aromatic crimson-tipped leaves, the snowy star of the white ochil, and that third starry flower the yellow loosestrife, the milk vetch, purple-, or pink-, or cream-coloured, backed by moss-like leaves and lilac blossoms of the lousewort, and overhung by the fragrant bells and cool green leaves of the lily of the valley. It would puzzle a gardener to surpass the elegance and delicacy of such a nosegay.

Offerings like these did our miller's maiden delight to bring at all seasons, and under all circumstances, whether of peace or war between the heads of the two opposite houses; and whenever there chanced to be a lull in the storm, she availed herself of the opportunity to add to her simple tribute a dish of eels from the mill-stream, or perch from the river. That the thought of Edward ('dear Edward', as she always called him) might not add somewhat of alacrity to her attentions to his wayward aunt, I will not venture to deny, but she would have done the same if Edward had not been in existence, from the mere effect of her own peace-making spirit, and a generosity of nature which found more pleasure in giving than in possessing. A sweet and happy creature was Cicely: it was difficult even for Mrs Deborah to resist her gentle voice and artless smiles.

Affairs were in this posture between the belligerents, sometimes war to the knife, sometimes a truce under favour of Cissy's white flag, when one October evening, John Stokes entered the dwelling of his kinswoman to inform her that Edward's apprenticeship had been some time at an end, that he had come of age about a month ago, and that his master for whom he had continued to work was so satisfied of his talents, industry and integrity, that he had offered to take him into partnership for a sum incredibly moderate, considering the advantages which such a connexion would ensure.

'You have more than the money wanted in the Belford Bank: money that ought to have been his,' quoth John Stokes; 'besides all your property in land and houses and the funds; and if you did advance this sum, which all the world knows is only a small part of what should have belonged to him in right of his father, it would be as safe as if it was in the Bank of England, and the interest paid half-yearly. You ought to give it him out and out; but of course you won't even lend it,' pursued this judicious negotiator; 'you keep all your money for that precious chap, Mr 'Dolphus, to make ducks and drakes with after you are dead; a fine jig he'll dance over your grave. You know, I suppose, that we've got the fellow in a cleft stick about that petition the other day? He persuaded old Jacob, who's as deaf as a post, to put his mark to it, and when he was gone Jacob came to me (I'm the only man in the parish who can make him hear) to ask what it was about. So upon my explaining the matter, Jacob found he had got into the wrong box. But as the chap had taken away his petition, and Jacob could not scratch out his name, what does he do but set his mark to ours o' t'other side; and we've wrote all about it to Sir Robert to explain to the Parliament, lest seeing Jacob's name both ways like, they should think 'twas he, poor fellow, that meant to humbug 'em. A pretty figure Mr 'Dolphus'll cut when the story comes to be told in the House of Commons! But that's not the worst. He took the petition to the workhouse, and meeting with little Fan Ropley, who had been taught to write at our charity-school, and is quick at her pen, he makes her sign her name at full length, and then strikes a dot over the *e* to turn it into Francis, and persuade the great folk up at Lunnun, that little Fan's a grown-up man. If that chap won't come some day to be tranported for forgery, my name's not John Stokes! Well, dame, will you let Ned have the money?' Yes or no?'

That Mrs Deborah should have suffered the good miller to proceed with his harangue without interruption, can only be accounted for on the score of the loudness of tone on which he piqued himself with so much justice. When she did take up the word, her reply made up in volubility and virulence for any deficiency in sound, concluding by a formal renunciation of her nephew, and a command to his zealous advocate never again to appear within her doors. Upon which, honest John vowed he never would, and departed.

Two or three days after this quarrel, Mr Adolphus having arrived, as happened not unfrequently, to spend the afternoon at Chalcott, persuaded his hostess to accompany him to see a pond being drawn at the Hall, to which, as the daughter of one of Sir Robert's old tenants, she would undoubtedly have the right of *entrée*; and Mrs Deborah assented to his request, partly because the weather was fine and the distance short, partly, it may be, from a lurking desire to take her chance, as a bystander, of a dish of fish: they who need such windfalls least, being commonly those who are most desirous to put themselves in their way.

Mr Adolphus Lynfield's reasons were obvious enough. Besides the *ennui* of a *tête-à-tête*, all flattery on one side and contradiction on the other, he was naturally of the fidgetty, restless temperament, which hates to be long confined to one place or one occupation, and can never hear of a gathering of people, whatever might be the occasion, without longing to find himself amongst them.

Moreover, he had, or professed to have, a passion for field sports of every description; and having that very season contrived, with his usual curious infelicity, to get into as many scrapes in shooting as shall last most sportsmen their whole lives – having shot a spaniel instead of a hare, a keeper instead of a partridge, and his own foot instead of a pheasant, and finally having been taken up for a poacher, although wholly innocent of the death of any bird that ever wore feathers – after all these woeful experiences (to say nothing of mischances in angling, which might put to shame those of our friend Mr Thompson), he found himself particularly well disposed to a diversion which appeared to combine in most choice union the appearance of sporting, which he considered essential to his reputation, with a most happy exemption from the usual sporting requisites, exertion or skill. All that he would have to do would be to look on and talk – to throw out a hint here and a suggestion there, and find fault with everything and everybody, like a man who understood what was going forward.

The weather was most propitious; a bright breezy sunny October day, with light snowy clouds, chased by a keen crisp wind across the deep blue heavens; and the beautiful park, the turf of an emerald green, contrasting with the brown fern and tawny woods, rivalling in richness and brightness the vivid hues of the autumnal sky. Nothing could exceed the gorgeous tinting of the magnificent trees, which, whether in detached clumps or forest-like masses, formed the pride and glory of the place. The oak still retaining its dark and heavy verdure; the elm letting fall a shower of yellow leaves, that tinged the ground beneath; the deep orange of the horse-chestnut, the beech varying from ruddy gold to greenish brown; and above all, the shining green of the holly, and the rich purplish red of the old thorns, those hoary thorns, the growth of centuries, gave to this old English gentleman's seat much of the variety and beauty of the American backwoods. The house, a stately ancient mansion, from the porch of which you might expect to see Sir Roger de Coverley issue, stood half-way up a gentle hill, finely backed by woods of great extent; and the pond, which was the object of the visit, was within sight of the windows, but so skilfully veiled by trees as to appear of much greater extent than it really was.

The master and mistress of the Hall, with their pretty daughters, were absent on a tour – is any English country family ever at home in the month of October in these days of fashionable enterprise? They were gone to visit the temples of Thebes, or the ruins of Carthage, the Fountains of the Nile, or the Falls of Niagara, St Sophia, or the Kremlin, or some such pretty little excursion, which ladies and gentlemen now talk of as familiarly 'as maids of puppy dogs'. They were away. But enough of the household remained at Chalcott to compose, with a few visitors, a sufficiently numerous and animated group.

The first person whom Mrs Deborah espied (and it is remarkable that we always see first those whom we had rather not see at all) was her old enemy the miller – a fisherman of so much experience and celebrity, that his presence might have been reckoned upon as certain – busily engaged, together with some half dozen stout and active coadjutors, in dragging the net ashore, amidst a chorus of exclamations and cautions from the various assistants, and the breathless expectation of the spectators on the bank, amongst whom were Mrs Thornby and Cicely, accompanied by a tall, athletic young man of dark complexion, with peculiarly bright eyes and curling hair, whom his aunt immediately recognized as Edward.

'How improved he is!' was the thought that flashed across her mind, as with an air of respectful alacrity he stepped forward to meet her; but the miller, in tugging at his nets, happened to look towards them, and ashamed that he of all men should see her change of feeling, she turned away abruptly, without acknowledging his salutation, and walked off to the other side with her attendant, Mr Adolphus.

'Drat the perverse old jade!' exclaimed John Stokes, involuntarily, as he gave a mighty tug, which brought half the net ashore.

'She's heavy, my good sir!' observed the pompous butler, conceiving that the honest miller's exclamation had reference to the sport; 'only see how full she is! We shall have a magnificent haul!'

And the spectators, male and female, crowded round, and the fishermen exerted themselves so efficiently, that in two minutes the net was on dry land.

'Nothing but weeds and rubbish!' ejaculated the disappointed butler, a peculiarly blank look taking the place of his usual self-importance. 'What can have become of the fish?'

'The net has been improperly drawn,' observed Mr Adolphus;

'I myself saw four or five large carp just before it was dragged ashore!'

'Better fling you in, Master 'Dolphus, by way of bait!' ejaculated our friend the miller; 'I've seen jacks in this pond that would make no more bones of swallowing a leg or an arm of such anatomy as you, if they did not have a try at the whole body, than a shark would of bolting down Punch in the show; as to carp, everybody that ever fished a pond knows their tricks. Catch them in a net if you look at 'em, and then they drop plump into the mud, and lie as still and as close as so many stones. But come, Mr Tomkins,' continued honest John, addressing the butler, 'we'll try again. I'm minded that we shall have better luck this time. Here are some brave large tench, which never move till the water is disturbed; we shall have a good chance for them as well as for the jacks. Now, steady there, you in the boat. Throw her in, boys, and mind you don't draw too fast!' So to work they all went again.

All was proceeding prosperously, and the net, evidently well filled with fish, was dragging slowly to land, when John Stokes shouted suddenly from the other side of the pond – 'Dang it, if that unlucky chap, Master 'Dolphus there, has not got hold of the top of the net! He'll pull it over. See, that great jack has got out already. Take it from him, Tom! He'll let all the fish loose, and tumble in himself, and the water at that part is deep enough to drown twenty such manikins. Not that I think drowning likely to be his fate – witness that petition business,' muttered John to himself in a sort of parenthesis. 'Let go, I say, or you will be in. Let go, can't ye?' added he, in his loudest tone.

And with the word, Mr Adolphus, still struggling to retain his hold on the net, lost his balance and fell in, and catching at the person next to him, who happened to be Mrs Deborah, with the hope of saving himself, dragged her in after him.

Both sank, and amidst the confusion that ensued, the shrieks and sobs of the women, the oaths and exclamations of the men, the danger was so imminent that both might have been drowned had not Edward Thornby, hastily flinging off his coat and hat, plunged in and rescued Mrs Deborah, whilst good John Stokes, running round the head of the pond as nimbly as a boy, did the same kind office for his prime aversion, the attorney's clerk. What a sound kernel is sometimes hidden under a rough and rugged rind!

Mr Adolphus, more frightened than hurt, and with so much of the conceit washed out of him by his involuntary cold bath that it might be accounted one of the most fortunate accidents in his life, was conveyed to the Hall; but her own house being almost equally near, Mrs Deborah was at once taken home, and put comfortably to bed in her own chamber.

About two hours afterwards, the whole of the miller's family, Mrs Thornby still pallid and trembling, Cicely smiling through her tears, and her father as blunt and free-spoken as ever, were assembled round the home couch of their maiden cousin.

'I tell you I must have the lawyer fetched directly. I can't sleep till I have made my will,' said Mrs Deborah.

'Better not,' responded John Stokes; 'you'll want it altered tomorrow.'

'What's that you say, cousin John?' enquired the spinster.

'That if you make your will tonight, you'll change your mind tomorrow,' reiterated John Stokes. Ned's going to be married to my Cicely,' added he, 'and that you may'nt like, or if you did like it this week, you might not like it next. So you'd better let matters rest as they are.'

'You're a provoking man, John Stokes,' said his cousin – 'a very provoking, obstinate man. But I'll convince you for once. Take that key, Mrs Thornby,' quoth she, raising herself in bed, and fumbling in an immense pair of pockets for a small old-fashioned key, 'and open the 'scrutoire, and give me the pen and ink, and the old narrow brown book, that you'll find at the top. Not like his marrying Cicely! Why I have always loved that child – don't cry, Cissy! – and have always had cause, for she has been a kind creature to me. Those dahlias came from her, and the sweet posy,' pursued Mrs Deborah, pointing to a nosegay of autumn flowers, the old fragrant monthly rose, mignonette, heliotrope, cloves and jasmine, which stood by the bedside. 'Ay, that's the book, Mrs Thornby; and there, Cissy,' continued Aunt

Deborah, filling up the cheque, with a sum far larger than that required for the partnership – 'there, Cissy, is your marriage portion. Don't cry so, child!' said she, as the affectionate girl hung round her neck in a passion of grateful tears – 'don't cry, but find our Edward, and send for the lawyer, for I'm determined to settle my affairs tonight. And now, John Stokes, I know I've been a cross old woman, but—'

'Cousin Deborah,' interrupted John, seizing her withered hand with a grip like a smith's vice – 'Cousin Deborah, thou hast acted nobly, and I beg thy pardon once for all, God bless thee! Dang it,' added the honest miller to himself, 'I do verily believe that this squabbling has been mainly my fault, and that if I had not been so provoking she would not have been so contrary. Well, she has made us all happy, and we must try to make her happy in return. If we did not, we should deserve to be soused in the fish-pond along with that unhappy chap, Master 'Dolphus. For my part,' continued the good yeoman, forming with great earnestness a solemn resolution – 'for my part, I've fully made up my mind never to contradict her again, say what she will. No, not if she says black's white! It's contradiction that makes women contrary; it sets their backs up, like. I'll never contradict her again so long as my name's John Stokes.'

The Two Drovers

SIR WALTER SCOTT

I

It was the day after Doune Fair when my story commences. It had been a brisk market; several dealers had attended from the northern and midland counties of England, and English money had flown so merrily about as to gladden the hearts of the Highland farmers. Many large droves were about to set off for England, under the protection of their owners, or of the topsmen whom they employed in the tedious, laborious and responsible office of driving the cattle for many hundred miles, from the market where they had been purchased, to the fields or farm-yards where they were to be fattened for the shambles.

The Highlanders, in particular, are masters of this difficult trade of driving, which seems to suit them as well as the trade of war. It affords exercise for all their habits of patient endurance and active exertion. They are required to know perfectly the drove-roads, which lie over the wildest tracts of the country, and to avoid as much as possible the highways, which distress the feet of the bullocks, and the turnpikes, which annoy the spirit of the drover; whereas, on the broad green or grey track, which leads across the pathless moor, the herd not only move at ease and without taxation, but, if they mind their business, may pick up a mouthful of food by the way. At night, the drovers usually sleep along with their cattle, let the weather be what it will; and many of these hardy men do not once rest under a roof during a journey on foot from Lochaber to Lincolnshire. They are paid very highly, for the trust reposed is of the first importance, as it depends on their prudence, vigilance and honesty, whether the cattle reach the final market in good order, and afford a profit to the grazier. But as they maintain themselves at their own expense, they are especially economical in that particular. At the period we speak of, a Highland drover was victualled for his long and toilsome journey with a few handfuls of oatmeal, and two or three onions, renewed from time to time, and a ram's horn filled with whisky, which he used regularly, but sparingly, every night and morning. His dirk, or *skene-dhu* (i.e. black-knife), so worn as to be concealed beneath the arm, or by the folds of the plaid, was his only weapon, excepting the cudgel with which he directed the movements of the cattle. A Highlander was never so happy as on these occasions. There was a variety in the whole journey, which exercised the Celt's natural curiosity and love of motion; there were the constant change of place and scene, the petty adventures incidental to the traffic, and the intercourse with the various farmers, graziers and traders, intermingled with occasional merry-makings, not the less acceptable to Donald that they were void of expense; – and there was the consciousness of superior skill; for the Highlander, a child amongst flocks, is a prince amongst herds, and his natural habits induce him to disdain the shepherd's slothful life, so that he feels himself nowhere more at home than when following a gallant drove of his country cattle in the character of their guardian.

Of the number who left Doune in the morning, and with the purpose we described, not a *glunamie* of them all cocked his bonnet more briskly, or gartered his tartan hose under knee over a pair of more promising *spiogs* (legs) than did Robin Oig M'Combich, called familiarly Robin Oig, that is, Young, or the Lesser, Robin. Though small of stature, as the epithet Oig implies, and not very strongly limbed, he was as light and alert as one of the deer of his mountains. He had an elasticity of step which, in the course of a long march, made many a stout fellow envy him; and the manner in which he busked his plaid and adjusted his bonnet, argued a consciousness that so smart a John Highlandman as himself would not pass unnoticed among the Lowland lasses. The ruddy cheek, red lips and white teeth set off a countenance which had gained by exposure to the weather a healthful and hardy rather than a rugged hue. If Robin Oig did not laugh, or even smile frequently, as indeed is not the practice among his countrymen, his bright eyes usually gleamed from under his bonnet with an expression of cheerfulness ready to be turned into mirth.

The departure of Robin Oig was an incident in the little town, in and near which he had many friends, male and female. He was a topping person in his way, transacted considerable business on his own behalf, and was entrusted by the best farmers in the Highlands, in preference to any other drover iin that district. He might have increased his business to any extent had he condescended to manage it by deputy; but except a lad or two, sister's sons of his own, Robin rejected the idea of assistance, conscious, perhaps, how much his reputation depended upon his attending in person to the practical discharge of his duty in every instance. He remained, therefore, contented with the highest premium given to persons of his description, and comforted himself with the hopes that a few journeys to England might enable him to conduct business on his own account, in a manner becoming his birth. For Robin Oig's father, Lachlan M'Combich (or son of my friend, his actual clan-surname being M'Gregor), had been so called by the celebrated Rob Roy, because of the particular friendship which had subsisted between the grandsire of Robin and that renowned cateran. Some people even say that Robin Oig derived his Christian name from one as renowned in the wilds of Loch Lomond as ever was his namesake Robin Hood, in the precincts of merry Sherwood. 'Of such ancestry,' as James Boswell says, 'who would not be proud?' Robin Oig was proud accordingly; but his frequent visits to England and to the Lowlands had given him tact enough to know that pretensions, which still gave him a little right to distinction in his own lonely glen, might be both obnoxious and ridiculous if preferred elsewhere. The pride of birth, therefore, was like the miser's treasure, the secret subject of his contemplation, but never exhibited to strangers as a subject of boasting.

Many were the words of congratulation and good luck which were bestowed on Robin Oig. The judges commended his drove, especially Robin's own property, which were the best of them. Some thrust out their snuff-mulls for the parting pinch – others tendered the *doch-an-dorrach*, or parting cup. All cried – 'Good luck travel out with you and come home with you. – Give you luck in the Saxon market – brave notes in the *leabhar-dhu*' (black pocketbook) 'and plenty of English gold in the *sporran*' (pouch of goatskin).

The bonny lasses made their adieus more modestly, and more than one, it was said, would have given her best brooch to be certain that it was upon her that his eye last rested as he turned towards the road.

Robin Oig had just given the preliminary 'Hoo-hoo!' to urge forward the loiterers of the drove, when there was a cry behind him.

'Stay, Robin – bide a blink. Here is Janet of Tomahourich – auld Janet, your father's sister.'

'Plague on her, for an auld Highland witch and spaewife,' said a farmer from the Carse of Stirling; 'she'll cast some of her cantrips on the cattle.'

'She canna do that,' said another sapient of the same profession – 'Robin Oig is no the lad to leave any of them, without tying St Mungo's knot on their tails, and that will put to her speed the best witch that ever flew over Dimayet upon a broomstick.'

It may not be indifferent to the reader to know, that the Highland cattle are peculiarly liable to be taken, or infected, by spells and witchcraft; which judicious people guard against by knitting knots of peculiar complexity on the tuft of hair which terminates the animal's tail. But the old woman who was the object of the farmer's suspicion seemed only busied about the drover, without paying any attention to the drove. Robin, on the contrary, appeared rather impatient of her presence.

'What auld-world fancy', he said, 'has brought you so early from the ingle-side this morning, Muhme? I am sure I bid you good-even, and had your God-speed, last night.'

'And left me more siller than the useless old woman will use till you come back again, bird of my bosom,' said the sibyl. 'But it is little I would care for the food that nourishes me, or the fire that warms me, or for God's blessed sun itself, if aught but weel should happen to the grandson of my father. So let me walk the *deasil* round you, that you may go safe out into the foreign land, and come safe home.'

Robin Oig stopped, half embarrassed, half laughing, and signing to those near that he only complied with the old woman to soothe her humour. In the meantime, she traced around him, with wavering steps, the propitiation, which some have thought has been derived from the Druidical mythology. It consists, as is well known, in the person who makes the *deasil* walking three times around the person who is the object of the ceremony, taking care to move according to the course of the sun. At once, however, she stopped short, and exclaimed, in a voice of alarm and horror, 'Grandson of my father, there is blood on your hand.'

'Hush, for God's sake, aunt,' said Robin Oig; 'you will bring more trouble on yourself with this *taishataragh*' (second sight) 'than you will be able to get out of for many a day.'

The old woman only repeated, with a ghastly look, 'There is blood on your hand, and it is English blood. The blood of the Gael is richer and redder. Let us see – let us—'

Ere Robin Oig could prevent her, which, indeed, could only have been done by positive violence, so hasty and peremptory were her proceedings, she had drawn from his side the dirk which lodged in the folds of his plaid, and held it up, exclaiming, although the weapon gleamed clear and bright in the sun, 'Blood, blood – Saxon blood again. Robin Oig M'Combich, go not this day to England!'

'Prutt trutt,' answered Robin Oig, 'that will never do neither – it would be next thing to running the country. For shame, Muhme – give me the dirk. You cannot tell by the colour the

265

difference betwixt the blood of a black bullock and a white one, and you speak of knowing Saxon from Gaelic blood. All men have their blood from Adam, Muhme. Give me my *skene-dhu*, and let me go on my road. I should have been half-way to Stirling Brig by this time – Give me my dirk, and let me go.'

'Never will I give it to you,' said the old woman – 'Never will I quit my hold on your plaid, unless you promise me not to wear that unhappy weapon.'

The women around him urged him also, saying few of his aunt's words fell to the ground; and as the Lowland farmers continued to look moodily on the scene, Robin Oig determined to close it at any sacrifice.

'Well, then,' said the young drover, giving the scabbard of the weapon to Hugh Morrison, 'you Lowlanders care nothing for these freats. Keep my dirk for me. I cannot give it to you, because it was my father's; but your drove follows ours, and I am content it should be in your keeping, not in mind – Will this do, Muhme?'

'It must,' said the old woman – 'that is, if the Lowlander is mad enough to carry the knife.'

The strong westlandman laughed aloud.

'Goodwife,' he said, 'I am Hugh Morrison from Glenae, come of the Manly Morrisons of auld langsyne, that never took short weapon against a man in their lives. And neither needed they. They had their broadswords, and I have this bit supple,' showing a formidable cudgel – 'for dirking ower the board, I leave that to John Highlandman – Ye needna snort, none of you Highlanders, and you in especial, Robin. I'll keep the bit knife, if you are feared for the auld spaewife's tale, and give it back to you whenever you want it.'

Robin was not particularly pleased with some part of Hugh Morrison's speech; but he had learned in his travels more patience than belonged to his Highland constitution originally, and he accepted the service of the descendant of the Manly Morrisons without finding fault with the rather deprecating manner in which it was offered.

'If he had not had his morning in his head, and been but a

Dumfriesshire hog into the boot, he would have spoken more like a gentleman. But you cannot have more of a sow than a grumph. It's shame my father's knife should ever slash a haggis for the like of him.'

Thus saying (but saying it in Gaelic), Robin drove on his cattle, and waved farewell to all behind him. He was in the greater haste, because he expected to join at Falkirk a comrade and brother in profession, with whom he proposed to travel in company.

Robin Oig's chosen friend was a young Englishman, Harry Wakefield by name, well known at every northern market, and in his way as much famed and honoured as our Highland drover of bullocks. He was nearly six feet high, gallantly formed to keep the rounds at Smithfield, or maintain the ring at a wrestling match; and although he might have been overmatched, perhaps, among the regular professors of the Fancy, yet, as a yokel, or rustic, or a chance customer, he was able to give a bellyful to any amateur of the pugilistic art. Doncaster races saw him in his glory, betting his guinea, and generally successfully; nor was there a main fought in Yorkshire, the feeders being persons of celebrity, at which he was not to be seen, if business permitted. But though a *sprack* lad, and fond of pleasure and its haunts, Harry Wakefield was steady, and not the cautious Robin Oig M'Combich himself was more attentive to the main chance. His holidays were holidays indeed; but his days of work were dedicated to steady and persevering labour. In countenance and temper, Wakefield was the model of old England's merry yeomen, whose clothyard shafts, in so many hundred battles, asserted her superiority over the nations, and whose good sabres, in our own time, are her cheapest and most assured defence. His mirth was readily excited; for, strong in limb and constitution, and fortunate in circumstances, he was disposed to be pleased with everything about him; and such difficulties as he might occasionally encounter were, to a man of his energy, rather matter of amusement than serious annoyance. With all the merits of a sanguine temper, our young English drover was not without his defects. He was irascible, sometimes to the verge of being quarrelsome; and perhaps not the less inclined to bring his disputes to a pugilistic decision, because he found few antagonists able to stand up to him in the boxing ring.

It is difficult to say how Harry Wakefield and Robin Oig first became intimates; but it is certain a close acquaintance had taken place betwixt them, although they had apparently few common subjects of conversation or of interest, so soon as their talk ceased to be of bullocks. Robin Oig, indeed, spoke the English language rather imperfectly upon any other topics but stots and kyloes, and Harry Wakefield could never bring his broad Yorkshire tongue to utter a single word of Gaelic. It was in vain Robin spent a whole morning, during a walk over Minch Moor, in attempting to teach his companion to utter, with true precision, the shibboleth *Llhu*, which is the Gaelic for the calf. From Traquair to Murder-cairn, the hill rang with the discordant attempts of the Saxon upon the unmanageable monosyllable, and the heartfelt laugh which followed every failure. They had, however, better modes of awakening the echoes; for Wakefield could sing many a ditty to the praise of Moll, Susan and Cicely, and Robin Oig had a particular gift at whistling interminable pibrochs through all their involutions, and what was more agreeable to his companion's southern ear, knew many of the northern airs, both lively and pathetic, to which Wakefield learned to pipe a bass. Thus, though Robin could hardly have comprehended his companion's stories about horse-racing, and cock-fighting or fox-hunting, and although his own legends of clan-fights and *creaghs*, varied with talk of Highland goblins and fairy folk, would have been caviare to his companion, they contrived nevertheless to find a degree of pleasure in each other's company, which had for three years back induced them to join company and travel together, when the direction of their journey permitted. Each, indeed, found his advantage in his companionship; for where could the Englishman have found a guide through the Western Highlands like Robin Oig M'Combich? and when they were on what Harry called the *right* side of the Border, his patronage, which was extensive, and his purse, which was heavy, were at all times at the service of his Highland friend, and on many occasions his liberality did him genuine yeoman's service.

II

> Were ever two such loving friends!
> How could they disagree?
> Oh thus it was, he loved him dear,
> And thought how to requite him,
> And having no friend left but he,
> He did resolve to fight him.
>
> *Duke upon Duke*

The pair of friends had traversed with their usual cordiality the grassy wilds of Liddesdale, and crossed the opposite part of Cumberland, emphatically called The Waste. In these solitary regions, the cattle under the charge of our drovers derived their subsistence chiefly by picking their food as they went along the drove-road, or sometimes by the tempting opportunity of a *start and owerloup*, or invasion of the neighbouring pasture, where an occasion presented itself. But now the scene changed before them; they were descending towards a fertile and enclosed country, where no such liberties could be taken with impunity, or without a previous arrangement and bargain with the possessors of the ground. This was more especially the case, as a great northern fair was upon the eve of taking place, where both the Scotch and English drover expected to dispose of a part of their cattle, which it was desirable to produce in the market, rested and in good order. Fields were therefore difficult to be obtained, and only upon high terms. This necessity occasioned a temporary separation betwixt the two friends, who went to bargain, each as he could, for the separate accommodation of his herd. Unhappily it chanced that both of them, unknown to each other, thought of bargaining for the ground they wanted on the property of a country gentleman of some fortune, whose estate lay in the neighbourhood. The English drover applied to the bailiff on the property, who was known to him. It chanced that the Cumbrian squire, who had entertained some suspicions of his manager's honesty, was taking occasional measures to ascertain how far they were well founded, and had desired that any enquiries about his enclosures, with a view to occupy them for a temporary purpose, should be referred to himself. As, however, Mr Ireby had gone the day before upon a journey of some miles' distance to the northward, the bailiff chose to consider the check upon his full powers as for the time removed, and concluded that he should best consult his master's interest, and perhaps his own, in making an agreement with Harry Wakefield. Meanwhile, ignorant of what his comrade was doing, Robin Oig, on his side, chanced to be overtaken by a good-looking smart little man upon a pony, most knowingly hogged and cropped, as was then the fashion, the rider wearing tight leather breeches and long-necked bright spurs. This cavalier asked one or two pertinent questions about markets and the price of stock. So Robin, seeing him a well-judging civil gentleman, took the freedom to ask him whether he could let him know if there was any grassland to be let in that neighbourhood, for the temporary accommodation of his drove. He could not have put the question to more willing ears. The gentleman of the buckskin was the proprietor with whose bailiff Harry Wakefield had dealt or was in the act of dealing.

'Thou art in good luck, my canny Scot,' said Mr Ireby, 'to have spoken to me, for I see thy cattle have done their day's work, and I have at my disposal the only field within three miles that is to be let in these parts.'

'The drove can pe gang two, three, four miles very pratty weel indeed,' said the cautious Highlander; 'put what would his honour be axing for the peasts pe the head, if he was to tak the park for twa or three days?'

'We won't differ, Sawney, if you let me have six stots for winterers, in the way of reason.'

'And which peasts wad your honour pe for having?'

'Why – let me see – the two black – the dun one – yon doddy – him with the twisted horn – the brocket – How much by the head?'

'Ah,' said Robin, 'your honour is a shudge – a real shudge – I couldna have set off the pest six peasts petter mysell, me that ken them as if they were my pairns, puir things.'

'Well, how much per head, Sawney?' continued Mr Ireby.

'It was high markets at Doune and Falkirk,' answered Robin.

And thus the conversation proceeded, until they had agreed on the *prix juste* for the bullocks, the squire throwing in the temporary accommodation of the enclosure for the cattle into the boot, and Robin making, as he thought, a very good bargain, provided the grass was but tolerable. The squire walked his pony alongside of the drove, partly to show him the way, and see him put into possession of the field, and partly to learn the latest news of the northern markets.

They arrived at the field, and the pasture seemed excellent. But what was their surprise when they saw the bailiff quietly inducting the cattle of Harry Wakefield into the grassy goshen which had just been assigned to those of Robin Oig M'Combich by the proprietor himself! Squire Ireby set spurs to his horse, dashed up to his servant, and learning what had passed between the parties, briefly informed the English drover that his bailiff had let the ground without his authority, and that he might seek grass for his cattle wherever he would, since he was to get none there. At the same time he rebuked his servant severely for having transgressed his commands, and ordered him instantly to assist in ejecting the hungry and weary cattle of Harry Wakefield, which were just beginning to enjoy a meal of unusual plenty, and to introduce those of his comrade, whom the English drover now began to consider as a rival.

The feelings which arose in Wakefield's mind would have induced him to resist Mr Ireby's decision; but every Englishman has a tolerably accurate sense of law and justice, and John Fleecebumpkin, the bailiff, having acknowledged that he had exceeded his commission, Wakefield saw nothing else for it than to collect his hungry and disappointed charge, and drive them on to seek quarters elsewhere. Robin Oig saw what had happened with regret, and hastened to offer to his English friend to share with him the disputed possession. But Wakefield's pride was severely hurt, and he answered disdainfully, 'Take it all, man -- take it all – never make two bites of a cherry – thou canst talk over the gentry, and blear a plain man's eye – Out upon you, man

– I would not kiss any man's dirty latchets for leave to bake in his oven.'

Robin Oig, sorry but not surprised at his comrade's displeasure, hastened to entreat his friend to wait but an hour till he had gone to the squire's house to receive payment for the cattle he had sold, and would come back and help him to drive the cattle into some convenient place of rest, and explain to him the whole mistake they had both of them fallen into. But the Englishman continued indignant: 'Thou hast been selling, hast thou? Aye, aye – thou is a cunning lad for kenning the hours of bargaining. Go to the devil with thyself, for I will ne'er see thy fause loon's visage again – thou should be ashamed to look me in the face.'

'I am ashamed to look no man in the face,' said Robin Oig, something moved; 'and, moreover, I will look you in the face this blessed day, if you will bide at the clachan down yonder.'

'Mayhap you had as well keep away,' said his comrade; and turning his back on his former friend, he collected his unwilling associates, assisted by the bailiff, who took some real and some affected interest in seeing Wakefield accommodated.

After spending some time in negotiating with more than one of the neighbouring farmers, who could not, or would not, afford the accommodation desired, Henry Wakefield at last, and in his necessity, accomplished his point by means of the landlord of the ale-house at which Robin Oig and he had agreed to pass the night, when they first separated from each other. Mine host was content to let him turn his cattle on a piece of barren moor, at a price little less than the bailiff had asked for the disputed enclosure; and the wretchedness of the pasture, as well as the price paid for it, were set down as exaggerations of the breach of faith and friendship of his Scottish crony. This turn of Wakefield's passions was encouraged by the bailiff (who had his own reasons for being offended against poor Robin, as having been the unwitting cause of his falling into digrace with his master), as well as by the innkeeper, and two or three chance guests, who stimulated the drover in his resentment against his quondam associate – some from the ancient grudge against the Scots which, when it exists anywhere, is to be found lurking in the

Border counties, and some from the general love of mischief, which characterizes mankind in all ranks of life, to the honour of Adam's children be it spoken. Good John Barleycorn also, who always heightens and exaggerates the prevailing passions, be they angry or kindly, was not wanting in his offices on this occasion; and confusion to false friends and hard masters was pledged in more than one tankard.

In the meanwhile Mr Ireby found some amusement in detaining the northern drover at his ancient hall. He caused a cold round of beef to be placed before the Scot in the butler's pantry, together with a foaming tankard of home-brewed, and took pleasure in seeing the hearty appetite with which these unwonted edibles were discussed by Robin Oig M'Combich. The squire himself lighting his pipe, compounded his patrician dignity and his love of agricultural gossip by walking up and down while he conversed with his guest.

'I passed another drove,' said the squire, 'with one of your countrymen behind them – they were something less beasts than your drove, doddies most of them – a big man was with them – none of your kilts though, but a decent pair of breeches – D'ye know who he may be?'

'Hout aye – that might, could, and would be Hughie Morrison – I didna think he could hae peen saw weel up. He has made a day on us; but his Argyleshires will have wearied shanks. How far was he pehind?'

'I think about six or seven miles,' answered the squire, 'for I passed them at the Christenbury Crag, and I overtook you at the Hollan Bush. If his beasts be leg-weary, he will be maybe selling bargains.'

'Na, na, Hughie Morrison is no the man for pargains – ye maun come to some Highland pody like Robin Oig hissell for the like of these – put I maun pe wishing you goot night, and twenty of them let alane ane, and I maun down to the clachan to see if the lad Harry Waakfelt is out of his humdudgeons yet.'

The party at the ale-house were still in full talk, and the treachery of Robin Oig still the theme of conversation, when the supposed culprit entered the apartment. His arrival, as usually happens in such a case, put an instant stop to the discussion of which he had furnished the subject, and he was received by the company assembled with that chilling silence which, more than a thousand exclamations, tells an intruder that he is unwelcome. Surprised and offended, but not appalled by the reception which he experienced, Robin entered with an undaunted and even a haughty air, attempted no greeting as he saw he was received with none, and placed himself by the side of the fire, a little apart from a table at which Harry Wakefield, the bailiff, and two or three other persons, were seated. The ample Cumbrian kitchen would have afforded plenty of room, even for a larger separation.

Robin, thus seated, proceeded to light his pipe, and call for a pint of twopenny.

'We have not twopence ale,' answered Ralph Heskett, the landlord; 'but as thou find'st thy own tobacco, it's like thou may'st find thy own liquor too – it's the wont of thy country, I wot.'

'Shame, goodman,' said the landlady, a blithe bustling house-wife, hastening herself to supply the guest with liquor – 'Thou knowest well enow what the strange man wants, and it's thy trade to be civil, man. Thou shouldst know, that if the Scot likes a small pot, he pays a sure penny.'

Without taking any notice of this nuptial dialogue, the High-lander took the flagon in his hand, and addressing the company generally, drank the interesting toast of 'Good markets' to the party assembled.

'The better that the wind blew fewer dealers from the north,' said one of the farmers, 'and fewer Highland runts to eat up the English meadows.'

'Saul of my pody, put you are wrang there, my friend,' answered Robin, with composure; 'it is your fat Englishmen that eat up our Scots cattle, puir things.'

'I wish there was summat to eat up their drovers,' said another; 'a plain Englishman canna make bread within a kenning of them.'

'Or an honest servant keep his master's favour, but they will come sliding in between him and the sunshine,' said the bailiff.

'If these pe jokes,' said Robin Oig, with the same composure, 'there is ower mony jokes upon one man.'

'It is no joke, but downright earnest,' said the bailiff. 'Hark ye, Mr Robin Ogg, or whatever is your name, it's right we should tell you that we are all of one opinion, and that is, that you, Mr Robin Ogg, have behaved to our friend Mr Harry Wakefield here, like a raff and a blackguard.'

'Nae doubt, nae doubt,' answered Robin, with great composure; 'and you are a set of very pretty judges, for whose prains of pehaviour I wad not gie a pinch of sneeshing. If Mr Harry Waakfelt kens where he is wranged, he kens where he may be righted.'

'He speaks truth,' said Wakefield, who had listened to what passed, divided between the offence which he had taken at Robin's late behaviour, and the revival of his habitual feelings of regard.

He now arose, and went towards Robin, who got up from his seat as he approached, and held out his hand.

'That's right, Harry – go it – serve him out,' resounded on all sides – 'tip him the nailer – show him the mill.'

'Hold your peace all of you, and be—,' said Wakefield; and then addressing his comrade, he took him by the extended hand, with something alike of respect and defiance. 'Robin,' he said, 'thou hast used me ill enough this day; but if you mean, like a frank fellow, to shake hands, and make a tussle for love on the sod, why I'll forgie thee, man, and we shall be better friends than ever.'

'And would it no pe petter to pe cood friends without more of the matter?' said Robin; 'we will pe much petter friends with our panes hale than proken.'

Harry Wakefield dropped the hand of his friend, or rather threw it from him.

'I did not think I had been keeping company for three years with a coward.'

'Coward pelongs to none of my name,' said Robin, whose eyes began to kindle, but keeping the command of his temper. 'It was no coward's legs or hands, Harry Waakfelt, that drew you out of the fords of Frew, when you was drifting ower the plack rock, and every eel in the river expected his share of you.'

'And that is true enough, too,' said the Englishman, struck by the appeal.

'Adzooks!' exclaimed the bailiff – 'sure Harry Wakefield, the nattiest lad at Whitson Tryste, Wooler Fair, Carlisle Sands, or Stagshaw Bank, is not going to show a white feather? Ah, this comes of living so long with kilts and bonnets – men forget the use of their daddles.'

'I may teach you, Master Fleecebumpkin, that I have not lost the use of mine,' said Wakefield, and then went on. 'This will never do, Robin. We must have a turn-up, or we shall be the talk of the countryside. I'll be d— d if I hurt thee – I'll put on the gloves sin thou like. Come, stand forward like a man.'

'To pe peaten like a dog,' said Robin; 'is there any reason in that? If you think I have done you wrong, I'll go before your shudge, though I neither know his law nor his language.'

A general cry of 'No, no – no law, no lawyer! a bellyful and be friends', was echoed by the bystanders.

'But,' continued Robin, 'if I am to fight, I've no skill to fight like a jackanapes, with hands and nails.'

'How would you fight, then,' said his antagonist; 'though I am thinking it would be hard to bring you to the scratch anyhow.'

'I would fight with proadswords, and sink point on the first plood drawn – like a gentlemans.'

A loud shout of laughter followed the proposal, which indeed had rather escaped from poor Robin's swelling heart, than been the dictate of his sober judgement.

'Gentleman, quotha!' was echoed on all sides, with a shout of unextinguishable laughter; 'a very pretty gentleman, God wot canst get two swords for the gentlemen to fight with, Ralph Heskett?'

'No, but I can send to the armoury at Carlisle, and lend them two forks, to be making shift with in the meantime.'

'Tush, man,' said another, 'the bonny Scots come into the world with the blue bonnet on their heads; and dirk and pistol at their belt.'

'Best send post,' said Mr Fleecebumpkin, 'to the squire of Corby Castle, to come and stand second to the *gentleman*.'

In the midst of this torrent of general ridicule, the Highlander instinctively gripped beneath the folds of his plaid.

'But it's better not,' he said in his own language. 'A hundred curses on the swine-eaters, who know neither decency nor civility!'

'Make room, the pack of you,' he said, advancing to the door.

But his former friend interposed his sturdy bulk, and opposed his leaving the house; and when Robin Oig attempted to make his way by force, he hit him down on the floor, with as much ease as a boy bowls down a nine-pin.

'A ring, a ring!' was now shouted, until the dark rafters, and the hams that hung on them, trembled again, and the very platters on the *bink* clattered against each other. 'Well done, Harry' – 'Give it him home, Harry' – 'Take care of him now – he sees his own blood!'

Such were the exclamations, while the Highlander, starting from the ground, all his coldness and caution lost in frantic rage, sprang at his antagonist with the fury, the activity, and the vindictive purpose, of an incensed tiger-cat. But when could rage encounter science and temper? Robin Oig again went down in the unequal contest; and as the blow was necessarily a severe one, he lay motionless on the floor of the kitchen. The landlady ran to offer some aid, but Mr Fleecebumpkin would not permit her to approach.

'Let him alone,' he said, 'he will come to within time, and come up to the scratch again. He has not got half his broth yet.'

'He has got all I mean to give him, though,' said his antagonist, whose heart began to relent towards his old associate: 'and I would rather by half give the rest to yourself, Mr Fleecebumpkin, for you pretend to know a thing or two, and Robin had not art enough even to peel before setting to, but fought with his plaid dangling about him – Stand up, Robin, my man! all friends now; and let me hear the man that will speak a word against you, or your country, for your sake.'

Robin Oig was still under the dominion of his passion, and

eager to renew the onset; but being withheld on the one side by the peace-making Dame Heskett, and on the other aware that Wakefield no longer meant to renew the combat, his fury sank into gloomy sullenness.

'Come, come, never grudge so much at it, man,' said the brave-spirited Englishman, with the placability of his country, 'shake hands and we will be better friends than ever.'

'Friends!' exclaimed Robin Oig, with strong emphasis – 'friends! – Never. Look to yourself, Harry Waakfelt.'

'Then the curse of Cromwell on your proud Scots stomach, as the man says in the play, and you may do your worst, and be d— d; for one man can say nothing more to another after a tussle, than that he is sorry for it.'

On these terms the friends parted; Robin Oig drew out, in silence, a piece of money, threw it on the table, and then left the ale-house. But turning at the door, he shook his hand at Wakefield, pointing with his forefinger upwards, in a manner which might imply either a threat or a caution. He then disappeared in the moonlight.

Some words passed after his departure, between the bailiff, who piqued himself on being a little of a bully, and Harry Wakefield, who, with generous inconsistency, was now not indisposed to begin a new combat in defence of Robin Oig's reputation, 'although he could not use his daddles like an Englishman, as it did not come natural to him'. But Dame Heskett prevented this second quarrel from coming to a head by her peremptory interference. 'There should be no more fighting in my house,' she said; 'there had been too much already – And you, Mr Wakefield, may live to learn,' she added, 'what it is to make a deadly enemy out of a good friend.'

'Pshaw, dame! Robin Oig is an honest fellow, and will never keep malice.'

'Do not trust to that – you do not know the dour temper of the Scots, though you have dealt with them so often. I have a right to know them, my mother being a Scot.'

'And so is well seen on her daughter,' said Ralph Heskett.

This nuptial sarcasm gave the discourse another turn; fresh

customers entered the tap-room or kitchen, and others left it. The conversation turned on the expected markets, and the report of prices from different parts both of Scotland and England – treaties were commenced, and Harry Wakefield was lucky enough to find a chap for a part of his drove, and at a very considerable profit; an event of consequence more than sufficient to blot out all remembrances of the unpleasant scuffle in the earlier part of the day. But there remained one party from whose mind that recollection could not have been wiped away by the possession of every head of cattle betwixt Esk and Eden.

This was Robin Oig M'Combich – 'That I should have had no weapon,' he said, 'and for the first time in my life! – Blighted be the tongue that bids the Highlander part with the dirk – the dirk – ha! the English blood! – My Muhme's word – when did her word fall to the ground?'

The recollection of the fatal prophecy confirmed the deadly intention which instantly sprang up in his mind.

'Ha! Morrison cannot be many miles behind; and if it were a hundred, what then?'

His impetuous spirit had now a fixed purpose and motive of action, and he turned the light foot of his country towards the wilds, through which he knew, by Mr Ireby's report, that Morrison was advancing. His mind was wholly engrossed by the sense of injury – injury sustained from a friend; and by the desire of vengeance on one whom he now accounted his most bitter enemy. The treasured ideas of self-importance and self-opinion – of ideal birth and quality, had become more precious to him, like the hoard to the miser, because he could only enjoy them in secret. But that hoard was pillaged, the idols which he had secretly worshipped had been desecrated and profaned. Insulted, abused and beaten, he was no longer worthy, in his own opinion, of the name he bore, or the lineage which he belonged to – nothing was left to him – nothing but revenge; and, as the reflection added a galling spur to every step, he determined it should be as sudden and signal as the offence.

When Robin Oig left the door of the ale-house, seven or eight English miles at least lay betwixt Morrison and him. The advance of the former was slow, limited by the sluggish pace of his cattle; the last left behind him stubble-field and hedgerow, crag and dark heath, all glittering with frost-rime in the broad November moonlight, at the rate of six miles an hour. And now the distant lowing of Morrison's cattle is heard; and now they are seen creeping like moles in size and slowness of motion on the broad face of the moor; and now he meets them – passes them, and stops their conductor.

'May good betide us,' said the Southlander – 'Is this you, Robin M'Combich, or your wraith?'

'It is Robin Oig M'Compich,' answered the Highlander, 'and it is not – Put never mind that, put pe giving me the *skene-dhu*.'

'What! you are for back to the Highlands – The devil! – Have you selt all off before the fair? This beats all for quick markets!'

'I have not sold – I am not going north – May pe I will never go north again – Give me pack my dirk, Hugh Morrison, or there will pe words petween us.'

'Indeed, Robin, I'll be better advised before I gie it back to you – it is a wanchancy weapon in a Highlandman's hand, and I am thinking you will be about some barns-breaking.'

'Prutt, trutt! let me have my weapon,' said Robin Oig, impatiently.

'Hooly, and fairly,' said his well-meaning friend. 'I'll tell you what will do better than these dirking doings – Ye ken Highlander, and Lowlander, and Border-men, are a' ae man's bairns when you are over the Scots dyke. See, the Eskdale callants, and fighting Charlie of Liddsdale, and the Lockerby lads, and the four Dandies of Lustruther, and a wheen mair grey plaids, are coming up behind, and if you are wranged, there is the hand of a Manly Morrison, we'll see you righted, if Carlisle and Stanwix baith took up the feud.'

'To tell you the truth,' said Robin Oig, desirous of eluding the suspicions of his friend, 'I have enlisted with a party of the Plack Watch, and must march off tomorrow morning.'

'Enlisted! Were you mad or drunk? – You must buy yourself off – I can lend you twenty notes, and twenty to that, if the drove sell.'

'I thank ye – thank ye, Hughie; but I go with good will the gate that I am going – so the dirk – the dirk!'

'There it is for you then, since less wunna serve. But think on what I was saying – Waes me, it will be sair news in the braes of Balquidder, that Robin Oig M'Combich should have run an ill gate, and ta'en on.'

'Ill news in Palquidder, indeed!' echoed poor Robin. 'Put Cot speed you, Hughie, and send you good marcats. Ye winna meet with Robin Oig again, either at tryste or fair.'

So saying, he shook hastily the hand of his acquaintance, and set out in the direction from which he had advanced, with the spirit of his former pace.

'There is something wrang with the lad,' muttered the Morrison to himself, 'but we'll maybe see better into it the morn's morning.'

But long ere the morning dawned, the catastrophe of our tale had taken place. It was two hours after the affray had happened, and it was totally forgotten by almost everyone, when Robin Oig returned to Heskett's inn. The place was filled at once by various sorts of men, and with noises corresponding to their character. There were the grave low sounds of men engaged in busy traffic, with the laugh, the song, and the riotous jest of those who had nothing to do but to enjoy themselves. Among the last was Harry Wakefield, who, amidst a grinning group of smock-frocks, hob-nailed shoes, and jolly English physiognomies, was trolling forth the old ditty,

> What though my name be Roger,
> Who drives the plough and cart—

when he was interrupted by a well-known voice saying in a high stern tone, marked by the sharp Highland accent, 'Harry Waakfelt – if you pe a man, stand up!'

'What is the matter? – what is it?' the guests demanded of each other.

'It is only a d— d Scotsman,' said Fleecebumpkin, who was by this time very drunk, 'whom Harry Wakefield helped to his broth the day, who is now come to have his *cauld kail* het again.'

'Harry Waakfelt,' repeated the same ominous summons, 'stand up, if you pe a man!'

There is something in the tone of deep and concentrated passion, which attracts attention and imposes awe, even by the very sound. The guests shrank back on every side, and gazed at the Highlander as he stood in the middle of them, his brows bent, and his features rigid with resolution.

'I will stand up with all my heart, Robin, my boy, but it shall be to shake hands with you, and drink down all unkindness. It is not the fault of your heart, man, that you don't know how to clench your hands.'

But this time he stood opposite his antagonist; his open and unsuspecting look strangely contrasted with the stern purpose which gleamed wild, dark and vindictive in the eyes of the Highlander.

''Tis not thy fault, man, that, not having the luck to be an Englishman, thou canst not fight more than a schoolgirl.'

'I *can* fight,' answered Robin Oig sternly, but calmly, 'and you shall know it. You, Harry Waakfelt, showed me today how the Saxon churls fight – I show you now how the Highland Dunnie-wassel fights.'

He seconded the word with the action, and plunged the dagger, which he suddenly displayed, into the broad breast of the English yeoman, with such fatal certainty and force, that the hilt made a hollow sound against the breastbone, and the double-edged point split the very heart of his victim. Harry Wakefield fell and expired with a single groan. His assassin next seized the bailiff by the collar, and offered the bloody poniard to his throat, whilst dread and surprise rendered the man incapable of defence.

'It were very just to lay you beside him,' he said, 'but the blood of a base pickthank shall never mix on my father's dirk with that of a brave man.'

As he spoke, he cast the man from him with so much force that he fell on the floor, while Robin, with his other hand, threw the fatal weapon into the blazing turf-fire.

'There,' he said, 'take me who likes – and let fire cleanse blood if it can.'

The pause of astonishment still continuing, Robin Oig asked for a peace-officer, and a constable having stepped out, he surrendered himself to his custody.

'A bloody night's work you have made of it,' said the constable.

'Your own fault,' said the Highlander. 'Had you kept his hands off me twa hours since, he would have peen now as well and merry as he was twa minutes since.'

'It must be sorely answered,' said the peace-officer.

'Never you mind that – death pays all debts; it will pay that too.'

The horror of the bystanders began now to give way to indignation; and the sight of a favourite companion murdered in the midst of them, the provocation being, in their opinion, so utterly inadequate to the excess of vengeance, might have induced them to kill the perpetrator of the deed even upon the very spot. The constable, however, did his duty on this occasion, and with the assistance of some of the more reasonable persons present, procured horses to guard the prisoner to Carlisle, to abide his doom at the next assizes. While the escort was preparing, the prisoner neither expressed the least interest nor attempted the slightest reply. Only, before he was carried from the fatal apartment, he desired to look at the dead body, which, raised from the floor, had been deposited upon the large table (at the head of which Harry Wakefield had presided but a few minutes before, full of life, vigour and animation) until the surgeons should examine the mortal wound. The face of the corpse was decently covered with a napkin. To the surprise and horror of the bystanders, which displayed itself in a general '*Ah!*' drawn through clenched teeth and half-shut lips, Robin Oig removed the cloth, and gazed with a mournful but steady eye on the lifeless visage, which had been so lately animated that the smile of good-humoured confidence in his own strength, of conciliation and contempt towards his enemy at once, still curled his lips. While those present expected that the wound, which had so lately flooded the apartment with gore, would send forth fresh streams at the touch of the homicide, Robin Oig replaced the covering, with the brief exclamation – 'He was a pretty man!'

My story is nearly ended. The unfortunate Highlander stood his trial at Carlisle. I was myself present, and as a young Scottish lawyer, or barrister at least, and reputed a man of some quality, the politeness of the Sheriff of Cumberland offered me a place on the bench. The facts of the case were proved in the manner I have related them; and whatever might be at first the prejudice of the audience against a crime so un-English as that of assassination from revenge, yet when the rooted national prejudices of the prisoner had been explained, which made him consider himself as stained with indelible dishonour when subjected to personal violence; when his previous patience, moderation and endurance were considered, the generosity of the English audience was inclined to regard his crime as the wayward aberration of a false idea of honour rather than as flowing from a heart naturally savage, or perverted by habitual vice. I shall never forget the charge of the venerable judge to the jury, although not at that time liable to be much affected either by that which was eloquent or pathetic.

'We have had,' he said, 'in the previous part of our duty' (alluding to some former trials) 'to discuss crimes which infer disgust and abhorrence, while they call down the well-merited vengeance of the law. It is now our still more melancholy task to apply its salutary though severe enactments to a case of a very singular character, in which the crime (for a crime it is, and a deep one) arose less out of the malevolence of the heart, than the error of the understanding – less from any idea of committing wrong, than from an unhappily perverted notion of that which is right. Here we have two men, highly esteemed, it has been stated, in their rank of life, and attached, it seems, to each other as friends, one of whose lives has been already sacrificed to a punctilio, and the other is about to prove the vengeance of the offended laws; and yet both may claim our commiseration at least, as men acting in ignorance of each other's national prejudices, and unhappily misguided rather than voluntarily erring from the path of right conduct.

'In the original cause of the misunderstanding, we must in justice give the right to the prisoner at the bar. He had acquired possession of the enclosure, which was the object of competition, by a legal contract with the proprietor, Mr Ireby; and yet, when accosted with reproaches undeserved in themselves, and galling doubtless to a temper at least sufficiently susceptible of passion, he offered notwithstanding to yield up half his acquisition for the sake of peace and good neighbourhood, and his amicable proposal was rejected with scorn. Then follows the scene at Mr Heskett the publican's, and you will observe how the stranger was treated by the deceased, and, I am sorry to observe, by those around, who seem to have urged him in a manner which was aggravating in the highest degree. While he asked for peace and composition, and offered submission to a magistrate, or to a mutual arbiter, the prisoner was insulted by a whole company, who seem on this occasion to have forgotten the national maxim of "fair play"; and while attempting to escape from the place in peace, he was intercepted, struck down, and beaten to the effusion of his blood.

'Gentlemen of the jury, it was with some impatience that I heard my learned brother, who opened the case for the Crown, give an unfavourable turn to the prisoner's conduct on this occasion. He said the prisoner was afraid to encounter his antagonist in fair fight, or to submit to the laws of the ring; and that therefore, like a cowardly Italian, he had recourse to his fatal stiletto, to murder the man whom he dared not meet in manly encounter. I observed the prisoner shrink from this part of the accusation with the abhorrence natural to a brave man; and as I would wish to make my words impressive when I point his real crime, I must secure his opinion of my impartiality, by rebutting everything that seems to me a false accusation. There can be no doubt that the prisoner is a man of resolution – too much resolution – I wish to Heaven that he had less, or rather that he had had a better education to regulate it.

'Gentlemen, as to the laws my brother talks of, they may be known in the bull-ring, or the bear-garden, or the cockpit, but they are not known here. Or, if they should be so far admitted as furnishing a species of proof that no malice was intended in this sort of combat, from which fatal accidents do sometimes arise, it can only be so admitted when both parties are *in pari casu*, equally acquainted with, and equally willing to refer themselves to, that species of arbitrement. But will it be contended that a man of superior rank and education is to be subjected, or is obliged to subject himself, to this coarse and brutal strife, perhaps in opposition to a younger, stronger, or more skilful opponent? Certainly even the pugilistic code, if founded upon the fair play of Merry Old England, as my brother alleges it to be, can contain nothing so preposterous. And, gentlemen of the jury, if the laws would support an English gentleman, wearing, we will suppose, his sword, in defending himself by force against a violent personal aggression of the nature offered to this prisoner, they will not less protect a foreigner and a stranger, involved in the same unpleasing circumstances. If, therefore, gentlemen of the jury, when thus pressed by a *vis major*, the object of obloquy to a whole company, and of direct violence from one at least, and, as he might reasonably apprehend, from more, the panel had produced the weapon which his countrymen, as we are informed, generally carry about their persons, and the same unhappy circumstance had ensued which you have heard detailed in evidence, I could not in my conscience have asked from you a verdict of murder. The prisoner's personal defence might, indeed, even in that case, have gone more or less beyond the *Moderamen inculpatae tutelae*, spoken of by lawyers, but the punishment incurred would have been that of manslaughter, not of murder. I beg leave to add that I should have thought this milder species of charge was demanded in the case supposed, notwithstanding the statute of James I, cap. 8, which takes the case of slaughter by stabbing with a short weapon, even without malice prepense, out of the benefit of clergy. For this statute of stabbing, as it is termed, arose out of a temporary cause; and as the real guilt is the same, whether the slaughter be committed by the dagger, or by sword or pistol, the benignity of the modern law places them all on the same, or nearly the same footing.

'But, gentlemen of the jury, the pinch of the case lies in the interval of two hours interposed betwixt the reception of the injury and the fatal retaliation. In the heat of affray and *chaude mêlée*, law, compassionating the infirmities of humanity, makes allowance for the passions which rule such a stormy moment – for the sense of present pain, for the apprehension of further injury, for the difficulty of ascertaining with due accuracy the precise degree of violence which is necessary to protect the person of the individual, without annoying or injuring the assailant more than is absolutely requisite. But the time necessary to walk twelve miles, however speedily performed, was an interval sufficient for the prisoner to have recollected himself; and the violence with which he carried his purpose into effect, with so many circumstances of deliberate determination, could neither be induced by the passion of anger, nor that of fear. It was the purpose and the act of predetermined revenge, for which law neither can, will, nor ought to have sympathy or allowance.

'It is true, we may repeat to ourselves, in alleviation of this poor man's unhappy action, that his case is a very peculiar one. The country which he inhabits, was, in the days of many now alive, inaccessible to the laws, not only of England, which have not even yet penetrated thither, but to those to which our neighbours of Scotland are subjected, and which must be supposed to be, and no doubt actually are, founded upon the general principles of justice and equity which pervade every civilized country. Amongst their mountains, as among the North American Indians, the various tribes were wont to make war upon each other, so that each man was obliged to go armed for his own protection. These men, from the ideas which they entertained of their own descent and of their own consequence, regarded themselves as so many cavaliers or men-at-arms, rather than as the peasantry of a peaceful country. Those laws of the ring, as my brother terms them, were unknown to the race of the war-like mountaineers; that decision of quarrels by no other weapons than those which nature has given every man, must to them have seemed as vulgar and as preposterous as to the noblesse of France. Revenge, on the other hand, must have been as familiar to their habits of society as to those of the Cherokees or Mohawks. it is indeed, as described by Bacon, at bottom a kind of wild untutored justice; for the fear of retaliation must withhold the hands of the oppressor where there is no regular law to check daring violence. But though all this may be granted, and though we may allow that, such having been the case of the Highlands in the days of the prisoner's fathers, many of the opinions and sentiments must still continue to influence the present generation, it cannot, and ought not, even in this most painful case, to alter the administration of the law, either in your hands, gentlemen of the jury, or in mine. The first object of civilization is to place the general protection of the law, equally administered, in the room of that wild justice, which every man cut and carved for himself, according to the length of his sword and the strength of his arm. The law says to the subjects, with a voice only inferior to that of the Deity, "Vengeance is mine". The instant that there is time for passion to cool, and reason to interpose, an injured party must become aware that the law assumes the exclusive cognizance of the right and wrong betwixt the parties, and opposes her inviolable buckler to every attempt of the private party to right himself. I repeat, that this unhappy man ought personally to be the object rather of our pity than our abhorrence, for he failed in his ignorance and from mistaken notions of honour. But his crime is not the less that of murder, gentlemen, and, in your high and important office, it is your duty so to find. Englishmen have their angry passions as well as Scots; and should this man's action remain unpunished, you may unsheath, under various pretences, a thousand daggers betwixt Land's-End and the Orkneys.'

The venerable judge thus ended what, to judge by his apparent emotion, and by the tears which filled his eyes, was really a painful task. The jury, according to his instructions, brought in a verdict of Guilty; and Robin Oig M'Combich, *alias* M'Gregor, was sentenced to death and left for execution, which took place accordingly. He met his fate with great firmness, and acknowledged the justice of his sentence. But he repelled indignantly the observations of those who accused him of attacking an unarmed man. 'I give a life for the life I took,' he said, 'and what can I do more?'

The Surgeon of Gaster Fell

ARTHUR CONAN DOYLE

I. HOW THE WOMAN CAME TO KIRKBY-MALHOUSE

Bleak and wind-swept is the little town of Kirkby-Malhouse,
harsh and forbidding are the fells upon which it stands. It
stretches in a single line of grey-stone, slate-roofed houses,
dotted down the furze-clad slope of the rolling moor.

In this lonely and secluded village, I, James Upperton, found
myself in the summer of '85. Little as the hamlet had to offer, it
contained that for which I yearned above all things – seclusion
and freedom from all which might distract my mind from the
high and weighty subjects which engaged it. But the inquisitive-
ness of my landlady made my lodgings undesirable and I
determined to seek new quarters.

As it chanced, I had in one of my rambles come upon an
isolated dwelling in the very heart of these lonely moors,
which I at once determined should be my own. It was a
two-roomed cottage, which had once belonged to some shepherd, but had long been deserted, and was crumbling rapidly
to ruin. In the winter floods, the Gaster Beck, which runs
down Gaster Fell, where the little dwelling stood, had over-
swept its banks and torn away a part of the wall. The roof was
in ill case, and the scattered slates lay thick amongst the grass.
Yet the main shell of the house stood firm and true; and it was

no great task for me to have all that was amiss set right.

The two rooms I laid out in a widely different manner – my own tastes are of a Spartan turn, and the outer chamber was so planned as to accord with them. An oil-stove by Rippingille of Birmingham furnished me with the means of cooking; while two great bags, the one of flour, and the other of potatoes, made me independent of all supplies from without. In diet I had long been a Pythagorean, so that the scraggy, long-limbed sheep which browsed upon the wiry grass by the Gaster Beck had little to fear from their new companion. A nine-gallon cask of oil served me as a sideboard; while a square table, a deal chair and a truckle-bed completed the list of my domestic fittings. At the head of my couch hung two unpainted shelves – the lower for my dishes and cooking utensils, the upper for the few portraits which took me back to the little that was pleasant in the long, wearisome toiling for wealth and for pleasure which had marked the life I had left behind.

If this dwelling-room of mine were plain even to squalor, its poverty was more than atoned for by the luxury of the chamber which was destined to serve me as my study. I had ever held that it was best for my mind to be surrounded by such objects as would be in harmony with the studies which occupied it, and that the loftiest and most ethereal conditions of thought are only possible amid surroundings which please the eye and gratify the senses. The room which I had set apart for my mystic studies was set forth in a style as gloomy and majestic as the thoughts and aspirations with which it was to harmonize. Both walls and ceilings were covered with a paper of the richest and glossiest black, on which was traced a lurid and arabesque pattern of dead gold. A black velvet curtain covered the single diamond-paned window; while a thick, yielding carpet of the same material prevented the sound of my own footfalls, as I paced backward and forward, from breaking the current of my thought. Along the cornices ran gold rods, from which depended six pictures, all of the sombre and imaginative caste, which chimed best with my fancy.

And yet it was destined that ere ever I reached this quiet

harbour I should learn that I was still one of humankind, and that it is an ill thing to strive to break the bond which binds us to our fellows. It was but two nights before the date I had fixed upon for my change of dwelling, when I was conscious of a bustle in the house beneath, with the bearing of heavy burdens up the creaking stair, and the harsh voice of my landlady, loud in welcome and protestations of joy. From time to time, amid the whirl of words, I could hear a gentle and softly modulated voice, which struck pleasantly upon my ear after the long weeks during which I had listened only to the rude dialect of the dalesmen. For an hour I could hear the dialogue beneath – the high voice and the low, with clatter of cup and clink of spoon, until at last a light, quick step passed my study door, and I knew that my new fellow-lodger had sought her room.

On the morning after this incident I was up betimes, as is my wont; but I was surprised, on glancing from my window, to see that our new inmate was earlier still. She was walking down the narrow pathway, which zigzags over the fell – a tall woman, slender, her head sunk upon her breast, her arms filled with a bristle of wild flowers, which she had gathered in her morning rambles. The white and pink of her dress, and the touch of deep red ribbon in her broad, drooping hat, formed a pleasant dash of colour against the dun-tinted landscape. She was some distance off when I first set eyes upon her, yet I knew that this wandering woman could be none other than our arrival of last night, for there was a grace and refinement in her bearing which marked her from the dwellers of the fells. Even as I watched she passed swiftly and lightly down the pathway and, turning through the wicket gate, at the farther end of our cottage garden, she seated herself upon the green bank which faced my window and, strewing her flowers in front of her, set herself to arrange them.

As she sat there, with the rising sun at her back, and the glow of the morning spreading like an aureole around her stately and well-poised head, I could see that she was a woman of extraordinary personal beauty. Her face was Spanish rather than English in its type – oval, olive, with black, sparkling eyes, and a sweetly sensitive mouth. From under the broad straw hat two thick coils of blue-black hair curved down on either side of her graceful, queenly neck. I was surprised, as I watched her, to see that her shoes and skirt bore witness to a journey rather than to a mere morning ramble. Her light dress was stained, wet and bedraggled; while her boots were thick with the yellow soil of the fells. Her face, too, wore a weary expression, and her young beauty seemed to be clouded over by the shadow of inward trouble. Even as I watched her, she burst suddenly into wild weeping and, throwing down her bundle of flowers, ran swiftly into the house.

Distrait as I was and weary of the ways of the world, I was conscious of a sudden pang of sympathy and grief as I looked upon the spasm of despair which seemed to convulse this strange and beautiful woman. I bent to my books, and yet my thoughts would ever turn to her proud, clear-cut face, her weather-stained dress, her drooping head, and the sorrow which lay in each line and feature of her pensive face.

Mrs Adams, my landlady, was wont to carry up my frugal breakfast; yet it was very rarely that I allowed her to break the current of my thoughts, or to draw my mind by her idle chatter from weightier things. This morning, however, for once, she found me in a listening mood and, with little prompting, proceeded to pour into my ears all that she knew of our beautiful visitor.

'Miss Eva Cameron be her name, sir,' she said: 'but who she be, or where she came fra, I know little more than yoursel'. Maybe it was the same reason that brought her to Kirkby-Malhouse as fetched you here yoursel', sir.'

'Possibly,' said I, ignoring the covert question; 'but I should hardly have thought that Kirkby-Malhouse was a place which offered any great attractions to a young lady.'

'Heh, sir!' she cried, 'there's the wonder of it. The leddy has just come fra France; and how her folk come to learn of me is just a wonder. A week ago, up comes a man to my door – a fine man, sir, and a gentleman, as one could see with half an eye. "You are Mrs Adams," says he. "I engage your rooms for Miss Cameron," says he. "She will be here in a week," says he; and then off without a word of terms. Last night there comes the young leddy hersel' – soft-spoken and downcast, with a touch of the French in her speech. But my sakes, sir! I must away and mak' her some tea, for she'll feel lonesome-like, poor lamb, when she wakes under a strange roof.'

II. HOW I WENT FORTH TO GASTER FELL

I was still engaged upon my breakfast when I heard the clatter of dishes and the landlady's footfall as she passed towards her new lodger's room. An instant afterward she had rushed down the passage and burst in upon me with uplifted hand and startled eyes. 'Lord 'a mercy, sir!' he cried, 'and asking your pardon for troubling you, but I'm feared o' the young leddy, sir; she is not in her room.'

'Why, there she is,' said I, standing up and glancing through the casement. 'She has gone back for the flowers she left upon the bank.'

'Oh, sir, see her boots and her dress!' cried the landlady wildly. 'I wish her mother was here, sir – I do. Where she has been is more than I ken, but her bed has not been lain on this night.'

'She had felt restless, doubtless, and went for a walk, though the hour was certainly a strange one.'

Mrs Adams pursed her lip and shook her head. But then, as she stood at the casement, the girl beneath looked smilingly up at her and beckoned to her with a merry gesture to open the window.

'Have you my tea there?' she asked in a rich, clear voice, with a touch of the mincing French accent.

'It is in your room, miss.'

'Look at my boots, Mrs Adams!' she cried, thrusting them out from under her skirt. 'These fells of yours are dreadful places – *effroyable* – one inch, two inch: never have I seen such mud! My dress, too – *voilà*!'

'Eh, miss, but you are in a pickle,' cried the landlady, as she gazed down at the bedraggled gown. 'But you must be main weary and heavy for sleep.'

'No, no,' she answered laughingly, 'I care not for sleep. What is sleep? it is a little death – *voilà tout*. But for me to walk, to run, to breathe the air – that is to live. I was not tired, and so all night I have explored these fells of Yorkshire.'

'Lord 'a mercy, miss, and where did you go?' asked Mrs Adams.

She waved her hand round in a sweeping gesture which included the whole western horizon. 'There,' she cried. *'O comme elles sont tristes et sauvages, ces collines!* But I have flowers here. You will give me water, will you not? They will wither else.' She gathered her treasures in her lap, and a moment later we heard her light, springy footfall upon the stair.

So she had been out all night, this strange woman. What motive could have taken her from her snug room on to the bleak, wind-swept hills? Could it be merely the restlessness, the love of adventure of a young girl? Or was there, possibly, some deeper meaning in this nocturnal journey?

Deep as were the mysteries which my studies had taught me to solve, here was a human problem which for the moment at least was beyond my comprehension. I walked out on the moor in the forenoon, and on my return, as I topped the brow that overlooks the little town, I saw my fellow-lodger some little distance off amongst the gorse. She had raised a light easel in front of her, and, with papered board laid across it, was preparing to paint the magnificent landscape of rock and moor which stretched away in front of her. As I watched her I saw that she was looking anxiously to right and left. Close by me a pool of water had formed in a hollow. Dipping the cup of my pocket-flask into it, I carried it across to her.

'Miss Cameron, I believe,' said I. 'I am your fellow-lodger. Upperton is my name. We must introduce ourselves in these wilds if we are not to be forever strangers.'

'Oh, then, you live also with Mrs Adams!' she cried. 'I had thought that there were none but peasants in this strange place.'

'I am a visitor, like yourself,' I answered. 'I am a student, and have come for quiet and repose, which my studies demand.'

'Quiet, indeed!' said she, glancing round at the vast circle of silent moors, with the one tiny line of grey cottages which sloped down beneath us.

'And yet not quiet enough,' I answered, laughing, 'for I have been forced to move farther into the fells for the absolute peace which I require.'

'Have you, then, built a house upon the fells?' she asked, arching her eyebrows.

'I have, and hope, within a few days, to occupy it.'

'Ah, but that is *triste*,' she cried. 'And where is it, then, this house which you have built?'

'It is over yonder,' I answered. 'See that stream which lies like a silver band upon the distant moor? It is the Gaster Beck, and it runs through Gaster Fell.'

She started, and turned upon me her great, dark, questioning eyes with a look in which surprise, incredulity, and something akin to horror seemed to be struggling for mastery.

'And you will live on the Gaster Fell?' she cried.

'So I have planned. But what do you know of Gaster Fell, Miss Cameron?' I asked. 'I had thought that you were a stranger in these parts.'

'Indeed, I have never been here before,' she answered. 'But I have heard my brother talk of these Yorkshire moors; and, if I mistake not, I have heard him name this very one as the wildest and most savage of them all.'

'Very likely,' said I carelessly. 'It is indeed a dreary place.'

'Then why live there?' she cried eagerly. 'Consider the loneliness, the barrenness, the want of all comfort and of all aid, should aid be needed.'

'Aid! What aid should be needed on Gaster Fell?'

She looked down and shrugged her shoulders. 'Sickness may come in all places,' said she. 'If I were a man I do not think I would live alone on Gaster Fell.'

'I have braved worse dangers than that,' said I, laughing; 'but I fear that your picture will be spoiled, for the clouds are banking up, and already I feel a few raindrops.'

Indeed, it was high time we were on our way to shelter, for even as I spoke there came the sudden, steady swish of the shower. Laughing merrily, my companion threw her light shawl over her head, and, seizing picture and easel, ran with the lithe grace of a young fawn down the furze-clad slope, while I followed after with camp-stool and paint-box.

It was on the eve of my departure from Kirkby-Malhouse that we sat upon the green bank in the garden, she with dark, dreamy eyes looking sadly out over the sombre fells; while I, with a book upon my knee, glanced covertly at her lovely profile and marvelled to myself how twenty years of life could have stamped so sad and wistful an expression upon it.

'You have read much,' I remarked at last. 'Women have opportunities now such as their mothers never knew. Have you ever thought of going further – or seeking a course of college or even a learned profession?'

She smiled wearily at the thought.

'I have no aim, no ambition,' she said. 'My future is black – confused – a chaos. My life is like one of these paths upon the fells. You have seen them, Monsieur Upperton. They are smooth and straight and clear where they begin; but soon they wind to left and wind to right, and so mid rocks and crags until they lose themselves in some quagmire. At Brussels my path was straight; but now, *mon Dieu!* who is there can tell me where it leads?'

'It might take no prophet to do that, Miss Cameron,' quoth I, with the fatherly manner which two score years may show toward one. 'If I may read your life, I would venture to say that you were destined to fulfil the lot of women – to make some good man happy, and to shed around, in some wider circle, the pleasure which your society has given me since first I knew you.'

'I will never marry,' said she, with a sharp decision, which surprised and somewhat amused me.

'Not marry – and why?'

A strange look passed over her sensitive features, and she plucked nervously at the grass on the bank beside her.

'I dare not,' said she in a voice that quivered with emotion.

'Dare not?'

'It is not for me. I have other things to do. That path of which

I spoke is one which I must tread alone.'

'But this is morbid,' said I. 'Why should your lot, Miss Cameron, be separated from that of my own sisters, or the thousand other young ladies whom every season brings out into the world? But perhaps it is that you have a fear and distrust of mankind. Marriage brings a risk as well as a happiness.'

'The risk would be with the man who married me,' she cried. And then in an instant, as though she had said too much, she sprang to her feet and drew her mantle round her. 'The night air is chill, Monsieur Upperton,' said she, and so swept swiftly away, leaving me to muse over the strange words which had fallen from her lips.

Clearly, it was time that I should go. I set my teeth and vowed that another day should not have passed before I should have snapped this newly formed tie and sought the lonely retreat which awaited me upon the moors. Breakfast was hardly over in the morning before a peasant dragged up to the door the rude hand-cart which was to convey my few personal belongings to my new dwelling. My fellow-lodger had kept her room; and, steeled as my mind was against her influence, I was yet conscious of a little throb of disappointment that she should allow me to depart without a word of farewell. My hand-cart with its load of books had already started, and I, having shaken hands with Mrs Adams, was about to follow it, when there was a quick scurry of feet on the stair, and there she was beside me all panting with her own haste.

'Then you go – you really go?' said she.

'My studies call me.'

'And to Gaster Fell?' she asked.

'Yes; to the cottage which I have built there.'

'And you will live alone there?'

'With my hundred companions who lie in that cart.'

'Ah, books!' she cried, with a pretty shrug of her graceful shoulders. 'But you will make me a promise?'

'What is it?' I asked, in surprise.

'It is a small thing. You will not refuse me?'

'You have but to ask it.'

She bent forward her beautiful face with an expression of the most intense earnestness. 'You will bolt your door at night?' said she; and was gone ere I could say a word in answer to her extraordinary request.

It was a strange thing for me to find myself at last duly installed in my lonely dwelling. For me, now, the horizon was bounded by the barren circle of wiry, unprofitable grass, patched over with furze bushes and scarred by the profusion of Nature's gaunt and granite ribs. A duller, wearier waste I have never seen; but its dullness was its very charm.

And yet the very first night which I spent at Gaster Fell there came a strange incident to lead my thoughts back once more to the world which I had left behind me.

It had been a sullen and sultry evening, with great, livid cloud-banks mustering in the west. As the night wore on, the air within my little cabin became closer and more oppressive. A weight seemed to rest upon my brow and my chest. From far away the low rumble of thunder came moaning over the moor. Unable to sleep, I dressed and, standing at my cottage door, looked on the black solitude which surrounded me.

Taking the narrow sheep path which ran by the stream, I strolled along it for some hundred yards, and had turned to retrace my steps, when the moon was finally buried beneath an ink-black cloud, and the darkness deepened so suddenly that I could see neither the path at my feet, the stream upon my right, nor the rocks upon my left. I was standing groping about in the thick gloom, when there came a crash of thunder with a flash of lightning which lighted up the whole, vast fell, so that every bush and rock stood out clear and hard in the vivid light. It was but for an instant, and yet that momentary view struck a thrill of fear and astonishment through me, for in my very path, not twenty yards before me, there stood a woman, the livid light beating upon her face and showing up every detail of her dress and features.

There was no mistaking those dark eyes, that tall, graceful figure. It was she – Eva Cameron, the woman whom I thought I had for ever left. For an instant I stood petrified, marvelling whether this could indeed be she, or whether it was some figment conjured up by my excited brain. Then I ran swiftly forward in the direction where I had seen her, calling loudly upon her, but without reply. Again I called, and again no answer came back, save the melancholy wail of the owl. A second flash illuminated the landscape, and the moon burst out from behind its cloud. But I could not, though I climbed upon a knoll which overlooked the whole moor, see any sign of this strange, midnight wanderer. For an hour or more I traversed the fell, and at last found myself back at my little cabin, still uncertain as to whether it had been a woman or a shadow upon which I gazed.

III. OF THE GREY COTTAGE IN THE GLEN

It was either on the fourth or the fifth day after I had taken possession of my cottage that I was astonished to hear footsteps upon the grass outside, quickly followed by a crack, as from a stick upon the door. The explosion of an infernal machine would hardly have surprised or discomfited me more. I had hoped to have shaken off all intrusion for ever, yet here was somebody beating at my door with as little ceremony as if it had been a village ale-house. Hot with anger, I flung down my book and withdrew the bolt just as my visitor had raised his stick to renew his rough application for admittance. He was a tall, powerful man, tawny-bearded and deep-chested, clad in a loose-fitting suit of tweed, cut for comfort rather than elegance. As he stood in the shimmering sunlight, I took in every feature of his face. The large, fleshy nose; the steady, blue eyes, with their thick thatch of overhanging brows; the broad forehead, all knitted and lined with furrows, which were strangely at variance with his youthful bearing. In spite of his weather-stained felt hat, and the coloured handkerchief slung round his muscular, brown neck, I could see at a glance he was a man of breeding and education. I had been prepared for some wandering shepherd or uncouth tramp, but this apparition fairly disconcerted me.

'You look astonished,' said he, with a smile. 'Did you think, then, that you were the only man in the world with a taste for solitude? You see that there are other hermits in the wilderness besides yourself.'

'Do you mean to say that you live here?' I asked in no conciliatory voice.

'Up yonder,' he answered, tossing his head backward. 'I thought as we were neighbours, Mr Upperton, that I could not do less than look in and see if I could assist you in any way.'

'Thank you,' I said coldly, standing with my hand upon the latch of the door. 'I am a man of simple tastes, and you can do nothing for me. You have the advantage of me in knowing my name.'

He appeared to be chilled by my ungracious manner.

'I learned it from the masons who were at work here,' he said. 'As for me, I am a surgeon, the surgeon of Gaster Fell. That is the name I have gone by in these parts, and it serves as well as another.'

'Not much room for practice here?' I observed.

'Not a soul except yourself for miles on either side.'

'You appear to have had need of some assistance yourself,' I remarked, glancing at a broad, white splash, as from the recent action of some powerful acid, upon his sunburnt cheek.

'That is nothing,' he answered, curtly, turning his face half round to hide the mark. 'I must get back, for I have a companion who is waiting for me. If I can ever do anything for you, pray let me know. You have only to follow the beck upward for a mile or so to find my place. Have you a bolt on the inside of your door?'

'Yes,' I answered, rather startled at this question.

'Keep it bolted, then,' he said. 'The fell is a strange place. You never know who may be about. It is as well to be on the safe side. Good-bye.' He raised his hat, turned on his heel and lunged away along the bank of the little stream.

I was still standing with my hand upon the latch, gazing after my unexpected visitor, when I became aware of yet another dweller in the wilderness. Some distance along the path which the stranger was taking there lay a great, grey boulder, and leaning against this was a small, wizened man, who stood erect as the other approached, and advanced to meet him. The two talked for a minute or more, the taller man nodding his head frequently in my direction, as though describing what had passed between us. Then they walked on together, and disappeared in a dip of the fell. Presently I saw them ascending once more some rising ground further on. My acquaintance had thrown his arm round his elderly friend, either from affection or from a desire to aid him up the steep incline. The square, burly figure and its shrivelled, meagre companion stood out against the skyline and, turning their faces, they looked back at me. At the sight, I slammed the door, lest they should be encouraged to return. But when I peeped from the window some minutes afterwards, I perceived that they were gone.

All day I bent over the Egyptian papyrus upon which I was engaged; but neither the subtle reasonings of the ancient philosopher of Memphis, nor the mystic meaning which lay in his pages, could raise my mind from the things of earth. Evening was drawing in before I threw my work aside in despair. My heart was bitter against this man for his intrusion. Standing by the beck which purled past the door of my cabin, I cooled my heated brow, and thought the matter over. Clearly it was the small mystery hanging over these neighbours of mine which had caused my mind to run so persistently on them. That cleared up, they would no longer cause an obstacle to my studies. What was to hinder me, then, from walking in the direction of their dwelling, and observing for myself, without permitting them to suspect my presence, what manner of men might they be? Doubtless, their mode of life would be found to admit of some simple and prosaic explanation. In any case, the evening was fine, and a walk would be bracing for mind and body. Lighting my pipe, I set off over the moors in the direction which they had taken.

About half-way down a wild glen there stood a small clump of gnarled and stunted oak trees. From behind these, a thin, dark column of smoke rose into the still evening air. Clearly this marked the position of my neighbour's house. Trending away to the left, I was able to gain the shelter of a line of rocks, and so reach a spot from which I could command a view of the building without exposing myself to any risk of being observed. It was a small, slate-covered cottage, hardly larger than the boulders among which it lay. Like my own cabin, it showed signs of having been constructed for the use of some shepherd; but, unlike mine, no pains had been taken by the tenants to improve and enlarge it. Two little peeping windows, a cracked and weather-beaten door, and a discoloured barrel for catching the rainwater, were the only external objects from which I might draw deductions as to the dwellers within. Yet even in these there was food for thought, for as I drew nearer, still concealing myself behind the ridge, I saw that thick bars of iron covered the windows, while the old door was slashed and plated with the same metal. These strange precautions, together with the wild surroundings and unbroken solitude, gave an indescribably ill omen and fearsome character to the solitary building. Thrusting my pipe into my pocket, I crawled upon my hands and knees through the gorse and ferns until I was within a hundred yards of my neighbour's door. There, finding that I could not approach nearer without fear of detection, I crouched down, and set myself to watch.

I had hardly settled into my hiding-place, when the door of the cottage swung open, and the man who had introduced himself to me as the surgeon of Gaster Fell came out, bareheaded, with a spade in his hands. In front of the door there was a small cultivated patch containing potatoes, peas and other forms of green stuff, and here he proceeded to busy himself, trimming, weeding and arranging, singing the while in a powerful though not very musical voice. He was all engrossed in his work, with his back to the cottage, when there emerged from the half-open door the same attenuated creature whom I had seen in the morning. I could perceive now that he was a man of sixty, wrinkled, bent, and feeble, with sparse, grizzled hair, and a long, colourless face. With a cringeing, sidelong gait, he shuffled towards his companion, who was unconscious of his approach until he was close upon him. His light footfall or his breathing may have finally given notice of his proximity, for the worker sprang round and faced him. Each made a quick step towards the other, as though in greeting, and then – even now I feel the horror of the instant – the tall man rushed upon and knocked his companion to the earth then, whipping up his body, ran with great speed over the intervening ground and disappeared with his burden into the house.

Case-hardened as I was by my varied life, the suddenness and violence of the thing made me shudder. The man's age, his feeble frame, his humble and deprecating manner, all cried shame against the deed. So hot was my anger, that I was on the point of striding up to the cabin, unarmed as I was, when the sound of voices from within showed me that the victim had recovered. The sun had sunk beneath the horizon, and all was grey, save a red feather in the cap of Pennigent. Secure in the failing light, I approached nearer and strained my ears to catch what was passing. I could hear the high, querulous voice of the elder man and the deep, rough monotone of his assailant, mixed with a strange metallic jangling and clanking. Presently the surgeon came out, locked the door behind him and stamped up and down in the twilight, pulling at his hair and brandishing his arms, like a man demented. Then he set off, walking rapidly up the valley, and I soon lost sight of him among the rocks.

When his footsteps had died away in the distance, I drew nearer to the cottage. The prisoner within was still pouring forth a stream of words, and moaning from time to time like a man in pain. These words resolved themselves, as I approached, into prayers – shrill, voluble prayers, pattered forth with the intense earnestness of one who sees impending and imminent danger. There was to me something inexpressibly awesome in this gush of solemn entreaty from the lonely sufferer, meant for no human ear, and jarring upon the silence of the night. I was still pondering whether I should mix myself in the affair or not, when I heard in the distance the sound of the surgeon's returning footfall. At that I drew myself up quickly by the iron bars and glanced in through the diamond-paned window. The interior of the cottage was lighted up by a lurid glow, coming from what I afterwards discovered to be a chemical furnace. By its rich light I could distinguish a great litter of retorts, test-tubes and condensers, which sparkled over the table, and threw strange, grotesque shadows on the wall. On the farther side of the room was a wooden framework resembling a hen-coop, and in this, still absorbed in prayer, knelt the man whose voice I heard. The red glow beating upon his upturned face made it stand out from the shadow like a painting from Rembrandt, showing up every wrinkle upon the parchment-like skin. I had but time for a fleeting glance; then, dropping from the window, I made off through the rocks and the heather, nor slackened my pace until I found myself back in my cabin once more. There I threw myself upon my couch, more disturbed and shaken than I had ever thought to feel again.

Such doubts as I might have had as to whether I had indeed seen my former fellow-lodger upon the night of the thunderstorm were resolved the next morning. Strolling along down the path which led to the fell, I saw in one spot where the ground was soft the impressions of a foot – the small, dainty foot of a well-booted woman. That tiny heel and high instep could have belonged to none other than my companion of Kirkby-Malhouse. I followed her trail for some distance, till it pointed, so far as I could discern it, to the lonely and ill-omened cottage. What power could there be to draw this tender girl, through wind and rain and darkness, across the fearsome moors to that strange rendezvous?

I have said that a little beck flowed down the valley and past my very door. A week or so after the doings which I have described, I was seated by my window when I perceived something white drifting slowly down the stream. My first thought was that it was a drowning sheep; but, picking up my stick, I strolled to the bank and hooked it ashore. On examination it proved to be a large sheet, torn and tattered, with the initials 'JC' in the corner. What gave it its sinister significance, however, was that from hem to hem it was all dappled and discoloured.

Shutting the door of my cabin, I set off up the glen in the direction of the surgeon's cabin. I had not gone far before I perceived the very man himself. He was walking rapidly along the hillside, beating the furze bushes with a cudgel and bellowing like a madman. Indeed, at the sight of him, the doubts as to his sanity which had risen in my mind were strengthened and confirmed.

As he approached I noticed that his left arm was suspended in a sling. On perceiving me he stood irresolute, as though uncertain whether to come over to me or not. I had no desire for an interview with him, however, so I hurried past him, on which he continued on his way, still shouting and striking about with his club. When he had disappeared over the fells, I made my way down to his cottage, determined to find some clue to what had occurred. I was surprised, on reaching it, to find the iron-plated door flung wide open. The ground immediately outside it was marked with the signs of a struggle. The chemical apparatus and the furniture within were all dashed about and shattered. Most suggestive of all, the sinister wooden cage was stained with blood-marks and its unfortunate occupant had disappeared. My heart was heavy for the little man, for I was assured I should never see him in this world more.

There was nothing in the cabin to throw any light upon the identity of my neighbours. The room was stuffed with chemical instruments. In one corner a small book-case contained a choice selection of works of science. In another was a pile of geological specimens collected from the limestone.

I caught no glimpse of the surgeon upon my homeward journey; but when I reached my cottage I was astonished and indignant to find that somebody had entered it in my absence. Boxes had been pulled out from under the bed, the curtains disarranged, the chairs drawn out from the wall. Even my study had not been safe from this rough intruder, for the prints of a heavy boot were plainly visible in the ebony-black carpet.

IV. OF THE MAN WHO CAME IN THE NIGHT

The night set in gusty and tempestuous, and the moon was all girt with ragged clouds. The wind blew in melancholy gusts, sobbing and sighing over the moor, and setting all the gorse bushes a-groaning. From time to time a little sputter of rain pattered up against the window-pane. I sat until near midnight, glancing over the fragment on immortality by Iamblichus, the Alexandrian Platonist, of whom the Emperor Julian said that he was posterior to Plato in time but not in genius. At last, shutting up my book, I opened my door and took a last look at the dreary fell and still more dreary sky. As I protruded my head, a swoop of wind caught me and sent the red ashes of my pipe sparkling and dancing through the darkness. At the same moment the moon shone brilliantly out from between two clouds and I saw, sitting on the hillside, not two hundred yards from my door, the man who called himself the surgeon of Gaster Fell. He was squatted among the heather, his elbows upon his knees, and his chin resting upon his hands, as motionless as a stone, with his gaze fixed steadily upon the door of my dwelling.

At the sight of this ill-omened sentinel, a chill of horror and of fear shot through me, for his gloomy and mysterious associations had cast a glamour round the man, and the hour and place were in keeping with his sinister presence. In a moment, however, a manly glow of resentment and self-confidence drove this petty emotion from my mind, and I strode fearlessly in his direction. He rose as I approached and faced me, with the moon shining on his grave, bearded face and glittering on his eyeballs. 'What is the meaning of this?' I cried, as I came upon him. 'What right have you to play the spy on me?'

I could see the flush of anger rise on his face. 'Your stay in the country has made you forget your manners,' he said. 'The moor is free to all.'

'You will say next that my house is free to all,' I said, hotly. 'You have had the impertinence to ransack it in my absence this afternoon.'

He started, and his features showed the most intense excitement. 'I swear to you that I had no hand in it!' he cried. 'I have never set foot in your house in my life. Oh, sir, sir, if you will but believe me, there is a danger hanging over you, and you would do well to be careful.'

'I have had enough of you,' I said. 'I saw that cowardly blow you struck when you thought no human eye rested upon you. I have been to your cottage, too, and know all that it has to tell. If there is a law in England, you shall hang for what you have done. As to me, I am an old soldier, sir, and I am armed. I shall not fasten my door. But if you or any other villain attempt to cross my threshold it shall be at your own risk.' With these words, I swung round upon my heel and strode into my cabin.

For two days the wind freshened and increased, with constant squalls of rain until on the third night the most furious storm was raging which I can ever recollect in England. I felt that it was positively useless to go to bed, nor could I concentrate my mind sufficiently to read a book. I turned my lamp half down to moderate the glare and, leaning back in my chair, I gave myself up to reverie. I must have lost all perception of time, for I have no recollection how long I sat there on the borderland betwixt thought and slumber. At last, about 3 or possibly 4 o'clock, I came to myself with a start – not only came to myself, but with every sense and nerve upon the strain. Looking round my chamber in the dim light, I could not see anything to justify my sudden trepidation. The homely room, the rain-blurred window and the rude wooden door were all as they had been. I had begun to persuade myself that some half-formed dream had sent that vague thrill through my nerves, when in a moment I became conscious of what it was. It was a sound – the sound of a human step outside my solitary cottage.

Amid the thunder and the rain and the wind I could hear it – a dull, stealthy footfall, now on the grass, now on the stones – occasionally stopping entirely, then resumed, and ever drawing nearer. I sat breathlessly, listening to the eerie sound. It had stopped now at my very door, and was replaced by a panting and gasping, as of one who has travelled fast and far.

By the flickering light of the expiring lamp I could see that the latch of my door was twitching, as though a gentle pressure was exerted on it from without. Slowly, slowly, it rose, until it was free of the catch, and then there was a pause of a quarter minute or more, while I still sat silent with dilated eyes and drawn sabre. Then, very slowly, the door began to revolve upon its hinges, and the keen air of the night came whistling through the slit. Very cautiously it was pushed open, so that never a sound came from the rusty hinges. As the aperture enlarged, I became aware of a dark, shadowy figure upon my threshold, and of a pale face that looked in at me. The features were human, but the eyes were not. They seemed to burn through the darkness with a greenish brilliancy of their own; and in their baleful, shifty glare I was conscious of the very spirit of murder. Springing from my chair, I had raised my naked sword, when, with a wild shouting, a second figure dashed up to my door. At its approach my shadowy visitant uttered a shrill cry, and fled away across the fells, yelping like a beaten hound.

Tingling with my recent fear, I stood at my door, peering through the night with the discordant cry of the fugitives still ringing in my ears. At that moment a vivid flash of lightning illuminated the whole landscape and made it as clear as day. By its light I saw far away upon the hillside two dark figures pursuing each other with extreme rapidity across the fells. Even at that distance the contrast between them forbid all doubt as to their identity. The first was the small, elderly man, whom I had supposed to be dead; the second was my neighbour, the surgeon. For an instant they stood out clear and hard in the unearthly light; in the next, the darkness had closed over them, and they were gone. As I turned to re-enter my chamber, my foot rattled against something on my threshold. Stooping, I found it was a straight knife, fashioned entirely of lead, and so soft and brittle that it was a strange choice for a weapon. To render it more harmless, the top had been cut square off. The edge, however, had been assiduously sharpened against a stone, as was evident from the markings upon it, so that it was still a dangerous implement in the grasp of a determined man. And what was the meaning of it all? you ask. Many a drama which I have come across in my wandering life, some as strange and as striking as this one, has lacked the ultimate explanation which you demand. Fate is a grand weaver of tales; but she ends them, as a rule, in defiance of all artistic laws, and with an unbecoming want of regard for literary propriety. As it happens, however, I have a letter before me as I write which I may add without comment, and which will clear all that may remain dark.

KIRKBY LUNATIC ASYLUM,
September 4th, 1885.

'Sir – I am deeply conscious that some apology and explanation is due to you for the very startling and, in your eyes, mysterious events which have recently occurred, and which have so seriously interfered with the retired existence which you desire to lead. I should have called upon you on the morning after the recapture of my father, but my knowledge of your dislike to visitors and also of – you will excuse my saying it – your very violent temper, led me to think that it was better to communicate with you by letter.

'My poor father was a hard-working general practitioner in Birmingham, where his name is still remembered and respected. About ten years ago he began to show signs of mental aberration, which we were inclined to put down to overwork and the effects of a sunstroke. Feeling my own incompetence to pronounce upon a case of such importance, I at once sought the highest advice in Birmingham and London. Among others we consulted the eminent alienist, Mr Fraser Brown, who pronounced my father's case to be intermittent in its nature, but dangerous during the paroxysms. "It may take a homicidal, or it may take a religious turn," he said; "or it may prove to be a mixture of both. For months he may be as well as you or me, and then in a moment he may break out. You will incur a great responsibility if you leave him without supervision."

'I need say no more, sir. You will understand the terrible task which has fallen upon my poor sister and me in endeavouring to save my father from the asylum which in his sane moments filled him with horror. I can only regret that your peace has been disturbed by our own misfortunes, and I offer you in my sister's name and my own our apologies.

'Yours truly,
J. Cameron.'

Fullcircle

JOHN BUCHAN

'Between the Windrush and the Colne
I found a little house of stone—
A little wicked house of stone.'

The October day was brightening towards late afternoon when
Leithen and I climbed the hill above the stream and came in sight
of the house. All morning a haze with the sheen of pearl in it had
lain on the folds of downland, and the vision of far horizons,
which is the glory of Cotswold, had been veiled, so that every
valley seemed a place enclosed and set apart. But now a glow had
come into the air, and for a little the autumn lawns had the tints
of summer. The gold of sunshine was warm on the grasses, and
only the riot of colour in the berry-laden edges of the fields and
the slender woodlands told of the failing year.

We were looking into a green cup of the hills, and it was all a
garden. A little place, bounded by slopes that defined its
graciousness with no hint of barrier, so that a dweller there,
though his view was but half a mile on any side, would yet have
the sense of dwelling on uplands and commanding the world.
Round the top edge ran an old wall of stones, beyond which the
October bracken flamed to the skyline. Inside were folds of
ancient pasture with here and there a thorn-bush, falling to rose
gardens, and, on one side, to the smooth sward of a terrace above

a tiny lake. At the heart of it stood the house, like a jewel well set. It was a miniature, but by the hand of a master. The style was late seventeenth-century, when an agreeable classic convention had opened up to sunlight and comfort the dark magnificence of the Tudor fashion. The place had the spacious air of a great mansion, and was finished in every detail with a fine scrupulousness. Only when the eye measured its proportions with the woods and the hillside did the mind perceive that it was a small dwelling. The stone of Cotswold takes curiously the colour of the weather. Under thunder-clouds it will be as dark as basalt; on a grey day it will be grey like lava; but in sunshine it absorbs the sun. At the moment the little house was pale gold, like honey.

Leithen swung a long leg across the stile.

'Pretty good, isn't it?' he said. 'It's pure authentic Sir Christopher Wren. The name is worthy of it, too. It is called Fullcircle.'

He told me its story. It had been built after the Restoration by the Carteron family, whose wide domains ran into these hills. The Lord Carteron of the day was a friend of the Merry Monarch, but it was not as a sanctuary for orgies that he built the house. Perhaps he was tired of the gloomy splendour of Minster Carteron, and wanted a home of his own and not of his ancestors' choosing. He had an elegant taste in letters, as we can learn from his neat imitations of Martial, his pretty *Bucolics*, and the more than respectable Latin hexameters of his *Ars Vivendi*. Being a great nobleman, he had the best skill of the day to construct his hermitage, and here he would retire for months at a time with like-minded friends to a world of books and gardens. He seems to have had no ill-wishers; contemporary memoirs speak of him charitably, and Dryden spared him four lines of encomium. 'A selfish old dog,' Leithen called him. 'He had the good sense to eschew politics and enjoy life. His soul is in that little house. He only did one rash thing in his career – he anticipated the King, his master, by some years in turning Papist.'

I asked about its later history.

'After his death it passed to a younger branch of the Carterons. It left them in the eighteenth century, and the Applebys got it.

314

They were a jovial lot of hunting squires, and let the library go to
the dogs. Old Colonel Appleby was still alive when I came to
Borrowby. Something went wrong in his inside when he was
nearly seventy, and the doctors knocked him off liquor. Not that
he drank too much, though he did himself well. That finished
the poor old boy. He told me that it revealed to him the amazing
truth that during a long and, as he hoped, publicly useful life he
had never been quite sober. He was a good fellow, and I missed
him when he died . . . The place went to a remote cousin called
Giffen.'

Leithen's eyes, as they scanned the prospect, seemed amused.

'Julian and Ursula Giffen . . . I daresay you know the names.
They always hunt in couples, and write books about sociology
and advanced ethics and psychics – books called either "The
New This or That", or "Towards Something or Other". You
know the sort of thing. They're deep in all the pseudo-
sciences . . . Decent souls, but you can guess the type. I came
across them in a case I had at the Old Bailey – defending a ruffian
who was charged with murder. I hadn't a doubt he deserved
hanging on twenty counts, but there wasn't enough evidence to
convict him on this one. Dodderidge was at his worst – it was just
before they induced him to retire – and his handling of the jury
was a masterpiece of misdirection. Of course there was a shindy.
The thing was a scandal, and it stirred up all the humanitarians,
till the murderer was almost forgotten in the iniquities of old
Dodderidge. You must remember the case. It filled the papers
for weeks. Well, it was in that connection that I fell in with the
Giffens. I got rather to like them, and I've been to see them at
their house in Hampstead. Golly, what a place! Not a chair fit to
sit down on, and colours that made you want to weep. I never
met people with heads so full of feathers.'

I said something about that being an odd *milieu* for him.

'Oh, I like human beings – all kinds. It's my profession to
study them, for without that the practice of the law would be a
lean affair. There are hordes of people like the Giffens – only not
so good, for they really have hearts of gold. They are the rootless
stuff in the world today – in revolt against everything and

315

everybody with any ancestry. A kind of innocent self-righteousness – wanting to be the people with whom wisdom begins and ends. They are mostly sensitive and tender-hearted, but they wear themselves out in an eternal dissidence. Can't build, you know, for they object to all tools, but very ready to crab. They scorn any form of Christianity, but they'll walk miles to patronize some wretched sect that has the merit of being brand-new, "Pioneers" they call themselves – funny little unclad people adventuring into the cold desert with no maps. Giffen once described himself and his friends to me as "forward-looking", but that, of course, is just what they are not. To tackle the future you must have a firm grip of the past, and for them the past is only a pathological curiosity. They're up to their necks in the mud of the present . . . But good, after a fashion; and innocent – sordidly innocent. Fate was in an ironical mood when she saddled them with that wicked little house.'

'Wicked' did not seem to me to be a fair word. It sat honey-coloured among its gardens with the meekness of a dove. The sound of a bicycle on the road behind made us turn round, and Leithen advanced to meet a dismounting rider.

He was a tallish fellow, some forty years old perhaps, with one of those fluffy blond beards that have never been shaved. Short-sighted, of course, and wore glasses. Biscuit-coloured knickerbockers and stockings clad his lean limbs.

Leithen introduced me. 'We are walking to Borrowby, and stopped to admire your house. Could we have just a glimpse inside? I want Jardine to see the staircase.'

Mr Giffen was very willing. 'I've been over to Clyston to send a telegram. We have some friends for the weekend who might interest you. Won't you stay to tea?'

There was a gentle formal courtesy about him, and his voice had the facile intonations of one who loves to talk. He led us through a little gate, and along a shorn green walk among the bracken to a postern which gave entrance to the garden. Here, though it was October, there was still a bright show of roses, and the jet of water from the leaden Cupid dripped noiselessly among fallen petals. And then we stood before the doorway, above which the old Carteron had inscribed a line of Horace.

I have never seen anything quite like the little hall. There were two, indeed, separated by a staircase of a wood that looked like olive. Both were paved with black and white marble, and the inner was oval in shape, with a gallery supported on slender walnut pillars. It was all in miniature, but it had a spaciousness which no mere size could give. Also it seemed to be permeated by the quintessence of sunlight. Its air was of long-descended, confident, equable happiness.

There were voices on the terrace beyond the hall. Giffen led us into a room on the left. 'You remember the house in Colonel Appleby's time, Leithen. This was the chapel. It had always been the chapel. You see the change we have made . . . I beg your pardon, Mr Jardine. You're not by any chance a Roman Catholic?'

The room had a white panelling, and on two sides deep windows. At one end was a fine Italian shrine of marble, and the floor was mosaic, blue and white, in a quaint Byzantine pattern. There was the same air of sunny cheerfulness as in the rest of the house. No mystery could find a lodgement here. It might have been a chapel for three centuries, but the place was pagan. The Giffens' changes were no sort of desecration. A green-baize table filled most of the floor, surrounded by chairs like a committee room. On new raw-wood shelves were files of papers and stacks of blue-books and those desiccated works into which reformers of society torture the English tongue. Two typewriters stood on a side-table.

'It is our workroom,' Giffen explained, 'where we hold our Sunday moots. Ursula thinks that a weekend is wasted unless it produces some piece of real work. Often a quite valuable committee has its beginning here. We try to make our home a refuge for busy workers, where they need not idle but can work under happy conditions.'

' "A college situate in a clearer air," ' Leithen quoted. But Giffen did not respond except with a smile; he had probably never heard of Lord Falkland.

A woman entered the room, a woman who might have been

pretty if she had taken a little pain. Her reddish hair was drawn tightly back and dressed in a hard knot, and her clothes were horribly incongruous in a remote manor-house. She had bright eager eyes, like a bird, and hands that fluttered nervously. She greeted Leithen with warmth.

'We have settled down marvellously,' she told him. 'Julian and I feel as if we had always lived here, and our life has arranged itself so perfectly. My Mothers' Cottages in the village will soon be ready, and the Club is to be opened next week. Julian and I will carry on the classes ourselves for the first winter. Next year we hope to have a really fine programme . . . And then it is so pleasant to be able to entertain one's friends . . . Won't you stay to tea? Dr Swope is here, and Mary Elliston and Mr Percy Blaker – you know, the Member of Parliament. Must you hurry off? I'm so sorry . . . What do you think of our workroom? It was utterly terrible when we first came here – a sort of decayed chapel, like a withered tuberose. we have let the air of heaven into it.'

I observed that I had never seen a house so full of space and light.

'Ah, you notice that? It is a curiously happy place to live in. Sometimes I'm almost afraid to feel so light-hearted. But we look on ourselves as only trustees. It is a trust we have to administer for the common good. You know, it's a house on which you can lay your own impress. I can imagine places which dominate the dwellers, but Fullcircle is plastic, and we can make it our own just as much as if we had planned and built it. That's our chief piece of good fortune.'

We took our leave, for we had no desire for the company of Dr Swope and Mr Percy Blaker. When we reached the highway we halted and looked back on the little jewel. Shafts of the westering sun now caught the stone and turned the honey to ripe gold. Thin spires of amethyst smoke rose into the still air. I thought of the well-meaning restless couple inside its walls, and somehow they seemed out of the picture. They simply did not matter. The house was the thing, for I had never met in inanimate stone such an air of gentle masterfulness. It had a personality of its own, clean-cut and secure, like a high-born old dame among the females of profiteers. And Mrs Giffen claimed to have given it her impress!

That night in the library at Borrowby, Leithen discoursed on the Restoration. Borrowby, of which, by the expenditure of much care and a good deal of money, he had made a civilized dwelling, is a Tudor manor of the Cotswold type, with high-pitched narrow roofs and tall stone chimneys, rising sheer from the meadows with something of the massiveness of a Border keep. He nodded towards the linen-fold panelling and the great carven chimney-piece.

'In this kind of house you have the mystery of the elder England. What was Raleigh's phrase? "High thoughts and divine contemplations." The people who built this sort of thing lived close to another world, and they thought bravely of death. It doesn't matter who they were – Crusaders or Elizabethans or Puritans – they all had poetry in them, and the heroic, and a great unworldliness. They had marvellous spirits, and plenty of joys and triumphs; but they had also their hours of black gloom. Their lives were like our weather – storm and sun. One thing they never feared – death. He walked too near them all their days to be a bogey.

'But the Restoration was a sharp break. It brought paganism into England – paganism and the art of life. No people have ever known better the secret of a bland happiness. Look at Fullcircle. There are no dark corners there. The man that built it knew all there was to be known about how to live . . . The trouble was that they did not know how to die. That was the one shadow on the glass. So they provided for it in the pagan way. They tried magic. They never became true Catholics – they were always pagan to the end, but they smuggled a priest into their lives. He was a kind of insurance premium against unwelcome mystery.'

It was not till nearly two years later that I saw the Giffens again. The May-fly season was near its close, and I had snatched a day on a certain limpid Cotswold river. There was another man on the same beat, fishing from the opposite bank, and I watched him with some anxiety, for a duffer would have spoilt my day.

To my relief I recognized Giffen. With him it was easy to come to terms, and presently the water was parcelled out between us.

We forgathered for luncheon, and I stood watching while he neatly stalked, rose and landed a trout. I confessed to some surprise – first that Giffen should be a fisherman at all, for it was not in keeping with my old notion of him; and second, that he should cast such a workman-like line. As we lunched together, I observed several changes. He had shaved his fluffy beard, and his face was notably less lean, and had the clear even sunburn of the countryman. His clothes, too, were different. They also were workman-like, and looked as if they belonged to him – no more the uneasy knickerbockers of the Sunday golfer.

'I'm desperately keen,' he told me. 'You see it's only my second May-fly season, and last year I was no better than a beginner. I wish I had known long ago what good fun fishing was. Isn't this a blessed place?' And he looked up through the canopy of flowering chestnuts to the June sky.

'I'm glad you've taken to sport,' I said. 'Even if you only come here for the weekends, sport lets you into the secrets of the countryside.'

'Oh, we don't go much to London now,' was his answer. 'We sold our Hampstead house a year ago. I can't think how I ever could stick that place. Ursula takes the same view . . . I wouldn't leave Oxfordshire just now for a thousand pounds. Do you smell the hawthorn? Last week this meadow was scented like Paradise. D'you know, Leithen's a queer fellow?'

I asked why.

'He once told me that this countryside in June made him sad. He said it was too perfect a thing for fallen humanity. I call that morbid. Do you see any sense in it?'

I knew what Leithen meant, but it would have taken too long to explain.

'I feel warm and good and happy here,' he went on. 'I used to talk about living close to nature. Rot! I didn't know what nature meant. Now—' He broke off. 'By Jove, there's a kingfisher. That is only the second I've seen this year. They're getting uncommon with us.'

320

'With us' – I liked the phrase. He was becoming a true countryman.

We had a good day – not extravagantly successful, but satisfactory, and he persuaded me to come home with him to Fullcircle for the night, explaining that I could catch an early train next morning at the junction. So we extricated a little two-seater from the thicket of lilacs, and he drove me through four miles of sweet-scented dusk, with nightingales shouting in every thicket. I changed into a suit of his flannels in a bedroom looking out on the little lake where trout were rising, and I remember that I whistled from pure light-heartedness. In that adorable house one seemed to be still breathing the air of the spring meadows.

Dinner was my first big surprise. It was admirable – plain but perfectly cooked, and with that excellence of basic material which is the glory of a well-appointed country house. There was wine too, which, I am certain, was a new thing. Giffen gave me a bottle of sound claret, and afterwards some more than decent port. My second surprise was my hostess. Her clothes, like her husband's, must have changed, for I did not notice what she was wearing, and I had noticed it only too clearly the last time we met. More remarkable still was the difference in her face. For the first time I realized that she was a pretty woman. The contours had softened and rounded, and there was a charming well-being in her eyes very different from the old restlessness. She looked content – infinitely content.

I asked about her Mothers' Cottages. She laughed cheerfully.

'I gave them up after the first year. They didn't mix well with the village people. I'm quite ready to admit my mistake, and it was the wrong kind of charity. The Londoners didn't like it – felt lonesome and sighed for the fried-fish shop; and the village women were shy of them – afraid of infectious complaints, you know. Julian and I have decided that our business is to look after our own people.'

It may have been malicious, but I said something about the wonderful scheme of village education.

'Another relic of Cockneyism,' laughed the lady; but Giffen looked a trifle shy.

'I gave it up because it didn't seem worth while. What is the use of spoiling a perfectly wholesome scheme of life by introducing unnecessary complications? Medicine is no good unless a man is sick, and these people are not sick. Education is the only cure for certain diseases the modern world had engendered, but if you don't find the disease the remedy is superfluous. The fact is, I hadn't the face to go on with the thing. I wanted to be taught rather than to teach. There's a whole world round me of which I know very little, and my first business is to get to understand it. Any village poacher can teach me more of the things that matter than I have to tell him.'

'Besides, we have so much to do,' his wife added. 'There's the house and the garden, and the home-farm and the property. It isn't large, but it takes a lot of looking after.'

The dining-room was long and low-ceilinged, and had a white panelling in bold relief. Through the windows came odours of the garden and a faint tickle of water. The dusk was deepening, and the engravings in their rosewood frames were dim, but sufficient light remained to reveal the picture above the fireplace. It showed a middle-aged man in the clothes of the later Carolines. The plump tapering fingers of one hand held a book, the other was hidden in the folds of a flowered waistcoat. The long, curled wig framed a delicate face, with something of the grace of youth left to it. There were quizzical lines about the mouth, and the eyes smiled pleasantly yet very wisely. It was the face of a man I should have liked to dine with. He must have been the best of company.

Giffen answered my question.

'That's the Lord Carteron who built the house. No. No relation. Our people were the Applebys, who came in 1753. We've both fallen so deep in love with Fullcircle that we wanted to see the man who conceived it. I had some trouble getting it. It came out of the Minster Carteron sale, and I had to give a dealer twice what he paid for it. It's a jolly thing to live with.'

It was indeed a curiously charming picture. I found my eyes

straying to it till the dusk obscured the features. It was the face of one wholly at home in a suave world, learned in all the urbanities. A good friend, I thought, the old lord must have been, and a superlative companion. I could imagine neat Horatian tags coming ripely from his lips. Not a strong face, but somehow a dominating one. The portrait of the long-dead gentleman had still the atmosphere of life. Giffen raised his glass of port to him as we rose from table, as if to salute a comrade.

We moved to the room across the hall, which had once been the Giffens' workroom, the cradle of earnest committees and weighty memoranda. This was my third surprise. Baize-covered table and raw-wood shelves had disappeared. The place was now half smoking-room, half library. On the walls hung a fine collection of coloured sporting prints, and below them were ranged low Hepplewhite bookcases. The lamplight glowed on the ivory walls, and the room, like everything else in the house, was radiant. Above the mantelpiece was a stag's head – a fair eleven-pointer.

Giffen nodded proudly towards it. 'I got that last year at Machray. My first stag.'

There was a little table with an array of magazines and weekly papers. Some amusement must have been visible in my face as I caught sight of various light-hearted sporting journals, for he laughed apologetically. 'You mustn't think that Ursula and I take in that stuff for ourselves. It amuses our guests, you know.'

I dare say it did, but I was convinced that the guests were no longer Dr Swope and Mr Percy Blaker.

One of my many failings is that I can never enter a room containing books without scanning the titles. Giffen's collection won my hearty approval. There were the very few novelists I can read myself – Miss Austen and Sir Walter and the admirable Marryat; there was a shelf full of memoirs, and a good deal of seventeenth- and eighteenth-century poetry; there was a set of the classics in fine editions, Bodonis and Baskervilles and such-like; there was much county history, and one or two valuable old herbals and itineraries. I was certain that two years before Giffen would have had no use for literature except some muddy Russian oddments, and I am positive that he would not have known the name of Surtees. Yet there stood the tall octavos recording the unedifying careers of Mr Jorrocks, Mr Facey Romford and Mr Soapy Sponge.

I was a little bewildered as I stretched my legs in a very deep armchair. Suddenly I had a strong impression of looking on at a play. My hosts seemed to be automata, moving docilely at the orders of a masterful stage-manager, and yet with no sense of bondage. And as I looked on they faded off the scene, and there was only one personality – that house so serene and secure, smiling at our modern antics, but weaving all the while an iron spell rounds its lovers. For a second I felt an oppression as of something to be resisted. But no. There was no oppression. The house was too well-bred and disdainful to seek to captivate. Only those who fell in love with it could know its mastery, for all love exacts a price. It was far more than a thing of stone and lime; it was a creed, an art, a scheme of life – older than any Carteron, older than England. Somewhere far back in time – in Rome, in Attica, or on an Aegean island – there must have been such places; but then they called them temples, and gods dwelt in them.

I was roused by Giffen's voice discoursing on his books. 'I've been rubbing up my classics again,' he was saying. 'Queer thing, but ever since I left Cambridge I have been out of the mood for them. And I'm shockingly ill-read in English literature. I wish I had more time for reading, for it means a lot to me.'

'There is such an embarrassment of riches here,' said his wife. 'The days are far too short for all there is to do. Even when there is nobody staying in the house I find every hour occupied. It's delicious to be busy over things one really cares for.'

'All the same, I wish I could do more reading,' said Giffen. 'I've never wanted to so much before.'

'But you come in tired from shooting and sleep sound till dinner,' said the lady, laying an affectionate hand on his shoulder.

They were happy people, and I like happiness. Self-absorbed perhaps, but I prefer selfishness in the ordinary way of things.

We are most of us selfish dogs, and altruism makes us uncomfortable. But I had somewhere in my mind a shade of uneasiness, for I was the witness of a transformation too swift and violent to be wholly natural. Years, no doubt, turn our eyes inward and abate our heroics, but not a trifle of two or three. Some agency had been at work here, some agency other and more potent than the process of time. The thing fascinated and partly frightened me. For the Giffens – though I scarcely dared to admit it – had deteriorated. They were far pleasanter people. I liked them infinitely better. I hoped to see them often again. I detested the type they used to represent, and shunned it like the plague. They were wise now, and mellow, and most agreeable human beings. But some virtue had gone out of them. An uncomfortable virtue, no doubt, but a virtue, something generous and adventurous. Before their faces had had a sort of wistful kindness. Now they had geniality – which is not the same thing.

What was the agency of this miracle? It was all around me: the ivory panelling, the olive-wood staircase, the lovely pillared hall. I got up to go to bed with a kind of awe on me. As Mrs Giffen lit my candle, she saw my eyes wandering among the gracious shadows.

'Isn't it wonderful,' she said, 'to have found a house which fits us like a glove? No! Closer. Fits us as a bearskin fits the bear. It has taken our impress like wax.'

Somehow I didn't think that the impress had come from the Giffens' side.

A November afternoon found Leithen and myself jogging homewards from a run with the Heythrop. It had been a wretched day. Twice we had found and lost, and then a deluge had set in which scattered the field. I had taken a hearty toss into a swamp, and got as wet as a man may be, but the steady downpour soon reduced everyone to a like condition. When we turned towards Borrowby the rain ceased, and an icy wind blew out of the east which partially dried our sopping clothes. All the grace had faded from the Cotswold valleys. The streams were brown torrents, the meadows lagoons, the ridges bleak and grey, and a sky of scurrying clouds cast leaden shadows. It was a matter of ten miles to Borrowby: we had long ago emptied our flasks, and I longed for something hot to take the chill out of my bones.

'Let's look in at Fullcircle,' said Leithen, as we emerged on the highroad from a muddy lane. 'We'll make the Giffens give us tea. You'll find changes there.'

I asked what changes, but he only smiled and told me to wait and see.

My mind was busy with surmises as we rode up the avenue. I thought of drink or drugs, and promptly discarded the notion. Fullcircle was, above all things, decorous and wholesome. Leithen could not mean the change in the Giffens' ways which had so impressed me a year before, for he and I had long ago discussed that. I was still puzzling over his words when we found ourselves in the inner hall, with the Giffens making a hospitable fuss over us.

The place was more delectable than ever. Outside was a dark November day, yet the little house seemed to be transfused with sunshine. I do not know by what art the old builders had planned it, but the airy pilasters, the perfect lines of the ceiling, the soft colouring of the wood seemed to lay open the house to a clear sky. Logs burned brightly on the massive steel andirons, and the scent and the fine blue smoke of them strengthened the illusion of summer.

Mrs Giffen would have had us change into dry things, but Leithen pleaded a waiting dinner at Borrowby. The two of us stood by the fireplace, drinking tea, the warmth drawing out a cloud of vapour from our clothes to mingle with the wood-smoke. Giffen lounged in an armchair, and his wife sat by the tea-table. I was looking for the changes of which Leithen had spoken.

I did not find them in Giffen. He was much as I remembered him on the June night when I had slept here, a trifle fuller in the face perhaps, a little more placid about the mouth and eyes. He looked a man completely content with life. His smile came readily and his easy laugh. Was it my fancy, or had he acquired a look of the picture in the dining-room? I nearly made an errand to go and see it. It seemed to me that his mouth had now something of the portrait's delicate complacence. Lely would have found him a fit subject, though he might have boggled at his lean hands.

But his wife! Ah, there the changes were unmistakable. She was comely now rather than pretty, and the contours of her face had grown heavier. The eagerness had gone from her eyes and left only comfort and good-humour. There was a suspicion, ever so slight, of rouge and powder. She had a string of good pearls – the first time I had seen her wear jewels. The hand that poured out the tea was plump, shapely, and well cared for. I was looking at a most satisfactory mistress of a country house, who would see that nothing was lacking to the part.

She talked more and laughed oftener. Her voice had an airy lightness which would have made the silliest prattle charming.

'We are going to fill the house with young people and give a ball at Christmas,' she announced. 'This hall is simply clamouring to be danced in. You must come both of you. Promise me. And, Mr Leithen, it would be very nice if you brought a party from Borrowby. Young men, please. We are overstocked with girls in these parts . . . We must do something to make the country cheerful in winter-time.'

I observed that no season could make Fullcircle other than cheerful.

'How nice of you!' she cried. 'To praise a house is to praise the householders, for a dwelling is just what its inmates make it. Borrowby is you, Mr Leithen, and Fullcircle us.'

'Shall we exchange?' Leithen asked.

She made a mouth. 'Borrowby would crush me, but it suits a Gothic survival like you. Do you think you would be happy here?'

'Happy,' said Leithen thoughtfully. 'Happy? Yes, undoubtedly. But it might be bad for my soul . . . There's just time for a pipe, Giffen, and then we must be off.'

I was filling my pipe as we crossed the outer hall, and was about to enter the smoking-room I so well remembered when Giffen laid a hand on my arm.

327

'We don't smoke there now,' he said hastily.

He opened the door and I looked in . . . The place had suffered its third metamorphosis. The marble shrine which I had noticed on my first visit had been brought back, and the blue mosaic pavement and the ivory walls were bare. At the eastern end stood a little altar, with above it a copy of a Correggio Madonna.

A faint smell of incense hung in the air and the fragrance of hothouse flowers. It was a chapel, but, I swear, a more pagan place than when it had been workroom or smoking-room.

Giffen gently shut the door. 'Perhaps you didn't know, but some months ago my wife became a Catholic. It is a good thing for women, I think. It gives them a regular ritual for their lives. So we restored the chapel. It had always been there in the days of the Cartertons and the Applebys.'

'And you?' I asked.

He shrugged his shoulders. 'I don't bother much about these things. But I propose to follow suit. It will please Ursula and do no harm to anybody.'

We halted on the brow of the hill and looked back on the garden valley. Leithen's laugh, as he gazed, had more awe than mirth in it.

'That wicked little house! I'm going to hunt up every scrap I can find about old Tom Carteron. He must have been an uncommon clever fellow. He's still alive down there and making people do as he did . . . In that kind of place you may expel the priest and sweep it and garnish it. But he always returns.'

The wrack was lifting before the wind and a shaft of late watery sun fell on the grey walls. It seemed to me that the little house wore an air of gentle triumph.

The Old Man

DAPHNE DU MAURIER

Did I hear you asking about the old man? I thought so. You're a newcomer to the district, here on holiday. We get plenty these days, during the summer months. Somehow they always find their way eventually over the cliffs down to this beach, and then they pause and look from the sea back to the lake. Just as you did.

It's a lovely spot, isn't it? Quiet and remote. You can't wonder at the old man choosing to live here.

I don't remember when he first came. Nobody can. Many years ago, it must have been. He was here when I arrived, long before the war. Perhaps he came to escape from civilisation, much as I did myself. Or maybe, where he lived before, the folks around made things too hot for him. It's hard to say. I had the feeling, from the very first, that he had done something, or something had been done to him, that gave him a grudge against the world. I remember the first time I set eyes on him I said to myself, 'I bet that old fellow is one hell of a character.'

Yes, he was living here beside the lake, along of his missus. Funny sort of lash-up they had, exposed to all the weather, but they didn't seem to mind.

I had been warned about him by one of the fellows from the farm, who advised me, with a grin, to give the old man who lived down by the lake a wide berth – he didn't care for strangers. So I

329

went warily, and I didn't stay to pass the time of day. Nor would it have been any use if I had, not knowing a word of his lingo. The first time I saw him he was standing by the edge of the lake, looking out to sea, and from tact I avoided the piece of planking over the stream, which meant passing close to him, and crossed to the other side of the lake by the beach instead. Then, with an awkward feeling that I was trespassing and had no business to be there, I bobbed down behind a clump of gorse, took out my spy-glass, and had a peep at him.

He was a big fellow, broad and strong – he's aged, of course, lately; I'm speaking of several years back – but even now you can see what he must have been once. Such power and drive behind him, and that fine head, which he carried like a king. There's an idea in that, too. No, I'm not joking. Who knows what royal blood he carries inside him, harking back to some remote ancestor? And now and again, surging in him – not through his own fault – it gets the better of him and drives him fighting mad. I didn't think about that at the time. I just looked at him, and ducked behind the gorse when I saw him turn, and I wondered to myself what went on in his mind, whether he knew I was there, watching him.

If he should decide to come up the lake after me I should look pretty foolish. He must have thought better of it, though, or perhaps he did not care. He went on staring out to sea, watching the gulls and the incoming tide, and presently he ambled off to his side of the lake, heading for the missus and home and maybe supper.

I didn't catch a glimpse of her that first day. She just wasn't around. Living as they do, close in by the left bank of the lake, with no proper track to the place, I hardly had the nerve to venture close and come upon her face to face. When I did see her, though, I was disappointed. She wasn't much to look at after all. What I mean is, she hadn't got anything like his character. A placid, mild-tempered creature, I judged her.

They had both come back from fishing when I saw them, and were making their way up from the beach to the lake. He was in front, of course. She tagged along behind. Neither of them took the slightest notice of me, and I was glad, because the old man might have paused, and waited, and told her to get on back home, and then come down towards the rocks where I was sitting. You ask what I would have said, had he done so? I'm damned if I know. Maybe I would have got up, whistling and seeming unconcerned, and then, with a nod and a smile – useless, really, but instinctive, if you know what I mean – said good day and pottered off. I don't think he would have done anything. He'd just have stared after me, with those strange narrow eyes of his, and let me go.

After that, winter and summer, I was always down on the beach or the rocks, and they went on living their curious, remote existence, sometimes fishing in the lake, sometimes at sea. Occasionally I'd come across them in the harbour on the estuary , taking a look at the yachts anchored there, and the shipping. I used to wonder which of them made the suggestion. Perhaps suddenly he would be lured by the thought of the bustle and life of the harbour, and all the things he had either wantonly given up or never known, and he would say to her, 'Today we are going into town.' And she, happy to do whatever pleased him best, followed along.

You see, one thing that stood out – and you couldn't help noticing it – was that the pair of them were devoted to one another. I've seen her greet him when he came back from a day's fishing and had left her back home, and towards evening she'd come down the lake and on to the beach and down to the sea to wait for him. She'd see him coming from a long way off, and I would see him too, rounding the corner of the bay. He'd come straight in to the beach, and she would go to meet him, and they would embrace each other, not caring a damn who saw them. It was touching, if you know what I mean. You felt there was something lovable about the old man, if that's how things were between them. He might be a devil to outsiders, but he was all the world to her. It gave me a warm feeling for him, when I saw them together like that.

You asked if they had any family. I was coming to that. It's about the family I really wanted to tell you. Because there was a tragedy, you see. And nobody knows anything about it except me. I suppose I could have told someone, but if I had, I don't know . . . They might have taken the old man away, and she'd have broken her heart without him, and anyway, when all's said and done, it wasn't my business. I know the evidence against the old man was strong, but I hadn't positive proof, it might have been some sort of accident, and anyway, nobody made any enquiries at the time the boy disappeared, so who was I to turn busybody and informer?

I'll try and explain what happened. But you must understand that all this took place over quite a time, and sometimes I was away from home or busy, and didn't go near the lake. Nobody seemed to take any interest in the couple living there but myself, so that it was only what I observed with my own eyes that makes this story, nothing that I heard from anybody else, no scraps of gossip, or tales told about them behind their backs.

Yes, they weren't always alone, as they are now. They had four kids. Three girls and a boy. They brought up the four of them in the ramshackle old place by the lake, and it was always a wonder to me how they did it. God, I've known days when the rain lashed the lake into little waves that burst and broke on the muddy shore near by their place, and turned the marsh into a swamp, and the wind driving straight in. You'd have thought anyone with a grain of sense would have taken his missus and his kids out of it and gone off somewhere where they could get some creature comforts at least. Not the old man. If he could stick it, I guess he decided she could too, and the kids as well. Maybe he wanted to bring them up the hard way.

Mark you, they were attractive youngsters. Especially the youngest girl. I never knew her name, but I called her Tiny. She had so much go to her. Chip off the old block, in spite of her size.

I can see her now, as a little thing, the first to venture paddling in the lake, on a fine morning, way ahead of her sisters and the brother.

The brother I nicknamed Boy. He was the eldest, and between you and me a bit of a fool. He hadn't the looks of his sisters and was a clumsy sort of fellow. The girls would play around on their own, and go fishing, and he'd hang about in the background, not knowing what to do with himself. If he possibly could he'd stay around home, near his mother. Proper mother's boy. That's why I gave him the name. Not that she seemed to fuss over him any more than she did the others. She treated the four alike, as far as I could tell. Her thoughts were always for the old man rather than for them. But Boy was just a great baby, and I have an idea he was simple.

Like their parents, the youngsters kept themselves to themselves. Been dinned into them, I dare say, by the old man. They never came down to the beach on their own and played; and it must have been a temptation, I thought, in full summer, when people came walking over the cliffs down to the beach to bathe and picnic. I suppose, for those strange reasons best known to himself, the old man had warned them to have no truck with strangers.

They were used to me pottering, day in, day out, fetching driftwood and that. And often I would pause and watch the kids playing by the lake. I didn't talk to them, though. They might have gone back and told the old man. They used to look up when I passed by, then glance away again, sort of shy. All but Tiny. Tiny would toss her head and do a somersault, just to show off.

I sometimes watched them go off, the six of them – the old man, the missus, Boy, and the three girls, for a day's fishing out to sea. The old man, of course, in charge; Tiny eager to help, close to her dad; the missus looking about her to see if the weather was going to keep fine; the two other girls alongside; and Boy, poor simple Boy, always the last to leave home. I never knew what sport they had. They used to stay out late and I'd have left the beach by the time they came back again. But I guess they did well. They must have lived almost entirely on what they caught. Well, fish is said to be full of vitamins, isn't it? Perhaps the old man was a food faddist in his way.

Time passed, and the youngsters began to grow up. Tiny lost something of her individuality then, it seemed to me. She grew more like her sisters. They were a nice-looking trio, all the same. Quiet, you know, well-behaved.

As for Boy, he was enormous. Almost as big as the old man, but with what a difference! He had none of his father's looks, or strength, or personality; he was nothing but a great clumsy lout. And the trouble was, I believe the old man was ashamed of him. He didn't pull his weight in the home, I'm certain of that. And out fishing he was perfectly useless. The girls would work away like beetles, with Boy, always in the background, making a mess of things. If his mother was there he just stayed by her side.

I could see it rattled the old man to have such an oaf of a son. Irritated him, too, because Boy was so big. It probably didn't make sense to his intolerant mind. Strength and stupidity didn't go together. In any normal family, of course, Boy would have left home by now and gone out to work. I used to wonder if they argued about it back in the evenings, the missus and the old man, or if it was something never admitted between them but tacitly understood – Boy was no good.

Well, they did leave home at last. At least, the girls did.

I'll tell you how it happened.

It was a day in late autumn, and I happened to be over doing some shopping in the little town overlooking the harbour, three miles from this place, and suddenly I saw the old man, the missus, the three girls and Boy all making their way up to Pont – that's at the head of a creek going eastward from the harbour. There are a few cottages in Pont, and a farm and a church up behind. The family looked washed and spruced up, and so did the old man and the missus, and I wondered if they were going visiting. If they were, it was an unusual thing for them to do. But it's possible they had friends or acquaintances up there, of whom I knew nothing. Anyway, that was the last I saw of them, on the fine Saturday afternoon, making for Pont.

It blew hard over the weekend, a proper easterly gale. I kept indoors and didn't go out at all. I knew the seas would be breaking good and hard on the beach. I wondered if the old man and the family had been able to get back. They would have been wise to stay with their friends up in Pont, if they had friends there.

It was Tuesday before the wind dropped and I went down to

the beach again. Seaweed, driftwood, tar and oil all over the place. It's always the same after an easterly blow. I looked up the lake, towards the old man's shack, and I saw him there, with the missus, just by the edge of the lake. But there was no sign of the youngsters.

I thought it a bit funny, and waited around in case they should appear. They never did. I walked right round the lake, and from the opposite bank I had a good view of their place, and even took out my old spy-glass to have a closer look. They just weren't there. The old man was pottering about as he often did when he wasn't fishing, and the missus had settled herself down to bask in the sun. There was only one explanation. They had left the family with friends at Pont. They had sent the family for a holiday.

I can't help admitting I was relieved, because for one frightful moment I thought maybe they had started off back home on the Saturday night and got struck by the gale; and, well – that the old man and his missus had got back safely, but not the kids. It couldn't be that, though. I should have heard. Someone would have said something. The old man wouldn't be pottering there in his usual unconcerned fashion and the missus basking in the sun. No, that must have been it. They had left the family with friends. Or maybe the girls and Boy had gone up country, gone to find themselves jobs at last.

Somehow it left a gap. I felt sad. So long now I had been used to seeing them all around, Tiny and the others. I had a strange sort of feeling that they had gone for good. Silly, wasn't it? To mind, I mean. There was the old man, and his missus, and the four youngsters, and I'd more or less watched them grow up, and now for no reason they had gone.

I wished then I knew even a word or two of his language, so that I could have called out to him, neighbour-like, and said, 'I see you and the missus are on your own. Nothing wrong. I hope?'

But there, it wasn't any use. He'd have looked at me with his strange eyes and told me to go to hell.

I never saw the girls again. No, never. They just didn't come back. Once I thought I saw Tiny, somewhere up the estuary, with a group of friends, but I couldn't be sure. If it was, she'd grown, she looked different. I tell you what I think. I think the old man and the missus took them with a definite end in view, that last weekend, and either settled them with friends they knew or told them to shift for themselves.

I know it sounds hard, not what you'd do for your own son and daughters, but you have to remember the old man was a rough customer, a law unto himself. No doubt he thought it would be for the best, and so it probably was, and if only I could know for certain what happened to the girls, especially Tiny, I wouldn't worry.

But I do worry sometimes, because of what happened to Boy.

You see, Boy was fool enough to come back. He came back about three weeks after that final weekend. I had walked down through the woods – not my usual way, but down to the lake by the stream that feeds it from a higher level. I rounded the lake by the marshes to the north, some distance from the old man's place, and the first thing I saw was Boy.

He wasn't doing anything. He was just standing by the marsh. He looked dazed. He was too far off for me to hail him; besides, I didn't have the nerve. But I watched him, as he stood there in his clumsy loutish way, and I saw him staring at the far end of the lake. He was staring in the direction of the old man.

The old man, and the missus with him, took not the slightest notice of Boy. They were close to the beach, by the plank bridge, and were either just going out to fish or coming back. And here was Boy, with his dazed stupid face, but not only stupid – frightened.

I wanted to say, 'Is anything the matter?' but I didn't know how to say it. I stood there, like Boy, staring at the old man.

Then what we both must have feared would happen, happened.

The old man lifted his head, and saw Boy.

He must have said a word to his missus, because she didn't move, she stayed where she was, by the bridge, but the old man turned like a flash of lightning and came down the other side of the lake towards the marshes, towards Boy. He looked terrible. I shall never forget his appearance. That magnificent head I had always admired now angry, evil; and he was cursing Boy as he came. I tell you, I heard him.

Boy, bewildered, scared, looked hopelessly about him for cover. There was none. Only the thin reeds that grew beside the marsh. But the poor fellow was so dumb he went in there, and crouched, and believed himself safe – it was a horrible sight.

I was just getting my own courage up to interfere when the old man stopped suddenly in his tracks, pulled up short as it were, and then, still cursing, muttering, turned back again and returned to the bridge. Boy watched him, from his cover of reeds, then, poor clot that he was, came out on to the marsh again, with some idea, I suppose, of striking for home.

I looked about me. There was no one to call. No one to give any help. And if I went and tried to get someone from the farm they would tell me not to interfere, that the old man was best left alone when he got in one of his rages and anyway that Boy was old enough to take care of himself. He was as big as the old man. He could give as good as he got. I knew different. Boy was no fighter. He didn't know how.

I waited quite a time beside the lake but nothing happened. It began to grow dark. It was no use my waiting there. The old man and the missus left the bridge and went on home. Boy was still standing there on the marsh, by the lake's edge.

I called to him, softly: 'It's no use. He won't let you in. Go back to Pont, or wherever it is you've been. Go to some place, anywhere, but get out of here.'

He looked up, that same queer dazed expression on his face, and I could tell he hadn't understood a word I said.

I felt powerless to do any more. I went home myself. But I thought about Boy all evening, and in the morning I went down to the lake again, and I took a great stick with me to give me courage. Not that it would have been much good. Not against the old man.

Well . . . I suppose they had come to some sort of agreement, during the night. There was Boy, by his mother's side, and the old man was pottering on his own.

I must say, it was a great relief. Because, after all, what could I have said or done? If the old man didn't want Boy home, it was really his affair. And if Boy was too stupid to go, that was Boy's affair.

But I blamed the mother a good deal. After all, it was up to her to tell Boy he was in the way, and the old man was in one of his moods, and Boy had best get out while the going was good. But I never did think she had great intelligence. She did not seem to show much spirit at any time.

However, what arrangement they had come to worked for a time. Boy stuck close to his mother – I suppose he helped her at home, I don't know – and the old man left them alone and was more and more by himself.

He took to sitting down by the bridge, humped, staring out to sea, with a queer brooding look on him. He seemed strange, and lonely. I didn't like it. I don't know what his thoughts were, but I'm sure they were evil. It suddenly seemed a very long time since he and the missus and the whole family had gone fishing, a happy, contented party. Now everything had changed for him. He was thrust out in the cold, and the missus and Boy stayed together.

I felt sorry for him, but I felt frightened too. Because I felt it could not go on like this indefinitely; something would happen.

One day I went down to the beach for driftwood – it had been blowing in the night – and when I glanced towards the lake I saw that Boy wasn't with his mother. He was back where I had seen him that first day, on the edge of the marsh. He was as big as his father. If he'd known how to use his strength he'd have been a match for him anyday, but he hadn't the brains. There he was, back on the marsh, a great big frightened foolish fellow, and there was the old man, outside his home, staring down towards his son with murder in his eyes.

I said to myself, 'He's going to kill him.' But I didn't know how or when or where, whether by night, when they were sleeping, or by day, when they were fishing. The mother was useless, she would not prevent it. It was no use appealing to the mother. If only Boy would use one little grain of sense, and go . . .

I watched and waited until nightfall. Nothing happened.

It rained in the night. It was grey, and cold, and dim. December was everywhere, trees all bare and bleak. I couldn't get down to the lake until late afternoon, and then the skies had cleared and the sun was shining in that watery way it does in winter, a burst of it, just before setting below the sea.

I saw the old man, and the missus too. They were close together, by the old shack, and they saw me coming for they looked towards me. Boy wasn't there. He wasn't on the marsh, either. Nor by the side of the lake.

I crossed the bridge and went along the right bank of the lake, and I had my spy-glass with me, but I couldn't see Boy. Yet all the time I was aware of the old man watching me.

Then I saw him. I scrambled down the bank, and crossed the marsh, and went to the thing I saw lying there, behind the reeds.

He was dead. There was a great gash on his body. Dried blood on his back. But he had lain there all night. His body was sodden with rain.

Maybe you'll think I'm a fool, but I began to cry, like an idiot, and I shouted across to the old man, 'You murderer, you bloody God-damned murderer.' He did not answer. He did not move. He stood there, outside his shack with the missus, watching me. You'll want to know what I did. I went back and got a spade, and I dug a grave for Boy, in the reeds behind the marsh, and I said one of my own prayers for him, being uncertain of his religion. When I had finished I looked across the lake to the old man.

And do you know what I saw?

I saw him lower his great head, and bend towards her and embrace her. And she lifted her head to him and embraced him too. It was both a requiem and a benediction. An atonement, and a giving of praise. In their strange way they knew they had done evil, but now it was over, because I had buried Boy and he was gone. They were free to be together again, and there was no longer a third to divide them.

They came out into the middle of the lake, and suddenly I saw the old man stretch his neck and beat his wings, and he took off from the water, full of power, and she followed him. I watched the two swans fly out to sea right into the face of the setting sun, and I tell you it was one of the most beautiful sights I ever saw in my life: the two swans flying there, alone, in winter.

Acknowledgements

H. E. Bates, 'The Mower' from *Seven by Five*, reprinted by permission of Laurence Pollinger Ltd and the Estate of H. E. Bates

Daphne Du Maurier, 'The Old Man' from *The Apple Tree*, reprinted by permission of Curtis Brown Ltd on behalf of The Chichester Partnership. Copyright 1952 by Daphne Du Maurier

Stella Gibbons, 'Christmas at Cold Comfort Farm' from *Christmas at Cold Comfort Farm and Other Stories*, reprinted by permission of Curtis Brown Ltd on behalf of the Estate of Stella Gibbons

Edith Somerville & Martin Ross, 'Philippa's Fox Hunt' from *Some Adventures of an Irish RM*, reprinted by permission of Curtis Brown Ltd and the Estate of Edith Somerville and Martin Ross

Dylan Thomas, 'The Enemies' from *Miscellany Three*, reprinted by permission of David Higham Associates Ltd and the Estate of Dylan Thomas

341

A selection of bestsellers
from Headline

THE LADYKILLER	Martina Cole	£5.99 ☐
JESSICA'S GIRL	Josephine Cox	£5.99 ☐
NICE GIRLS	Claudia Crawford	£4.99 ☐
HER HUNGRY HEART	Roberta Latow	£5.99 ☐
FLOOD WATER	Peter Ling	£4.99 ☐
THE OTHER MOTHER	Seth Margolis	£4.99 ☐
ACT OF PASSION	Rosalind Miles	£4.99 ☐
A NEST OF SINGING BIRDS	Elizabeth Murphy	£5.99 ☐
THE COCKNEY GIRL	Gilda O'Neill	£4.99 ☐
FORBIDDEN FEELINGS	Una-Mary Parker	£5.99 ☐
OUR STREET	Victor Pemberton	£5.99 ☐
GREEN GROW THE RUSHES	Harriet Smart	£5.99 ☐
BLUE DRESS GIRL	E V Thompson	£5.99 ☐
DAYDREAMS	Elizabeth Walker	£5.99 ☐

All Headline books are available at your local bookshop or newsagent, or can be ordered direct from the publisher. Just tick the titles you want and fill in the form below. Prices and availability subject to change without notice.

Headline Book Publishing PLC, Cash Sales Department, Bookpoint, 39 Milton Park, Abingdon, OXON, OX14 4TD, UK. If you have a credit card you may order by telephone – 0235 831700.

Please enclose a cheque or postal order made payable to Bookpoint Ltd to the value of the cover price and allow the following for postage and packing:
UK & BFPO: £1.00 for the first book, 50p for the second book and 30p for each additional book ordered up to a maximum charge of £3.00.
OVERSEAS & EIRE: £2.00 for the first book, £1.00 for the second book and 50p for each additional book.

Name ....

Address ....

....

....

If you would prefer to pay by credit card, please complete:
Please debit my Visa/Access/Diner's Card/American Express (delete as applicable) card no:

Signature .... Expiry Date ....